UNFASHIONABLY LATE

Vic Fieger

ISBN-13: 978-0692281680
ISBN: 0692281681

For everyone who wasn't invited to the party

UNFASHIONABLY LATE

Hello, notebook. Looks like we're going to be friends for a while, so I guess it's best to get the introductions out of the way. Granted, this is more for me than you. Just have to sum up what this is all about to help myself come to terms. Ready? Here goes.

My name is Audrey Perlmutter. I'm 29 years old. I am the school librarian at Braun Elementary in Ridgeway, Massachusetts. I have small eyes, a big nose, and an annoying voice. And I am a virgin. Alright. I said it. I said the V-word (well, wrote it.) I guess I'm going to have to get used to using it because I'm probably going to need to use it a lot now. I'm going to have to change a lot of things.

First off, you'll have to forgive my handwriting. I'm actually much better than this, but I'm writing in this cursive-like script because it's my own personal shorthand system. I can fit more words on the page, it's quicker, and it keeps what I'm writing a secret. I've learned growing up that if I don't write things in code it's an invitation for other people to go through it. I absolutely must keep the contents of this diary under lock and key. Oh yeah, forgot to mention that you're a diary now. Congratulations. First day on the job and you've been promoted.

You can probably tell that I've had to keep a lot of things hidden from my family over the years, as I've been kept on a pretty short leash. The result is that I've been kept in line pretty well for all of my life. I never broke the law, and always did my best to follow the rules. I'm too polite. I'm too considerate. I can't assert myself. I have to push myself to do anything that I feel might inconvenience others, even momentarily. But, I'm probably being a little harsh on my family, and I'm just looking for somebody else to blame for my own faults.

Ah. See? Right there. I'm also too hard on myself. Perfect example.

Today, the reason for the secrecy is my roommate Willow. We're in a tiny two-bedroom apartment on Reilly Street. My room is a little sliver with just enough space for me to keep all of my things, which is just right for me, because I don't have a lot of stuff. A couple of bookcases, a file cabinet, a dresser in the closet, and some boxes under the bed and I'm all set. I don't accumulate loads of clothes or knick-knacks, though I do have

1

a problem throwing things out. It actually is rather cramped in here, and I can't really stay awake in the room long without going stir crazy, but it does its job.

Willow, probably the only other person who stands a chance of coming across this diary, might read it if she could. She seemed pretty trustworthy when we first met at my last job, but now I know better. By my count, she still owes her half of the rent for four months total. I don't really want to bring it up because she still works at the supermarket and only makes ten dollars an hour. I can afford it a lot more than she can now that I'm working at the school, so I like to think I'm helping out a friend.

Maybe "friend" is too strong a word for Willow. "Ally" would be more appropriate. We don't share enough to be friends. She and her boyfriend Wes had broken up for two weeks at one time, but I didn't know about it for months.

As far as friends go, I'm lucky enough to get to work with Lynn, who's teaching a second grade class for the first time this year after completing her duties as a teacher's aide. As much as I love my other friends, she's the one who I consider to be my closest. She finds the strange things I do to be humorous and interesting when others would just roll their eyes at how dull I am. Yesterday when she pressed me for what I did over the weekend, I told her that I was going to draw cartoons at one point, only to be distracted when I found some amusing videos on the internet. Somebody had uploaded a bunch of episodes of a Japanese kids' show where people dressed up as marine life and vegetables beat the tar out of each other with blunt objects. I couldn't focus on drawing under those circumstances, so I used the pen and paper to practice signing my first name so I could get it just right if I ever get to be a contestant on *Jeopardy!* On Sunday, I went to the hardware store to buy some right-angle brackets, as I have a leaning bookcase that needs to be de-parallelogrammed.

See, now, most people would hear that and think I'm boring, which I suppose is actually rather true. Lynn heard that and thought it was amazing that I would practice signing my name for a game show I'll probably never be on. Lynn is friendly and considerate to everyone she meets, whereas I try to be considerate by getting out of the way and minding my own business. Where we really part ways is her sunny "I can do anything if I believe in myself" outlook. I'm too logical for that, I have to play the odds. If I didn't have Lynn around, I'm pretty sure I'd be completely lost.

Right now, another teacher is in the hospital recovering from being in a car accident. Her name is Natasha, and we actually weren't that close, to be honest. We talk every so often, but it's all business. We kind of have that in common: only talking when we have something to say. Sometimes I fear I identify a little too much with the lyrics to "Psycho Killer."

Natasha is very, I guess it's okay to say this here, robotic. If there's a good way to read that, then that's how I mean it. I have nothing against her at all, but even I crack a smile every so often. I don't think I've ever heard her laugh. I'd want a whole crowd of her to help out in a disaster, but not as an audience for a stand-up routine. She's a no-nonsense type who's sure of everything, with so much quiet assuredness that she could karate chop a district attorney and get away with it.

Last night, she and her husband Rob were hit head-on as they were driving home from a restaurant, and luckily nobody was hurt. Still, Natasha got carted off to the hospital for one reason or another. She's right as rain and expected to return to work in a day or two, as soon as she can get them to release her. When I first heard about the accident, I didn't really think anything of it. I just accepted it for what it was and went back to re-shelving the returned books. I was unaffected by it, or so I thought.

A few of us stopped by the hospital after work: Lynn, Rosi, Zena, and myself. I thought I'd be ready for what I would see, after all, there wasn't even an injury. We walked in, and I saw Natasha in that bed wearing a hospital gown. Right behind her were those flowers on the nightstand. That image has stayed with me since. It may have been the flowers. The message they conveyed to me was that of the grave.

Natasha was so close to death last night. Just because she's fine now doesn't mean things couldn't have gone much worse. If her car had been traveling only a few miles per hour faster, or had the other car been pointed just a few degrees to the left, then who knows? It could have been all over for her. I never would have gotten the chance to know her better. Just today, I found out that she's married. I never even stopped to consider that she might continue existing beyond her time at school, let alone have a husband.

A chill washed over me. I was standing in a hospital, in a room with four other people, but I felt as if I was alone. I heard what everyone was saying, but very little of it was registering in my brain. All the sights and sounds for the next few minutes were like white noise. I'm sure that I looked as if I had completely checked out, and on any other day someone (probably Rosi) would have tried to snap me out of it, "Earth to Audrey"-style. They most likely figured I was in shock from what was going on around me at that moment. I suppose I was, even if it wasn't for the reasons that would be considered appropriate. I was being selfish, thinking about myself and my life.

What have I been doing all this time? I feel like I never have anything to look forward to.

I regained awareness of the world around me just in time to hand Natasha the card we all signed. It had a rabbit on the front and the inside bore the legend, "HOPPY to hear you're doing well!" Don't ask me. I didn't buy it, I just signed it.

Natasha said goodbye to us in her *Dragnet*-esque monotone, "Thank you for visiting me. Thank you for the card with the bunny on it." We walked down a hallway on the way back to the elevator, past a long stretch of windows showing overcast skies. Normally, I walk faster than everybody else. I guess I have a longer stride than most and I usually want to get where I'm going as quickly as I can. Tonight I lagged behind the others, staring out those windows, walking as if I had forgotten something and I wanted to go back and get it.

Once I got into the elevator, it came to me. I knew what I had forgotten.

Lynn and I went to a spot just down the street from the hospital for a quick meal. The place was mostly empty, so we had enough privacy at our little booth for a sensitive topic. I couldn't order a thing. The thought of losing anyone I know at any given moment robbed me of any appetite I might have had otherwise. These can't be the exact words I said, but it came out something like, "I saw Natasha sitting up in that hospital bed, and I realized something: I could lose any of my friends or family at any time, for any reason. It could be a gun, a car crash, a fire, just falling down stairs, anything can happen. Any one of us can die at any time, even me.

"I realize now there's so much I haven't gotten to do yet. I've never traveled overseas. I've never smoked marijuana. I've never learned to dance. There are a lot of things I've been meaning to get to. Now, I think I need to get started. Lynn, I'm going to need your help on some of them. I can't do it all alone."

Lynn asked where I wanted to start. Okay. Deep breath. Inhale. Exhale. Ready, Audrey?

"First…"

It's too embarrassing, but I force it out.

"I need to have sex."

Lynn looked genuinely shocked. "Wow. Uh. Okay. But, just the other day weren't you saying you weren't into guys?"

"I'm not. In fact, the more I'm around them, the more they repulse me. But, the act itself, that is something I want to experience, preferably with someone who I actually

4

like. Even if it's just once. I don't want to get into a relationship, because there's no way that would work. I just need to cross this off of my list. And let's face it, I'm not getting any younger. I just need a casual encounter, you know? No strings."

"Penetration, right?"

"Uhhhh, yeah, you could put it that way."

Lynn let out the most relieved-sounding noise I've ever heard, and told me she thought I was asking her to be my first. Then she proposed a trip to Amsterdam, because prostitution is legal and regulated there. She says she's sure they "have something for the ladies, too."

"Do you think maybe we could try it the normal way first? You know, before we resort to crossing an ocean to pay for it?"

"Huh? OH! OH MY GOD, I'M SO SORRY! It's just, you know, you were talking about pot and seeing the world, and I thought you— I didn't mean to imply that you're hopeless! Aud, I'm SO sorry!"

Not off to a very good start, are we?

I'm going to pencil in Amsterdam as Plan Z.

On the way back home, I stopped at a pharmacy and picked up a big, thick heavyweight of a notebook (that would be you) in order to keep a diary of my progress on this and other fronts. I've already decided that tomorrow I'm going to have my first coffee. Tell you about it tomorrow.

APR 22 (WED)

I had my first coffee this afternoon. I'll get to that later, though.

Today I went in to work trying to project a new attitude and feeling ready for a change. Maybe I won't change my life, but I can at least change its course. At my desk I made a short list of the things I wanted to do for the first time, (drink coffee, take ballroom dancing lessons, go to Europe, visit that library in Vermont that I always wanted to see) but I ran out of ideas pretty quickly. I jotted everything down in my shorthand script, since I didn't want someone like, say, Rosi or Zena catching on if either of them happened to stop by and a wandering eye caught sight of my yellow notepad. I consider them friends and all, but I just want to keep things a secret for the obvious reasons. If only Lynn knows, then that's fine, but if one of those two finds out I'm still a

5

virgin, there's no telling if it would spread or not.

Rosita would not let me hear the end of it if she were to find out. She has this tendency to be a little insensitive, but in an oblivious sort of way. She's a bit of an absent-minded ditz and makes a supremely clumsy move every now and then. Even though she's still a teacher's aide and we only met in September, there's no doubt that she's a sincere and caring person. If she were to let a secret slip, it'd be by accident while she was discussing something completely unrelated. That's how I found out that Lynn re-gifted that Garfield Chia Pet I gave her for her birthday. Rosi somehow managed to spill the beans on that one while we were discussing head lice inspections.

On the other hand, Zena is an outright gossip. She was a hair stylist for a short spell before she became the school nurse, and she still does hair in her spare time for some extra cash. She can't keep secrets about her customers here at the school, so there's no way she'd be able to resist telling a bunch of them about me, figuring I wouldn't find out. But, things like that often have a way of getting back to you, or those who know you. I'd never say it out loud, but I do envy her. She's quite a temptress, and has never had any trouble finding a new fling when she's up for it, which is often. I'll never have her looks or her charm, but there's no doubt she could help me out. Still, the risk may be too great so I had better keep quiet.

Lynn did some recon, and found that only two men in the entire school are currently not spoken for: Winston and Jeff. I was not really into this "find someone at work" idea to begin with, because I don't want to have to come back and see my one-night stand every day. I don't think that would be a situation worth getting into. Also, there are a couple of problems with her two candidates. The first is that Lynn was not aware that Jeff is gay.

Winston DeVilbis is also out of the question. I don't even want to have to write about him, because it feels like I'm spilling something greasy all over the page. Winston is the vice principal who came to the school in September. He got transferred here from a tiny podunk as a last-minute replacement for his late predecessor. I don't know what constitutes requirements for a position as a vice principal in a town with an official population of "PLEASE! DON'T MOVE AWAY! WE'RE BEGGING YOU!" but I doubt it's much, seeing as how he's only in his early thirties.

Winston's almost universally-beloved around here. I don't think I've ever seen him at a time when he wasn't in the midst of a conversation. (That can't be what they're paying him for.) All the women would take him in a second, except for me and Natasha. And he'd probably have to take all the younger women, including Natasha, before he'd get to me. Maybe I can't stand him because he's the type who gets everything he wants and never seems to work for any of it. I really do not find him attractive, though. I think his personality is absolutely unbearable. People who are cocky and full of themselves are the ultimate turn-off for me.

You might be waiting for me to bite the bullet and admit that I can't stand him because I could never, um, "win the attentions of" somebody who I've heard even Lynn refer to as "cute." Really though, I think he would try to sleep with me, eventually. He strikes me as the type who wants to sleep with any woman just because he can. Like I said though, I'd have to be the last woman in the district he hasn't bedded yet before he'd consider it. Then again, maybe he knows how disgusted I am by him. He doesn't try flirting with me like he does with Zena or Rosi. Instead, he almost seems like he's trying to take me down a peg in the most subtle, barely detectable way he can. Though, that could be due to the fact that I've had to correct his understanding of "a.m." and "p.m." a couple of times. What kind of educator can't even keep that straight? Okay, I'll give him a break, maybe he's dyslexic. Nothing wrong with that.

Oh, I forgot about Principal Canada. Winston seems to grate on her nerves as well, but it was the superintendent's decision to put him here, so we're all stuck with him.

No, Principal Canada isn't a bank, she's the principal and her last name is Canada, a name that has always interested me. My best guess is that when some escaped slaves from the South got to choose their own last names, they wanted to name themselves after the country that they fled to. I can only imagine the ribbings she's gotten over the years for it. What really puzzles me is her first name: Miriam. How did she get a more Jewish first name than I did? I've been told that I was named for either Audrey Hepburn or Audrey Meadows, depending on which parent I asked. I should just be grateful it wasn't from *Little Shop Of Horrors*. "I'm a mean, green mother from outer space." That should be my new motto. Except that I'm none of those things, (though Willow might debate that last one.)

Work was uneventful, thankfully. On the way home, I stopped for that coffee. All day I was wondering where I should go for it and what I should get. I recalled that a few weeks ago, they were giving out free sample sizes of cappuccino at the supermarket, and I did enjoy the smell. At the time, I never thought I'd drink one, but that's what I ended up doing today.

Okay. My mind was made up: cappuccino it would be. So, I ended up at that Starbucks near the corner of Ward and Alexander. I was kind of dreading it as I approached, knowing that this could set the tone. Of all the things I'm now intent on doing for the first time, this would be the first. The first first. Though it wouldn't really have much of a bearing on anything else in a logical sense, I was crossing my fingers in the hope that I'd like this. I wanted to come away from this with a good feeling.

I went in and stood in line. After ten minutes, I came to the conclusion that I was standing in the line for people who had already ordered. I went around to the other line, the one that actually led to the register. Batting a thousand so far.

When I got to the front, I just flat out asked for a cappuccino, nothing added. That's it. It must have been pretty obvious to the cashier that this was my first time at one of these places. When she asked my name, I said "Jessica." I've been thinking on it for a while, and that name seems okay. But "Audrey"? The first syllable is the very sound of disappointment. What on earth could an audrey be anyways? It sounds like a burden. The "dr" of the second syllable brings to mind "drag", "draw", "drape", "drab." Is an audrey a sack of rocks you carry slung over one shoulder? Maybe it's an obsolete piece of farm machinery, gathering rust and cobwebs. "You kids stop running around over there. I don't want anybody climbing on top of that audrey! It hasn't been touched in decades and it could crack up and fall apart at any second!"

But everybody knows what a Jessica or a Jennifer is: they're girls' names. What else could they be? Maybe I'd like to be a Vanessa or a Veronica. My first instinct for classifying things is the alphabet. I feel that when it comes to evoking feminine sex appeal, you can't go wrong with J or V, which should be no coincidence as they're the newest and therefore youngest letters of the alphabet. X is perfect, but X names are so rare that they're not believable. Lucky Zena got a Z name, so she wins again. Truth be told, A isn't really that bad. It's a leader, it's looked-up to, it's sharp and assertive... just not when it's making the sound that begins "awful" and "awkward". That is A on the toilet.

I was so occupied with thinking about what my official fake name should be that I almost missed the one I already picked once it got called. Whoever wrote "Jessica" on the cup left a lot to be desired in the penmanship department, having written "Jes" followed by a squiggly incoherent tail with a dot for the non-existent I. I picked up the coffee and headed for the exit so I could drink in privacy.

As I approached the door, a man with two children in tow came in. I'd guess the kids were probably ten and twelve, if you pressed me for numbers. The father was asking the kids what they wanted. The older girl named something very specific, even using the correct Starbucks cup size jargon. These kids who couldn't even be teenagers yet were already coffee aficionados. How does something like that even happen?, I thought. If I had kids, there's no…

Damn. Damn, damn, damn.

"If I had kids." What if I get pregnant? Suddenly, after all this time, I find myself wanting to have sex and now I remember what it's really for. I have some research to do. I'm going to have to look into getting a hold of some birth control, because the last thing I need is a couple of caffeinated squirts in "Buzzed on Colombian" T-shirts jonesin' for some Folger's crystals.

I brought my cappuccino to the strip mall across the street. I sat on a bench and pretended to check messages on my phone while I drank it. I don't have a smartphone, all mine can do is calls and texts, but that's all I need. The coffee's taste did not live up to the promise of the aroma. I only got through half of it. Off to a great start.

Mom called about an hour ago. I told her about the cappuccino and she told me I went about it all wrong, not adding milk or cream or sugar. No wonder you didn't like it, she said. Well, I had to start somewhere, right? How am I going to know if I want to add dairy products or whathaveyou if I don't try the normal stuff straight up? It's not farfetched to think maybe I would have actually liked it better without anything added to it.

She was curious about why I had coffee for the first time today. Obviously, I could never tell her the whole truth, so I just kept it to "I just decided I should be trying new things." I didn't sense that she was onto me, she seemed to take it all at face value. I find it's easier to just do things and tell her about them after it's already done, or just never tell her at all. The less time she has to try to talk me out of making big decisions, the less I have to hear about it.

I have no idea how far I'll get with a few of these before she catches on. I'll probably end up giving myself away at some point by mentioning, "I have a doctor's appointment in the morning, Mom, so I should get going…"

"What are you seeing the doctor for, Audrey?"

"I'm getting vaccinated."

"How come you need vaccines?"

"They're for… my upcoming trip. To Europe."

"You're going to Europe!? Have you even thought this through? Do you realize how dangerous this could be? What if something happens to you? How would we ever know? Something like this will cost a fortune, how will you ever pay for it?"

And so on.

I'm certain that objective Number One would drive her over the edge. Maybe I should start preparing answers for the inevitable questions I'll be asked: What if I get pregnant? What if I get a disease? What if I go home with a guy and he kills me? What if I bring somebody to my place and he then knows where I live and stalks me for a while and then kills me? What if somebody sets me up with a blind date and then when I show up at the restaurant, my blind date kills me?

Though I would not appreciate being killed, if that were to happen I doubt there'd be much I could do about it after the fact. Of course, that's not the point of the questions. These questions are asked in order to seed as much doubt in my mind as possible in order to scare me away.

On the bright side, there's the possibility that she doesn't know I'm still a virgin, in which case she might not care. Thankfully, if there's one thing my parents absolutely never talk with me about under any circumstances, it's sex. I've got to keep it that way.

APR 23 (THU)

When I arrived at school today, George the custodian was out in front with Jaws, his bolt cutters. Jaws is kind of a legend around here, picking locks off of kids' lockers for years. The very first week I interned here, a few snickering little rat turds were throwing fries from their lunch trays across the cafeteria and George told them that if he caught them doing it again, he'd use Jaws to sever their Achilles tendons. A bit too specific of a threat to be laughed off, if you ask me. That's the sort of thing you have to think about beforehand, rather than just conjure up on the spot.

Today, Jaws was taking the chain off of a bike which had been in the rack out front since September. I asked where the bike's owner was, and George told me he had no idea. He was just told to dispose of the abandoned bicycle.

I made an impetuous decision. I told George that I'd take the bike off his hands, and he was more than happy to let me take responsibility for it. I haven't ridden a bike since I was about twelve, but now I figure I can do this for fun and exercise every once in a while. I brought it inside and left it behind the library counter all day, hoping nobody would notice, and got away with it.

Now that I think about it, I honestly do not know why I wanted a bike other than it being free. I never wanted one before, and I'm pretty sure the law says I have to wear a helmet. Well, tough. I'm breaking the helmet law. I'm not gonna ride this thing around all the time, so I think I can get away with it.

It was Thursday, which means Lynn's class came in to return their books and check out new ones. While the kids were milling about, Lynn came over to me with some news. She subtly pumped Zena for some opinions on clubs in the area.

"I told her it was for me. Since Brian and I are through, I'm putting myself back on the market anyway," Lynn said. Not a bad cover story. Brian had been Lynn's boyfriend since before we met. Then, out of nowhere, it was over. I didn't want to pry into their business, so I'm not certain why they split, but it seems pretty final.

According to Zena, the best club in Ridgeway is Regent over on Siegel Street. We'll go tomorrow night. Friday. Perfect. I'm going to a nightclub for the first time.

Lynn thought it would be a good idea to round up as many women as we could in our general age bracket to come with. The more, the merrier, right? Maybe we could walk down hallways and staircases in slow motion while the first thirty seconds of "How Soon Is Now?" plays in the background.

Natasha is already back from her stay at the hospital. She'd never milk a minor incident for all she could. Even though I knew clubbing wasn't her thing, I went out of my way to ask her if she was interested in coming. She declined. Also, she's married. That slipped my mind again, and I didn't even remember until I began writing this paragraph. Lynn says Rosi is in, and Jeanette the kindergarten teacher is out. That just left Zena. I caught her on her way out at the end of the day, just as she was locking up the nurse's office.

I asked if she was free tomorrow night and if she wanted to come to Regent. I acted like I didn't know Lynn had spoken with her at all: "Lynn's on the rebound and had this idea that she was going to pick up a new guy there. I thought maybe you could come with us and maybe help her out, ya know? Give her some tips and such?"

Zena was kind of hesitant at this point. She checked her smartphone calendar to see if she had any prior engagements.

"And, perhaps," I added, "you might be able to help me out as well? I'm not really good at this sorta thing and I was hoping that maybeeeee… you know."

That made her smile. She said she'd be there. I have to say, I was over the moon at that moment. If anyone can help me, it's her. But, my enthusiasm was dampened a little by her next words.

"To tell the truth, I haven't been going out as much anymore. I guess since I'm thirty now, I'm slowing down a bit. Getting up there in years. Audrey, treasure your youth while you still have it."

I said I'm twenty-nine. Zena's eyes immediately assumed a look of half-awe and half-terror, like she'd just recognized me from a WANTED poster. I get that a lot.

I rode my new bike home from school. It was pretty satisfying, particularly the part where I went sailing past a small traffic jam. One driver yelled, "Cheater!" He must have been pretty mad that I was going faster than he was. Or, maybe he just thinks anyone riding a bicycle must be Lance Armstrong.

Willow was not in when I came home, but Wes was. He was splayed out on the couch like a Dali clock. His snoring was loud enough to nearly drown out the endless 30-second loop of music that accompanies the DVD menu for *Supersize Me*. I went into my room to plan for tomorrow.

Haven't decided what to wear yet, may need some advice on that one. I'll probably ask the others for help on that one at the school tomorrow. I won't bother Lynn tonight, since she mentioned stopping by her folks' place to watch a Red Sox game. She's actually a Mets fan, but her dad's okay with it as long as they both stay in their own leagues and both hate the Yankees.

Big day tomorrow. I'm going into this like it's already mine. Audrey Perlmutter is officially available and looking for a male. Let the games begin.

APR 25 (SAT)

I went to a nightclub for the first time last night and didn't come back until about 2 a.m., so forgive me for not finding the time to write yesterday. In fact, you should expect that I won't have something to say every day. Probably for the best, because I do seem to be writing an awful lot so far.

Once I got home from work, I picked out an outfit (lilac blouse and black skirt) and took a two-hour nap. Got up, showered, got dressed, and sat around anticipating. Told myself a lot of things like, "This is already yours!" The regular sort of upbeat motivational bullshit. Saying it and meaning it are two different worlds, neither of which have much in the way of gravity.

I took the bus to the general area where Regent is and showed up early as I always do. I stood across the street, keeping watch for any of the others. Zena and Lynn showed up on the next bus, then Rosi's brother came by to drop her off. Lynn was compelled to do a last-minute check on my hair and warpaint. She picked a tiny speck of lint off my collar.

"There. Good to go," she said, sounding very satisfied. Ah, yes. That lint could have ruined everything for me.

Zena had hit the crosswalk button during Lynn's fussing with my appearance (which I'm now thinking was a clever ruse to steal my lint,) and called for us to get a move on while the WALK sign was still lit. "Let's get a move on. You ready? Audrey?"

"I'm a mean, green mother from outer space," I said, sounding dead-serious. Nobody had any reaction at all. They didn't get it. Now they must all think I'm genuine weirdo, because unless you know the source material, how else do you interpret something like that? Crossing that one off the list of potential catch-phrases.

Lynn asked if there was a chance we could get turned away at the door. There wasn't a line at the door when we showed up, so that didn't seem like it would be the case. Zena reassured her that we met the dress code and that a group of four women aren't going to get sent away. Sure enough, we weren't. The guy manning the door stamped each of our right hands and in we went. Once I was done scrutinizing my stamp to try to decode what its smeared ink said ("Regent," believe it or not) I looked up and got my first impression.

It was terrific. I was in a building with hundreds of other people my own age and I didn't see a single person who was baseball-capped, flip-flopped, or pajama-panted. All night, the only time I saw a brand name of liquor, it was on a bottle rather than a shirt. I won't lie, I was frightened at first. It was like walking into a movie theater halfway through the first act: a big, bright, flashing screen in a dark room full of strangers and loud, throbbing music. The dancefloor was huge but mostly empty. It was still early yet, so I decided to wait until it filled up some more and have the anonymity of a crowd to keep me from standing out. Rosi picked out a table near the wall to establish a "base camp".

I wasn't ready to drink yet. I didn't know what it would do to me and I didn't want to get sick my first night out, so the whole night I only had two glasses of water. I stayed at the table for about thirty minutes, waiting for the crowd to thicken. The bass was loud. I mean, I expected that, but this was really loud. I couldn't hear my own voice at times, and in certain spots, the vibrations in my throat were overridden by the ones coming from the music. Hear? I couldn't even FEEL myself talking. I couldn't feel my ears pop. I must have tried a hundred times. This must be like that quiet room that absorbs so much noise that you go insane from not hearing yourself speak. That is, except for the part about being quiet.

I kept an eye on the door the whole time I was at the table, looking to cross any prospects off of my list if they came as part of a couple. I'd have to say a little more than half the guys who filed in were spoken for already. Are they just trying to ruin things for the rest of us? Well, I suppose Regent isn't a club meant for just singles.

I was just about to make my way onto the dancefloor when I saw Zena waving me over. "Hey! Audrey Two!" is what I could make out from my limited lip-reading capabilities. Oh, so she did get the line from earlier. Fantastic. Now I only feel like two-thirds a weirdo.

From what I could gather, she wanted to show me some dance steps. Or maybe she was just looking out for me, and wanted to keep me close. Either way, I didn't really pay attention. I had found a good groove with a left-left-right-right pattern that I spent the night perfecting and adding occasional arm gestures to. I slipped up a few times, but nobody cares, really. As long as there were no time signatures with odd numbers in them, I was good. I may be tone-deaf, but I have great rhythm.

I still felt out of sync with everybody else. Glancing over at Zena, I realized what it was: I wasn't smiling. I had to fix this, and tried to put a huge smile on my face. Thankfully, the big screen helped me on this point, as the visuals being presented were pretty absurd. There were clips of *Teletubbies* and *Sesame Street* interspersed with black-and-white footage of a speech being delivered by Franklin Roosevelt. Then, for four seconds, all the lights came on. No! This wasn't part of the deal!

Okay. It's back to normal. Just part of the show. With my face, I needed this place dark if I wanted to get anywhere. Plus, the music was enough to block out my voice, so I had that going for me, too. It may have sounded like a woodpecker stuck in an Atari, but it was working in my favor.

I glanced over in the direction I last saw Zena, but couldn't place her. By now, things were getting mighty crowded and my dancing had become bobbing in place. Four people surrounded me, each facing the other way, so they wouldn't necessarily know someone was right there. I was down to a patch of territory roughly the size of an LP sleeve. I kept my arms frozen to my sides to minimize the chance of accidental hand-rump contact. It didn't work. I must have grazed my hand against about thirty butts, male and female, before the night was through. Everyone seemed to understand. There is hope for this species yet.

14

I was on the dancefloor for nearly an hour, the second half of which was spent trying to navigate my way through the crowd and back to the table. It took a while, but I was finally able to follow in the wake of somebody more experienced at this than me. I sidled and squeezed my way through, only to find Lynn still drinking at the table with a note written on a napkin.

"I'll be at someone else's place tonight. Don't wait for me." The signature was a flowing Z with a couple of loops at the corners.

Well, Zena had no trouble, at least. Looking over the room again, I came to the conclusion that this was going to be a LOT harder than I thought. Despite my efforts to keep tabs earlier, I had no idea who was taken and who wasn't. This is especially vexing for me, as introductions are what I'm worst at. Plus, I should at least be able to hear what others are saying. I've decided that having my voice heard is worth having my words heard.

Things were looking kind of dangerous now. Lemon wedges were all over the floor, begging to be photographed and submitted as Exhibit A should somebody get injured. There were more than a few ice cubes, too. Rosi was nowhere to be seen, and Lynn was getting pretty plastered. I figured I should stay at the table and keep an eye on her until our remaining party member resurfaced.

We ended up leaving about thirty minutes past midnight. Rosi and I practically carried Lynn to the bus stop and up to her door. Drunk Lynn sure seems to hate Brian a lot more than sober Lynn. He was called every name in the book during our trip home, including a few new ones Lynn invented, like "nang" and "brench."

Honestly, I knew nothing was going to happen on the first night. Rome wasn't burnt in a day, after all. I went home, where I knew I'd end up, and crawled into bed alone, like I knew I would. I went out that night with the attitude of knowing it was already mine, that I was going to make at least some progress. But, it was all for show. What I really knew was that things weren't going to work out immediately and that I still have a long road ahead of me. I just can't turn off the logic. When you know something, you know it. If I'm going to change my mind on something, I have to be convinced, not just encouraged.

It was a pretty good Saturday though, the weather in particular. April's finally starting to live up to its promise.

I decided to make a list of everything I have going for me. It will help me to look on the bright side.

1. I'm only 29, but I look young for my age on top of that. It could be that I have good genes, as far as that goes. I'm pretty sure staying away from drinking and smoking my whole life have helped out, though. Guess it wasn't all a waste.

2. I guess I've got a reasonably good body. Nothing to write home about, but my frequent exercising has kept my weight in check. Mom's now concerned that I'm anorexic because I "only" weigh in around the 120 - 125 range. No matter what it is I'm doing, there *has* to be something wrong with it.

3. I don't have thick or bushy eyebrows. That has to be a plus, right? I dunno, that's kind of a reach.

4. I'm smart. I'm good with words and math and geography. Not exactly something guys are looking for, but good news is always welcome.

There's a few more I thought of, but like that last one they're not really pertinent to achieving the goal, so I'll leave them for now. I'll check in on that list again later if I come up with anything.

Looking back at Regent, I'm certain I know what my problem is: I don't know how to approach any of these people because I have no idea what any of their individual statuses are. Who's taken? Who's available? Who's just here to dance? I have no leads. What I need is a third-party, a mutual friend who can introduce me to guys he or she knows.

Maybe there's a singles-only place around here that... yeah, never mind. As if that would stop them. Steady couples would march right in, brazen as fucking daylight, and demand to be served. Probably make a lot of noise about "I thought this was a free country!" and start comparing themselves to Rosa Parks. And the owner would cave to them because, hey, "the customer is always right." Imagine if companies really did adhere to the edict of "the customer is *always* right." Capitalism would collapse in a day.

- "Two-hundred dollars? But the ad in my paper said they were only fifty cents! Swear to God!"
- "What do you mean my lottery ticket didn't win? There must be something wrong with your machine."
- "Hi, I bought a donut here three weeks ago, but when I took it home to eat it, it

turned out to be just this rusty old nail. You have to give me a free one now, since I already paid. And another free one as an apology."

I get the sense that a lot of couples feel that they're on a higher private plane than singles, even if it's only because they have a trump card: they can shame people into shutting up. Sex is used as a weapon to try to silence those of us who aren't as sexually active, usually through a childish changing of the subject. It's like the fable of the caterpillar that was picked up by a child, looked down at its peers on the ground, and thought it had turned into a butterfly. It is never explained why we're supposed to feel inferior, but we do, even though that caterpillar looks pretty deluded from this angle.

I suppose the unspoken assumption is that any opposition must be motivated by jealousy, and therefore should be dismissed without addressing it directly. "You're just jealous," is the final refuge for those who have no sound argument to make when faced with criticism, a one-size-fits-all answer for any situation. Probably the best example of this in my life is my relationship with Willow. Even though the rent is split down the middle, she pretty much has most of the apartment to herself due to the presence of Wes. Because they're a couple, they should be afforded their privacy. Of course, if I were to start bringing a guy over from time to time then it would be Willow's turn to make herself scarce. (If that were to happen, I have no doubt that the first thing I'd hear would be "I never agreed to that!")

At times, when I'm cooped up in my room, I'll have to go to the bathroom. On the way back, I'll get another drink of water. Then, an hour later, the process repeats. Leaving my quarters for the bathroom means that I have to pass through the back of the living room. Therefore, I have to do my best to sneak by Willow and Wes. I try my hardest to avoid detection because I don't want to irritate them by intruding on their business.

After one of those nights, Willow came up to me the next day and accused me of going to the bathroom just to spite her. I'd like to think I was polite in suggesting that maybe, if they wanted to make sure I didn't walk in on anything, they could stay in Willow's room rather than in what is supposed to be neutral territory.

"Hey, don't try to punish me for your jealousy," was essentially her response to that.

This is where I ended up. I'm living in a world where I am accused of urinating out of jealousy.

So, there was a sudden shake-up today.

The kids were all cooped up at an assembly, so Lynn, Rosi and Zena stopped by the library to talk about Friday night. Natasha came along just to listen, perhaps wanting to feel more like part of the group. I really should get to know her better, and I get the feeling she wanted to come with us but her marriage got in the way. I was a bit distracted by the papers I was filling out at my desk and didn't want to participate at first, as I was a little worried about coming across insensitive, maybe slipping and saying the wrong thing in front of Natasha. She goes to church every Sunday, so I didn't want to be the one to say something that would offend her. Still, once things got going I was dragged in and yakking away with the rest of them.

Zena told us about the guy she met, but she doesn't think she wants to see him again. She says he "can't keep up" with her. Rosi went on for a couple of minutes about the men there that night, and how she didn't like a single one. Maybe she didn't know that Lynn and Brian were through, because she made a point of mentioning that she and I were the only two who, quote, "weren't gettin' any!" I responded, saying something along the lines of, "Well, someday I'll get my chance." In the midst of the rousing conversation, I didn't even realize what I had said until after it came out.

There was a short silence. Zena broke it by asking what I meant by "someday."

Shit.

Loyal Lynn tried to throw up a distraction. "Hey! Did anyone notice they haven't refilled that vending machine since February? It hasn't had orange soda in ages! Which one of you likes orange? Rosi? No, it's Natasha, right?"

"I should have known! I should have known!" Rosi squealed, as if she were trying to avoid bursting into laughter. Zena looked kind of concerned. Natasha looked the way she always looks.

Lynn again: "Hey! What about that kid who got into the elephant pit at the zoo yesterday? Anyone see that on the news?"

Zena asked if I was a virgin. Lynn shouted something about an internet video of a bank robber slipping on a patch of ice.

I looked over to make sure the door was shut. I couldn't even look at them. I closed my eyes and said, "Yes. I am. But you absolutely must keep it a secret from everyone. Okay? Can you promise me that?" They all said my secret was safe with them. As if I had a choice anymore.

I opened my eyes and Zena's look of concern seemed to have become one of amusement. "I feel now like I always kind of knew, but never thought about it before," she said. "The concept of Audrey having sex is one that never occurs naturally. You need something like this to come up to force it into your mind, otherwise the two ideas never cross paths." Just for the record, I was still sitting about eight feet away.

Natasha stepped forward in my defense, telling the other two to knock it off. "I didn't do it until I was about Audrey's age. I wanted to make absolutely sure I waited for a man who truly loved me."

"Natasha, we ARE the same age. You're only four months older than me. Happy belated thirtieth, by the way."

"Oh. I thought you were twenty-three."

They were clearly having fun with me. Maybe even Natasha wasn't serious for once. I had to put an end to this. "Come on, somebody could hear us. Can we please not discuss this at work?"

So we discussed it after work. They really wanted to know what was going on with me, so I gave in, but only on the condition we go somewhere with a better degree of privacy. We went straight from work to the park by the reservoir. It's mostly thought of as a small beach, so it's usually deserted before the summer kicks into gear. The five of us took a picnic table and I kept my eye on an elderly man walking his dog along the shore. I was worried he might have that super hearing-aid from one of those two-minute commercials that ends with the words "Call now!"

Rosi caught me eyeing him. "Jeez, Audrey. You're being a little paranoid. You're really that ashamed of this?"

"I'm not ashamed. I'm afraid. If people find out about this, I'll be a laughing stock," I said, hoping to jog a bit of self-awareness in her.

So, I told the four of them the condensed version of the last fifteen years of my life, again on the condition that they wouldn't breathe a word of it. Well, here's how it happened...

For some reason, I've never felt any physical attraction to anybody based on their appearance, male or female. I still don't know why that is. As a teenager, I did feel like I got along well with a few of my male friends, and actually thought they might be interested in me. But whenever the wheels came off one of those notions, the boy in question would go back to being just another normal person to me. It's kind of like I felt attraction *towards* them without being attracted *to* them, if that makes sense. I only liked a guy if I thought there was a chance we could be more than friends, but that never came to be. With my friends coupling off and drifting away from me, I felt left out and needed the companionship more than anything.

Zena threw this out: "Audrey, if you have no sexual attraction to guys, I think you may be a lesbian."

"You don't understand. I just don't feel anything for anybody. I've never been aroused by the sight of another person."

Rosi seemed to think this was a bit too melodramatic to be true. "Okay," she said, "so what are you thinking about when you play with yourself?" She's not exactly the best at toning down the language at sensitive moments, but that was actually a bit better than I would have expected.

It should have been harder for me to admit it, but without hesitating, I just calmly said, "cartoon characters."

"Oh yeah! You read those black-and-white Japanese comics. I remember now! So, is that like porn for you?"

"Ummm, sometimes. Anyway..."

I suppose I always read the signals the wrong way, because I just never got asked out. If I did the asking, there was always an excuse. To this day, I've never even been on a date.

Out of the blue, Rosi became very angry at this point. "You mean you didn't even go to the prom? That's terrible! My prom was one of the best times I ever had! No girl should have to miss her prom!"

"Well," I said, "some do. Life ain't Hollywood."

In college, I felt like I could put if off, and wait for somebody to make the first move. If someone else approached me, I'd be willing to give them a chance, but it never happened. I don't know why. Instead, I had to cope by convincing myself that I wasn't missing out on anything and just suppress it all. I just assumed eventually things would work out in their own time. Well, time's up. I've waited too long without doing anything about it.

Piercing as always, Natasha asked, "So what is it you *are* after?"

"At this point, it's all about the sex. Just the experience, the physical sensation and all that goes with it. I don't want to hurt anyone by leading them on when I don't want a relationship. But I need to do something for myself," I said in my best 'wistful' voice, trying to turn the profane into the profound.

Natasha had a follow-up question. "Then why don't you just pay somebody? If you're afraid of breaking the law, there are countries where it's legal."

"That is Plan Z," I sighed.

"If any of you have suggestions," Lynn said, "I'm making it my new project to get Audrey laid. Any help at all is welcomed." I was so thankful upon hearing this that I wanted to give her a hug, in spite of the fact that my mission was now a project. That makes it sound a lot more difficult, doesn't it? A mission is going to the store to pick up last-minute ice and cups for the party. A project is getting there and back in reverse gear.

Rosi, still seeming to be incensed by the prom, stood and announced she wanted to help. It would be a great excuse to do more clubbing, she said, and also that it would be like "a fun game." I have no idea how I'm supposed to react to a statement like that.

Zena said she's not letting us do this without her. Now we're getting somewhere. Anything Zena has to offer on this subject I want to hear. Natasha says she's there for me, even though she's not sure she can give me much in the way of help.

So, that's that then. My secret got out, but it was contained. Somehow I've gathered a small team to keep an eye out for opportunities and lend me their support in my journey. Things are looking up. I am now really starting to believe that this is going to happen. I am going to have sex.

I have the best friends I could ever ask for.

UPDATE. Rosi just texted me. Says she wants to have day-glo yellow T-shirts made, with the words "AUDREY DE-VIRGINIZATION PROJECT" on them.

UPDATE 2. Another text. Make that "FIRST ANNUAL AUDREY DE-VIRGINIZATION PROJECT."

APR 28 (TUE)

Fate must be smiling on me. I finally got in touch with Angela again.

Ange and I were close friends all throughout school, reaching back to when I was eight. We were close the whole time, but we did drift apart a little bit in high school when all my friends started dating. Since graduation, I've seen her only a handful of times, when she'd visit her family for holidays back in our hometown of Railhead. She went to college in Rochester and stayed there after getting her sheepskin, but just today I found out she lives in Massachusetts again, and right here in Ridgeway, to boot.

The other day, I sent out a bunch of texts to my old friends from Railhead, trying to get back in touch with them again. I felt guilty, like I'd been neglecting them all these years even though I had their numbers. They all just live so far away now, so I never really saw the purpose. Of course, since the incident last week, I've had to re-evaluate my stance on only seeing my friends when it happens to come about on its own. The only two who've gotten back to me so far are Lexy (still living out in Long Beach) and Angie. Ange just called this morning and left a message for me, telling me to visit her new place.

Ange and her steady guy Lew (they've been living together for about eight years now, I think) have a nice third-story apartment in the Almaburg neighborhood. They've only been in Ridgeway for a few weeks now. Seems Lew just began a new job at Mt. Hope Bay Hospital, and Ange doesn't need to be anywhere in particular for her job. She composes and records original music for the backgrounds of political commercials. She has to make sure that the image of the candidate gets associated with bright, positive music and that you hear an ominous, chilling drone whenever the opponent is being discussed (which always happens over low-res, slow-motion footage of the subject at a debate, strangely enough.)

Ange and I are a case study in how two people with so much in common can take very different paths once they've been taken out of a high school environment. Without any schedules or rules to adhere to, I fell flat on my face, as following the rules was the only thing I'd ever been taught. It seems like everywhere she went right, I went wrong. I don't have a thing against her, because she's never been anything but a friend to me and she's the most wonderful person. Still, I feel a little gypped, mad at the system. In high school, I was genuinely shocked to find she (and all of my other friends) had started smoking pot. I've been offered it plenty of times since, but have always had to refuse, maybe out of a misplaced sense of pride, but mostly a fear of getting caught and facing the consequences. Ange didn't just stop at marijuana, though. She would dice up her medication tablets into fine dust and snort them. One time I was present for a powdered-drink-snorting session. I think it was the blue flavor of Kool-Aid with the octopus in a top hat on the packet. He was a magician.

"What the hell? This can't end well, this just can't," I'd think. I was genuinely concerned for her future at the time. Now, we sat together in the same room about a decade later. On one side of the table, the beautiful young professional with a steady of eight years, both gainfully employed, living together in a gorgeous new apartment and going out to parties regularly. On the other... um, me. I should have broken the rules. I shouldn't have played it safe all my life. Maybe I'd just end up in the same place I am now, but I would have at least enjoyed the ride once in a while.

We had some time to catch up with each other. Ange filled me in on everything I mentioned above. My turn. Okay, this won't be hard. I had already gone through it before, so I spilled my guts to Ange the same way I did to Lynn. I was getting good at this now.

"You know, I've been to Amsterdam, and they've got this district called de Wallen that's nothing but sex workers," she said, almost instantly.

Why do people keep saying that? I'm starting to think there's something about myself that my friends aren't telling me.

Ange just may be the key to this whole thing. She's out and about all the time. She has to know all the clubs and secret hotspots for meeting and hooking up. As much as I appreciate everything the girls at work are doing for me, they pretty much travel in very small circles, except for Zena, who has burned more than a few bridges. Any help I can get is welcomed.

A couple of hours later, Ange was driving me to her yoga class in Rehoboth, about 20 minutes away. She had asked if I wanted to join her, as she does this on an almost nightly basis. We stopped over at my place, I ran in to change my clothes, and grab a beach towel and a bottle of water. She had a spare yoga mat in her car for just such an occasion. I hadn't intended on ending up doing this today, but there I was. I guess this is the way things go sometimes when you act impetuously: you find yourself being driven to Rehoboth for your first "hot yoga."

I thought that "hot yoga" was a figure of speech. I was told it would be upwards of 100 degrees Fahrenheit in there, but I didn't know that was literal. Or on purpose. I thought it would just feel like 100 degrees once I was finished. When Ange explained it to me, I thought we would be listening to relaxing music in a setting where I might work up a sweat, but hey, exercise does that. Might get a little hot under the collar, that's to be expected though.

"Sweating out the toxins," as she put it.

"I've heard that before. Is there any scientific veracity in that phrase?"

"Probably not."

We showed up, and I had to take off my shoes and socks before we even got into the class. I spent a couple of minutes looking for matching clean socks in my drawer, all for naught. Ange opened the door and ARE YOU KIDDING ME? Did this door open up a portal to Satan's personal fart storage facility? Okay. Calm down. It can't be this bad the whole time. Put my mat down here, towel and... already sweating. Good omen.

The instructor led us in a chant and I think I hit a good note. I should write that note down so I can practice later. Maybe I can help fill out the stereo-scape for some a cappella group that's sounding a little thin. I'll just do that one note while they're busy doing the hard stuff and nobody will even notice. Then, the instructor came over to us one by one while we were doing our first pose and left a couple of maroon blocks next to each of us. Turns out that these were blocks which would be necessary for doing a few poses. Because of the temperature and humidity, I was initially certain that they were sauna bricks.

I was hoping I'd be able to show off a little bit. I can reach my arms all the way around my back to the other side no problem. Never a challenge for me to apply my own sunscreen back there. Also, I can put both my legs behind my head at the same time, a skill I learned when I was underwater, believe it or not.

Note to future generations who decode this tome: If you're going to learn to put both your legs behind your head at once, do not try to do so underwater your first time. I now know that I was very lucky.

Somewhere around the second "downward dog" I noticed my towel was suddenly too short to accommodate my body. How could it be shrinking? Maybe I was just being stretched out? Also, the towel kept getting gradually nudged forward bit by bit and I had to go back a few times and re-align it with Ange's. Sort of broke the flow, but if I didn't then I would have been behind the instructor by the end of class. I'm glad I got water from the tap instead of wasting the cold stuff in the fridge. It was pretty much fit for bathwater by the time I took my first sip (which was only about two minutes in.)

It wasn't long at all before I was starting to struggle. My thoughts were pretty much on a downhill slope after only ten minutes. I don't want to sweat out my toxins! I want them back! Come back, toxins! I can't... I... What?... Snagglepuss?... What are you doing here?... With my.... Hey... That's my gravy boat... Give it back... It's mine...

No!... I WON'T go to Jo-Ann Fabrics... I am not going... to... Jo... You,... You pink bastard! This isn't cartoons, this is *prime time!*

Oh dear. I think everything after "toxins" came out of my mouth, and the person next to me heard it. Also, I was pretty sure I was dehydrating by now. My head was throbbing. I had no more energy. Just had to lie down and rest for a little while.

And then I could not get back up.

I was not serene.

The instructor turned the lights out for some reason. I lied there in the dark, on a mat, in a room full of strangers while one woman watched over us all and made sure we were all kept in line. I was back in preschool.

When the class finally ended, I had enough energy to get back up (once the doors were opened and temperature began returning to a reasonable level, of course.) Looking around, it became clear why my spot had not been taken by the time we arrived: I was closer to the radiator than anyone else in the room. I estimate that I only lasted about half an hour. Ange said she was impressed, and that I actually kept it up twice as long as she did her first class.

On the way home, Ange mentioned that she might be up for going to Europe with me. Maybe in August, though. She's pretty busy as it is, and in July she's going to a music festival out in California. Lexy's going to join her there. I think I might consider going with her just to see Lexy again, even though it doesn't sound like the sort of thing I'd enjoy. Well, we'll see.

Yeah, who am I kidding. That ain't happenin'. Imagine me in a field in California in July with tens of thousands of screaming drug-fueled college kids. Possible causes of death: dehydration, suffocation, over-exposure to the word "awesome." I'm not adding "Leave my sunburned corpse for the coyotes" to my list anytime soon.

As for right away, Angela said she'd be more than happy to take me out to Cambridge this Friday. There's a late-night gathering where she's planning to meet up and catch up with a lot of people she knows in those parts. I guess she DJs in her spare time and she's made more than a few trips out to the Boston area over the years for it.

"I'll know pretty much everyone there," she claims. "I'll introduce you to some guys."

That was exactly what I needed to hear. Friday it is.

APR 29 (WED)

Some fourth-graders were chatting in the library today and I happened to overhear them. They were curious about what happened to Hunter Burnside's bike.

"It was in the bike rack a few days ago and now it's gone!" one panicked kid said.

"I heard some big kid stole it 'cause he was running from the police and he used it to get away," said another one.

"They must have given it to Hunter's family to remember him by," hypothesized another.

"Or, a librarian took it because it was free," a nearby 29 year-old woman thought to herself with a twinge of guilt. I guess I won't be riding that bike to work now.

I was able to join Lynn and Rosi in the lounge while their classes were at lunch and recess. Lynn found the details of my yoga class rather humorous. I'm glad I didn't get carted off in an ambulance. Lynn would have died laughing.

Throughout my recounting of the events, Rosi was eating her sandwich slowly, and with a look of suspicion, as if I might try to steal it from her at any moment. I don't want that thing, somebody's already eaten half of it. I asked what was up.

"You weren't gonna tell me? You told Lynn, but I found out by accident."

It took a few seconds before I realized what she meant. "Rosi, I wasn't going to tell anyone. And I didn't. For years. I only told Lynn because I know I need help with this. The fewer people you tell a secret to, the smaller the chance it will get out. Plus, I've only known you for about eight months. It's nothing personal."

"Well, I guess I understand."

I further explained that not even my parents knew, and she seemed to feel validated by that. She felt like she was in on some really covert stuff now. She wanted to get walkie-talkies and matching sunglasses for everyone in our secret little cadre. "Operation Audrey De-Virginization Project" she christened it. Oh yeah, that's real secretive. I would have gone with something like "Operation Cherry Blossom", anything that at least tries for subtlety.

Rosi wanted code names, too. Hers is Mai Tai. Lynn wants to be Mrs. Met. I couldn't come up with one right away. I thought maybe I could do something that related back to my name. I've always been interested in things with hidden meanings like that. Okay, let's see…

In German, Perlmutter means "one who sells mother of pearl." In English, it means "Okay, aaaaaand how do you spell that?" Not that it does any good. Half the time, a wayward A sneaks in, or a couple of Ds set up camp on land that is clearly property of the T family. So: mother of pearl. Nacre. Mollusks. Pearls. Oysters. Okay, I don't like where this is going. What else is related to mother of pearl? Oh! There was a Roxy Music song called "Mother of Pearl" ! Now think, what other Roxy Music songs are there? "More Than This", "Love Is the Drug", "Avalon". Ah. Got it. Perfect.

I gave them my answer. "Code name: Virginia Plain." No one's going to accuse me of being delusional. Or so I thought.

"What exactly is your mission objective?", Rosi asked as if she were a general sitting at a table with a huge map and little plastic tanks. She actually sounded a bit like

26

Natasha there.

"I guess I'd have to say: have sex. That is objective number one. I need to make up for lost time, so I'd like to do it with... let's say, seven guys minimum," I said. Then I said, "Why are you laughing?"

When Rosi regained her composure a little bit, she pointed out that she heard the average number of sex partners an average American has in a lifetime is around four, and that I've got some ground to make up. I wanted to explain how averages tend to be misleading when you have certain numbers you can't go beyond, such as zero. But, that wouldn't have accomplished anything. Ya gotta pick your battles.

Lynn said that she's been thinking it over and suggested I should consider looking for a boyfriend rather than casual sex. That is simply not in the cards. I'm aware that I ain't pretty, but I'm also dull and lack confidence. If I have to wait for someone who wants to be around me night and day, spending time with me, having conversations with me, then I'll be waiting forever. I'm done waiting. Besides, I can't even imagine how a relationship with me would last any longer than a few hours. What a trainwreck that would be.

Later, on my way home, a woman and her son walked past me. I recognized the kid as a second grader. He had an iced coffee in his hand. I suppose the logic is that coffee with ice in it isn't as unhealthy and fattening as a milkshake or a soda, but that's only true until you drench it with cream and sugar. Then it's a milkshake with caffeine in it. Kids drinking coffee. What a golden age we live in.

I stopped at the pharmacy to pick up those birth control pills I was thinking about, only to find out I need a prescription. I honestly had no idea. I guess the pill is a hot commodity out there. Back-alley drifters must be downin' those things like Skittles. Looks like I have to schedule a doctor's visit now, which I hate because of all the red tape I have to deal with. Once it's all over and done, I'm never sure how much money it's going to cost. It just doesn't seem worth it, but this time there's something I want. I just hope I don't have to prove anything to get it. I can't even fake a convincing sneeze.

I figured that if I couldn't get the pills yet, I might as well take care of things on the other end. Wouldn't hurt to get condoms, just in case I find myself with somebody who doesn't have any of his own. Can't be too careful with that. I figured I'd splurge and went for the box of twelve, seeing as how I'm always the eternal optimist (if that wasn't obvious by now.)

As I walked up to the register, my path took me past a white wire rack bin overflowing with enough colors to scar a chameleon for life. The sign read, "WOMEN'S UNDERWEAR $2 EACH". One-hundred pairs of panties, no two alike, were piled in a manner that only a multi-car collision could love. I actually gave it a look-see for a few seconds before realizing what I was doing and backed off. There's nothing really wrong about buying underwear from a bin I guess, as long as you wash before wearing. But, it still doesn't seem... "correct." Anyone off the street can touch it and yes, I know that's true of most clothes but I shouldn't have to point out why undies have to be held to a separate standard.

True, even the six-packs I buy have to be handled before being sealed up in their plastic bags, but out of sight, out of mind. I've never really strayed too far from plain white cotton. You could say I'm pretty utilitarian (derived from Latin "utia" meaning "cheap", and "litarus" meaning "skate".) At some point, I should consider adding a bit of color to my top drawer, but I haven't got a clue what to get. What, if anything, is right for me? It's the same reason I don't have any art or photos on the walls of my room: what am I supposed to do, look at them all the time? "Yep! Still the same as yesterday!" Just doesn't seem worth the trouble.

Now that I think about it, I guess the lingerie on the plastic hangers is free for anyone to handle as well, but something about bins is very unappealing. Just a week ago, that thing probably had off-brand boxes of fruit snacks in it. Can't say that about hangers.

Brought the condoms to my room when I got home and took one out to see what level of protection I was dealing with. I performed a stress test and tried to stretch it to a breaking point, but it held fast. Even blew it up like a balloon just to make sure no tiny holes escaped my vision. To think, it worked so well and it seemed thinner than a plastic Stop & Shop bag. Damn, science. You really dropped the ball on that whole global warming thing, but you can sure get it right when you friggin' *want* to.

Willow and Wes are playing a video game in the living room tonight, so I'm in solitary again. Mom called around 7:30. She said she wants me to see my physician Dr. Yiu with regard to my alleged weight problem. I don't know why she refuses to let that go. My BMI says I'm healthy. If this were Europe, I'd be a "medium." I wasn't the least bit worried, until she brought up the possibility that unexplained weight loss may be a symptom of cancer. Alright, you win, I said. Now I have to make two appointments to see doctors. Wheeee.

I did some looking online for something to do in Providence. It looks like there's a dance club that has an event every Tuesday night. The venue's website had a mock flyer on the front page ending with this line: "Everybody gets laid or a free T-shirt."   I know, I know. It's not meant to be taken literally. Still, it's at least worth looking into, just because not much else is going to be happening on a Tuesday. When a chance presents itself, I have to take it.

APR 30 (THU)

I heard once that if ten average straight young men and women, five of each, met for the first time in the same place that each of the men would immediately be sexually attracted to four of the women. Four of the women would each feel the same way about only one of the men. I feel like I must be the fifth woman in each case.

For some reason, I just don't find men attractive. I don't. Honestly, they all look the same to me. I can't recognize a person from their facial features unless I get to know them really well. There are teachers who have been at this school longer than I have who I still wouldn't be able to pick out of a police line-up.

I'm not sure what my "type" is. I guess I like people who like me. I can't really deny the narcissism inherent in that statement. I'm pretty sure that if somebody who didn't strike me as a knuckle-dragger showed genuine interest in me, I'd warm up to him without much trouble.

One thought has been nagging me since Monday, and I suppose that if I write about it, it might be therapeutic. It helps put things in perspective, seeing what I can admit to myself outside the safe confines of my own thoughts. It's been that way so far. When I was in the park a few days ago with Lynn and the others, I made mention of the fact that I have an inconvenient fetish. I can only get turned on by Japanese manga comics, the ones that are always printed in only black and white. I think I can attribute this to practically being raised by television. It's the reason why I've always liked drawing, even if I'm not necessarily that good at it. I think most people's fetishes must have some influence on the way they live their lives. I did want to become an author or a librarian, after all. It probably wouldn't be a shock to anyone that guys who are into feet are the most likely to look for work in shoe stores. When you start looking at every job through this lens, it's hard to stop.

Anyhow, I mention this because Rosi brought a newspaper to lunch today and wanted everyone to read their horoscopes. "They're all pretty good today, so you can't lose! What's your birthday?" I told her it's July 13, and she was amazed because that's the same as her brother's birthday. "What are the odds of that?" she asked. (Pretty sure it's 1 in 365.25)

My horoscope predicted that new friendships would soon present themselves and something about the planet Venus. Oh, so that's what I felt governing my interpersonal relationships around 9:35 last night: Venus. I should have known. I asked if Rosi could hand me the facing page so that I could do the Jumble. It was a really easy one for me, took about thirty seconds. Some of the comic strips were on this page as well, so I took a moment to read them.

Rosi saw me reading and asked me, "See anyone you like?"

"No, I've never really been into newspaper strip guys. I just like reading them. Unless you were joking, in which case, ha."

Rosi folded up the paper and rolled it into a tube so that it looked like a diploma from Hobo Tech. She gave me a quick donk on the head with it, and pressed the issue further as if she were intrigued by this kink of mine. "C'mon, I'm open-minded. Who are you into right now? Who's your big crush?"

I showed her a volume of *Yoichi-san no Hanafuda* I had stashed in my purse. I pointed out Junichi, the character I really like.

Open-minded Rosi then told me that was weird and that I am weird. "That's weird, Audrey. You're weird. There's two other guys on this page who are way hotter than him! What do you see in this average-looking guy?"

I said I didn't know exactly. I've never been into the really hot types of guys. We all have our likes and our own individual tastes. So, I guess I just like normal-looking, everyday people. I'd just like a regular relationship with someone I have a lot in common with. That's all I've really wanted. I just want things to be normal, and I guess real life is close enough.

Lynn, who was watching all this, had a theory: "I think something's been building up inside you for a long time. It wasn't just the car crash, though that may have been the last straw that set it all off. You've just been going through life without this thing and finally the denial of your natural urges reached a tipping point.

"I know how you feel, though. That happened to me once. There was this woman down the street from where I grew up, and she had a cat named Marco. Once in a while, when it was time for her to feed him, she'd go outside and call for him if he wasn't around. And this happened for, like, years. I couldn't take it anymore. One night, she's out there shouting 'Marco! Marco!', and I just lost it and went to my window and yelled 'POLO!' Mom was furious, but it was worth it."

What? I saw the connection, but that was the first comparison she could draw to her own life? You lucky, lucky woman, you.

She's right, though. During those frozen years I practically had no sex drive at all. I thought I came to terms with it all, but instead I was just putting it off. Who knows, maybe all this is coming to light now because I need some form of closure. I could be trying to reconcile my ambivalence towards males by giving it all another chance. There may not be any going back now.

I'm through living in only black and white. It's time to put a little color into the mix.

MAY 2 (SAT)

Went to the party in Cambridge with Angela last night. I spent a big chunk of daylight in bed today, since we didn't show up there until around one this morning. Ange kept texting somebody who was already there, asking if things had started to get going yet. Delay after delay kept us bouncing around Boston, popping in and out of a series of bars. The first one we went to had a pool table, and Ange was itching to play. The balls were all over the table, but nobody was present. It was a coin-op ball retrieval system, so someone had to have paid and left. We sat there, Ange with her beer and me with my anticipation, for twenty minutes according to my oft-checked cell phone. The game remained untouched.

"Okay. I'm done. Grab a stick and let's play," she said. We got up, re-racked the balls, and Ange broke.

The balls made their clacking mating calls. "HEY! That was *our* game!" was the immediate response from across the room.

Twenty minutes. This world. I've heard of playing chess by mail, but until yesterday, not billiards. Ange gave the game-neglecting urchins money for the next round and they let us finish without further hassle, though they kept staring at our game as if we were going to drop everything and take off at the count of three. You already have the money, what could we be trying to escape from?

There was really nothing of note at any of the other bars we stopped at. At the last one, I let out a yawn as I tried to keep myself busy with my pen and a nearby napkin. When you start seeing me play Tic Tac Toe against myself, that's when you know I'm bored beyond help. Ange thought I was tired. I assured her, it was just because I was waiting. We'd been out and about for three hours now. At this point, I was sure the night was going to be a complete snooze.

Ange decided 1 a.m. was late enough, and she drove me to the party and I was alert as ever again. Didn't expect what I saw: it was a bunker-like building so non-descript that it wouldn't have looked out of place no matter what it was zoned for. Brick, concrete, windows, and a sense that it had been unoccupied for at least a year. We walked around to the back. There was a person who couldn't have been described as anything but "a bouncer" checking IDs. Well, this must be the place, I thought. Looks deceive. In we went.

I was not expecting what I saw inside. There was one single colored light moving around in a figure-eight pattern. I'm pretty sure the rest of the lighting was from ordinary house lamps. The DJ's songs all had the exact same tempo and bass line, so they kind of bled into one long slog of a medley. Instead of a giant screen like the one at Regent, there was a regular-sized TV in the corner with the DVD player's "Insert disc" logo bouncing around. The wall had an old tapestry that was either orange and filthy or just colored a filthy orange. This place looked more like a suburban basement rec room than a club. In fact, I'm convinced this wasn't a club at all. I may have been in the home of squatters.

To be honest, I liked it much more than Regent. Everyone here seemed to know each other. The atmosphere wasn't slick and flashy, it was a lot more comfortable. There was no shortage of places to sit down, and I felt like if I did, I wouldn't stand out for being alone. Strangers might actually come up to me and start a conversation here, if they could hear me over the bass. Also, instead of getting my hand stamped, the woman by the door who took my admission fee just drew a smiley face with an eyebrow piercing on my right hand. I think the piercing was to detect counterfeiters.

Even though it was more than an hour past midnight, those messages Ange got were right: this place hadn't even gotten going yet. I estimated about thirty people in the room, not counting the people tending the bar and the DJ. About half of them were lined up against one wall in impregnable little chemical bonds of two and three. Everybody on the dancefloor seemed to be coupled up as well. But wait a minute, that one guy doesn't seem to be with anybody. And there's another one. They're not with any girls, and they…

Oh. Never mind. I should have realized something was up when I saw them wearing the only two balloon animal hats in the room.

May as well start dancing, I thought. Nothing else for me to do. Back to left-left-right-right, with minor embellishments as I saw fit. Kept that up for a while as the room began filling up, slowly but surely. I hadn't even noticed the influx until I decided to turn around and see where Angela was.

Ange was still in the same chair she sat down in upon arrival, talking to somebody now. I kept watch out of the corner of my eye for a minute or two, then I heard her call out, "Audrey!" and she signaled me over to meet her friend.

His name was Tim, and Ange had known him for a while now. I don't think she mentioned how they met. He had glasses and, uh, I don't really know how else to describe him. Like I mentioned before, I'm not good with faces. I just met him last night and the room wasn't well-lit, so if I saw him in a public place again, I probably wouldn't recognize him. If I had to provide a description, I'd say he seemed like... not the type of guy I would dislike. He was dressed well enough for casual Friday at the office, build was a speck or two on the smaller side of medium, hair was short and straight but mussed up just barely enough to be alluring. Um, what else? Did I mention glasses already?

Okay, it sounds like I wasn't immediately taken by his appearance. I never am. But, we exchanged a few words, he said I was pretty good at dancing. (Oh! Going out of his way to tell a white lie just to give me a compliment! I kinda like where this is going.)

Then he said, "Sit down." Not a domineering "Sit down," but an inviting and almost-sensual "Sit down." The tone of those two words spoke volumes to me. It was the way someone might say something like, "I really like you," or, "So, are you seeing anyone right now?" or,... I dunno, maybe something like, "Angela told me you're looking for someone to lose your virginity to and I'd be more than happy to oblige, so why don't we get out of here and make it happen?" That's what it sounded like to these ears.

So I sat down.

He wanted me to turn away from him. I complied and faced Ange in the chair next to me. I didn't see Ange's face as it was obscured by the bottom of a cup for the one half-moment I was able to concentrate. Tim's hands were on my shoulders now. He was giving me a neck rub that slowly worked its way into a backrub. I'd seen it flaunted before my eyes hundreds of times, this time I was experiencing it.

This was happening so fast, and it was perfect. I wasn't worried about anything. I didn't feel the least bit self-conscious. As far as I was concerned there was nobody else in the room. Maybe even the city. I don't think I was even aware of whether I was indoors or outdoors anymore. Tim may or may not have said something about how I felt tense, but my flight data recorder was out to lunch.

After a while, he stopped. He got up and told me to give him a hug, in a sympathetic and caring tone that wasn't too far removed from "Sit down." I was a little hesitant now. Why does he want me to hug him? Now I was starting to think that Ange really did explain my predicament to him, and that he seriously does want to, uh, "help" me. I don't care if Tim knows I'm a 29 year-old virgin. If he wants to change that, then the whole room can know, for all I care! I hugged him, and asked if he was going to lift me up and carry me outside. Instead, the massage went on, and he began working my back while my body was pressed against his.

This is it. This is really gonna be it, isn't it?

When he let go of me, we started dancing and talking. He asked how I knew Ange, and I told him we met when I was only eight.

"Angela's the greatest, isn't she?" he said. Somebody nominate this guy for "Understatement of the Year"!

"Oh, yeah! She's the best! I wish Angie was just made out of chocolate so I could eat up every last little bit of her!" What the hell was that? I don't even know what I meant by that! All I knew was that I already owed her everything.

Everything I just wrote, going all the way back to where Angela shouted my name, probably all played out in less than two minutes. They were the best two minutes of my life.

Tim kept dancing with me for ten more seconds before something caught his eye and he walked away without a word. He went over to talk to a couple he recognized and, from what I could hear, probably hadn't seen in a while. Oh, alright then. I'll just keep my place over here and wait for you to come back, I thought. So I just kept dancing in place. Left-left-right-right. Left-left-right-right. Over and over, on and on.

I kept it up for quite a while, maybe ten minutes.

Angela came by and said she was going into the smoking room. I was not aware there was a smoking room. Turns out that really ugly tapestry on the far end of the room was actually a really ugly curtain. Tim was already heading in. Therefore, so would I.

The smoking room (or, more accurately, "the cloud of smoke with a room around it") continued the rec room motif. It even had a lizard in a glass case under a hot lamp. Tim was in the corner with empty spots on either side. Given how every other seat in the room was taken, I considered this to be quite the stroke of luck. Ange sat by his left side and I plunked down on his right. The room was pretty close to the speakers, so it was harder to hear what was going on, particularly during the parts where our DJ's sleeve scraped against the mic.

Ange asked if I wanted to hit a joint she just rolled. I kindly refused her. Not yet. If things go the way I hope they do, I want to be at peak awareness. I don't want anything clouding my mind tonight.

Tim and Ange were chatting, I couldn't make out what it was all about. At one point, he got in close to her to whisper something, something that I wasn't supposed to hear. Okay, that has to be about me, right? Don't worry. He's probably asking Ange if

I'm in for something long-term or just available for the night. Whenever there was a break in the conversation, I tried to get in on it. I asked Tim if he was seeing anybody.

He said, "No." That was it.

"Aw, that's too bad," was my reply. Then a short pause. Then he started talking to Ange again. It went like that every time I tried to join the discussion, not that I would have been able to hear much of it anyways. He really did not want to talk to me. Okay, I can take a hint.

Ange got up to hit the line for the bathroom. I used that as my excuse to leave the room as well. It wasn't going the way I wanted after all. Once I got back out to the dancefloor, it was packed. They really jammed 'em in since I was last out here.

I managed to squeeze my way over to a stool against the wall, and I just sat there for a couple of minutes, waiting for Ange to get back so she could introduce me to somebody else. But, a funny thing happened as I sat on that stool: the entire city of Cambridge, give or take, entered the room at a steady clip. I was trapped. I couldn't get up and go anywhere even if I wanted to. I've seen coffins with fewer people per square foot than this room. The dancefloor at Regent was little league compared to this.

Pulled out my phone. The time was a little after 2:45. I needed air. I don't know how, but I managed to get to the door, and slip out. As refreshing as it was to escape that crowd and get myself to the relative cool of the outside, the symbolism of the act was not lost on me.

There was a line out here now. The appointed bouncers were not letting anyone else in until more people like me came out. I would have a long wait ahead if I hoped to get back in and commandeer Ange to drive me home, so I texted her instead. It took about a quarter-hour, but she managed to extricate herself.

On the way home, I expressed my disappointment regarding Tim. Ange said she couldn't believe what she saw happening right in front of her. She was stunned. Wait, she wasn't expecting something like that? Something just didn't seem right. Why was he so affectionate and touchy-feely at first, then suddenly so distant?

I had to know. "What did you tell Tim about me before we met?"

"Nothing," Ange declared. "I just pointed to you dancing over there and said, 'You should meet my friend Audrey.' That's it." Well, that doesn't give me much to go on.

Ange then added, "He thought you were on drugs."

I beg pardon? "He thought I was on drugs? What are you talking about?" I asked.

"When we were in the smoking room, he asked me if you were on ecstasy. I guess it was just because of the way you were dancing, and something you said about chocolate." I guess that explains the whispering.

"Oh, yeah, I kinda said that I wish you were made of chocolate so that I could eat you. It was meant as a compliment." Ange laughed like I'd never heard her laugh before. She sounded like she was going to hyperventilate.

So, Tim thought I was fueled by ecstasy. Did he lose interest in me because he found out that I wasn't? If I had known, I would have pretended. I could have put my face up against the bathroom door and said, "I love this door. This is the best door because it lets me go pee. It's my favorite door." Was he even the least bit interested in me at all, or just being friendly in an "I know we met ten seconds ago, but I want to put my hands all over your neck and back" manner? Well, whatever. It's clear he wasn't into me once we went into the smoking room so, ashes to ashes.

I feel like I had something great and lost it. I suppose I never actually "had" him to begin with. No use in wishing it could have gone the other way, because it wouldn't have. It wasn't my choice to make.

Tim, I won't forget you.

Before I got out of the car, I had to clear something up. "I don't actually wish you were literally made of chocolate, Ange. I still love ya, though."

"I know, Audrey."

MAY 3 (SUN)

Went to lunch with Zena today. She took me to a Greek place on the other side of town, across the street from Marathon Park. There's another first for me: Greek cuisine. Not something on my list, but there's always room for more things as they become available (so long as I want to do them.) The restaurant was more like a deli counter with booths and tables, sort of how you'd imagine a fast food place for Greek eat-in.

There was a review taped up on the front door. It wasn't from a major newspaper, but from nearby Quinella University's school paper. It contained this little gem: "I eat here all the time. The food is great and you never get sick afterward!" How can I argue with a ringing endorsement like that? The picture window had "WE DELIVER" written on it. Of course I was inside, so from that vantage point it said "REVILED EW." Not very good for subliminal marketing. I wonder if anybody else caught on to that yet.

I ordered a chicken kebab wrap, but ended up with beef instead. On top of that, the receipt said I had ordered a gyro. How that happens boggles the mind. I suppose I should have counted my blessings, as I still got a type of kebab. If they had mistakenly given me a kabob I would have been furious.

Zena said, "You should go up and say something. If they got your order wrong, then it's their fault. You don't have any reason to feel nervous about it." It wasn't that I was nervous, though. I just didn't want to end up spending fifteen minutes trying to get my beef replaced with chicken when my only evidence said I ordered something else entirely. It was just easier to take what I got.

Just then, one middle-aged man who didn't seem like the rowdy type began making a big stink about something. "Hurry up, I'm wasting away!" he whined loud enough for everyone in the restaurant to hear. He then added, "This place wasn't even my first choice, either." Oh yeah, good plan. That'll make the food cook faster. Always works when I'm boiling eggs. He hadn't even entered the building when I got my food, and that was less than five minutes ago. I waited for my meal for almost ten minutes.

Inconsiderate, obnoxious people are everywhere. What if I end up getting stuck with a piece of shit like that?

I didn't bring it up, but Zena felt an urge to assuage my concerns about my looks. She may have seen my reluctance to have my order rectified as another sign of how my appearance affects my confidence.

Zena says my nose isn't big. She says it's long. Not Pinocchio long, but more vertically-oriented. She says it "looks longer than it is," and that it's accentuated by my hairstyle, which she claims also makes the shape of my head look longer than it should. She does know hair, though. She still makes money on the side doing haircuts and coloring and the like for her friends and family. I've never had anything too different from what I've already got in that arena, so I wouldn't pass up a chance for something new there, provided I don't come back looking like I should be onstage singing with Fred Schneider.

I noticed there's a mole just a squidge below the far corner of Zena's right eye. It's a beauty mark mole, circular and dark, clearly defined. It has an exotic quality about it, like an accent on the eye. I have a mole in the middle of the empty space on my cheek, floating on its own like a punctuation mark miles from the nearest word. It's light and patchy, and only serves to enhance the splotchy color of my skin, which comes out clearer in photos than mirrors. Further inspection reveals I've got two big ones on my midriff, a smattering of tiny ones on my arms that you can only find if you're looking for them, and a dark black hole of one just above my right knee. I'm not too worried about that last one, though, because I don't want anybody seeing my knees anyways.

To me, that mole of hers represents so much of who she is. Zena seems to be the type of woman who can turn any imperfection into an asset. Her confidence shields her from everything by disarming anything negative at the source. Not that there's anything to criticize, really. (I guess that helps.)

If only I could be like her. When you're that gorgeous, people go out of their way to help you. Opportunities present themselves. Doors open for you. I need more doors to open for me, even if it only succeeds in taking a few pounds off my key ring.

Once the meal was over, we sat on a bench in the park for a while. Zena made me an offer: she said she'll do my hair whenever it's convenient for me. She's convinced she can do wonders for me. She does a good job on her own hair, so if she can get me even a little closer to where she is, it's money well spent. I want this done before I go to that place in Providence on Tuesday, so that didn't leave a lot of time. She has a prior engagement Monday evening, but she says she'll be happy to take care of me tomorrow morning, as long as I don't mind being a little late coming in to work that day. Well, if anyone there can afford to be late once, it would be me.

I felt compelled to ask Zena a rather personal question. I asked when she lost her virginity. I dunno why, perhaps the relative privacy of the mostly empty park drove me to it. I've known her since I first started working at the school, and she now knows much more about my personal life than I do about hers, given recent revelations. I guess that was enough for me to feel safe asking.

"Nineteen," she said. She wasn't the least bit shy about it.

I was in disbelief. I still am, really. She wasn't just saying that to make me feel better, was she? Anyone, Lynn, Natasha, Angela, Rosi, even Willow, anybody else I wouldn't have flinched at "nineteen." But Zena Swanson of all people?

"I'm not just saying that to make you feel better, either. It's true." Of course, she had to tell me that the first time is a disappointment for most people. Yeah, yeah, I know, I know. But, hunger is the best spice, as they say. As long as I climax and don't yell "Pigs! In! Spaaaaace!", I'll consider it a success.

She picked her phone out of her purse to reply to a text message as she asked me, "Are you sure you're ready, though?"

"Am I ready? I've been waiting for this for fourteen years!"

Without flinching or unfixing her gaze, she replied, "I didn't ask that. I asked if you're ready." I hate when people do that.

Got a call from Mom. She wanted to know if I made that doctor's appointment yet. Argh.

I almost wanted to tell her about what I was up to with Angela on Friday night. Part of my mind said, "This is important! Why not tell her? Your mother should hear about this sort of thing." Of course, the other parts all said, "No, no, you go ahead. I'm sure it'll work out great for you, like when you told her about the time you peed in the woods behind the park when you were fourteen and she said 'Oh God, I can see the headlines now.'" Instead, I just acted like nothing interesting was going on, answering all sorts of questions about how I was doing with the usual words beginning with N: no, nah, nothing, nope, normal. Some might find that suspicious, but for me it's par for the course.

MAY 4 (MON)

What a day this was. Started out great, then after a while it all went to hell.

I took Zena up on her hairstyle offer. It meant getting up an hour earlier than usual so she could squeeze it in. The whole thing took longer than I thought it would, and we were both late coming in that day. It would have been easier and smarter to get it done some other time, but I wanted to look my best for my trip to Providence tomorrow.

If the early hour was a problem for Zena, she sure didn't let on. It was a lot of fun talking with her the whole time about this and that. I had a few more questions for her that I wanted to ask yesterday.   "What's with that leg thing when you're kissing?" was one. I could have done a better job phrasing that, couldn't I?

She was understandably confused. I tried to clarify: "When you're kissing someone and you fold up one of your legs at the knee for no reason that I can discern. Why is that? Why are we supposed to do that?"

Zena thought about it for a sec, concluding, "I think it's because the guy is usually taller, so the girl has to stand on her toes, and… that makes it easier somehow."

"I wanna do that. I wanna do the leg thing. Even if I turn out to be the taller one." That's how I operate. Before I throw a list away, I take out a pen and cross off the last thing, just for the feeling of completion. Necessity isn't a prerequisite for satisfaction.

Eventually, the "Well, what do you think?" part of the operation came. I went to the bathroom mirror but it must have been malfunctioning because there was a very attractive young lady staring back at me. I don't know how to describe what Zena did, but it was perfect. She sorta, how do I put this?, re-engineered my hair and retrofitted it to my head

40

without de-lengthifying it. It looked fuller and shinier and I was even told my straight center part was in a zigzag now. I didn't bother looking back there with a second mirror, I was too overjoyed and couldn't wait to get back to Braun Elementary.

I didn't hate how I looked. I smiled the whole day. I couldn't pass by a reflective surface without going for another look. Maybe it was my mood, my hair, or just my imagination, but everyone seemed to be treating me differently. If anybody was happier than me, it was Lynn. Seeing me smiling on my own was probably like getting high for her. She even came to the library to check in on me a couple of times when she had the chance to.

"Just checking to see if you're still happy!" she said once.

"You're sure you're not just making sure I didn't bring any boys in here, Mom?" She told me she might have to start doing that if things kept up the way they've been today. If only, huh?

Winston tried to flag me down in the hall as I was coming back from lunch. He noted that both Zena and I happened to be late today. I simply said that it was because she gave me a ride, which was true even though it avoided the real question. The reason why Zena gave me a ride would be obvious to anyone who was paying attention, but Winston just couldn't be bothered to present any theories without anything more than circumstantial evidence.

As we parted ways he warned me, "I'm gonna be keeping an eye on you," in a voice that almost sounded like he was flirting.

I returned the thought, saying, "You wouldn't be the only one." Game, set, match: Audrey.

I couldn't stand to go home when the school day was over. Looking the way I did now, I had to go out and be seen. Rosi volunteered to join me at Il Costo for a light early dinner, drinks on me. She ordered something called a "Corpse Reviver." I hope that it wasn't meant as a tribute to me.

Rosi was curious as to whether the new hairstyle was the first step on the road to a complete image overhaul. Good question. I hadn't really thought of it that way, but I'm willing to try anything short of unnecessary cosmetic surgery. I sort of forgot where I was and wondered aloud if there was still a chance that someone would find me attractive enough to date someday.

"Of course! There's plenty of people out there who'll think you're great just the way you are!" she said.

"But, in order to get them interested in me, I just have to change everything about who I am."

"You're caught in a vicious oxymoron, then."

I explained to Rosi that she meant "paradox," and that an oxymoron is a combination of contradictory words. She said I was lucky that I was buying the drinks. It hadn't occurred to me that might offend her and so I apologized. I can't stand it when people are rude and I don't want to be seen that way. I try my hardest to be nice to everyone, but they often don't catch on because I don't smile a lot. I guess being cheerful is integral to one's bedside manner.

"I think people are put off by your expression. You don't come off as being friendly because you always look like a boxing glove is heading directly for your face. You need to smile more, like you did today." Well, that was because of my new look, really. Give me a reason to smile and I'm good to go. It just doesn't come naturally to me.

My phone rang. It was Doctor Yiu's office, calling back regarding my appointment. Couldn't quite hear what the receptionist on the other end was saying, so I stepped outside for a little bit. It was noticeably more humid out than earlier, and the wind was stronger. Picked up on that musky aroma that precedes a summer storm. I didn't want my new hair getting drenched in the rain. Turns out I didn't need to worry.

When I came back to our table, Rosi's eyes were fixed on the baseball game on the TV behind the bar. I got her attention by saying that Winston of all people was being friendly to me today. She turned around to reply, but only got one word out. Her eyes grew to the size of two CDs. It was an "Uh-oh" look if I ever saw one, to put it mildly.

"What? What's wrong?" I asked.

She pointed to what I thought was the space above my head. Judging from the look on her face, I turned around expecting to see Winston standing right behind me. Nothing there.

"No, not behind you! Your hair, it's… um, not… good no more!"

I didn't like the sound of that. I rushed to the bathroom so I could consult a mirror, and found that their reflective powers had returned to normal. There she was again: me.

What the fuck? How could it all come apart so quickly? So that was all it took, huh? Some wind and a little humidity and it's all over, after only a few hours. On one hand, I knew it was too good to last. On the other, this couldn't be what was supposed to happen. Though I have no experience in hairdressing, I don't think I'm going too far out on a limb to allege that, somewhere along the line, Zena made an "oopsie." Technical term, I saw it in a book.

Rosi gave me a lift home. After a brief and minor quibble with Willow over the usual minutiae (dishes in the sink, clothes on the floor, carnivorous fungus in the fridge,) I decamped to my room. Stared at my hair in my mirror. There's actually a reason I wear my hair the way I always do: it covers my ears. As you've probably surmised by now, my ears are ghastly, sticking out at a cruel angle. They are the worst aspect of my appearance, but thankfully they're easily obscured.

One thing that person in the mirror and I don't have in common: she's pretty keen on making eye contact. Just who is she, anyways? How am I supposed to talk sense into her when she's always mimicking me?

And how can I blame her for all of my problems?

I reserved a rent-a-car for Providence tomorrow. Maybe there's some way Zena can give me a tune-up that will at least get me another few hours.

MAY 6 (WED)

Zena was not able to salvage my hair. I went to the nurse's office yesterday so she could take a look at it, but it was no good. She couldn't give me another treatment so soon because that would be too harsh on my hair, and now she was having no luck trying to get it to do anything she wanted it to. "It's almost like the treatment didn't work at all," she said. "It's like it only made your hair sick and now it's built up an immunity." She says that if anything good is to be divined from this, it's that I have very "stubborn" hair. Hooray. It's nice to know I'll have a fun challenge ahead of me when I start tearing it out. I had no choice but to go to Providence on Tuesday looking like my usual self.

Rented a car and took a twenty-minute drive to the little big city. I'm not sure how I feel about a car whose name is synonymous with "Killed In Action," though. They must have a dark sense of humor, because they would have changed it otherwise. On top of that, the A in the logo doesn't even have a crossbar so it looks like a lambda, the Greek equivalent of an L. Disturbing.

The club, as it turned out, was not a club after all, but a bar. There was a small dancefloor, but nobody would be dancing tonight, as there were stools and mic stands all over the place for a performance later on. I got there early, and was greeted by the artist who owned and ran the place. It had just opened, so there were only two other customers so far. I looked around, trying to kill time.

There were a few works of art around with price tags on them. I liked the screen-print of a bulldozer and asked the woman in charge if I could buy it. She was more than happy to part with it, and made a big deal in front of the few patrons present. "I sold a piece of art!" she said. It came across sounding like maybe this didn't happen very often. She let me take it right off the wall and I brought it outside and put in the backseat of the Kia. For the rest of the night whenever she saw me, she pointed out that I bought the screen-print to whoever was nearby, almost like trying to talk me up in front of them.

But, it was still early yet. I saw there were some copies of the *Providence Phoenix* under the bar. I asked and the bartender let me have one. Figured I could thumb through it for something to do while waiting for the place to fill up a little more. There was an insert for "adult" services with a photo of a nearly-nude guy on the cover. I was interested in taking a look just to see what was being peddled, but I wouldn't dare in public. I skimmed all the way through to the back in no time and found a crossword. Well, nothing else to do for the moment, so I took out my pen and got to work.

The bartender, about my age I'd guess, came over and began chatting with me about the crossword. He said that if I came to any that had me stumped I shouldn't bother asking him, because he isn't very good even though he tries the *Phoenix* puzzle every week. Well, he's interested enough to try. He was a pretty friendly personality. I didn't care much for all the tattoos, but he was a decent enough person that I could see myself with him. But, uh-oh, that necklace he's wearing is the same as the woman who owns the place. I'd better cross that possibility off my list. Then, an idea.

Aha, I thought, I can use this. My crossword will be an ice-breaker. I can ask for some help with clues I can't get. Maybe someone will even want to finish it with me. I'll get to know someone that way. Audrey, you are a genius. Now, I just gotta find a few clues that someone can help me with. Oh! Perfect! Here's one asking for a "Provo sch." Three letters, ending with "YU". I'm not from Providence, but most of these others were, so they might be able to identify a certain Providence school. I'm sure that'll work, won't it?

I tried it a couple of times and got nowhere. Then, a guy came up to me and asked "Are you doing the crossword?"

"Yeah."

"My name's John, I'm from Rehoboth."

"Oh! No kidding! I'm from Ridgeway!"

"Oh, okay." And he walked off. What the hell? Me saying I'm from Ridgeway was enough to drive him away? What's wrong with Ridgeway? I swear, I have no idea what's going on sometimes.

Six people with guitars and a stand-up bass were now gathering over on the dancefloor to begin their show. A short film was being projected onto the wall behind them, over and over in a loop about ten minutes long. The place crowded up a bit more, but I was lucky enough to get a seat right next to three guys right at the end of the bar. Most of the other men around looked like they were there with their girlfriends, or were out of my age range, or were dressed like complete schmucks. These three seemed okay, so I pulled the "Can you help me with this clue?" again, and they couldn't. My artist friend then pointed out that I bought her bulldozer, and said I should tell them about it. But, by this point, the band on the dancefloor was doing "Ring of Fire", so the conversation-making was getting a bit difficult.

Nothing came of the shouting and straining to hear that followed, but I wasn't giving up yet. There had to be another clue they could help me with. So, I looked and—

"Oh my God! A crossword puzzle! That's like... I can do that, I think!"

Those were the words of the woman who sat down on my other side right then. She was pretty drunk, and I had plenty of time to make that call since she sat there talking to me for the next twenty minutes being the least-helpful crossword buddy the English-speaking world had to offer.

"What's this clue say?" she asked. "Rattler's relative? What the fuck does that mean?"

I explained that it meant the answer was a type of snake, in all likelihood. Three letters, so probably either "BOA" or "ASP".

"Asp? Like... A-S-P? What the fuck is an asp?"

I thought my explanation about the clue would have been enough context to glean that an asp is a snake (particularly the part when I used the word "snake".) "It's a type of snake," I repeated, practically shouting over "Folsom Prison Blues".

"But, but the clue is... 'Rattler's... Relative'."

What did I do to deserve this? I tried to lay it out as clearly as I could and even mentioned that an asp is the type of snake thought to have killed Cleopatra. At this juncture, I wouldn't have been surprised if the next thing out of her mouth was "Cleopatra *died?*" But instead, she somehow steered the conversation away from the puzzle entirely.

"You know, the thing about me is… is, is when I want something I *go* for it. I don't let anything get in my way, I'm like… like, *zoom!* I'm all about… doing things. I do things." Well, that's me being generous again. The actual tirade was far less coherent.

Once she decided to be kind enough to split, it was time for me to refocus my attentions, but my artist friend behind the bar had a surprise. While I was having my ear bent about whether or not asps exist, she had been talking to the guys next to me. Now, she had obtained another *Phoenix* and pulled out the insert.

The band had taken a break now, so she shouted out, "Excuse me, everyone! We have a celebrity in the bar tonight! This guy over here is on the cover of the adult section for this week's *Phoenix!*" Much hooting and hollering ensued. I froze.

I didn't know which of the three guys she was talking about. I didn't care. Whichever one it was, he was a model. What chance did I have with any of them? I couldn't bear the thought of trying to talk to them again. I stepped outside without saying another word to anyone, threw away my *Phoenix*, and got in the car. My forehead hit the edge of the upside-down steering wheel. I sat there for a few minutes, eyes fixed on the wheel, silently cursing myself.

I'm a coward. It's hopeless. I can't approach anybody. I drove the rental home miserable, defeated, disappointed in myself. I wanted to cry, but I couldn't. I never cry. I think it's because of that damn medication I have to take to "level out" my moods.

I was halfway home when it hit me. "Provo sch." is "BYU", Brigham Young University. "Provo" isn't a nickname for Providence, you moron; it's Provo, Utah. No wonder nobody knew. Idiot. Miserable, cowardly idiot.

As for today, nothing of any interest happened. It's for the best.

UPDATE. I just now realized it's not a bulldozer. I was calling it a bulldozer all damn night. It's a steamroller.

MAY 8 (FRI)

I knew that, at age 29, losing my virginity would be a difficult thing to accomplish. It's a difficult thing just to say. It's such a clunky, unnatural phrase. It doesn't roll off the tongue, it climbs. "Lose" is a bad thing. Nobody intends to lose something. Loss is an

46

accident. Sex is something you want to happen, right? The first time is a milestone, and milestones aren't mistakes. You don't come home from school one day when you're sixteen, check the mail, and find out that you accidentally got your driver's license.

I suppose the fact that it wasn't always a unisex word could explain a lot of this. But nowadays, we're not talking about the hymen exclusively. When you think about it, "virginity" isn't even an actual thing. It's a concept defined by an absence of something. It doesn't even sound like a real word! It's like they added the wrong suffix. "Virginhood" would be better, but not by much. I bet the first appearance of the word "virginity" had a note in red ink scrawled next to it reading, "Go back and fix later."

I don't know what I'm going to do with that steamroller. I don't want to see it every day, reminding me of what happened in Providence every time I glance in its general direction. I think I'll give it to Ange next time we cross paths. She can have it as a housewarming/thank-you gift. "Thanks for helping me out with what may be the most important thing I've ever done. Here is a picture of a steamroller for you."

Speaking of Ange, I got a call from her a few hours ago. She said she's in Boston and, from the background murmurs, it sounded like she was at a party. She said, "We were just playing this drinking game that involves a phone book, and I started going through the 'escort services' section. Are you up for that?"

"A drinking game? No, I'll pass." Yeah, I knew what she meant, but I reflexively tried to delay the inevitable. I probably don't need to explain that Ange wanted to see if I'd be interested in a male escort. I told her I'd think it over.

Sure, it's not ideal. It's not necessarily the route I was hoping for, but an opportunity is an opportunity. It would be foolish of me to pass it up if it presents itself, right? Just get the first one this way, then go back to the original plan. I can't afford putting things off anymore.

Plus, I trust Angela. I'd trust her with my life. I know that if there was any real danger here, or any possibility of me getting arrested, she wouldn't have even brought it up. Anyone she's acquainted with should be able to tell by now that Angela knows what she's talking about. I can't even recall any times she's made any huge mistakes, aside from leaving a pint of milk in the pocket of her winter jacket all summer.

I can do this. Ange and I can have a strategy meeting, plan out the logistics, the time and place, whether or not I should bring snacks, sunscreen, etc.

Okay. This is it, then. I'm gonna do it. This is going to happen.

UPDATE. No, it's not. I can't do this.

I can't go through with it. It's not the illegality, but that's related to the problem. How do I know what happens to the money? These phone book "services" aren't on the up-and-up, so as far as I know, my money could end up helping to support some things I find unacceptable. I know that there are plenty of independent sex workers out there who aren't connected to human trafficking, so I have no problem with them. But still, I can't bring myself to do it. This is a risk I can't take.

That was what the Amsterdam idea was all about, wasn't it? Making sure that everything is above board. Even if it comes to this, I'm doing it the legal way. That's just the way I have to do things.

Also, what kind of drinking game requires a phone book?

MAY 9 (SAT)

Every spring, I've told myself, "Someday when it's neither too warm nor too cool, I will rent a car and drive to the Canadian border in Vermont so I can see that library I've heard about." Today was the day I finally followed through on that.

A long time ago, I saw a story on the news about a building that's directly on the official border between Canada and the United States. You could walk right in and, without leaving, find yourself in another nation. It's in the town of Derby Line, about a five-hour drive from Ridgeway. I felt this would be a perfect diversion for taking my mind off of sex for a while, just taking a nice drive down the highways and appreciating the sights and the fresh air. Plus, nothing's gonna happen for a few days anyway, as it's my time of the month. Maybe a long car ride isn't the best of ideas, but the solitude brings me a bit of peace of mind.

I picked up the car at 9 a.m. I threw in my map books, my camera, and a few CDs since the only radio station that I can stomach would probably be out of range in no time. It plays jazz during the day and country music at night. Strange, right? How could they get that exactly backwards? Country isn't my thing, but I like having jazz as ambient music, as long as nobody's singing.

The route I planned out wasn't as straight a shot as it could have been. It's kind of angular, bending to avoid toll roads and state highways going through towns. It's a long enough drive as it is, I don't want a bunch of town square traffic lights gumming up the works. That ended up happening anyway as, about halfway through, I took a slightly wrong turn which led me through the center of Greenfield. It was a perfect excuse for a pit stop, though.

I took the same interstate all the way from Greenfield up to Derby Line, the entire length of Vermont. I have to say, driving through Vermont was not as pleasant as it may sound. Every so often you see a square blue sign in the distance, and you expect it to let you know there's a rest area coming up. As you get closer, you see it's actually informing you that this highway was built as part of the Eisenhower Interstate System. Gee, thanks for heads-up, bladder-tease.

There were a lot of sights that only I'd be interested in. Saw a license plate with eight characters today. Didn't think those existed. It was a vanity plate from North Carolina. I don't know what I would get for a vanity plate. Maybe something really confusing like "FFEFEEF", so that I would have an easier time fleeing the scene of minor parking lot fender-benders. What I'd really want to get is something that expresses a little bit about myself in code, but still decipherable if you think about it long enough. That's why I like puzzles and riddles. Flat-out trivia is only good if you can win money. If someone asks a trivia question usually you either know it or you don't, so if there's no prize, what's the point? Puzzles are things you can figure out, and there's a sense of achievement when you do. They play with you when no one else will.

For instance, "I 0 10IS" could be "I love tennis" because "love" is the tennis term for a score of zero. I don't play tennis, though. That was just an example.

After about three hours in Vermont, I finally made it to the last exit before Canada, filled up the tank at the first gas station I saw, and asked for directions. As I got closer to my goal, I started seeing a lot of signs with the words "BORDER PATROL" on them, and then I nearly had a panic attack: I don't have a passport.

What if I got stopped? What if I had to be taken in for questioning? What if they wouldn't let me into the library? I would have gone all this way for nothing! My only option was to play it cool. I just had to act like a normal citizen of Vermont driving a car with a Massachusetts plate. Didn't want to end up in a holding cell with smugglers trafficking in over-the-counter Canadian drugs and vestigial silent U's.

I saw the library sign, and felt a bit of relief that I had found it without accidentally joining a queue of cars going through customs. Pulled into the parking lot and, when I walked around to the front, I saw a plaque that was half-English, half-French. I didn't stop to read it, I just threw open the doors and marched in. "Excuse me, is this the famous library that's half in Canada, half in America?" I asked the librarian in a normal volume of voice. She confirmed it was, and that I was now in Canada. She had a French accent. Even the way she pointed down at my feet was kind of French-like.

I looked down at the floor and saw nothing. I looked behind me. I had walked right past a strip of black electric tape. I did it. I didn't even notice it, but I had walked right into another nation. Just like that, I had visited another country, without even needing a passport. I went around the system without breaking any rules and got what I wanted.

I wandered around for a few minutes, looking at the Canadian ceiling and Canadian walls, like I was expecting something really great to happen. I don't know why. I was probably just awestruck by the fact that I had made it. I wasn't expecting to turn the corner and see Niagara Falls. There were a lot of French books, though.

I saw a clear plastic box for donations and threw in a five. Upon closer inspection, I noticed all the money in the box was American. Hmm, I guess maybe Canadians don't have the sort of access to the library that we do. I went back to the electric tape and stepped over it and back a few times, just flaunting it, I guess. The tape hit the wall and resumed in the next room over, so I followed it and saw there were three people in there using computers. Oops. I probably should have remembered that this is a library and I need to be quiet. I guess I was kind of loud earlier.

The computers are all on the American side of the border. Maybe there was a legal reason for that, since there was plenty more space for that on the northern side of the room. I walked along the line, slaloming from one country to the other, with a big smile on my face. I must have been giggling a bit, too. You'd think the locals at the computers would be used to this sort of thing by now, but my behavior in particular must have stood out to them. I probably came across like a first-class geek, all giddy over a black line on the floor. I brought a digital camera which I got secondhand from my sister. Snapped a couple of photos of the line, trying to be as low-key as possible. That way, I'd be able to prove to people that I saw an important length of tape today.

And then, I was off. Just got into the car and got back on the road. Two five-hour trips just so I could spend twenty minutes dipping in and out of Canada in only the most literal sense. Now it's just a memory. All the joy and excitement of anticipation is gone. Granted, I never thought anything really enjoyable was going to come of it. I wasn't expecting to get some kind of prize, or have a life-altering experience, or even see something breathtaking. I got just about what I thought I would get out of it. Just another item crossed off of my list, now. It was a symbolic victory, but I'll take it.

Mom called, and I told her about my daytrip. Of course, she felt it was all pretty silly. I guess most people would. I mentioned my plans to Lynn yesterday and even she gave off an "Okay then, if that's your idea of a good time, have fun" vibe.

I told Mom I took a few pics of the electric tape border and that I'd email them to her if she wanted to see them. She said, no, that's okay. I sent them anyways.

MAY 10 (SUN)

Laundry is where I draw the line. Willow and I may share dishes, floors, tables, appliances, and other things I can't be bothered wracking my brain for at the moment, but we do not share clothing. She does hers, I do mine, and never do they cross paths.

I went down to the laundromat today. Took the taxi down there, had the clothes washed and dried, took the taxi back, all at my own expense. That's how it always worked before. But when I got back, Willow was a little pouty. "You didn't ask if I had any clothes that needed to be cleaned and folded," she sneered.

Eh? When was that part of the deal? She argued that since I was going down there anyways, I should have saved her the effort of having her wash and fold her own things. I asked if we were now supposed to take turns doing this, week by week. She said she would prefer if I handled it myself.

Then she pulled out the lazy person's favorite sentence: "But you're so much better at it than I am!" (Well, I can't deny that if she were responsible for laundry we'd be on first-name basis with the local HAZMAT team.)

"Willow, when was the last time you did anything for yourself?" I asked, genuinely wanting to know the answer so that I could pin down the date for a first anniversary party. Summer needs more holidays anyways.

"I do things for myself all the time! Just last week, I called out sick from work so I could spend the whole day smoking and catching up on my Netflix stuff."

I couldn't be bothered trying to clarify my question. I asked if she would consider going to the laundromat with Wes so they could fold her clothes together. She asked him to help with that once and they fought about it for a week. No mistake about it, those two were cut from the same sloth.

That whole interaction put me in a dour mood. I've always had to do everything by myself without someone to keep company with. Every week, I just wait at the laundromat with nobody to talk to. I just bring a sketchpad or a book and wait for the machines to finish up their jobs, then fold everything without any help. Companionship, that's what I've needed all this time.

Searched online for any nearby clubs that I might want to check out. Even looked for ones in the town of Sandwich on Cape Cod, just playing a hunch that there might be a Club Sandwich. There is not. Somebody had better get on that.

There's one club just around the corner from Regent that looks interesting. Sounds interesting, too. From the photos I saw online, there's a sign out front that doesn't even look like a sign. It's simply a shiny blue slab of metal with no words or pictures or information on it, and it is shaped like a trapezoid. The club is called "the club whose name is a blue trapezoid." That's not what it's called informally, that is its official legal name. No capital letters. I assume they wanted the blue trapezoid itself to be the name of the club, but that would be unfeasible.

If I owned a club, I would call it The Terrible Name. When people ask me about it, I would pretend to be ashamed, as if I had no say in the matter. "Yeah, yeah, I know. Don't blame me. It wasn't my choice."

I made up my mind to give my phone number to someone there. I even wrote it down on a few prepared pieces of paper in stark and angular digits. Used those open-topped 4's just to make sure they couldn't be mistaken for 9's. (I worry a lot, you know.) Maybe I should make business cards, with my own little tag line. I could even make my phone number the answer to an algebra problem, just as a screening mechanism. (Rosi has said I'm "adorkable," which I'll accept as a compliment only because I know that's how it was intended.)

This isn't over until I say it's over, and I say: it's not over.

MAY 11 (MON)

After I gave a thorough mulling-over of Angela's proposal, my mind was made up. There was no way I could go through with it. I know she meant well, but I had to tell her how I felt about the whole thing.

I wrote down what I wanted to say to Ange on my notepad in the library. In my shorthand, I jotted down that I wasn't comfortable with the possibility of giving my money to any sort of organization that could be connected to human trafficking. The last sentence I wrote down was "I couldn't live with myself knowing someone might be sold into slavery just because I had to have sex."

Rosi walked in to pick up a new book for Mrs. Sanders to read to her class. She asked if I had any suggestions. I fessed up to not having read many of the children's novels in my own library recently.

Ed Perregrin's class was in the room at the time, getting their books for the week. Ed is the sort of insecure male who might see a fourth-grader wearing a T-shirt bearing the words "I'm an awesome kid" and feel threatened enough to challenge him to arm-wrestling.

Rather than miss out on a chance to be an asshole for attention, Ed decided to wedge himself into the private conversation Rosi and I were having. As he tried to distract us with banal small talk, his eyes darted all over what I had laid out on the counter, searching for something to ask questions about. If you were to ask Ed where the nearest mailbox is, he'd reply "Why?" as if he didn't know what you needed a mailbox for.

Then, a target was sighted. He practically slammed his face down onto my notebook and saw my secretive gibberish, spelling out what I planned to say to Ange in words and symbols only I (and you, notebook) can understand. He noticed the last two words: "h sx."

"What's this! Does this say 'have sex'? You writing something about having sex?" he said in an effort to embarrass me. Uh, genius, your kids are on the other side of the room, ya know.

I calmly replied, "The X represents the 'sh' sound. I'm writing about having sushi." I prepared that escape tunnel ahead of time, just in case.

He exhaled a disgusted scoff and then trumpeted, nay, broadcasted, "I don't eat bait. You're not getting any raw fish in my mouth."

Rosi, almost as if on cue, said, "Yeah, some men just can't handle raw meat. Remind me not to invite you to eat out anytime soon." Holy double-entendre. Sex *and* meat. Attacking his masculinity on two fronts at once? Damn, Rosi, you cold. Ed grunted softly and slunk away in a manner reserved for men who have been thusly zinged by a young woman.

I just used the words "thusly zinged."

"Sushi" might actually be a good code word. Well, on second thought, I may want to go for sushi with the girls sometime, and that has the potential to get confusing. Ridiculous-sitcom-premise-level confusing.

After school, I stopped over at Ange's place to give her the steamroller picture. I also talked with her in regards to the escort proposal and gave her my feelings on why I thought it was a bad idea. The human trafficking angle is very important to me. I just couldn't risk having my money end up supporting that. If I really have to pay for my first time, it has to happen in a first-world country where it is legal and regulated (like The Netherlands.) At least, that's what I told her, but I left something out.

I don't want to admit that it has to be like this yet. I feel like it would be resigning myself to the fact that I'm just that unattractive. Ange must have called me at exactly the right time and I wasn't in a proper frame of mind to put everything in perspective, but this would essentially be giving up. How could I have any confidence in myself knowing I all but conceded that nobody would touch me unless it was a business transaction? I don't think I'd even be able to enjoy it under those circumstances. I was using a righteous sense of justice as cover for my selfish pride.

Ange said she actually looked over the phone book again, and couldn't find anything but female escort services anyway. I probably should have known better.

I collapsed onto Ange's couch and asked her some questions about Tim, just out of curiosity. I just couldn't get over how well I thought I was doing with him. I wanted to know more about this man who gave me my first morsel of physical attention.

"You know," Ange said, "you might still be able to fuck him."

"No, that ship has sailed. It's pretty clear he wasn't interested. Just getting him to talk to me was an exercise in futility." I must have sounded a bit down when I said that, given what Ange said next.

"I hope you're not gonna start recklessly accumulating cats, because I'm allergic to them."

"Don't worry. I'm allergic to buying food for anything that can't return the favor." (Willow being the clear exception.)

Ange took me out for another long, aimless drive. It really brought my spirits up after longing needlessly over Tim. I've always liked riding in the passenger seat. You have someone to talk to, the scenery changes, and there's rarely something to distract from the conversation. I'd have to say most of the best conversations I've had were ones where I was sitting in a passenger seat. Granted, so was the scariest one, that being the one that ended with the words "GRANDPA, BRAKES!"

Angela insists that my unique sense of style and intellect are my appeal. (Oh yeah, intellect. I'm surprised they're not getting into fist-fights over who saw my intellect first.) "I know there's plenty of guys out there who'd want to do you. I just don't know how I'm going to sell you yet," she said.

Sell me? I suppose she could commission an ad agency to produce a series of over-directed high-concept commercials. Maybe show a city street accompanied by the sharp echo of my shoes as I walk down the sidewalk, out of frame. My shadow is the most you ever see between close-ups of onlookers' faces. The men look intrigued. The women, silently fuming. Finally, we see a very well-dressed guy (presumed to be gay and therefore knowledgeable about fashion) speak up, cattily saying "Who is *that*?" Jump cut to a black screen displaying the word "Audrey" in bold white letters. No further information is given. They'll just have to wait, speculate, and gossip.

I told Ange about the club I saw online yesterday. She's glad to hear that I wasn't going to let Providence keep me from getting back out there and trying again. "Remember, you haven't failed in your mission until you decide to quit. It's like the stock market: as long as you don't sell, you haven't really lost yet. It can get better." Of course, this was coming from a person who "invested" fake money in a penny-stock for an economics class project in high school and then saw the company fold three days later.

Still, I had to agree. "The show's not over, so don't pull the curtain out from under me yet. I'm feeling a little down today, but my goal is still the same. I refuse to give up on the first good thing I've had to look forward to in a long time."

We go back a long way, Angela and I. She's used to seeing me as the distraught pessimist who considers joy to be always out of reach. This must be new for her. She was smiling ear to ear when I told her about my plans for Friday. By writing off the escort service, it's almost like I was ahead of her in terms of optimism for the first time. I want her to know that I really am trying to improve myself. I want to make her proud to have me as a friend.

"That was a pretty good line about the curtain back there," she said.

"Thanks, I've been saving that."

MAY 12 (TUE)

Second grade had a field trip to Roger Williams Park Zoo, so Lynn was out of the picture today. Natasha says her parting words included instructions on how her possessions should be divvied up in the event that she didn't return. I was to receive the furniture. Don't know if I'd have anywhere to put it, but she texted me around four to say she's alive, so the problem solved itself.

Speaking of bequeathing things, Zena dropped off a couple of books for me today. She says they were her sister's, but I have my doubts. They're self-help books. I hate self-help books. They all contradict each other with unverifiable non-scientific information that doesn't account for variations depending on the situation, and it's all presented as solid fact. There are no gray areas. The combatively upbeat attitude of "This way is the right way!" foghorns itself on every page, leaving no oxygen for Plausibility and Reason, the commanders of the Bringdown Brigade.

I'm actually quite worried looking at these, due to their age. One has pink and seafoam triangles and a yellow squiggly stripe on the front cover, so it's just dripping 1991-scented ooze. It's called *Meeting and Making the Most Of It!* (Exclamation point theirs.) Judging by its cover, I'd say the info within is probably as stale as an episode of *Full House*. If I see the phrase "has the hots for" in this book, I'm—

Oh dear Lord, there it is. And there are single-panel comics by that editorial cartoonist who died ten years ago. One has a girl holding a food processor and saying to her friend, "I thought you said we were going to a mixer." I get it. Ha. So much of the information in this refugee from Dr. Huxtable's sweater closet is outdated to the point of absurdity. Blind dates? Asking out people you just met in public settings? Didn't everyone stop doing those things once the media made it clear to us all that there is both a murderer and another murderer hiding behind every tree, fencepost, and blade of grass in this country? Remember, kids, the only way to be safe is to date people you already know, preferably within your own family.

Worst of all, the book is clearly for teenagers. This wouldn't help me one bit. Well, I figured I'd be positive and give it a chance. The thing is more dated than I am, after all, so there has to be something in this steaming pile that's of some use. Hello, what's this boldfaced header over here say?

*"**RULE #1:** Just Be Yourself!"*

And I was done with that book.

All that talk from yesterday about sushi had stirred up a craving in Rosi. I stayed in the library and tidied up at the end of the day while I waited for her to swing by so we could go to Lucky Cat. Ran out of tidying to do, so I thumbed through the other book for a little while and noticed a small "ZS" on the inside back cover in blue ballpoint. I suppose it's possible that Zena has a sister whose name begins with Z as well. But she doesn't. I can't prove anything, but I know that has to be right.

It was a little reassuring. Everyone starts somewhere, even Zena. Nobody gets the go-ahead from society to just skip their first five or six boyfriends and start with number seven. I may not know what Zena was like as a teenager, but she felt the need to buy books on the topic, so maybe she was even more insecure than me. The problem is that teenage Zena and I are in the same boat, and I am no teenager.

Rosi showed up while I had my face buried in that book. She twisted Natasha's arm until she agreed to join us. Natasha just doesn't get out of the house that much. I can relate, but I guess she has more incentive to be with her husband than I do to get home to Willow. I showed them both the paperbacks Zena palmed off on me. Rosi glanced at the titles. She picked up the second book, asking "I get the first one, but what the hell is some Chinese artist named Ming Ling gonna help?"

Natasha corrected her. "That says *The Art of Mingling*."

At Lucky Cat, Natasha made it clear to us that she wasn't going to touch anything raw. Rosi jabbed a shiny slab of mackerel with a fork and shoved it up to Natasha's face as if she might actually change her mind and eat it. All Rosi got for a response was a stern "Please get that away from me." She obeyed. How the hell does Natasha do that? Had that been me, Rosi would have kept poking the fish against my closed lips for five minutes straight before I finally snapped and murderized her.

Rosi had a thought: "I think maybe we should find a guy for you who works at the school. Somebody who you're already familiar with."

"Nah. Lynn already did her research on that. They're all married, engaged, gay, or in league with Satan," I told her.

Rosi asked who the gay one is. Seriously? Out of those four choices, her interest was piqued by "gay"? I told her it was Jeff, the teacher's aide for Mr. Lowell's class.

"Him? Well, I guess I could see that, but how are you so sure?" she asked.

"Chuck told me. He says Jeff made a pass at him once."

Rosi didn't know who Chuck was, so Natasha jumped in. "Chuck was the guy who ran the computer lab until he left during December break. He was pretty needy, always doing something to get people to look at him. The kids loved it, though. I heard he got a good gig in Texas. Best place for him. Lots of hot rocks for him lie on."

Rosi thought a bit more, and came out with, "What about Pedro the music teacher?"

Natasha shot that notion down without delay. "Pedro's getting married, didn't you hear?"

"Seriously? Pedro the Human Bumper Car? So, I guess his days of plowing into every woman he sees are over now."

Well, that explains that. I've always thought he was called that because of a series of traffic accidents. You learn something new every day.

Natasha's laser-focused gaze was on me now. "You know, Audrey, those books about dating aren't going to help you." I explained to her that I agreed but I couldn't just tell Zena I didn't want them. She's kind enough to want to get involved, so how can I refuse her help when she offers it? Then I'd just look like an ingrate.

While Natasha and I were on the same page, Rosi offered an opposing view on Zena's books. She insists that there could be at least some helpful information in them for helping me overcome my alleged (and I insist these were her words and not mine) "fear of guys."

She added, "It's like that Aimee Mann song, 'Boys Are Scary.'" I wanted to point out that the song is "Voices Carry," but that would be correcting her again, so I brushed it off.

"That's not the case," I told her. "I have a fear of asserting myself, not just with men but with everybody. I always feel like I'm walking on eggshells when I approach people. Remember when you thought I was spying on you because you were having that long chat with the fifth grade teacher Mr. Love in the hallway and I was just standing there for ten minutes?"

"Oh yeah, you had to push that book cart past us and you didn't want to interrupt. I kind of wished you had. A girl can only feign interest in a homemade foosball table for so long."

"Well, I kept thinking one of you was going notice me eventually. Trust me, Rosi. If the opportunity presents itself, I will go for it. I'm not terrified of men. If anything, they're terrified of me. That's why I've never been asked out, I suppose."

Natasha had a thought: "So, in a way, you're asserting yourself now in your own life because you think the delay has gotten to be too long to tolerate anymore. You're done waiting for a solution to present itself." I suppose she's right, in a way. I guess that's a sign that I'm on the right track.

I got home and saw a sock on the doorknob. Not just any sock, but one of mine. Was Willow trying to make some point here about laundry? I collected it and walked in.

I couldn't see where she was, but Willow yelled out, "HEY! DIDN'T YOU SEE THE SOCK?"

"What? Why are you yelling?" I shouted.

"GET THE FUCK OUT!!"

"Why? I live here. I pay half the rent."

"LEAVE!!!"

"Why should I?"

An arm emerged from the other side of the couch and flailed angrily at me. "THIS IS PRIVATE! NOW GET OUT!!!"

Oh, I get it now. Wes was over and they were fornicating in the living room. The sock thing was supposed to be like a necktie. I left and went for a walk. Why did I do that? I should have just went right to my room. Instead, I blindly did what Willow wanted for the sake of being cooperative, even though she wasn't showing me any respect. I'm still quite certain the fact that it was my sock was supposed to indicate that this was revenge for me not backing down on my laundry stance.

I don't know how Willow and Wes got together, but they deserve each other. I'm tempted to ask how they met, but I'm afraid of what the answer might be. Probably something really mundane like, for instance, they knew each other from a previous job. Something like that wouldn't be of any help to me. What I need is advice for approaching people, because there aren't any single guys among the ones I know. Maybe I should look at those books after all.

I know that if there were some surefire way to break the ice, things would be going my way. That's what I need to work on. I just haven't had a chance to get my foot in the door. I'm not afraid of men. I've just never had any experience, so I lack the confidence I need. I may be walking on eggshells but, when you get right down to it, I don't have an egg to stand on.

MAY 13 (WED)

My doctor's appointment was at the inconvenient hour of 11:00 a.m. No use going to school before or after that, so I made it a personal day. I think that a doctor's visit should count as a sick day, but I don't make the rules on that.

As always, nothing of any interest for reading material in the waiting room. Almost all of the magazines were about golf, yachting, and business. Whichever doctor was responsible for all these isn't exactly humble. There were one or two copies each of *Sports Illustrated* and *National Geographic*, and one of those thick, five-pound "women's" magazines that carries its own acrid scent, kinda like what you'd expect if the perfume counter at JC Penney got up and ran across the mall to get sick in that store that sells incense and potpourri. The volume of full-page ads (and I do mean "volume" as there are so many that they can be measured in three dimensions no problem) in these types of mags is pretty ludicrous. I thumbed through it, eventually reaching the table of contents somewhere around what I estimate to be page 41. If that's not enough of a space-waster, I saw an article beginning with a two-page photo spread. On the next page, the article proper began with a comically-enormous drop cap T. Eyeballing it, I estimate that the T and the negative space it encompassed on either side took up about one-third of the page. That's not an exaggeration. It was bigger than the photo it shared the page with.

Around 11:10, the nurse called me in to record my height and weight, then left me to my own devices. I was there for a long while, sitting on the bed-like piece of furniture and staring at my knees. I know I've made it clear by now that I'm not fond of my face, but my knees disappoint me a little more. The shortest skirts I own all stop strategically at knee-level. I figure if they're halfway-covered then from a distance nobody will be able to tell if something's wrong. Up close, a person would have to look down and the skirt would block the view. If it were feasible in this day and age, I'd always wear longer skirts and put on long bloomers for underwear. Maybe I should buy rollerblades and tote them around over my shoulder in the summer so that I can wear kneepads without worry.

They just have a, ugh, "knobby" quality to them. (There's another word I don't care much for the sound of.) They ruin things. I think I've got nice legs otherwise, but the knees ruin things. They're like that one note in Für Elise that absolutely has to be a mistake, even though it's always there no matter who plays it. It'd be nice to wear short shorts and show off my legs in the summer, but as things are I'd just be too self-conscious to relax and enjoy it.

In this world, there are those of us who wait, and those who make us wait. Boy, am I ever familiar with that. Had to keep myself busy while I was by myself for all that time, so I made my own fun. I stripped myself naked so I could see how much all of my clothes weighed. Then I saw how much they weighed with a stethoscope on top of them. I got dressed again and used the height-measuring thingie that pulls down from the ceiling to see how high I can jump. I have a fourteen-inch vertical leap. I tried creating a new dance. I was trying to make anagrams from the medications listed on a poster (acinvantone = "cat in an oven") when Dr. Yiu finally made her entrance.

The doc gave me all the usual tests. My blood pressure is perfect, she says. Lovely. I heard her mumbling as she went over my record on her computer. She used the words "attention deficit." Oh, that's still on there from when I was in elementary school? You'd think some of these things would have been erased when I turned eighteen. Even juvenile offenders get that much. I was able to read something on the monitor while her back was turned. It read, "Perlmutter, Audrey: never smoking, never ETCH, single, no kids."

"ETCH"? What does ETCH stand for? Some secret code term for heartburn, maybe "Eats things can't handle"? Maybe it's some nebulous collection of initials representing drinking and types of drugs or whatever.

She asked if I have any issues with my medication. I said "No," despite my sneaking suspicion that it prevents me from crying. That's nothing important, right? Better one that I'm used to than a new one with a laundry list of potential "uh-oh"s, like the ones on that poster. (Side effects may include complications related to killing you.) She asked whether or not I smoke. Again, I said "no."

She reached over and put her hand on my knee. She asked if I have a boyfriend. Ummm, what does that hafta do with… ohhh. That's the polite way of asking if I'm sexually active, I assume. I told her I didn't. Oh crap. I think I figured out what ETCH is. No matter where you go, no matter what you do, there's always a reminder.

I could have taken this opportunity to just outright ask her a few things about birth control and STDs and all that. But I kept silent. Sure, she's a doctor and I only see her about once a year and this is exactly the time and place for it, but I was too embarrassed to draw attention to it. Even though she's probably already aware of it, I just couldn't let her know I'm still in the dark at the age of twenty-nine.

She scheduled another appointment for me in a few months without asking if I wanted one. I probably won't show. It's all been good news so far, I wouldn't want to ruin it.

Willow was not pleased to see me home early, even if it was just by thirty minutes. After the events of yesterday, she certainly wasn't in the mood for more of my walking-into-my-own-home-unannounced shenanigans. She wasn't having a private moment or anything. In fact, Wes was passed out under a blanket composed of two burger wrappers and a bottle cap.

Look at that. Is that what I really want? He's about as sexy as a bagged snack food that rhymes with "vetoes." I can only hold out hope that I can do better than that.

It was kind of chilly out. Didn't want to turn the heat on in the middle of May, so I went to my room and crawled into bed for warmth. Got out again just long enough to grab a manga off the shelf. Read a couple of chapters, touched myself, dozed off for an afternoon nap.

I woke up with a headache and a sense of dread. I could hear the others playing a video game in the living room now. I felt compelled to put my ear to the empty slit between the door and the floor. I heard Wes ask Willow if I'm schizophrenic and if he should be afraid of me.

This is where I live. What an etching mess I've made for myself.

MAY 16 (SAT)

One step has been made. It was a small step forward, but forward is the right direction.

Last night I went to the club whose name is a blue trapezoid, just like I said I would. Rosi and Lynn joined me. Lynn's assignment was to keep an eye out for any guys who showed signs of not being there with a girl already. Rosi's job was to keep an eye out for pairs or small groups of guys that she could lure in. My unofficial objective was to keep an eye on Lynn and her alcohol intake. She says she can't help it, that it's her Irish ancestry that keeps her popping Cork and Dublin' over.

Upon arrival, the club was hard to distinguish from Regent. Everything was so loud and bright and dark all at once. Not the atmosphere I thrive in. Well, I'd done it before so no matter, time to get started. The night may be young, but it can still be tried as an adult.

Agent Mai Tai informed me she was going to do some scouting. She also informed me that Natasha found out about the code names and wants to be "The Sentinel." Great, now everybody's probably going to want one. If word of this gets back to Angela, soon I'll have an Agent Wigglebunny in my roster of operatives.

I didn't let anything hold me back this time, and jumped right onto the dancefloor. Was I nervous? Yes. But, I'm always nervous. I'd done this before. It wasn't the first day of school any longer. While I attempted to dance just barely enough to blend in with the crowd, I observed to see how others were handling the situation.

I noticed a young lady who approached someone from seemingly out of nowhere. She just touched his shoulder and off they went, shaking up a storm. Elsewhere, I saw a woman about my age pull over a guy and force him to dance with her. She grabbed him by the collar and tried to get him to take his jacket off. Since it was buttoned, it wouldn't budge very far and he kept dancing with his arms bound by his own clothes. It was such a spectacle that I had to watch. Their encounter only lasted about a minute before she lost interest and walked off.

In both cases, the message was clear: I should just find a guy who didn't seem to be with anyone, get his attention, and let the rest happen on its own.

I tapped the shoulder of a male wearing black jeans and a long-sleeve plaid aneurysm in colors that made it resemble a test pattern for The Vomit Channel. He turned and looked at me. Then he returned to his previous state. That went exactly how I expected it would.

I kept looking around, trying to find available prospects. Suddenly, one guy wearing sunglasses who was being led around by a lass stopped in front of me and began dancing. He was less than five feet in height and very... uh, "energetic," maybe? I don't know how that much natural energy could be crammed into such a tiny package, because he moved like he had the casts of three Broadway shows about breakdancing teenagers inside him, struggling to get out. Impressive it may have been, but also really funny. I'm adding him to my emergency list of things that make me laugh.

He didn't seem to be dancing with me so much as *at* me. He came off like a deaf person firing off a barrage of obscene sign language insults in the middle of his aerobics routine. Wait, was he even looking at me? He had shades on, so I couldn't tell. I think it's more likely he couldn't see much of anything and just picked an open spot to show off so that others could gather around and marvel. I just happened to be standing there already. I walked off and it didn't change a thing for him.

Lynn came over and told me she saw the whole thing. From her angle it looked like he was doing a "nuthouse mating dance." I think that's what she said, it was difficult to hear. I tried shouting, "How many drinks have you had so far?" She held up four fingers. I could only hope that didn't represent liters.

Oh dear. I realized something then. That woman was trying to get that jacket guy's wallet, wasn't she?

The evening went on with me seeking out anyone who looked like they weren't already joined to someone by the invisible red thread. Glints of light were few, far between, and fleeting. Then, miracle of miracles, came the words I never thought I'd hear.

"__y! D_ __u wa__ __ _an__?"

It was still very loud and hard to make out anything he was saying, but that's an approximation of what I heard. Given that limited audio clue, his lip movements, and the context, I could tell he was asking me to dance. Hey, y__ d__'t __ve t__sk m_ ___ce!

I pretty much went for broke, and threw everything I had into my dancing. I can't explain exactly what I did, but the pattern was like something a chimpanzee may have devised if he were given paint, a canvas, a pair of shoes, and an experimental drug that induces a feeling of invincibility. I even spun around a couple of times, because I am a dork. After about ten minutes of non-stop dancing, I had worked up a sweat and needed to sit. Luckily, he did, too.

I wanted to talk to this guy. The music had other ideas, though. I couldn't hear him say his name, something beginning with an F, I think? I did make out that he had to be somewhere in the morning and he and his friends were about to leave. Wait! Hold on! Crap. I forgot to bring my prepared scraps of paper with me. Luckily, I at least had a pen for just such an occasion. I seized a napkin from the bar and wrote my phone number along with my name just to make sure he knew it. He punched it into his smartphone as he turned to leave.

With that, I decided to call it a night and collected the others. Rosi was pretty tired. Lynn's relation to the floor was surprisingly perpendicular. Before we even made it back outside, my text alert sounded. Opened up my phone and saw this:

"Audrey i really like ur style. b sure 2 txt me sometime!"

Right after his message was his phone number. It was the most beautiful number I've ever witnessed. The 4 was a rescue ship on the horizon in full sail, the 8 a selfless Buddha appearing in Hell. I didn't hesitate to add it to my phone's list of contacts. One problem: I didn't know his name. I listed it in my contacts under the name "phone number." Yes, I labeled somebody's phone number "phone number" in reference to the person rather than the actual number. Rosi said that was "the most Audrey thing" she has ever seen.

Lynn puked in a trash can.

On the bus home, I looked over the number only about thirty or so times, trying to make words from it on the phone keypad despite the strategically placed pair of ones standing in the way. Things are going my way now. It's progress. I have made progress. But do I have momentum? I'm going to text this person on Monday. This morning I called up Lynn and texted Zena about this, and they both say I should wait three days. Any sooner and I look desperate, any later and I look like I'm not interested. The weekend gives me a perfect excuse for this. Monday it is.

MAY 17 (SUN)

I come from a small town. I was raised in a little asphalt spot known as Railhead. If you use a compass to draw a circle whose arc passes through Boston, Providence, and Worcester, then Railhead is the little hole you leave behind. So close to the big cities, but well beyond a leisurely, casual trip to any of them.

Railhead is exactly what its name suggests: the end of the line. The town's coffers are mostly filled by speeding fines. Nothing is open past ten at night, and if your commute to work is less than a quarter-hour long, you're not making enough to live on. All the convenience and sense of community of the countryside coupled with the beauty and charm of the suburbs.

The reason I bring this up is that it was Mother's Day today, so I drove out to my hometown to see the folks. This isn't something I look forward to. The first reason is the drive. It is such a bore. It reminds you that there really isn't anything to do when you're more than three miles outside of Boston or Ridgeway. What with all the private property, you may as well be driving through a desert. You can go twenty minutes down a state highway, and the only businesses you'll pass are of the "What good does that do me?" variety: real estate agencies, insurance, other real estate agencies, etc. Very little in the way of gas stations or bookstores. There isn't much of anything going on in these parts. Boston skews the average for the whole state, and outsiders tend to think we're just a sprawling city that's open 24 hours a day. I suppose that's just another unfair myth about Massachusetts, like the one about getting rid of the letter R when it follows a vowel. We are not wasteful people who throw out the letter R, we simply move it to the end of the word "idea."

I drove by what passes for a watering hole in these parts. The marquee out front read: "Ugly Christmas Sweater Contest: Friday 5/22. $50 Prize."

God almighty. (Or, as it says in the Hebrew-to-English dictionary, "gadol: mighty.") Ugly Christmas Sweater Contest? Is that what passes for a night on the town here? If things are bad for me on the love front now, I'd be navigating the Straits of Dire if I still lived here. There just aren't any opportunities for meeting new, available people your own age in these inbred little flyspecks. If you want love, you either make all your connections in high school, or you do what my little sister Rebecca did and get the hell outta Dodge.

I'm sorry, I just had to check the calendar. It is still May. Ugly Christmas Sweater Contest. Geez…

The second reason I dread visiting my family is that I never have a thing to say to them. Tonight was a fine example of that. In the same white house on First Street where I grew up, we all sat in the living room: Dad, Mom, and me. Mom asked the same questions as always, wanting to know if anything of note is happening at work and what I'm up to lately. Just gave her the same old news as always: reading, 'riting, 'rithmetic, running the rat race, regular routine.

Well, I got that guy's number on Friday night, so I suppose I could talk about that, I thought. Did I? Of course not. It would have been a good time to mention that I'm trying to date, but I couldn't bring myself to do it. I wasn't sure how they'd react. Instead, I just "uh huh"-ed and "yeah"-ed my way through Mom's lengthy diatribe about her job, one of those conversations that contains phrases like "*and* there's methyl isocyanate leak!"

I was considering telling them about the phone number. I really was. Maybe I would have even brought up Tim. But I was hesitant, waiting for an opening as always, hoping there would be a breach in the discussion. Mom went on about her co-workers, and I was hoping a thin beam of light would signal the presence of a crack that I could wedge my words into.

Luckily, I didn't find one. She did mention something about one of the women she works with, I forget the name. I think Mom's claim about her was, "Some women just lack any sort of moral grounding. Anyone who's slutty enough to sleep with someone on the first date has absolutely no self-respect."

And that was the end of that.

I wonder if Norman Bates had a sister who was put up for adoption. I should check my birth certificate, just in case.

I've always been uncomfortable around my parents, even though they're the two people who have been closer to me than any others over the entire course of my life. They had such great expectations for me, ever since I read my first sentence at the age of two. I was supposed to be the prodigy who would set the world on its ear, building supercomputers or discovering a cure for people complaining about why there isn't a cure for every disease known to man yet.

Maybe it's just my well-fed paranoia talking again, but I just feel like I'm disappointing them. Just by sitting there. Not being great. Brazenly existing. I feel guilty. After everything they did for me, all I can come back with is "school librarian." The thought of it drove me to ask Mom if she was disappointed that I didn't turn out as great as everybody expected.

She said she wasn't, but it came with a caveat, of course. She's convinced that I haven't reached my full potential due to my disability. Oh, right, I haven't mentioned that yet, have I? Well, notebook, let me explain…

When I was growing up, I was told that I had ADHD. My mother, my school nurse, and my psychiatrist all agreed. I had ADHD, and that was it. Then I grew up and found out that there was a big panic at the time where schoolchildren across the country were being diagnosed as such even when many of them clearly weren't. By the time I heard this, my mother had already been reading about something at the recommendation of my new psychiatrist. It was called Asperger's syndrome, and they were both convinced I had this now.

Today, everybody has heard of Asperger's, and we all know it's considered to be a form of autism, but a "high-functioning" form. Once this became "popular" in the same way that ADHD did, I realized that I probably didn't have Asperger's either, and wrote it off as another rush to judgment. I can't convince Mom otherwise, but she assures me that I don't have to worry about being "a late bloomer" on account of it.

Hearing this again made me groan at a barely audible level. "My head hurts," slid out of my mouth involuntarily.

"Audrey, do you need an aspirin?"

"Sure. Just one. Hockey puck-sized, please."

The main road leading out of town is a long, tempting gunbarrel through a sparse commercial zone. It has a magnetic pull that slowly drags your foot down onto the accelerator, until you pass a "SPEED LIMIT 30" sign and notice what you're doing. This is how Railhead pulls in cash from the outside world: drivers speed up on this stretch and get ticketed. Maybe it's the road and its accompanying lack of scenery that invites you to go faster without even realizing it. I think it's just as likely that people can't leave town fast enough.

MAY 18 (MON)

I dug through my CDs in the box under my bed today. Haven't done that in a while. I got a song in my head and wanted to listen to it, so I went hunting for the disc. While I was going through them all, I got the urge to look through my Fawn Clayton discs again. I was waiting for something (more on that later) so I read all the liner notes she wrote for the re-releases, just for something to read.

Fawn Clayton was the guitarist and lyricist for an all-female band from the late Seventies called Wax Dolls. For some reason, she speaks to me like no other artist. While she may not be the most poetic songwriter I can name, or even the most clever (though she comes close,) her songs are the only ones I feel I can identify with. I hear her singing and think, yes! That's exactly how I feel! Her career path resonates with me as well. Fawn didn't sing a note, not even back-up, on the first album; just played guitar and wrote most of the words. She wasn't confident in herself and didn't feel she had the chops to take the mic. After that, she sang lead on one song for the second album, and two songs on every album after that. Then, as one would expect, she did lead vocals for every song in her solo career. Talk about overcoming your shyness.

Fawn, how do you do it? How did you get it so right? I wouldn't say she's my hero, because she's just another person when you get right down to it. If we were to meet, I'm sure I'd like her a lot less and she wouldn't think much of me. I think about it from time to time and I don't think I've ever really had a "hero," just people whose work I've admired. I just have a hard time putting anyone on a pedestal. We're all human, after all.

You'd think being this close to the end of the school year would be enough to keep Monday from getting to you. Everyone around here has yet to get the memo on that one, it seems. Not me, though. I had somebody's phone number.

Talked with Lynn at lunch about how everything went Friday night. She thanked me for helping her get home again. I tried my hardest to express concern about her drinking without sounding like a nag. "Trust me," she said, "I don't have a problem. I only drink with friends. You won't see me ending up like Mack." Mack is a custodian who everyone on staff knows drinks on the job, due to his frequent stumbling and breath issues. He hasn't been fired because nobody has been able to prove it yet. (Though if they ever do find proof, I bet it will be 80 proof.)

True enough that Lynn hasn't had any issues at work, but she did need my help earlier in the year. She rang me up to help with her lesson plans coming back from the Christmas break. It was New Year's Day and she had put it all off 'til the last minute. Also, she was hung-over. Well, always glad to help out a friend. It was a breeze, really. I'm just lucky she teaches second grade. Had it been a high school lesson plan, she would've been shit-faced outta luck.

I waited until I was back home to send a text to "phone number." It was a simple one: "Hey, are you there?"

He got back to me only about three minutes later. A-OK so far! The lines of communication are open. Now to come up with something I could discuss with him. I suppose I could have asked him what his name was, but I feel I can probably drag this one out long enough that eventually I'll come across it again before I have to use it.

I told him I was at home, just having come back from my job. He was still at work, texting stealthily at his desk. I asked what his company does. I don't remember what his explanation was exactly, but it contained the word "solutions," so it's bullshit.

We went back and forth a few times. It was all pretty bland small talk so far. Had to come up with some angle I could use on him, something interesting. Time for this ingénue to use her ingenuity. Oh, you heard me, I'm pulling out the accent marks. I sent him one that said: "Have you ever had Indian food?"

He said he hasn't, so I told him I haven't either and suggested we go out for it some time this week.

"ok when?" he replied.

"Are you free on Wednesday?" was the last thing I sent to him.

Then I waited. I went through my CDs. I read those liner notes. I found the disc I was looking for, ripped the song and added it to my mp3 player. I walked to the pharmacy, bought a candy bar, walked back, ate it. He must be busy, I thought. Maybe he got caught texting. I sat at the kitchen table and doodled in a sketch pad for a little bit. Nothing fancy, just amateur prouns and decorative initials.

Willow came back from work and threw herself on the couch. She let out a moan in the form of my name. "Audreyyyy…"

She sounded a little sick. I got up to see what was wrong. She informed me that she wasn't feeling well and wanted to know what I was making for dinner.

"Probably just Japanese curry," I told her.

"No, I don't want that. Make something else." This came as a bit of a shock, as I don't believe I've ever made dinner for the both of us before. Usually she does her thing and I do my thing. I had to know why she expected a sudden shake-up in the order of things.

Willow told me she had a headache and that Wes was off doing something with his friends tonight. Under these circumstances, she assumed it fell on my shoulders to prepare a meal for the both of us. How come I'm never around to vote on these matters? I realize that most voters overlook the local elections, but I think I would have remembered seeing the "YES on Audrey making dinner!" signs in a few front yards around town.

I don't know why I did it (Ooh! Ooh! I know! Because you're a push-over?) but I made a bowl of ramen noodles for each of us. Willow expressed her gratitude with a heartfelt "Ramen? What are we? Penniless college students?" For the record, when she said this her head was resting on a pillow only six inches from a day-old McDonald's cup whose bottom quarter was brown and soggy from absorbing a forgotten few tablespoons of cola.

I thought I had her in a decent humor, having prepared a pseudo-meal for her, so I took the opportunity to ask a question. "Willow, would you say I'm attractive?"

"Okay, sure: you're attractive."

I believe it was one Charles Brown who was once quoted as saying, "Good grief."

I still haven't heard back from "phone number." I suppose he's just going to get back to me later. If there's one thing I've learned in the last month, it's that it's okay to be late.

MAY 19 (TUE)

The school day just dragged today. It was one of those chronological irregularities where the last sixty minutes of the day crawl on long enough to accommodate a screening of *Eight Elderly People Play Monopoly: the Director's Cut*. At lunch, Rosi talked me into going shopping with her, so that's what kept me out of the apartment for the afternoon. According to her, I needed new clothes to help with my manhunt. "I really want to see you try on some clothes!" were her exact words at one point. Time for me to go out and buy myself something pretty affordable.

Rosi was borrowing her brother's car, which looked like it was still in production, ninety-five percent finished being assembled by nanobots. Something like this usually ends up being stripped for parts and sold off to be crushed in an arena by a monster truck. This one could be done in by a really determined pogostick.

She wanted to pick up a milkshake, so we went to a drive-thru. As we sat at the window, she told me to look in my mirror. "Check out the woman at the wheel behind us. Tell me you're not better looking than her." I couldn't see her. All I could see in the passenger-side mirror was that the car had a Cadillac logo, so she had to be at least sixty.

Rosi got her milkshake, and off we went. "I don't want you saying you're ugly. You're not. There's nothing wrong with you, Aud. You're just, um,... plain."

"Plain," I said in a way that can only be punctuated with some non-existent symbol halfway between a question mark and a period. Not that I was arguing. I've admitted it myself (plenty of times,) but having someone else confirm it for you can sting a little.

"Not 'bad' plain, just average," she said. "There's nothing wrong with average. I only say 'plain' because I can't think of a better word. Think about this milkshake, for instance. People say 'vanilla' as a put-down, meaning something's bland or unremarkable. But vanilla goes with everything! It's a perfect complement to any other ice cream flavor!"

"Rosi, that shake is strawberry, not vanilla."

"I said I wanted you to *think about* the milkshake. I never said it was a vanilla one," she replied. I thought I understood what she meant up until then.

We pulled up to a strip mall on the edge of town. Once Rosi finished her drink, she brought me into the department store. While we made our way around the aisles in search of a place to start, she mentioned that she was surprised we were getting along so well and so suddenly. For her first few months at Braun, she just thought of me as "that nervous chick" in the library. She didn't even know I was the librarian and just thought I rented a room there or something. She even said, "We never really hung out before. It's like we have a special bond now that I know your secret. I could destroy you if wanted to. But, I won't, for I am a kind and loving soul as long as you don't cross me. If you do, I'll cut ya like glass! Ooh, look! Strappy sandals! I need these!"

She pulled me over to the shoes and assured me she was joking. "You don't have to worry about your secret getting out. I assure you, I have everything under control." Uhhh, alright. Odd choice of words.

While she was inspecting the shoes, I let myself wander over to the Women's Outerwear department, just beyond Women's Shoes and across from Men's Stupid-Looking Hats. I looked through some of the tops and, wait, what's going on with these sizes? M, XL, M, M, S, L, XS… Everything was out of order! I figured I'd just arrange that one short rack and I'd be satisfied. There we go, XS to XL. That was out of the way now, but then I turned around to see the skirts in similar chaos. I had just started to line them up numerically, when Rosi tapped me on the shoulder and asked why I wasn't looking at clothes.

First on the list: I needed a new dress for clubs and parties. Figured I should just let my guide do the legwork for me while I stood by and acted as mannequin, ducking in and out of the changing room every few minutes. She was a little annoyed that I didn't want her in there with me, but I have my reasons.

We narrowed it down to two dresses. Rosi suggested I just buy both, but I think she knew that wasn't gonna happen. She was certain she saw a pair of shoes that would go well with either one, and ran off to fetch them. An elderly-ish salesperson who was passing by saw me holding the dresses. She asked if I was looking for something for my prom. I told her I'm twenty-nine.

"Oh! Well. If he's a senior, I say, 'close enough!' That was old enough when I was growing up, you know. You *go*, girl!" She walked off. She clearly didn't understand what I meant. If only I could have reciprocated.

I ended up getting the purplish-maroon one. I also got the shoes Rosi picked out. For swimwear, she talked me into a hot pink bikini that was exactly the same hue and brightness as a campfire made entirely of road flares. I agreed to that one only as part of a strategy of relenting on something completely unreasonable for future leverage at an unspecified time. Alright, that's enough for today, I said. Off to the register, then.

Turned around and what do I see but the women's underwear section. No. Not today. Maybe there really isn't any good reason for me to feel so uncomfortable there, but with Rosi at my side? I know she'll go out of her way to embarrass me in public. It's too perfect for her to pass up. No way. Ain't happenin'. Made up my mind. I'm putting the underwear off for another—

"Audrey! Oh my God, we HAVE to buy you underwear, too!"

I must have hurt a great many people in a past life.

I went quietly since any attempt to escape would likely be met with increasingly louder calls of "Audrey! Hey, Audrey! The lingerie section is over here!" until finally the entire store would know my name and possibly even my age and mailing address.

"I think this is a good color for you," Rosi said as she pushed an electric purple object into my hands. Ugh. It was essentially a rubber band with a strip of cloth running from front to back. Why even bother? If the underwear is about wearing as little of it as possible, just save your cash and don't wear any instead of shelling out for what is basically just air on a G-string. I'm certain this is the result of a decades-long strategy by clothing manufacturers to save as much money as possible on fabric.

Rosi bounced from rack to rack, trying to sell me on something. I suggested that we should just skip this, my reasoning being that if somebody sees me in my underwear then we're past the point of no return and he's not going to suddenly not have sex with me just because he doesn't like my undies. "No guy is gonna show me the exit before I show him my entrance," I argued.

She slapped me on the cheek, but it was only about a 2 on a scale of 1 to 10. "I'm gonna slap you!" she then added. I asked her not to say that if she has already done it.

It wasn't hard to see that Rosi was getting a little frustrated with me now. She wanted me to just pick out something I liked. This would usually take a while for me, given how finicky I am with, well, everything. I didn't want her to lose her temper, so I quickly grabbed a six-pack of cotton briefs wrapped in plastic. She squinted at them in disbelief. Then I got the same treatment.

"You are making this so much harder on me than it has to be," she groaned. The fact that one pair had a pattern of red hearts didn't impress her in the least. Miscalculation on my part.

While she was bringing me back to my place, Rosi asked if I'm a nymphomaniac now. I'm not sure of the official rules, but I think I would need to have sex at least once in order to qualify. My problem is that I have a one-track mind. (Huh. With only one track, no wonder I'm still a single. Maybe I should consider acquiring a B-side.)

"You know when you're in the backseat on a long car ride and you have to pee? And, eventually, you reach that tipping point where the thought of urination goes from being unavoidable to all-consuming? That's where I am now."

The metallic jackhammer-rattle of the car became louder as we made the turn onto Reilly Street. Rosi said I need to start promoting myself. I have to learn how to "sell" myself. That sounds familiar. I asked what aspects I should focus on. She said she couldn't come up with one. Well, at least we're on the same page there.

I bid her farewell as soon as the car rolled to a stop. Couldn't wait to get out of that time bomb. "Remember: self-promotion!" she shouted as I ran up the front steps. I felt bad abandoning her in that casket on wheels, but no sense in a second person dying.

"Nymphomaniac." I wouldn't have phrased it like that. I just get fixated on ideas from time to time, and this time it happens to be sex. This one's practically normal.

There are only two ways to put an end to these phases I go through: either I get what I want, or decide that it's never going to happen and give up. And then, in the case of the latter, sometimes the process repeats.

UPDATE. Do all milkshakes start as vanilla and then have strawberry or chocolate flavor added to them? Is that what she meant? And why am I still thinking about that?

MAY 20 (WED)

I had a vivid dream last night. Sometimes, I'll hurriedly jot down a few notes when I wake up so that I won't forget the entire thing. From what I retained, it went like this:

I'm in a public space, probably a park. Other people are everywhere enjoying themselves. I'm on the ground, trying to drag myself forward because my legs don't work. Can't feel anything below my waist. I'm shouting, trying to get peoples' attention so somebody can help get me to a hospital. I can't tell if they can't hear me and aren't aware I'm there, or are all just doing a fantastic job of ignoring me.

I see everyone is coupled together, holding hands. I'm shouting something like, "Hey! Take *my* hand! Can't you see *I'm* the one who needs help!?" I get tired of this, and push myself over so I can lie on my back. I stare up at the sky and it's gray now. Voices and noises have all faded away. Just a few raindrops come down, and there's that smell that always shows itself just before a rainstorm on a warm day.

I keep staring up, accepting what's next, but instead I feel a hand on the side of my neck. There's nobody to be seen. Another hand slowly runs its fingers down my cheek. I never get up, yet somehow I'm standing up. All I see is the grey sky, but it still isn't raining. I get the sense that whoever helped me up wants me to repay him.

I pat my pockets, but I have nothing with me. No purse and no money. I have nothing to give in return. I look all around me, trying to find this person, but I'm alone. I shout out, "I have money! It's at home, I'll go get it! I just don't have any with me, but I promise I'll get it for you! I promise I have something to give in return." I'm panicking, because I'm not getting an answer, and I don't even know where I am anymore. I don't know how to get back to where I was, or how to get anywhere at all.

All I see is the gray sky, green grass, and an empty stretch of road. There are no cars, no buildings, no signs, and certainly no people. I have no idea which way to go. It's a complete toss-up as to which direction will get me back to civilization sooner. I figure, okay, I can do this now. After all, I've been healed, and I can walk again. So that's what I do.

Sounds like a pretty bad movie, huh? Maybe a short student film, without the frontal nudity. Also, not very subtle.

If life were a movie, and I had a part, I'm sure I would be somebody who got pushed out of the way by the bad guy as he runs down the street with the good guy in hot pursuit. I would be "Woman #2" or some such. My résumé might read like this:

- Other Maid, *Motel Las Cruces*
- Aide to Senator Bitpart, *Eagle's Elegy*
- Woman Running From Blowed-Up Dinosaur, *The Grapes of Wrath 3D*

I know I'm not a star. We can't all get to be the leaders, even though that's what everybody considers themselves to be. I don't mind being further down the ladder. I'm even cool with not necessarily being part of the main cast, but instead being someone they need to help out in a jam every so often, a dependable sort who pitches in when she's needed as long as it's appreciated. Along the outside edge but not an outsider. I don't think that's asking too much.

In the lounge, Rosi handed me her tablet and had me scroll through a bunch of pictures she found on a website devoted to collecting and cataloging dating website profile photos of very unattractive people. (That's about as diplomatic as I can make it.) Her aim was to make me feel better about my own looks. It did do some good, but I didn't much care for having to be compared to extreme outliers.

Plus, I felt kind of sick looking at these photos. I know Rosi's heart was in the right place, but I hate having to think that somewhere in this world, a person actually put the time and energy into creating a website for making a spectacle out of people who've no doubt already had very hard lives due to their looks. This is your labor of love, huh? My stomach had a knot in it, just knowing some slimy, heartless maggot could devote a portion of his or her (but, let's face it, his) life to this sort of cruelty.

Rosi graciously put the gadget away and unfurled her lunch bag, just before saying something that's stuck with me for the rest of the day. "You've been talking a lot about sex," she said at a low volume, "but I almost never hear you say anything about guys."

"What are you implying?"

"Well, isn't there anyone you know who you have a crush on?"

I told her no.

"Any celebrity crushes?"

Again, no.

"Come on, really? I know you like that Tim guy from Cambridge. Just the look on your face when you told me about him gave it away."

That's true, I admitted.

I don't know. If love at first sight is a real thing, I'm sure I'm immune. Back in school, I could only get interested in a boy if we got to know each other for a while beforehand. You know: working on the school paper, backstage at a play, things like that. We'd get along just fine, then I'd ask him out, he'd decline, and I wouldn't be interested anymore.

Don't get me wrong, I'm not too good for them. I'm sure as hell no looker. Aside from my more prominent features (nose, eyes, ears,) I've also got a couple of lumps on my head that never seem to go away, thankfully obscured by my hair. If the top of my head was the North Pole and the Prime Meridian was aligned with the center of my face, then I'd estimate the lumps are somewhere around British Columbia and Mongolia. And then there's that one horrid mole, of course (Uruguay.)

I could never share this with anyone but a notebook, but I've always longed to be gorgeous. Just like being happy or wealthy, I think we all secretly yearn to be beautiful, even if it's not socially expedient to say as much. I'd like to be in a burlesque show or something similar, to be sexy and be the one in the spotlight, even if it's just for a few minutes at a time. That's not wrong, is it? I won't be adding it to my list anytime soon, though. I know nobody wants to see that happen.

Sure, the outside edge is okay, but it would be nice to be on the inside once in a while. I feel beautiful on the inside. The trouble is getting someone else to feel.

Rosi assures me that it's not strange to not be turned on by physical appearance alone. "I think I get where you are. You might just have this tic where you like someone 'for his mind,' or something like that. I respect that. After all, they say love is blind, don't they?" Maybe. In my case, maybe it's just looking the other way.

MAY 22 (FRI)

He's not writing back, is he? I know I had the right number because we texted back and forth on Monday. I was the last person to say something. It's four days later. I'm sure he would have remembered by now, and if he forgot, then he wasn't really interested anyway.

I screwed up. I asked him out too soon. One little mistake and it all falls to pieces, like the Spanish high-wire walker who was killed by his fear of spiders.

Maybe it's a misunderstanding. Maybe he's waiting for me to write. I sent him another text this morning, asking how he's doing. So far, no reply.

I guess all I can do is keep waiting. I'm not going to erase "phone number" from my list of phone numbers just yet. I have to hold out hope. Plus, I'm afraid that if I did that, it might generate a botched line of code that would erase all of my phone numbers.

My worrying over this had gotten the better of me. I started getting a little queasy around lunchtime. It was enough to get me to pay a visit to the nurse's office today, just to lie down for a spell. Zena fixed me up with a bottle of Pepto to put me in the pink and asked if maybe it was psychosomatic.

I thought about it, and maybe it wasn't just the texting thing. I told Zena that it's possible that I've been worrying myself sick over my age. "People tell me I look young, but let's be honest about it. Society expects people my age to have already gotten it out of our systems by now."

"Gee, thanks," she responded. Oh. Whoops.

I had to clarify that I didn't quite mean it in that way. There's a world of difference between the two of us: she's beautiful and outgoing with plenty of experience. She already has lots to look back on.

She tried convincing me that my situation isn't so bad. Some guys actually see it as a good thing: they'd be turned on by it. The V-word even appears in all sorts of porn titles. However, I'm pretty sure that word is used to denote youth above everything. I have doubts that any of those alleged virgins are my age or above.

"It's only desirable up to a certain age," I argued. "After that, it's just a sign that something's wrong with you. I'm twenty-nine. In certain regions of the world, everyone would be wondering why I don't have any grandkids yet."

"You're lucky you live in Massachusetts," Zena told me. A friend of hers from another part of the country says that if a woman in her state isn't married by the age of twenty-seven, everyone thinks it's because she's crazy. I happen to know there's a similar stigma in Japan where the age is a firm twenty-five, thanks to unmarried women beyond that age being compared to Christmas cake (because nobody wants them after the 25th.)

"I just feel like… I may be out of time. Who am I kidding. Nobody wants to be a thirty-year-old woman's first boyfriend."

"Hey, cheer up," Zena said. "You still have a lot ahead of you. Good things come to those who wait." Well, I'm not expecting perfection. I can settle for less.

A kid burst into the room right then to get her medication. Zena's voice switched over to that syrupy, kid-friendly nurse's voice, speaking the way you'd expect Mr. Rogers to talk to a kid in a doctor's waiting room: "Hey, Frieda! How's it going? I have your acinvantone right here!"

The squirt got her tablet and a tiny plastic cup of water to wash it down. She saw me over on the bed, lying down on the job, and asked, "What's Miss Pearlharbor doing over there? Is she sick?"

"Oh, she's fine, honey. She just has a tummy ache. That's all."

Frieda got her fix and bid us adieu. "Bye, Miss Swanson. Bye, Miss Pearlharbor. I hope your belly-aching stops soon."

I got up to leave. Zena was snickering.

"Yeah, okay. I get it. She thinks my name is Pearlharbor. Hilarious."

Angela texted me around noon, asking if I wanted to go to the driving range with her. Okay, why not. A while ago, she mentioned going golfing sometime and I agreed instantly even though I've never had any interest in the sport at all. Well, the new Audrey does new things, so...

I don't like that. "New Audrey". There's always been a sort of confusion in phrases like that, seeing as how "old" is the opposite of both "new" and "young". The "new Audrey" is older than the "old Audrey". I'll have to come up with something else. "The Audrey of today" might work, but it makes me sound even older, like I'm a product being marketed to housewives in 1958.

I met Ange at her place at 5:30, but I had an agenda of my own. We loaded a couple bags of clubs into her car and set out for a little place on the edge of town, in the well-to-do Horizon Gardens neighborhood. Right after turning the first corner, I asked if I could possibly try some marijuana.

For years, friends of mine from school and my previous job have been offering me pot, and I always refused, but this is the Audrey of today: the Audrey who welcomes new concepts into her life, the Audrey who takes risks, the Audrey who doesn't care what MacGruff the Crime Dog has to say!

Ange pulled over into the parking lot of a bowling alley and hauled a duffel bag out of her trunk. She grabbed what she needed out of it, and got back into the car with her "merchandise", as people who aren't very good at being discreet always call it. I thought she'd be over the moon at the thought of me, of all people, smoking for the first time. And she was going to be right there, present for my maiden voyage INTO THE MIIIIIIIIIIIND!!! (That was supposed to be read in Jimi Hendrix's voice, with a lead guitar solo in the background.)

Instead, she seemed like she was just going about business as usual, stuffing one of those pipes called a "bowl" and handing it to me with a lighter. She started the car back up and off we went. Ange told me I had to light the pot in the bowl and inhale while keeping my finger over a hole in its side. I then release my finger while inhaling. How do I know when the right time to release is, though? And how do I push fire down into a bowl? All while the car is moving? Man alive, that guy who works at the Gulf station must be a lot more on the ball than I give him credit for.

After almost burning myself twice, Ange saw I was having problems and suggested I'd probably do better with a joint. Ah, that's more like it. That's what I had in mind, nice and simple, much easier to navigate. She pulled out some rolling papers and managed to throw one together with surgical precision at the next red light. She explained to me that I was supposed to hold the smoke in my lungs for as long as I could handle for the best results. I was sure that I was doing it right, but it didn't seem to be doing anything for me. Everything was the same as usual. I was just as aware of my surroundings and lucid as always. Oh! Wait, is that... am I... No, false alarm. I thought I was paranoid for a few seconds before remembering I'm always paranoid.

We drove past our destination, and instead pulled over to the wooded area by the far side of the reservoir. Got out and made our own path down through the trees to a cement embankment. We burned through a second joint, and I was still unsatisfied. Nothing. I wasn't calmer, I wasn't happier, all that changed was that I was getting a tingling sensation in my throat that I wasn't that fond of. Someone more of a hypochondriac than myself would have immediately diagnosed it as the makings of something malignant.

I didn't want to disappoint Ange, so I had to fake it. At one point when we were talking about one thing or another, I giggled and pretended I'd lost my train of thought, claiming I was distracted by the unprovoked mental image of a stereotypical French guy in a beret playing an accordion. That's believable, right?

We had one of those more "serious" talks. She wants to know more about what I'm looking for, in regards to sex. Me, I could go on for hours about my problems if you let me, but I tried to keep it to a minimum lest I bore her with my whining. I feel at ease with Ange in a way I don't with anybody else right now, not even Lynn, the first person I opened up to since the hospital visit. With Lynn, I feel like I have to choose my words a little more carefully, like I have to "translate", you could say. Ange has known me forever and I feel that she knows exactly what I'm talking about. On the other hand, I have to vulgarize my speech a little, using words that I normally wouldn't just to appear hipper.

I wonder if Angela knows how much I look up to her. She's never been anything but good to me, and I don't think there's any way I can ever repay her. I feel like an incompetent shadow that's always six steps behind, trying to catch up. I can't even get high properly. I don't know where she finds the patience, and now she's trying to help me lose my virginity at the age of twenty-goddamm-nine. I'd petition the Vatican to have her canonized, but they'd probably nominate me instead, thinking I could be a poster girl for celibacy.

We never did make it to the driving range. Come to think of it, it's Memorial Day, so they may have been closed anyhow.

Aside from having my first recreational drug usage, I also played the lottery for the first time. We went to a restaurant and sat at the bar. Ange ordered a beer and I ordered a plate of pesto scampi, as Monday is their night for shrimp specials. If everyone at my bat mitzvah could see me now.

There was Keno at the bar and I figured, what the hell. I wanted to put in the absolute minimum, so I played one number for one game and wagered one dollar. So, which number should I choose out of the eighty available? I picked 1. 1 because it's my first lottery game. 1 because I'm betting one dollar. 1 for the letter A, for Audrey. That's me, by the way.

Twenty numbers are drawn each game, so I had a one-in-four chance of winning. For such a small bet, my reward would be only $2.50. Subtracting what I spent, I had a twenty-five percent chance of coming away a buck and a half richer. Did I win? Of course not, you big silly. The lottery wasn't set up to lose more money than it makes. This wasn't actually my first time playing the lottery, technically. I have gotten plenty of scratch tickets in birthday cards over the years, so it's really only my first time giving them my money. Luckily, I've won about sixteen bucks on those scratch cards over the years, so I'm still fifteen dollars ahead of them. Who says you have to be in it to win it?

Ange brought me home the roundabout way, dipping in and out of all the neighboring towns, so we had plenty more time to talk. I wanted to avoid it for fear of being a downer, but I did tell her about the guy who stopped returning my texts, whose name I didn't even get. Just as that heavy, negative feeling began grabbing a hold of me, Ange spoke up.

"Wow. That's remarkable. I've never heard of that happening before in real life," she said. "I gotta say, I am really impressed."

Say what? Did she say "impressed" or "depressed"?

"You went to a club, met a guy, hit it off with him immediately, and exchanged phone numbers. That's great! Seriously, you're the first person I've known who's actually done that."

Is she humoring me, or what? I hadn't thought of it like that before. Geez, I must be making some progress, then.

We parted ways about 9:30. Before she dropped me off, she mentioned something about taking me to a club she goes to sometimes. Already looking forward to it. It's not over.

MAY 27 (WED)

Rosi had a gift for me today. She stopped by before classes started and left it on my counter with this note:

"I notice you don't seem to collect anything, so maybe you could start with this. A lot of people buy these and line them up against the wall. Maybe it helps them get their ducks in a row! LOL -Rosi"

It was a miniature rubber duckie wearing a straw hat and holding a cane under its wing. He must think he's in Vaudeville. Unfortunate. Vaudeville was notoriously anti-duck. I opened up a drawer under the counter and stuffed him as far back as I could. I didn't have the nerve to keep looking at the innocent, wide-eyed collectable. Bad memories.

Rosi and Lynn stopped by before lunch, and the duck's absence was noticed immediately. I couldn't give Rosi the wrong idea, so I told her that it's just because I hate ducks. She didn't understand how I could feel that way, saying "Duckies are cute. Especially rubber duckies."

I had to explain the duck incident from when I was a kid. "You know how sometimes you'll call me 'Aud' for short?"

Lynn figured it out. "Oh. Like 'odd duck.'"

"Okay," Rosi said, "so some dumb kids called you an odd duck. Get over it, already."

"'Odd duck' eventually became 'ugly duckling,'" I explained. "It dogged me all the way to fifth grade, when somebody left a rubber duck in my desk one day."

I put Vaudeville down atop my computer monitor to let Rosi know that I appreciated her gesture, and would stick it out (for now.) Boy, I'm a blast to have around, aren't I?

We went to the teachers' lounge, and passed by Mrs. Burris taping her kids' newest creations to the wall around her classroom door. The kids had drawn pictures of their pets and wrote three-sentence bios of them.

"Callista is a gray cat. She likes sitting in boxes and jumping onto chairs. She loves plaing with her toy mouse."

"Squeakers is my dog. He is very shagy. When I come home from shool, he barks becus he is happy to see me."

"Captain Bloodlust is the hamster of death. He is ravenous and will bite you if you try to touch him. He fears no mortal."

Something tells me a boy was responsible for that last one.

As we were giving the drawings a quick skimming, Winston walked by and gave us each a hasty acknowledgment for a greeting.

"Rosi. Lynn. Aud."

We continued making our way to lunch. Lynn wondered if he had been listening in on our conversation in the library from the hall. "That would be pretty disappointing if that were the case," she said. I wouldn't say that. With the faith I have in him, he could never disappoint me. He can only surpass my expectations.

Natasha was already in the lounge by the time we got there, getting a soda out of the automat-style vending machine with the little individual sliding windows and the products on a series of rotating shelves. The school's machines only carry water and flavored water now, so we keep this one hidden here, away from the students. Our late vice principal Tench owned it and would restock it with soda he got from the wholesale supermarket, but now that he's gone, I have no clue as to who's maintaining it. I'd guess George the head custodian, but he doesn't exactly seem much like the type who'd care enough to waste his time on any technology more advanced and/or less gruesome than a mousetrap.

All this recent worrying about the path I've taken in life has gotten me thinking about my job. I honestly don't know if there'd be a possibility of me becoming a writer at some point, but it sure seemed like a long shot years ago, so I figured working in a library would be more feasible. The others were chatting about their respective students all acting up today, energized by the sight of summer on the horizon. They weren't too pleased with their kids' behavior.

"How come you wanted to be teachers?" I asked the others.

Lynn was more than happy to announce she's always wanted to be a teacher, "ever since I was a kid!" Well, at least somebody around here is living the dream.

"I wish to reward the good and punish the wicked," was Natasha's entire response.

"Huh? Oh, gee, sorry. Wasn't listening," said Rosi, who was writing roller derby pseudonyms in her notepad:

- Loni Murderson
- Elizadeath Impaylor
- Congresswoman Maxine Slaughters
- Jane Bad-all
- Penelope Deadly-Ward

- The woman who is going to kill you
- The Ulcer Twins: Mary-Hate and Smashley

"How about Fawn Slayton?" I suggested. Nobody got it, and I had to explain who Fawn Clayton is to them. Philistines. I'm lucky I didn't go with "Naoko Take-Ouchie." They would have buried me alive.

I wonder if I made the right choice with my career. Maybe I should have gone to art school and become an illustrator instead. I suppose there's a chance I could still be an author. I don't know what to write about, though.

I also pondered exactly what it is that makes me dislike this job. It's certainly not the responsibilities, or the hours, or being in a room full of books. Why am I so dissatisfied with working in a school library?

Mrs. Harmon-Lewis from second grade entered the room at that moment. "Oh, Audrey, there you are. I'm sorry, but one of my students just threw up in the library."

"Isn't your class supposed to be in at one o'clock?"

She explained that her students were still in their classroom. The kid in question was on his way to the bathroom but felt the need to puke on the library carpet rather than the tiled hallway, so that it wouldn't be in peoples' way. Thoughtful li'l scamp.

This afternoon, Rosi texted me with this one: Butch Casualty. I know when I'm beat.

MAY 30 (SAT)

I hate hate HATE my voice so much. Aside from my knees and my ears, I think my voice is the most unsexy aspect of my being. It's just a tad nasally, but it has this sharp, barking quality to it that may not break glass but could punch a few holes in some discount drywall.

My mp3 player has a microphone function on it. I used it to practice fine-tuning my speaking voice, recording myself speaking as normally as possible in a variety of different ways, none of them requiring *too* much strain on the way I normally form my words. You know what they all sounded like? Forty different varieties of me, each attempting to sneak into a restricted area disguised as a different delivery person.

There's only one voice-modulating technique I can come up with that's close to being half-good. I try to keep the back of my tongue as still and as rock solid as I can while letting the tip flow as freely as possible. It is hard to perform, maintain, and endorse. I'm better off just giving up on that one.

Yesterday I did the laundry, went to the store, one of those days. Got a text from Ange around ten at night asking if I wanted to stop over. Well, I had nothing else planned. Ange was drinking a bottle of beer when I showed up. She kept offering them to me all night, but I kept refusing. I must have refused about eight beers and she must have drank every last one of them. She was in the middle of sorting through a tangled mess of cables for her stereo equipment. She was going to DJ a wedding on Sunday, all the way down in Connecticut.

She was alone that night. The peril of being on-call beckoned Lew to the hospital. We discussed the possibility of Lew knowing anybody over there who was looking for a date. Ange sat there, extricating wires from her bundle one by one. "He told me he couldn't think of anyone. We'll find someone for you, though. I'm sure of it." She took a final, bottle-emptying swig and added, "This may be one of the most difficult puzzles I've ever had to deal with."

"Uh, they're only wires," I said, hoping that's what she was referring to.

She held up another beer, neck pointed at me. I declined. She asked if I was interested in something from her liqueur cabinet instead. "Trust me. If you're going to mingle, you need to start drinking."

I put a sly spin on my tone and asked, "In that case, do you know how to make a cherry cordial?" She said she didn't. I may have lobbed that one a little too high.

Ange thought we should be doing more things together, as getting involved in more activities would improve my chances of meeting someone. She suggested that I join her bowling team. They're called "The Slam Dunks" and they have a cartoon mascot on their shirts. He's a goofy-faced basketball. Again, this is for a bowling team.

I expressed concern that it might not make a difference, as everyone my age is already taken.

"Did someone take your cookies?" Ange said with a grin. I didn't get it and she explained that this was a joke from when she was in college. She and her friends decided that if you add "And someone took my cookies!" to the end of a litany of grievances, you can then plausibly blame all of your life's problems on Cookie Monster. There's a self-help book right there, waiting to be written.

She opened the beer and went on. "The thing is this: in college and shit, people would always ask me to help them with things. And I want to do it. I want to help people because it all comes back to you. Good karma. But, a lot of the time, they don't want to help themselves.

"When you told me about that guy at the club, and how you started texting each other, I was really surprised. You really shocked me. I never thought that sort of thing would happen to you. You're serious about this. That makes me want to help." That actually made me feel kinda good. We untangled wires and sorted equipment until about 2 a.m. I wasn't sure how much help I could be but I want to help her, too, whenever I can. I was a little concerned about how she planned to make the wedding on time, but she always comes through. That's how she is.

I woke up about seven times before finally getting out of bed. I've just been going through the motions all day: paying the bills, cleaning the bathroom, arguing with Willow. I thought about it all day, and I don't know how I'm going to meet anyone who's available.

I need some new ideas. I've got to come up with a new strategy for this. I'm not sure if I've got what it takes. It might be too late for me.

And someone took my cookies.

MAY 31 (SUN)

Rosita stopped by unannounced. She said she had a great idea that I should try out, and needed me to get my laptop. She pulled up a website for a speed-dating service.

I have to give her credit on this one. So far, I've been able to ascertain that my biggest problem is that I can't assert myself. Also, I don't know who is taken and who is available, and I wouldn't know how to keep a perfect stranger locked in conversation long enough to make an impression. This takes care of all these problems for me. Everyone there is available and looking, and you're pretty much forced to pair up and take turns in an orderly manner for a set amount of time. Like clockwork. What's the downside and where do I sign up?

Signing up was the downside, of course. Rosi was quite aware that I hate "social media", and that I especially did not want to sign up for any online dating services. Buuuuuuuuut… if I wanted to participate in this speed-dating thing, I had to fill out an online profile.

She told me, "I know you want to keep your anonymyny, but I couldn't sign you up for the speed-dating without writing this profile for you. It was supposed to be a surprise, but I need you to answer these questions." Yes, she said "anonymyny." She brought up my profile and I got a look at how well-concealed my true identity would be from prying eyes.

My username is "yerduA0713".

Are you frigging kidding me!? "Anonymyny", my ass! That's just my name spelled backwards followed by my birthday! You even capitalized the A, idiot! I politely pointed out her error in judgment.

"Are you frigging kidding me!? 'Anonymyny', my ass! That's just my name spelled backwards followed by my birthday! You even capitalized the A,... you... crazy person!"

Rosi's defense was that there are probably thousands of Audreys in this world born on July 13.

"Okay," I asked, "how many of them are in a position to be utilizing a speed-dating service? And how many of them would have profiles that also give my current age and my state of residence?" Well, this was all a little late for me to be bringing up now. I'd just have to hope that nobody I know would come across this, but it's not a major website that everyone's heard of, so the odds are in my favor. Plus, I suppose I can just delete my profile whenever I want, right? If they don't allow that, I'll tell them I'm actually a man. A man who just got married. And then died. They'll have to take me at my word. They wouldn't want to risk setting somebody up with newlywed corpse. The local news would turn that into a two-month-long story.

"Just fill in all that stuff I left blank, and we'll be good to go," Rosi said. So far, she had only filled out my age, city, and hair color. "I didn't want to make any assumptions regarding your ethnic background. Jewish is considered white, right?" Some questions you just can't begin to answer. Okay, let's look over this thing. They're almost entirely multiple choice. That might be a problem.

#2: If I found a $100 bill on the street, I would...

Why, "Give it to charity," of course. Isn't that what everybody does?

#3: On Friday night I am...

There's no option for "Riding out the night in cabin fever solitude while my roomie and her boyfriend play *Bad Guy Killer II* in the living room." I'll choose "Dancing at a club" as that is partially true as of late.

#6: People find me irresistible because...

...It is Opposite Day? Man, they do not give me any appropriate options here.

Guess I'll pick "My razor wit." Why the hell not.

#8: My favorite type of book is…

No "Reference." No "Manga." These options are getting further and further away from how I'd choose to answer the question. How can I be so out of sync with my peers and still be so dull at the same time? Okay, "Non-fiction" wins.

#9: When it comes to keeping secrets, I…

Am I applying for a job at a nuke plant? Who wrote these questions? Anyone filling out this form is giving personal details about themselves to a privately-owned company so that they may be displayed on a website. How's that for keeping secrets?

#11: When my lover is "in the mood," I slip on…

Knowing my luck, a banana peel at the top of a staircase. Oh, what's this last question? I can fill out Number 12 in my own words?

#12: If I had to choose a panel of any three people, dead or alive, to make all of my decisions for me, I'd choose…

"Alive."

Once all the questions were filled out (to the best of my ability to do so,) two steps remained. First, I had to write a short bio. Oh, how I loathed this. Rosi suggested I just write anything at all that will work to my advantage, true or not.

"Honesty is the best policy," I said. "Besides, if I don't tell the truth, then it won't really…"

Rosi prodded at the unfinished explanation, wanting to know, "It won't really what?"

I said, "I just want someone to like me for who I am, I guess. A friend of mine suggested that I get a hold of a male escort service a couple weeks back, and I couldn't go through with it. If I pay somebody, then he wouldn't really want to do it with me, he'd just be doing his job. That wouldn't feel right. I want to matter to somebody. I want to feel beautiful."

"Audrey, I thought you didn't want a relationship. It really sounds like you do!" Oh boy, she was getting that giddy squeal in her voice again. I could hear it sneaking up.

"I wouldn't be able to maintain one. I like my privacy too much. Trust me, it wouldn't work," I argued.

Rosi still insisted I wasn't being entirely forthcoming. I guess she isn't completely off the mark. I mean, if I do meet someone and we do get along well and have a lot in common, then I certainly wouldn't try to stop anything good from happening. But, let's be realistic. That's a pretty big "if." That's an "if" that affects the tides.

I still didn't want anyone to know this profile was mine, so I was vague with the truth. I didn't lie, but I didn't specify.

"I work in a library in Ridgeway. I like to go for walks, read, and exercise. My favorite food is Japanese curry and my favorite game is Scrabble. For music, I really like Fawn Clayton, The Smiths, Vince Guaraldi, and Wax Dolls."

Rosi said I should add that I can put both my legs behind my head at the same time. I did not add that.

Then, the last piece of the puzzle: a photo. So much for plausible deniability. I explained to Rosi that I didn't have any photos of myself, for reasons that should be obvious. No problem, she said, she'll take one with the camera on her tablet.

I really didn't want this. Cameras hate me. They're heartless, cruel little bits of machinery, feeding on tiny seedlings of delusion before they can blossom into confidence. They bring out things that even the harsh, unforgiving bathroom light is humane enough to let slip by. Rosi said she'd fix my make-up perfectly so that the picture would come out fine. In fact, while my guard was down, she snapped a candid so she could study which of my features needed the most attention. She looked at her tablet. She looked for four minutes straight.

She finally spoke up. "Maybe the lighting isn't right here. Nothing to worry about, though."

In the photo, my cheeks looked splotchy and bumpy in a way I've never seen them before. My eyes looked sunken in. One of my moles stood out, and something unidentifiable appeared on my neck, as if it were just passing through that very moment. My parentheses… the less said, the better. My nose breathed a sigh of relief, as it had come out looking relatively good compared to what its neighbors just went through.

Rosi sat me down and put so much make-up on me that I went up a weight class. I tried to keep still as she caked all manner of whatever she found in the bathroom cabinet, and possibly a few things from the fridge, all over my face. This is what I have to go through just to sign up for a website that arranges meetings that then might lead to actual dates.

"This is beyond belief," I said. "What did I do to deserve this? Even prisoners get conjugal visits."

Rosi's eyes lit up. "I got it!" she announced. "You could get a pen pal in—"

"NO."

She sighed and shot me a look. "First, he can't be a complete knuckle-dragger.

Now, he can't be a prisoner. You know, for a beggar, you sure are choosy."

I insisted on doing the mascara and eyeliner myself. Too close for comfort in too sensitive an area, and it always puts me on edge. I see those moments as perfect opportunities for earthquakes or nearby car crashes to do permanent damage.

Once Rosi finished applying the cosmetics (maybe she ran out?) we found a spot with okay-ish lighting and took a few pics. After that, she told me to choose any one of the six shots for my profile. Any one I wanted. I chose one. She told me I was not allowed to choose that one.

"You're not smiling," was her reasoning. Well, that was the point. Smiling brings out the parentheses. Of the remaining five, I just went for the one where they were least prominent. We put the photo up on the site, and we were good to sign up.

There was a Jewish-only event listed for the 18th, for ages 22 to 31. Good, I'll take it. Leaves me with just enough time to prepare. The big drawback is that it's in Boston. I hate getting to and from that city. It's always such an ordeal. Gathering everything up for a day at the beach requires less preparation. Plus, at the beach, you'll eventually find a place to park.

It's reassuring to know that Rosi's still looking into possibilities. I suppose I need to be doing more of that myself. Instead, I've been fretting over this one person not sending me a text. I'm done waiting. He's history. But, I think I'll still keep his number in my phone's contacts list for a while longer, just in case.

Rosi thinks I shouldn't be too quick to rule out the prison pen pal idea, and asked if she could send out a few letters on my behalf. She has this way of telling jokes that makes it sound like she's really going to go through with the more extraordinarily stupid ideas. I'm kind of worried now.

New month. New page on the calendar. June: the month of the pearl. Beautiful weather out today. Cloudy, windy, seventy degrees Fahrenheit. My favorite.

That entire paragraph didn't have a single complete sentence in it. It didn't even have any verbs. Starting off on the right two left feet again, I see.

Had to help Mrs. Reedbuck staple a bunch of pieces of construction paper to the corkboard by the library today. The fifth-graders who read above a certain number of books in a month get their names on the board the next month. In January, their names are on little snowflake-shaped cutouts. February has hearts, March has shamrocks, and so on. June has vague, non-committal attempts at polygons in pastel colors. Not sure how else to describe them. Why not suns? It's not like you should bother saving that shape for July or August. Well, never mind. That's just me being a know-it-all again.

I never really liked being around Mrs. Reedbuck for a very specific reason: I think I'm going to end up looking like her in thirty years. I can foresee everything that has happened to her coming for me also. Her wrinkly neck, her thick glasses, her stooped hobbling walk, her silver hair. It's a damn shame that has to happen. It's a damn shame I automatically think about myself when I see her.

She's only in her sixties. I don't think humans were meant to live past forty. Just think back to ye days of olde, when people had a high possibility of passing in their thirties. You'd die young and leave a beautiful corpse. Well, maybe not. That's just the saying. Taking what some of those diseases did to you into account, it probably wasn't what you'd call "beautiful," to be kind.

What happens after a certain age is natural decomposition. Our bones get weak. Our hair loses color and thins out. Our organs figure "I think I've done enough" and get lazy. I don't want my body crapping out on me. Sometimes I'll sleep with the closet light on just to make sure my eyelids aren't slacking while I'm unconscious.

Zena left another book for me. This one was wrapped in a brown paper lunch bag with a piece of scotch tape. I'm convinced she was trying to make it look like she was leaving pornographic literature for me. Depending on your definition, she very well could have been: *23 Sex Positions For Beginners.* Why twenty-three? Were they all so crucial that they couldn't have left three by the wayside? They couldn't strain themselves to dig up two more for something divisible by five? Maybe they could just show two of the ones they already had from different angles and give them new names, and nobody would care enough to complain. Here's two names now that I just made up: "The Pelican's Revenge" and "The Cube of Inevitability". Done.

I'm starting to think it's easier to just give me books than to take them to the donation bin downtown. I appreciate the thought and all, but what possessed her to give me this? It's kind of like, "Yeah, I know you're deaf and you can't listen to music, and you've been kind of down about it lately, so... I got you a book about music! Now you can read about everything you're missing! Not bad, huh?"

The book lacks photographs, but has line drawing illustrations. They're not really up my alley, though. The male and female look like they just came back from a casting call for *Body Hair: the Animated Series.* The book was printed in 1995, but I'm willing to bet the drawings were from a much earlier incarnation. Imagine 1980's Bob Vila and 1960's Sally Struthers and you're nine-tenths of the way there.

The book came with another note helpfully pointing out that it once belonged to her sister. Uh huh. I looked at the inside of the back cover. There it was again: "ZS". Sure. Her "sister" (wink.)

Speaking of names, I got an amusing piece of junk mail today, addressed to "Aubrey Pearlmudder." Wow, hitting all the bases on that one. This might go down in the hall of fame, alongside the college professor who called me "Rodney" to my face and that bat mitzvah bracelet for "Andre" (it was written in Hebrew.) I hope it's just a coincidence that all of these are boys' names. Although, I do hear there was a song about a girl named Aubrey, so I suppose it could be unisex. I still have my suspicions, though. There must have been a typesetter's error somewhere along the line with that name, someone at the press wasn't minding his p's and q's that day.

JUN 2 (TUE)

I think I know part of the problem: I like driving, but I hate cars. Trust me, this is going somewhere.

Driving is great because it's the perfect excuse to do nothing. Everybody wants something from you, you always have be somewhere at a certain time, you have a schedule to meet. But, there's a catch: in order to meet all the obligations that people expect from you, you have to get there first. For instance, you don't get out of work until, say, five. Your neighbor wants to know if you can drive him to the train station to catch the 5:12 leaving Greenton. You don't really want to do it, but guess what? You can't! The station is less than ten minutes from your home, but your job is all the way over in Redhill, a good 45-minute haul to Greenton. He understands and doesn't hold anything against you, that's just the way the ball bounces.

When you're driving, (almost) nothing can touch you. You're sealed up with your CD playing and nobody to interrupt your thoughts. Nobody expects you to multi-task to suit their needs. It's pretty much perfect. On the other hand, I think owning a car is a complete hassle. There's so much to take care of and keep an eye on, so many parts that can conk out at any moment and things that can go wrong out of nowhere. I don't even like the way they look, and they all look the same to me. I can't tell one from another.

"My car's right over there, it's the Nissan," someone will say to me in a parking lot.

"Is that the blue one?" I'll ask, going by nothing but which one I think she was pointing at.

Thankfully, I live in a city with a small but effective bus system and almost everything I need is within walking distance. I don't need a car, so I don't have one. I have a driver's license, so I rent one when I need to.

Now, let's apply the same paradigm to men. When I'm getting groceries or going to the bank or the post office or whatever, I feel like I've landed on another planet, like I'm intruding on another species' culture. I'll see couples strolling hand-in-hand like they're Paul and Paula, when they look more like Test Subject #43 and Suspected Accomplice in Escape. What the hell does either one of them see in the other? Even celebrities (make that *especially* celebrities) turn me off. To me, the different varieties of men are like a rainbow made from all the dull shades of green and brown and greyish-blue that never get used in a giant box of crayons. I may not know sex, but I know what I don't like.

The point: Just because I'm not drooling over guys all the time doesn't mean I wouldn't enjoy the act of sex itself. The physical sensation would still be immensely enjoyable, right?

It can't be my fault, can it? If I can't find any of these people physically attractive, how am I to be blamed? You can't make a straight person gay, or vice versa.

So what was it about Tim? Why is it that he set me off so?

When I first saw Tim, I wasn't immediately struck by him or his appearance because, well, that's just how I am. He even had glasses on, and I'm not really "into" glasses. But when he got his hands on me, the effect was instantaneous. It was so fast even someone with the memory of a goldfish would think "I remember back when you two first met, and now you... um... hold on, lost my place..." And when I was in his arms for those few seconds, every pore, hair, and nerve I have was moaning, "Please, PLEASE let him be the one!" But it wasn't in the cards. I thought he really liked me, so I really liked him.

When I saw Ange on Friday night, she suggested I may be "asexual with heterosexual leanings". I suppose that's possible, but I've got enough obstacles in my way as it is. I don't need to start drawing in a new square on surveys that ask for sexual orientation. I'll say I'm straight. Tim got me all hot an' bothered, and I'm after straight sex, so I'm straight. No need to complicate it.

One other thing I'm worried about: what if I don't like it?

I didn't like the coffee. I didn't like the pot. I didn't like the yoga. Maybe I just don't like anything. Maybe I'm a bitter, insufferable shrew who's amused and delighted by nothing. That could be what I'm all about: nothing. Nothing really looks good on me.

JUN 4 (THU)

To add to the list of things I'm worried about: my hair. I'm only 29 and I'm finding grey hairs now. One day, I'll wake up with a white stripe dividing my scalp in half, and leave the house only to be followed by a bouncing French skunk. "Come back, mon petit bookworm! I want to fill you up with love like ze chef making ze éclair!"

Don't look at me like that, notebook. You know that's what he was thinking.

I was thumbing through my manga early this morning, when Rosi appeared in the library holding the Ridgeway Courier-Post. Miriam and Jeff walked in behind her. She opened up the paper on my desk and said, "Can you show these two the Jumble thing?" by which she meant I should provide the answers to the daily scrambled word puzzle at a speed that most people find inhuman.

Despite my hair worries, I was feeling unusually upbeat and I kind of wanted to showboat, but I acted like she was pushing me into it. She silently mouthed "self-pro-mo-tion" to goad me into it and I said okay. I grabbed a Post-it and a pen, and told her to read me the first one.

M-O-G-A-E. I came back with "OMEGA."

"That didn't even take two seconds!" Jeff remarked. Rosi was delighted by the audience reaction. She gave me another one.

G-Y-L-F-I-N. Easy. "FLYING."

"I'm amazed," said Miriam in a tone of voice I've never heard from her before. "That was even faster. How do you do it?" I explained that once I knew there was an I, an N, and a G, I could make "ING" from them. That left the letters in "FLY" remaining, so I just stuck both parts together.

Miriam asked if I had seen the puzzle earlier in the day, and Rosi challenged them to give me a word themselves. Miriam stared at the wall behind me and came out with A-E-G-R-L.

"LARGE or REGAL or GLARE or LAGER." Of course, I knew she was thinking of LARGE because she was certainly looking at the "LARGE BOOKS HERE" sign for items that won't fit in the return slot.

"Okay," Jeff announced, "how about Y-U-A-D-E-R?"

"Jeff, I think I'd know my own name."

On their way out I heard Miriam reminding Rosi that she's supposed to have the serial numbers for all the computers in the lab ready for tomorrow's inventory. "Don't worry! I have everything under control!" she replied. Why do I feel like I've heard that somewhere before?

Lynn's class came in today, right on schedule. While her kids were browsing for their books, she planned to churn out some photocopies of her science quiz on marine life. I said it looked a little confusing, as she had drawn an elephant at the top of the page, and I'm pretty certain they're not aquatic creatures. She told me it was a whale.

Huh. That was embarrassing. I just badmouthed her whale-drawing prowess. In public, no less. I hoped nobody overheard.

The way I saw it, it was an elephant's head, with the whale's jaw, fin, and tail becoming the elephant's ear, tusk, and trunk respectively. She admitted it wasn't her finest hour and asked if I could draw a whale for her instead. Wouldn't hurt to give it a go.

I had just barely touched my pencil to a piece of scrap paper when a kid placed a book on my counter. It was David, a bespectacled half-pint who smiles like he just got back from winning the grand prize at the 6th Annual County-Wide Ear-Wigglin'

Showdown. I ran his book through the system, and bid him farewell.

I whispered to Lynn, "Sheesh, that kid's a little too happy, don't you think? Always has a look on his face like the next words out of his mouth are going to be 'Hey, everybody!' How does he keep it up all day?"

She said that he doesn't. He just really likes coming to the library because that's where I am. Of course. That's the way it works, isn't it? There's a male who can't take his eyes off of me, but it turns out he's a member of the Pee-Wee Casanova Front.

"You know how kids are at that age," Lynn continued, "they'll get a crush on anyone who's nice to them. He doesn't know any better." I understood what she intended to say with that remark, and so elected not to take umbrage.

My whale was a goofy-looking cartoon one with a black eye, an X-shaped bandage, and a tooth missing from his smile. Lynn asked why he looked like he just lost a fight.

"Because he did. He went two rounds with a giant squid," I explained.

"So why is he smiling?"

"His manager's cousin bet a small fortune on the squid. He threw the fight."

Lynn couldn't decide which scenario was stranger: me having that story prepared ahead of time or coming up with it on the spot. Regardless, she taped my whale over hers and wrote "illustration by Ms. Perlmutter, age 29" next to it. Always glad to help.

Speaking of helping, I was about to leave for the day when Rosi showed up, requesting my assistance with her inventory task. She needed to collect and record various different pieces of info on each machine in the computer lab: serial, manufacturer's key, IP, etc.

That room has about thirty computers. I asked how many she had done already. "Oh, half a dozen, I guess." (*Perlmutter's Dictionary* defines "half a dozen" as "what people say to make five or six sound like ten or twelve.")

It took us about an hour, going from monitor to monitor, writing down long strings of letters and digits. I thought I'd ask Rosi if she was seeing anyone right now. She said she's still available.

"You're right when you say that everybody's already taken. Pretty much the only young guys I know right now are all here at the school: Aristide Love, Winston, and Jeff. I really like Mr. Love, but he's married. And Winston is way out of my league. I lose my cool a little when he talks to me. The other day he asked me if I heard any good jokes lately. I couldn't remember any, so I told a knock-knock joke. The last line was 'Howard you like a nice Hawaiian Punch?' That may have been the lamest thing I've said in years."

She asked if I had any good ones. I looked around suspiciously. Got up, went to the door to make sure the hall was empty and all the kids had gone home. I went back over to Rosi and said, "Why do they say fish is brain food?"

"I don't know. Why?"

I looked around again to be sure no one would hear, then whispered, "Because they travel in schools."

"That is a kids' joke. Why were you whispering like it was obscene or offensive?"

"That's what makes it funny."

She recommended that I don't use that one at any parties.

After Rosi and I parted ways, I legged it back home. Not long after I arrived, I got a call from Mom.

She wants to know if there's anything in particular I'd like as a gift for my upcoming birthday. I said I couldn't think of anything. I say that every year, and I usually mean it.

Well, this year is different, but what the hell am I supposed to say?

JUN 6 (SAT)

This time of year is when that park by the reservoir starts filling up with families looking for a day at the beach without the hassle of travel. I had to have some time to myself in the outdoors though, so I pedaled over to St. Hyacinth's Shrine, a Catholic church in the Upper Ridgeway neighborhood. It boasts a large churchyard with lots to look at: sculptures, an altar and pews for outdoor services, a rosary, and a bunch of patio stones carved to look like the forty-eight contiguous states. If the remaining two were in proportion, Alaska would be over near a small shrine filled with candles, and Hawaiian Islands would, appropriately, be floating in a nearby pond.

Often, I find this place isn't very relaxing on really nice days. There'll be too many people and too much noise. Fortune must have been smiling on me today, because I had the whole grounds to myself at first. Normally, I am the type who might fly all the way to the Himalayas and take a day-long hike just to visit a shrine called Tranquility Sanctuary, only to arrive on the day they're giving out vuvuzelas at the "Harleys Help the Homeless" motorcycle rally across the street. The weather must have been keeping the rest of world at bay. It was my favorite type of atmosphere: very warm, windy, humid, and cloudy, like a rainstorm was going to break out at any moment. Never did, though. I would have been in deep if it had, given my mode of transport.

It was just what I needed to clear my head after all I've been through the last few weeks. For about thirty minutes it was silent, save for the leaves rustling in the wind, and I was able to enjoy wandering around in the outdoors free of distraction. Suddenly, I hear my name being called from above.

"Audrey Perlmutter. I have been watching you and your sinful ways displease me. Get off my lawn."

Wait. I know whose monotone that is. I couldn't see her anywhere, so I shouted, "Okay, Natasha, I know it's you. Get out here and make yourself plain!"

"Forget it. I'd never catch up to you." Oh, *ha ha.*

She emerged from behind a tree and descended the nearby flight of granite stairs. "I'm sorry. I thought it would be funny. I didn't mean it." I didn't realize she was capable of this sort, well, ANY sort of mischief. Guess there's still a few surprises out there after all. Turns out that this is her church. She comes here for confession on a monthly basis. In fact, that's where she was before we ran into each other.

We made our way past the shrine on the proposed site of Alaska. It's filled with lit candles and a stained glass window tribute to Mary. There's a metal honor system box asking for three dollars if you wish to light a candle. I took them up on it. That must have jogged something in Natasha's brain, because she then lit up a cigarette and belatedly asked if I minded. "Of course not," I answered. "I work in an elementary school. If that's the worst smell I have to put up with on any given day, then it's a relief."

I couldn't think of anything to discuss with her. We don't have many interests in common, and I haven't been doing anything interesting recently, aside from conspiring to sin. That topic is off-limits. With Natasha nearby, I had to make sure I held my tongue so as to keep proper decorum in the presence of the religious iconography. I've never been much for maintaining icon tact. Eventually, she mentioned there was a saint with my name. I've heard that before and asked what St. Audrey is known for. I didn't get an answer on that because she changed the subject, saying, "Maybe I shouldn't have brought it up… Say, do you need a ride home?" I told her I'd take a rain check.

Willow was out when I came home, so I had the chance to watch some television. Saw, by my count, the same commercial for that erectile dysfunction pill six times. Might have to stop watching TV for a while. I know they're actors, but seeing those couples rubbing it in my face just makes me depressed and angry. Come to think of it, about eighty percent of the ads on cable news are for pills. We may not have flying cars, but *The Jetsons* turned out to be more prescient than anyone could have imagined.

I don't exactly envy the women in those ads, though. The males always look twice as old as the females. You could probably record new audio and reuse the footage for ads selling a "Make Your Own Grandchildren" kit.

Later, I invented my own non-alcoholic mixed beverage:

"Liquid Water"

ingredients: 12 oz. cold water, ice cubes.

1. Pour water into glass.

2. Add ice cubes to taste.

I was finishing up my drink when I heard Willow's unmistakable "miffed" walk climbing the stairs outside. She burst in and went straight to her room without a word, shutting the door behind her. Wes appeared in her wake, and they soon engaged in heated conversation on opposite sides of the door, while I sat six feet from Wes and continued watching a crime documentary.

Seems they had an anniversary and Willow was not pleased with her gift. "You didn't even give me a pair of jeans! This is one leg! You gave me a *jean*. You gave me a single jean!"

"Come on, baby, it's what they're wearing in Japan right now! They think it's totally punk rock!"

"What the fuck made you think I like punk rock!?"

"C'mon, Willow, I'm starving. I thought we were going to McDonald's."

"I thought you were going to McShut The Hell Up!" That one almost got me to laugh, but I was able to keep cool, lest they redirect their anger towards me.

It was obvious by now that I wouldn't get to enjoy my murder, so I retired to my room. Those things always end the same way anyhow: the boyfriend did it. I figured that if I minded my own business and let things in the living room play out on their own that maybe tonight the boyfriend would be the victim instead.

JUN 7 (SUN)

I've had this on my mind for a while now, maybe it's time that I address it. In the very first entry I wrote, I went out of my way to graft a certain word to myself.

"Virgin." What is it about that word? Why have I stuck myself with it like a tattoo artist's needle? I suppose it's possible that I've been pulled in by the taboo, assigning myself a word with any sexual connotation at all just so I can eradicate my statelessness. Or, maybe I'm just trying to "reclaim" it, no longer running from it and instead trying to dull its impact.

"Virgin" is not a nasty word made up for a group of people as a means of dehumanizing them. Rather, it became an insult through its own definition. It means the same thing in vitriol as it does in neutrality. What's more, there is no other noun for it, no polite synonym that deflects the energy. Even Latin cannot save you. It's a word used in popular culture with a disparaging, often abusive, tone. It's a punch line.

A joke can be a funny thing: sometimes you're in on it, and sometimes it's on you. I can take a joke, we all have to laugh at ourselves. None of us are special. But when you're already hurting, it feels like being kicked when you're down. I know the sentiment traditionally isn't directed at me, particularly due to gender roles and accompanying presumptions. You know how the old saws go: males want to have sex and females don't, boys are supposed to and girls aren't. But really, the underlying meaning is still the same: no one has ever loved you and no one probably ever will. Therefore, your life isn't worth living. And, on top of that, you're ugly.

What's there to lose after that, except for the obvious?

But, when you look at the dictionary definition and strip away the cultural significance, you're left with this:

virgin \'vûr·jin\ *noun* : a person who has not had sexual intercourse

That's it. That's the word as just a word. But, as an entire sentence called out at someone (whether true or not,) we know what it really means.

You look at the definition and you want to say, "So what the hell is wrong with being a virgin, anyway? Why is that so shameful? Is comparing yourself to me on this one count the only way you can feel like you've accomplished anything in life? If you're so superior, why don't you grow a spine so you can mouth off to somebody who deserves it for once?"

Maybe that's what it all comes down to: societal expectations. I'm a person as complex as any other, and I don't want the world defining me with short, easy one-word ideas. When you control the language, you control the argument. I don't want to be controlled in such a manner.

Here's an example of how language colors our thoughts. When people who speak

English as a first language see the word "red," we all pretty much think of the same color: the color of stop signs and blood and cherries. Lighter shades of red are called "pink" and "peach." Darker ones are "brown" and "maroon." Now consider the color blue. Sure, there are specific names for different types of blues, but none of them have caught on to become as regularly-used and commonly accepted as "pink" and "brown" are. When see different shades, we call them "light blue" and "dark blue." Nothing else has come close to achieving equal footing with "blue". Even "indigo," neither a primary nor a secondary color and therefore absent from the color wheel, still seems like a made-up term for bluish-purple that was created to provide a much-needed vowel in the acronym "ROY G. BIV." Because we don't have good, solid words for these colors, "blue" has to fill the gaps and therefore encompasses a much wider variety of hues and tints.

Thus you can see that words are not just labels, but entire concepts. Words have their own back stories and auras and textures. Even though they're synonyms, I'd much rather be thought of as "clever" than "crafty." It's preferable to be "old-fashioned" instead of "obsolete." And it's better to be known as a "nonconformist" than a "loner."

So then, why fixate on the word? If I'm trying to unmoor myself of the emotional ballast of being a "virgin," why invoke it so much? Or at all?

Because I need a goal. Because there has to be a finish line off in the distance for me to focus on. Because I am a woman obsessed, brimming with a twitching monomania. When I want something, it consumes me. I become my obsessions. But this time I already am my obsession, and it's rather unbecoming.

Whether it's my first time or thousandth time shouldn't matter, as the objective is the same. Still, I'll write it out right here in a cryptic cursive shorthand: Audrey Perlmutter is a virgin. It's a disaster to say out loud, with a mess of the more abrasive consonants grappling for elbow room amid a smog of "er" sounds. But it means something, too. At this moment, I choose to have it mean that there is a woman with a lot to look forward to. I may be inexperienced (some might say "green,") but if you think of it that way, then it comes across as sunny, sanguine, and even a little "blue."

So, like they say, "Sticks and stones."
I don't even have to finish that line. We all know what those words really mean.

<u>JUN 8 (MON)</u>

It was Rosi's birthday today, so a lot of the staff came down to the library after classes for a small celebration. We don't do this for every birthday, this was just because Lynn brought an ice cream cake in. I got to write "HAPPY BIRTHDAY, ROSI" on the cake in icing. Rosi surprised me by instantly recognizing that the icing work was mine, due to the presence of the comma. Winston chimed in and suggested that maybe Lynn wrote it, and that I just added a comma to make people think I was responsible. The older women in the room lauded him for his brilliant but completely inaccurate deduction. "Oh, he's so clever!" was heard at one point. I don't even know if that guy's serious anymore. Maybe he's secretly a stand-up comic filming a TV series without us knowing it.

Okay, I suppose that's a little crazy. Most women do find him attractive, so there's no way he's a comedian.

Rosi's twenty-six now. All day she was unhappy about that, as she considers this the final year of her "mid-twenties."

"My time in this world is fleeting," she said, seeming to mean it seriously. I know she's only four years shy of where I am, so the sentiment would sound almost as strange coming from me. Still, I have a lot more left to do than she does. She asked me if this birthday means her "spring is over."

"You know, how they say 'autumn of life' and 'May-December romance' and such. If January 1st is the day you're born, and life expectancy is 72 years, where am I?" she asked. Good question. I did some quick calculations and estimated that she's 132 days in to her "year," you could say. I informed her that she's somewhere around May 11.

"Are you going for a May-December, then?"

She laughed in disbelief, and assured me that if she's dating a man that old, "it had better be Christmas every day, if you know what I mean!"

Some more calculating put my "year" at about 151½ days, right at the tail end of the month. "Does that put you in May or June?" Rosi asked.

"Well, I'm May, or I'm May not."

"You're such a geek, Audrey."

Zena was present for the festivities, which was unusual as she doesn't often mingle amongst the teachers. This time there was cake, so the presence of sweets may have been enough to tip the scales on that decision.

I told Zena that I had an idea for something sexy I could say to a guy to let him know I'm interested in sleeping with him. She giggled a little and said, "Sorry, sorry. It's just that you're so cute the way that you said that, like you're still a teenager or something." Not really what I wanted to hear.

I asked her how this sounds: "First, I say, 'I just bought new bed sheets.' Then I pause for a few seconds like I'm expecting him to say something and add, 'Feel free to jump in at any time.'"

"You really want my advice on that?"

"Yeah."

"Don't ever say that. But go tell it to Lynn, she'll think it's hilarious."

She dug into her slice from the upper left corner (bearing the left half of the H) and remarked on Winston's attempted put-down from earlier. How the hell did he get his job in the first place? He doesn't have the same last name as the superintendent, so I'm guessing somebody married somebody else's sister somewhere along the line.

Zena had a theory: she thinks that Winston actually likes me. Her explanation for this leaves much to be desired. "When you were a kid, didn't you ever hear that if a boy teases you it's because he likes you?"

Ah. So the idea is that he's teasing me because he actually has a crush on me. I have a more likely theory: glass running shoes will be "in" this fall.

"Think about it," Zena continued between bites, "if he had no interest in you, he'd act like you weren't even there."

"So if he said you're garbage and you'll never amount to anything, that would make you like him more?"

"Audrey, you're way too sensitive."

Well, admittedly, Zena's logic makes sense but only if you take away the context. Winston is very popular and photogenic. He could have anyone he wanted, so why would he have any interest in me? If her assessment had any truth to it, maybe he's just trying to win me over because he can't stand the fact that there's a young woman left in this city who can't stand the sight of him. That's more his M.O.

I still think Zena's wrong about him, though. Either way, I don't want to be talked down to. I'm better than that. I deserve better, even I know that. I deserve to be treated like an equal. If someone's trying to win me over with mind games and damaging my self-esteem, then that's a relationship already standing in line for the scrapheap, give or take a consonant.

Speaking of not being treated right, I still had some unfinished business.

I sent one more text to the guy who gave me his number. It read: "If you didn't get my last text, sorry I took so long to get back to you. If you did, sorry I wasted your time. Wish I could have seen you again."

Of course, by now, that would be a lie.

JUN 9 (TUE)

Had another one of those heavy-handed bad metaphor dreams. This time, I was running the last leg of a relay race, but the person handing me the baton never showed up. So I guess I wasn't really "running", to be precise.

Ange told me about "lucid dreaming" a while back: the phenomenon wherein one becomes aware of the fact that one is dreaming and can then exercise a degree of editorial control over what happens. I may have to give it a try, if only so I can have the chance to tell my subconscious, "Okay! I get it! Can't I have a dream that doesn't read like a sketch from the *Sigmund Freud Variety Hour*?" Oh God, what a horrible show that would be. Like *Saturday Night Live*, but with fewer penis jokes.

Speaking of Freud, I've read that feelings of sexual inadequacy can often take the form of dreams where everybody can fly except the subject. I've had the opposite. I've had dreams where I'm the only person on Earth who can fly. You'd think it would be enjoyable and empowering, but instead I'm very careful and always looking over my shoulder. If anyone else finds out that I have this new ability, I know the already-sickening frequency at which I hear the phrase "can you do me a favor and" would triple.

"Audrey, can you do me a favor and deliver these party invitations for me? I'd mail them, but stamps cost money and you're right here, so... Yeah, just drop them off at their addresses. Yours isn't in there because I mailed it and it'll probably get lost."

Not naming any names, I'd expect these sorts of requests to be mainly originating from those who ask me to hand them the remote control, even though it's a five-foot amble from where they sit, and I'm in the kitchen. (Counterpoint: "Yeah, but you're already standing up.")

Lynn brought her class in for a last-chance research session on their reports. They each had to do a report giving information and history on any state in the union, as long as they each chose a different state and none of them were Massachusetts. Rosi was around, too. I don't know why. I didn't think teachers' aides were allowed to come and go as they pleased, but she seems to be operating on her own schedule. Months ago, I walked past the gymnasium and I swear I heard her arguing with Coach Bucket during a gym class game of basketball, yelling "NO FOUL! NO FOUL! C'MON, COACH, ARE YOU CRAZY?" She may have had money on that game.

The kids began to come up to check out their books in a slow drip. Rosi was lamenting that our journeys into clubland were not occurring as often as she first envisioned.

"We're not going out nearly as much as I hoped we would! Besides, Audrey still needs—"

"Child!" blurted Lynn, reminding her of a kid in earshot.

Rosi acknowledged the warning and went on. "Audrey still needs to G-E-T L-A-I-D."

Lynn tried to maintain a nonchalant grin, and through clenched teeth hissed, "The kid can spell those words, dummy. She's in second grade and is checking a book out of the library."

Tried my best to salvage this wreck by adding, "Don't worry, I won't forget to pick up my check this week. I'll get *paid*." Whether or not the kid caught or understood any of what we were discussing was beside the point, as she could always ask an adult and that would spell D-I-S-A-S-T-E-R.

After she went on her way and the next kid put his book on the counter, I suggested to Rosi, "Maybe you should just not talk about S-U-S-H-I in front of the L-A-R-V-A-E."

Almost automatically, she said, "Why would I talk about sushi in front of larvae?" Saw it coming. Thank heavens I used coded terms.

"It's secret code, remember?" I said.

Lynn snickered and pointed out that all codes are secret. "So, isn't 'secret code' an oxymoron?" she asked.

"No," Rosi challenged her, "an oxymoron is when two things that are supposed to be opposites have the same meaning. Like 'knuckle up' and 'knuckle down.'" Uhhhh no, but close.

Still, Rosi was right. We weren't going to clubs all that much, were we? I pointed out that Ridgeway's options are rather slim. I didn't really want to go to Regent again and my research into other options turned up a lot of places that looked even less desirable. Boston has more to work with, but it's never an easy go.

"Getting to and from Boston is a real pain," said Lynn. "If you drive, there's no guarantee you'll make it out alive, and even parking garages are a crapshoot. The train is fine for this sort of thing, but the schedules are inconvenient. Plus, if you're planning on leaving after 11:30, you're stuck if you came by train. Even the subways stop around midnight. It's almost as if the city's trying to keep out-of-towners from coming in and spending money."

"It's like having Joh Bjelke-Petersen for a mayor," I was tempted to add before it occurred to me that nobody else would have a clue what the hell I was saying.

That's one part of the problem: not much in the way of opportunity. Perhaps I shouldn't dwell on it too much, as I've come to the conclusion that the clubs are not really my thing. I'm too self-conscious and paranoid for that type of atmosphere. I'm pretty sure that the type of guy I could see myself with wouldn't be spending his time in a boozy blacklight trap anyway.

My reluctance to go clubbing again speaks to my other big problem: lack of confidence. I've never had any experience in love before, so I feel undesirable. It feels like only rejection awaits me. I can't be more confident if I don't make any progress towards my goal. I can't make any progress if I don't assert myself. I can't assert myself if I'm not confident enough. I am stuck in an "oxymoron."

JUN 10 (WED)

I worry a lot. No, really! I worry about my future. I worry about money. I worry about whether I remembered to lock the door before I left. I worry about whether or not things that didn't happen actually happened. But more than anything else, I worry about what other people think of me.

I'm worried about looking like someone who only shows up when she wants something. Natasha's collision in April was a huge turning point, and I had to start setting some new things in motion. I never really thought to contact Angela again before that, and I never gave any thought to trying to have sex before that. As a result, I'm worried that Ange might think I only bothered re-establishing communication so that I could use her to help me. Then there's Natasha, who I haven't really done a whole lot with before. We haven't gone to any clubs or anything like that, but I also know that's not her style. If I suddenly needed her help, would she know that I'm not trying to take advantage of her?

Well, it rained today, and it was coming down pretty hard once classes were over. I figured I could cash in that free ride home from Natasha, so I swung by her classroom before she could escape without me. There's a laminated construction paper placard on her door spelling out "Mrs. Przybysz." I have no clue how it's pronounced, but the kids call her "Mrs. P." Natasha's only been married for a year, so last year she was "Miss W." and I was often "Miss P." Now, to avoid confusion, I've been demoted to just "the librarian."

Turns out, Natasha wouldn't be leaving for a while yet, as she was keeping one of her students after class. She told me she'd be happy to give me a ride when the kid's punishment was over. Once the brat finished paying his debt to society, he gave a stern notice to his teacher.

"Ya know, you can't tell me what to do! You're not my parents!"

Natasha, cold as ice (as always,) answered, "No, I'm not. But, if your parents wish to discuss your behavior, I'd be more than happy to speak with them."

The student thought he was calling her bluff. "You wouldn't want my dad to come down here!"

Natasha tore out a prepared page in her notepad, folded it up and handed it to Tyler. "Here you are. Give that note to your dad so he'll know I'm interested in speaking with him once he has the time."

Tyler walked out of the room. "He'll *be* here!" the third-grader threatened. Oh no! He will? I hope I stay home that day so he doesn't get me!

As we walked down the hallway, Natasha informed me that Tyler's father has in fact come down to the school to speak with her before. Following a second term in which Tyler's report card looked like the results of a Burger King health inspection, the kid's dad came down to throw a fit, claiming Natasha was not doing her job. She pointed out that 24 of her other 28 students were getting nothing but A's and B's.

"I told him that if he didn't think I was doing a good job, he should consider taking it up with the other parents to see if they agreed."

"You think he'll be back?" I asked.

"Absolutely not. Especially since I wrote that note for Tyler to give him. If he knows I want to see him, he'll never return."

"Ah, of course. But not because he doesn't feel he has control of the situation. He just doesn't want to give you the satisfaction."

"Precisely."

We got to the front door just as it started coming down in sheets. Natasha had an umbrella, of course. My long walking stride makes it hard for me to keep pace with others to begin with, but I really had to slow down if I wanted to stay dry.

She explained to me how she and her husband are getting by with only one set of wheels for the moment: "This is Robbie's car. I'm dropping him off at work in the morning now." Ah, she calls him "Robbie." I've always felt a little bad for guys named Robert who get called "Rob." It's okay as a proper noun, but it's a hell of a verb to be associated with.

It was a quick ride to my place. Once we were out of the parking lot, she wasted no time in bringing up something that she heard me say not too long ago. "Audrey, I understand that you haven't had any intimacy before and that you want to make up for lost time, but… I did overhear what you were saying to Zena the other day, about the 'jumping into your bed sheets' line. I was seriously hoping you were above that kind of thing. I hoped that once you found someone, you'd be ready to settle down and think about committing to him." Even though Natasha was speaking in her usual steady drone, her words were emotional kerosene. I could sense that she had lost a lot of respect for me.

What the hell, Natasha. If you wanted to live your life that way, then fine. Try seeing things from my perspective. I'm not hurting anyone, I thought.

She was already good enough to do me this favor, so I didn't really have the nerve to defend myself. With nothing else to say, I sighed an apologetic and ashamed-sounding sigh and just let her have this one. I hate being brought down to sighs.

"Audrey, I have to say that while I'm not in favor of what you're doing, I understand your reasons. But, I want you to remember that there are consequences to everything." At a red light, she pulled a pack of smokes out of her purse and lit one up. After her first drag, she added, "But, I guess that's what makes life enjoyable. We all have our vices, I suppose."

We pulled up to my building. I thanked Natasha and was about to get out of the car, when she stopped me and said, "I wasn't going to do this before, but I've changed my mind. I know someone that I can set you up with for a blind date."

A blind date! Could my ears be deceiving me, the way they did back when I liked that Blues Traveler album? After all this, I'm finally going on a date! This is progress. *Real* progress, not like the phone number guy!

Natasha said that the male in question is her cousin Willis, so she wants to make sure that I don't "use" him. Sure, I'm fine with that. Though if he wants to "use" me, I guess that wouldn't be my fault, would it? Well, whatever happens is fine with me, because I'm going on my first date. Finally.

I agreed to Natasha's conditions, and thanked her for everything. She says she'll call Willis and see when he's available.

Since manga characters don't count, I don't think I've ever spent any significant amount of time around a man who I knew was gay before. Well, no longer. An emergency meeting was called for the fifth grade teachers. I did not know why, but Miriam asked if I would mind postponing my lunch to keep an eye on their kids at recess. So, I found myself standing in the courtyard on a cloudy day next to the typically reserved Jeff, who was also called on for this. It was a neat experience, like we were buddy cops. Maybe prison guards would be more accurate. (Elementary school is still school, after all.)

From the courtyard, the school looks like a giant air conditioner riddled with smaller air conditioners. The playground equipment is all plastic in tertiary colors, and includes all of the kids' favorites such as "Steering Wheel Sticking Out Of A Plastic Wall Panel™" and "A Ladder™". There's a ruin of an old metal swing set without any swings. That's too bad. I used the swing set like mad when I was a kid, but I haven't been on one since. I could use a good swing once in a while. Read into that what you will.

Jeff explained why all the teachers were unavailable: Jim Lowell, who Jeff is teachers' aide to, told him that Ed forgot where he was the other day and said something a little naughty in front of his class. All the fifth grade teachers were meeting to go over the rules and such regarding that sort of behavior and what is and isn't acceptable.

Ah. Of course it would be Ed. I told Jeff about how he was straining to read my shorthand note out loud with his class in the room.

Jeff didn't seem the least bit surprised. "He's probably in that meeting right now, insisting that the parents of the kid who ratted him out are waging a secret campaign to remove him from his job." No argument here. Nothing's ever Ed's fault. He always claims some shadowy cabal is plotting against him. All laughs and joking until someone calls him on his bullshit, then it's time to huff and puff and pretend to be outraged. With that sort of attitude, he'd be a perfect Congressman for a state with more giant balls of twine than electoral votes.

There are only a few guys on staff who I can stand to be around, and Jeff's about my age. Too bad that he's not into the ladies. This was nice, whiling away some time with a guy I can just talk to. Things got a little quiet for an uncomfortable few minutes, and I figured this was probably one of those times where I should practice making conversation for its own sake, but I had no idea what to say to him. I came extremely close to crossing a line and possibly offending by invoking a stereotype when I tried to break the ice. "Do you watch *Sex and the City?*" I asked exactly one half-second before regretting it. I have no idea what possessed me to ask that, seeing as how I've never seen the show myself.

"I haven't watched much of either one since I lost my binoculars," he said.

Genius. It was the best possible answer to the question. Linguists and humorists could work in tandem for a year on a better response and never find one. And I ruined it by blurting out my obnoxious laugh where the first "ha" sounds like I only caught it halfway through. It's such an irritating sound that I always want to follow it up with, "I swear I wasn't making fun of you. That's really how I laugh!" I'm sorry, Jeff. I'm sorry I ruined your punch line.

He asked why I brought it up. Oh no. Don't say "because you're gay." Say anything except "because you're gay." Whatever you say, it cannot be "because you're gay."

"Because you're…"

Ohhhh, way to go. Gotta finish that sentence now. What can I possibly follow that up with? "Slender"? "Dressed well"? "Kinda yaoi-ish, hint-hint"?

I stalled instead. "Because you're… a… Oh, look at that bird! Is that a cardinal? It's so red!" I pointed up at the trees. Jeff looked for the cardinal. There was no cardinal.

He asked if I liked working at the school. I told him I'd rather be at a regular library. Anything to get me away from all these battalions of shrieky snot-harvesters. Speak of the devil, no sooner do I say that than a little altercation (read: beatdown) broke out before our eyes. Oh boy, we're gonna have to rush over there and shout "Break it up!" now, aren't we?

We leapt into action and began prying apart two kids in a tussle. It was gruesome. It was like one of those cartoons where two brawlers turn into a noisy dust cloud with brief glimpses of body parts, moving along at a leisurely pace, waiting to cross the street at the WALK signal. It was too chaotic for me to keep track of what happened when. I think at one point I said, "Hey! Stop that!" or something like it. Real hard-boiled stuff.

One of our little pugilists wasn't sorry in the least. His arms were crossed. Uh-oh, universal symbol for either "we got a biiiiig toughy over here," or "I'm doing an ad for my new cable reality show." Maybe it was my imagination, but the other fifth grader seemed to have a nascent beard in the works. The less said about that, the better.

Jeff gave the students the usual lines, telling them to knock it off in a stern but calm tone. "I don't have to do what you say!" said Arms-Crosser McGee.

"No," Jeff said, "but you don't *have* to go to school here, either. Now don't let this happen again, or Principal Canada's hearing about it." The kids made tracks in opposite directions, McGee stomping off and mumbling what sounded like an entire sentence made entirely of non-transcribable grunts.

Jeff brushed his hands together as if he had just finished a strenuous task, which was pretty humorous given how sharp the creases in his pants still were. "They're probably threatened by my strong masculine presence. One time I bent a Q-tip at a right angle to show them who's boss. Took me twenty minutes but it was worth it. I barely even had to use my teeth." As much as I enjoyed spending time with Jeff, I don't think I should seek out opportunities to hang out with him. I haven't got anything against him, I just don't want people thinking I'm a... let's just say "hag".

Rosi brought her tablet to the library again. This time she had a video she wanted me to watch. "I'm only doing this because you need to know. I was digging up some info on that club we went to last month, and, well..."

The title of the video was "Crazy Woman Dancing At the club whose name is a blue trapezoid." I was the title character. It was shaky smartphone footage of me dancing with that phone number guy. It was only forty-four seconds, but I couldn't watch it all, and I hit the pause button.

Rosi took her tablet back. "You only have three more seconds left to watch. Don't you want to see them?" I did not.

"If it makes you feel better, the video's been up for three weeks and it only has 124 views," she said. Well, I'd be lying if I said I wasn't concerned about something just like this happening. But, I'm concerned about a lot of unlikely things that don't happen as well. I suppose I should take this as a lesson that if things go wrong, they won't be as awful as I fear they'll be.

UPDATE. Angela texted me. She has an idea for a TV show: a Saturday morning cartoon called *Hippo Campus* about hippos in college. The jokes are mostly about how they eat a lot. In one episode, they try to cram themselves into a phone booth, but only one of them can fit, and he gets stuck. She wants to know if I can draw hippos for some concept sketches.

JUN 12 (FRI)

People are proud of some strange things. Today, I overheard Coach Bucket telling

George a story about a nasty skiing injury he got on his leg last year. I don't get why so many people talk about injuries. It's a pretty popular discussion topic. Rarely a Thanksgiving or a Passover goes by when I don't hear an uncle relating a new tale of belt sander-related agony or fishhook-induced blood-lettings. One of our more popular legends is of how my grandfather called an ambulance for his neighbor, who cut off his finger with an electric hedge trimmer. I always assumed it must have been his dialing finger.

I've never been injured. I consider myself to be quite lucky in that aspect of life, at least. However, if I were to attend an informal gathering where everyone was sharing anecdotes of bodily harm, I'd be unable to contribute anything. Oh, if only a malfunctioning elevator door could snap my arm in two. Then I'd be in business! Come to think of it, I don't have many entertaining tales from my past at all. My best story is probably the time I witnessed my cousin bait a balloon-selling clown at a parade into a fistfight. The clown, wearing a pointed party hat, blew his top after being subjected to a series of insults lobbed by my drunken kin including what sounded like "maniac in a cone".

Maybe most people feel this way, but it's hard to come to grips with the fact that I'm just not interesting. I wouldn't be able to hold the room's attention at a party. I haven't done anything that the average person would want to hear about. Sometimes I've wondered if the reason I've always been alone is because I don't really have anything to offer that would draw anyone in. I don't think that should disqualify me. What has anyone else ever done?

Around 10:30, Lynn texted me with an idea: I should practice my conversation tactics for speed-dating by having a rehearsal session. She explained that she and the others could take turns pretending to be males that I'd come across. I was not sure about this idea, but my morbid curiosity pushed me into going along with it. A concept such as that was brimming with possibilities for devolving into chaos.

After school, Lynn brought the usual suspects over to the library. We decided my "dates" should proceed alphabetically: Lynn, Natasha, Rosi, and Zena.

Rosi interjected, "If it's alphabetical order, shouldn't we use last names?"

Very well. The new line-up was: Lynn Mackenzie, Natasha Przybysz, Rosi Sandoval, and Zena Swanson. Much better. I took my seat at the table. Lynn stuck a Post-it with "AUDREY!!" scrawled on it to my jacket. "That's your nametag!" she explained. I suppose the exclamation points were to make me stand out and grab people's attention, but instead it just looked like I was being shouted down by office supplies. Zena looked at the clock on her phone to time it to the second. On "Go," Lynn rushed over to the chair like she was running a race. She extended her arm for a handshake. I know not why.

"Hello, I'm Audrey. Nice to meet you."

"I'm... crap, I forgot to make up a name. I'm Lynnnnnnn, uh, Linda. I'm Linda. Oh shit, that's not a boy's name... I'm... Warren!"

"Why Warren?" I asked.

"Because that's the name my mama gave me!" Of course. How could I be so foolish?

There was a bit of silence until I realized that I was supposed to be initiating conversation. So, I asked Warren where he was from. I asked if he'd seen any good movies recently. I asked where he would want to go on vacation if he could go anywhere in the world. I asked if he ever had any interesting injuries.

"*BUZZZZ! No!* Don't bring that up," Zena called out from the sidelines. "One minute."

I rode out the last minute discussing the weather. Zena let out another "Go," and Natasha took Lynn's seat.

"Hi. Nice meeting you. I'm Audrey."

"I'm Cristobal. I own rats and a komodo dragon."

I asked Cristobal what his job is. He said he works at a slaughterhouse, where he uses a mallet to "make the cows fall down." I asked what his favorite holiday is. He said it was Thanksgiving, "because 'Thanksgiving' spelled backwards is 'murder'."

Lynn broke in, telling Natasha to quit trying to ruin the rehearsal.

"No, this is good," said Zena. "Audrey's probably gonna run across a few of these, and she needs to learn how to handle them. Keep going."

I asked Cristobal to describe what he considers to be a perfect date. He responded by giving me a short list of singers he thinks deserve to be tortured. I figured it was best if I played along and kept him happy. "Okay! That's great! The guy from Path to Ascension? Really? Hmm, never thought of that one. Good call," essentially summed up my responses. I have to say, Natasha was genuinely scaring me. She very well might be spot-on with her impression, and I could likely end up crossing paths with people like that at some point. I can only hope the straitjacket manufacturers of today still take pride in their work.

"Go."

Now it was Rosi's turn. She had chosen the character of a rowdy Australian named

Ray-Ban.

"Me mates call me 'Fingers' because I've got ten of 'em. And they all wanna get to know ya better. They want the 'inside story,' if yer catchin' me drift."

"Uhhhh, hello. I'm Audrey."

"Look, Audrey. I'm not gonna lie. I've got a shiny sports car and a shedload o' me dead grandfather's cash. Anywhere you and your boobs wanna go, we're there."

I would rather not recount the next three minutes of conversation.

Lynn finally came over to the table and told Ray-Ban that speed-dating is not an excuse for sexual harassment and that he had to leave. He demanded his money back and stormed out while murmuring accusations of discrimination against people who can fake only Australian accents. I sat at the table alone, wondering if we would keep going for the full five minutes in light of Ray-Ban's early departure. We did.

Natasha apologized, saying, "I think I may have loosened the cap on that one."

After eighty seconds of silence, Zena finally sat down and introduced herself as Kevin. We were finally back to normal. This time, the first question was for me: Kevin asked what I did for work. I've always hated when people ask me that. Who cares about my job? I'm sick of having to define myself in terms of what I do for money. I'm not here to serve other people. Maybe I'm just worried that the word "librarian" makes me sound too, for lack of a less-appropriate term, bookish. I just told Kevin I work at an elementary school.

"Oh, so you must really like kids, huh?"

Uh-oh. Is this a trap? If I say "no," he might be put off if he has kids. Or worse yet, *wants* them. [*Insert ominous thunderclap*.] If I say "yes," that might scare him off if he's not in it for the long haul.

Instead, I came out with, "Well, my cousins are okay, but it's hard getting used to the ones I'm not related to." Not bad, if I do say so myself. The rest of our talk went pretty smoothly. When the five minutes were up, Zena congratulated me and said she was impressed with how I handled everything, particularly how I side-stepped that question about kids.

Rosi came back into the room and wanted to know if we were gonna go another round. She promised she wouldn't assume the persona of an asshole this time. I declined, feeling we had gotten as far as we were gonna get today. I was also getting a little scared about who I might end up being matched with, thanks to the ideas Natasha and Rosi were filling my head with. I shouldn't be picky, but I don't think it's unreasonable to dread being paired with a Cristobal or a Ray-Ban or a Rug Doctor (just guessing that's what

Rosi's next character would be named.)

Zena joined me for the first half of my walk home. She expressed concern about her own prospects, as she hasn't had been in a steady relationship for almost a year now. I told her she has nothing to worry about.

She asked me how I do it, how I've gone so long without anyone to help me through. Lord help me, I don't know why, but I took that question seriously.

I opened up and said, "You convince yourself that you're not missing out on anything. You look at all the places where everyone else went wrong and say, 'Whew! Dodged a bullet there!' You just avoid as many reminders as possible, even though they're everywhere. You say that something good's gonna happen any day now and that it'll come in its own time. In short: you just get really good at lying to yourself." I reminded Zena that she wasn't "active" until the age of nineteen, so she has to know what it's like from her high school days.

"Well, while that's true, and I didn't even date until I was eighteen, I could have been a little more honest with you. I spent my high school years at a boarding school for girls."

"Oh. But your freshman year in med school, you didn't…"

"I also had to repeat the third grade. Turned nineteen in October of my freshman year."

"I see." Yeah, that would have painted a more complete picture.

Zena tried to reassure me. "Look, don't worry. My sister had lot of trouble with guys, too. But, eventually she managed to get the hang of it." Hmmmm. Her sister, eh? The one who allegedly bought those books because she needed so much help?

"Oh, really? What's her name?" I nonchalantly asked.

"Zoe."

Son of a

JUN 15 (MON)

It's the last full week of classes, and everyone is already as good as gone. I spent the day rounding up older books that nobody's checked out all year so we can make room for some new ones in September. What a drag, finding the books nobody wanted and just tossing them out. I suppose it's not a waste, as they end up getting donated to a local shop for used books, but I can't imagine how those places stay in business. Of course, some unwanted and aged books get legacied in, like the Dickens section or the seventy-eight or so volumes of *The Wizard of Oz*. Why not send them to the middle school where they stand a chance of being read? These pre-teens never lay a finger on those dusty relics, but hey they have a rep, so let 'em stay. Unfair.

On the chopping block was our copy of *The Forty-Eight States*, a state-by-state intro to US geography from the days when kids' books all had illustrations that looked like stills from *The Andy Griffith Show*. I wanted to keep this one for myself, but orders are orders.

Zena appeared about fifteen minutes before my break. She said Winston wanted to see me in his office. I said she should tell him I'm dead.

"Audrey, that would be a lie."

"Only in a technical sense." I was going to miss my break today, wasn't I?

Winston's office is a tribute not just to himself but to the very concept of vanity. There are plenty of framed photos all over the desk of him shaking hands with and posing alongside local politicians who could never hope to get any further than the state Senate. Wait, do I capitalize "senate" if it's not the real Senate in Washington? You know what, I will, since I'm feeling merciful.

When I see photographs, my first thought is often that somebody had to take them. In cases like this, the person behind the camera had to be asked outright if they would mind snapping a pic of two people shaking hands. As a result, here's a vice principal of an elementary school hobnobbing with some seat-filler taking a break from passing laws limiting neon sign wattages. Wow, thinks the cameraperson, how could anyone let this moment slip by undocumented? The National Archives would never forgive me.

Winston wasn't even in his office when I arrived, even though I was the one summoned there. Like I said: those who make us wait. I passed the time by imagining a conversation between our acting vice principal and the state rep from the made-up town of Singlehorse (who has the voice of Wallace Shawn in *The Princess Bride*.)

"Thanks for your help, DeVilbis. Too bad you live seven towns away, I could use more constituents like you."

"Always glad to do a solid for an upstanding man of the people like yourself, Representative Bacdore. But, you don't need me in your town. I'm not even registered to vote."

"Hey, who cares about that? I always run unopposed! Ha ha ha!"

"Voting isn't my scene. It's more of an activity for people who aren't blessed with my stunning looks and raw animal magnetism. It gives them something to do which makes them feel as if their lives have some consequence."

"Whoa, careful there, DeVilbis! Those are my voters you're talking about!"

"Relax. I called them 'people', didn't I? Now, roll up your sleeves, already. This kid isn't going to bury himself."

"You'd think a straight-A student would know to be more cautious around traffic this time of day. Hasn't he heard of 'liquid lunch' before?"

"It was his fault for getting in your way, sir. You had your turn signal on and were clearly going to go down his driveway."

Winston surfaced after about ten minutes, settled himself behind his desk as if I weren't even there, and checked his email. About two minutes of this lapsed before he finally addressed me. I was informed that he decided our reference section needed slimming down. He cited the internet as the reason for this proposed change, and told me to get going on ordering a new computer that we can't afford.

I argued that a new computer for the library was completely unnecessary, as none of the kids use the one we have now. After all, it's an elementary school, the kids don't have free reign on the internet. Plus, we have an entire computer lab for research purposes.

Winston could not be swayed. I asked what Miriam said about spending money on another computer, and a brand new model at that.

"This isn't her decision. This is coming from me."

Oh dear. You moron.

He wasn't finished doing back flips in the minefield yet, and added, "This is my decision to make. When I say how things are going to get carried out, you have to do what's expected of you, right?" A few seconds ticked by. "Well? Right?" he added. He wanted me to answer what was clearly a rhetorical question? What kind of dick does that?

Okay, fine, you want an answer, so here it is: "Not unless *her* orders contradict them." I emphasized the word "her" to remind him of his place in the pecking order.

I was expecting and hoping he would explode and tear into me, as I could have used a laugh. Instead, perhaps realizing the limits of his powers, he made a closed-mouth chuckle which usually translates to English as, "I've been bested, but I can't let on."

"I should have expected this attitude from you," he said. "Even back in Railhead, you always had to go against the grain."

Uh, what? He knows me from before? He sounded like he was trying to drop a huge bombshell on me and really catch me off-guard. I just deadpanned it as if everything he said was completely expected.

He went on. "Why was that? Why did you always have to be the odd duck?"

I set all controls to "non-chalant" and replied, "Oh, you went to school with me?"

"Well, I was a few years ahead of you. I graduated before you even made it to high school. My sister was in your grade. That's how I always heard about you, from what she'd tell me. In a way, you and I were both pretty well-known there. Even if we didn't cross paths you were probably familiar with my name."

"No, sorry. Winston is the sort of name you remember, especially after reading *Nineteen Eighty-four*. Which team were you on?"

He was peeved now. "I wasn't on a team. How can you not remember me?"

"I just tend not to remember people from my past that I wasn't close to. I don't even remember ninety percent of the people in my own grade," I explained, knowing it wouldn't help.

He had moved beyond peeved. We had arrived at irked. "I was the prom king."

He didn't just say that, did he? He's in his thirties and he's still proud of that? I hope he doesn't put that on his résumé. (Who am I kidding? Of course I hope he does, it would be hysterical.)

He made it very clear that my orders were to get a new computer for the library, and that a few of our older encyclopedia sets had to go. I'm a little impressed with the restraint he showed in that he didn't end his dictates with "I hath spoken!" or even "Chop chop!" Admittedly, a couple of those encyclopedias are outdated and have been taking up too much valuable real estate for a while now. Compared to the newer ones, they only excel if, say, a fourth-grader suddenly gets the urge to find the name of the mountain range separating East Germany from Czechoslovakia. They're not the newest or the shiniest, but they're only about thirty years old. That isn't too old. Still full of useful knowledge. Still a lot to offer, even if everyone really does want yet another computer that would just end up being a vehicle for Minesweeper instead of real research.

Why is it like this? Why does the informative and still-mostly accurate *The Forty-Eight States* get the boot while other things children would never voluntarily read are allowed to skate by on the coattails of *A Christmas Carol*?

Went back to the library. I began cleaning out my stuff from behind the counter. I didn't have a lot, pretty much just office supplies, a couple volumes of *Yoichi-san no*

Hanafuda, and those three books Zena gave me. In the back corner of one drawer was the duck. The odd duck in the straw hat, silently mocking me as part of his comedy routine. I hated him at that moment. I wanted to put him in a microwave. I wanted to turn him into a pin cushion. I wanted to make that inanimate chunk of Chinese plastic suffer.

"Odd duck." Odd duck, huh? I figured I could take him to the janitor's shed and hide him in the wood chipper. Maybe I'll introduce him to Jaws.

But I couldn't do it. I couldn't kill innocent Vaudeville Duck. He didn't mean to upset me. All he wanted to do was entertain. Surely, someone out there would appreciate him.

Rather than break my duck, I chose to hide him at the bottom of my purse, deep enough that I wouldn't have to see him every time I looked in there. At the end of the day, he was covertly joined by *The Forty-Eight States*. On the way home, I stopped at one of those book stores I mentioned earlier and slid the book out of my purse when I was out of sight. I brought it up to the register and paid for it as if I had just taken it off the shelf. The cashier priced it at only $4.80. She said it would have been a flat five, but wanted to make up for the missing Alaska and Hawaii.

JUN 16 (TUE)

I'm not going to order a new computer. Granted, I already made up my mind yesterday, but now it's a certainty.

Even though it wasn't their day of the week to visit, Lynn's class (as well as the other second graders) stopped in to listen to the drama teacher from the high school read them a few stories. Just another one of those things we have to improvise in the final days of the year to keep the tykes occupied once their lessons are through and their brains are already on vacation. Last year, the third graders were all gathered in here to watch a CGI dinosaur movie, then they all had a three-hour recess. It was dubbed "Dinosaur Day" only after the fact. "Yeah! Dinosaur Day! We're gonna do nothing, then watch a movie, then go outside and do nothing! I've been waiting for this since September!"

While the kiddies were distracted by their storyteller, I brought Lynn up to speed on my debacle with Winston over the reference section. We decided the best plan of action would be to run everything past Miriam, seeing as how she'd have to approve buying the computer eventually.

Come to think of it, that may have been Winston's idea all along: make it look like

I'm a reckless spender full of bad ideas. That way, he could take Miriam's side and better his standing in her eyes. Or, maybe I'm over-thinking it and he just likes telling people to do stupid things that he thinks are brilliant.

Between his two books, the reader had a bit of an intermission. During this break, I called that David kid over and asked him to bring a note to the principal's office. He was happy to oblige. That's right, David. You love me but you can never have me. Therefore, you shall do my bidding until you wise up.

Ten minutes or so passed before an announcement came over the speaker calling for me to report to Miriam's office. All the students present gave their obligatory "Oooooooooooh!" to signify their belief that I was in trouble. What is it those kids all think I did that warrants punishment, as if I were their peer? Well, it actually isn't that hard to imagine Rosi and I both sitting in Miriam's office, bruises on our arms, each of us shouting "She started it!"

When I got there, Winston was already waiting for me. Hmph. Should've dawdled a little along the way and made him wait this time. Miriam asked me a few questions. I had more than a few answers, all of them basically different ways of saying "Is this new computer idea awful or what?"

It turns out Winston was true believer after all, as he argued that we needed the computer for students to use for research. I pointed out that maybe these pre-teen kids should be using books for that sort of thing, as they have internet access at home where their parents can monitor them, but all the books they need could be here. Plus, you can't check a computer out of the library and bring it home with you to read later. I couldn't help using the moment to point out that our fifth-grade history textbooks still refer to the break-up of the Soviet Union as "oncoming."

Miriam thought I made a better case, even if she didn't necessarily agree that buying new textbooks was the best plan at the moment. Winston couldn't concede a single point. Eyes were narrowing. They were both dug in, even though we all knew the winner of the argument was a foregone conclusion. It was a staring contest reminiscent of a McDonald's and a Burger King on opposite sides of the street, each one waiting for the other to be the first to stop flying the flag at half-staff in the wake of NASA's latest "boo-boo."

Miriam told me that I was not to make any changes to the reference section, nor was I to order a computer. She sent me on my way while the two of them would finish their friendly little chat. My pleasure.

Given what he said yesterday, it's easy to assume Winston was pretty proud of his years in high school, being the big fish in the little koi pond. His version of troublemaking was probably the bland, predictable variety: drinking beer on school property, cutting class for fast food, the outgoing senior class prank. ("Ha ha! Oh man, I can't believe we actually glued a toupee to the statue in front of the school! Some people will see this, and they're gonna be furious! That'll show 'em!")

Meanwhile, I was the only student who drew editorial cartoons for the school paper. I wrote pieces for the school's news program on cable access. Because I was held back a year in preschool, I was already eighteen when I entered my senior year, so I threatened to run for the local school board when a couple of teachers started getting under my skin about my news stories. The things I did actually upset the powers that be. Some of the faculty members at Railhead High hated me and they had no way to stop me because I worked within the system. When you get right down to it, I was more of a troublemaker than anybody.

Winston is more like the Winston from *Nineteen Eighty-Four* than he could ever fathom: a cog in the machine who wanted to rebel and have his day in the sun, only to get quashed in the end and be like everybody else. Just another casualty of the system. Today I worked within the system again, and I used it to thwart him. For today, I was his superior.

Ange and I went out for sushi (real sushi, not code-word sushi.) She had two places in mind and couldn't choose, so she thought we should eat half our fill at one and finish up at the other. Strange way of doing things, but that's the sort of thing that happens when she's around. She ordered a glass of champagne at the first place. I don't think there's an occasion, she just wanted one. So, my first alcoholic drink is the alleged greatest beverage ever devised, huh? This is the drink that is like "tasting stars"? This is the hallowed refreshment used to celebrate only the most momentous of milestones? Okay, I guess I could have a sip.

I didn't like it.

Our deal was that I'd pay for the food at the first place, and she'd pay at the second. I never know how to handle the tip. If I include it with the bill, it might look like I didn't leave one because there isn't one at the table, and vice-versa. That's always been one of my paranoid nagging doubts. I try to tip well, though. I almost always tip around twenty percent, because I know the wages these people are paid aren't nearly enough to live on. I may not have been a waitress, but I've been in a similar place, and I still consider them to be my own kind: human. Plus, even though I'm good with numbers, it's still a lot easier to divide by ten and double than to divide by twenty and multiply by three.

Got an email from the speed-date organizers. The event is off "due to a high number of cancelations." Not entirely certain I believe that. Seems a little more likely that not enough folks signed up for the thing, but admitting that would make them look bad. Rather than refunding my money (because this is the Twenty-first Century, when everybody gets 'store credit' in lieu of refunds,) they've given me a promotional code that will allow me to sign up for the next one for free.

Come to think of it, that would be a great idea for a scam. Step one: get people to pay to attend events you never plan on holding. Step two: tell them it's canceled but don't refund their money. Just give them a free pass to the next one. Step three: repeat the cycle until everyone gets frustrated enough to just give up. I'm not even sure there's anything illegal about that as long as the minimum number of attendees for an event is never met. Just set it at some ridiculously high number like, say, five thousand.

Looked over their schedule on the website. The only other one they have for my age group is 29 to 41. It isn't Jewish-only and it's in July at an Irish pub in Boston called Paddy O'Furniture's. After that, there's nowhere I'll fit in until September.

Le sigh. Okay, fine. At least I'll probably be the youngest and youngest-looking one there.

JUN 17 (WED)

The students were enjoying another three-hour recess. Four days of school left after today so why bother?

I had plenty of time to finish up gathering the tomes that were being sent off to a nice book barn upstate. Lynn helped out a little, since her class was outside running out the clock. She seemed to be taking the news of the speed-dating cancelation better than I thought she would. Maybe she just felt I needed more time to prepare. Gotta say, I wouldn't blame her if that were the case. My feet were getting a little chilly, and I was wavering on whether or not this was such a great idea, but options aren't exactly throwing themselves at me.

Rosi and Jeanette stopped in to play "Throw a Beanbag at a Ceiling Fan," a little game they invented. It sounds cerebral, but the rules are actually quite simple. Easy to learn, impossible to master. Jeff somehow found his way in while my back was turned.

He was thumbing through a few biographies, probably just for something to do. I don't know how, but I think the library may have become the new alternative teachers' lounge for the younger set.

Lynn wanted to take advantage of our temporary freedom from the students by putting some music on. She scrolled through the songs on my computer, and found a title she liked. "Oh! This sounds promising: 'It's Going To Happen'." She hit play and began dancing to the brassy, upbeat tune, all the while smiling.

"Yeah, Audrey! It's going to happen! Happens all the time! It's going to happen!" she said, echoing the chorus.

Lynn is three-quarters Irish. I didn't have the heart to tell her she was dancing to a song about her own people dying in a hunger strike.

I was finishing up packing up the books when Winston showed up. Oh boy, three days in a row dealing with this guy. Well, at first he was surprisingly pleasant, perhaps because Miriam tore him up so thoroughly that he was lucky to get out with any of his chromosomes intact. He wanted to apologize for the events of earlier this week. Fine. Accepted. Next.

After that, he wanted to know what I plan to do over the summer. I still don't know, myself. I told him I'm going to take a vacation, still without even bothering to look in his direction. Take a hint. Of course, he had to know where I was planning to go.

"Europe," I said curtly, hoping he'd be able to read between the lines and get lost. Did he? Of course not. They *never* get lost. They can't figure out my body language and yet, allegedly, *I'm* the one with Asperger's.

"Ah, Europe," he said. "I've been there: Ireland, Morocco, Amsterdam, Sweden. All great places. If I could go back to any one country, it would have to be Amsterdam."

I've been trying really hard to avoid correcting people on trivial details. I used to think I'd be helping them avoid embarrassing faux-pas in the future, but all I do is create one right then and there, and it's never appreciated. And that's exactly why I couldn't hold back this time.

I was as calm and polite as I could be when I informed Winston of the fact that Amsterdam is not a country. He insisted he was right, and that it's "one of the Nether Lands." I also said that Morocco isn't in Europe. Now he was mad.

Winston stormed right over to his hated reference section to get a world atlas. The room had grown silent as he flipped through it in a state of rage, searching for a map of Europe. I heard a faint giggle or two. He found what he wanted and brought the book back over to me.

"THERE!" he said, slamming his finger down on the corner of the page. "Morocco's right there! Is this or is this not a map of Europe?"

I tried to explain, saying, "It's a map of Europe and surrounding places. They couldn't just put water where Africa is, that would be inaccurate."

He still argued that Morocco is part of Europe because it's on the map. Jeanette called out to us, saying that Canada and Mexico must be new U.S. states, then. That got a few laughs.

Even though it wasn't my joke, Winston was determined to take it out on me. He headed for the hallway, but couldn't resist getting the last word: "This is why nobody likes you." Oh, I wouldn't go that far. I seemed to be effortlessly winning the crowd's favor today, even if it is by default.

I dunno, I feel a little bit bad about it all. Still, I wouldn't put it past him to eventually come back to stop in and say something like, "Hey, jump so I can see how high you can jump. Ha! I can jump higher than you! See? You're not so smart after all! Ha-ha-ha!"

Lynn called me around seven. She wanted to know the name of the speed-dating service I signed up for. Ah, I see now. It looks like she wants in. She says she's going to sign up for the same one I did on July 2nd, that way we can go together. I suppose I'd feel more at ease if I'm not alone, so why not? Maybe her signing up will be enough to keep this one from getting canceled, too.

I just looked at the site to see if she finished her profile yet. In her bio, she mentions that her interests are "baseball (Go Mets!), running, adding 'cha cha cha!' to ends of songs on the radio." Yeah, that's Lynn alright.

It just occurred to me that at some point in his adult life, Winston did not know which of Earth's continents he was on.

JUN 18 (THU)

It was such a nice day out. After school, I needed an excuse to get out of the apartment, so I decided to ride my bike for a while, just to see where it took me. I went up Reilly street and passed a beauty salon with a sign advertising something called "permanent make-up." Permanent make-up? We really are living in a sci-fi movie world now, aren't we?

I piloted the bike down to the Quinella University campus (school motto: "D's Get

Degrees... Oh What The Hell, F's Get Degrees, Too.") to visit the library there. It's closer than the Ridgeway Public Library and I haven't really been to either one in a while. Not since fall, in fact. It's the perfect time of year for it now: the students have mostly pulled up stakes, so I didn't have to make my way through a hailstorm of hackeysacks just to get to where I was going.

I didn't really spend a lot of time there. I guess in the end I only went inside because I was already in the neighborhood. Saw the strangest flyer on the bulletin board, though, for something called "MBC." It read:

"The next cult meeting will be June 26 at The Dungeon. Prepare to bow down to your master!"

There's something you don't see every day. Well, I thought, this is clearly a joke, because no self-respecting cult would refer to themselves as a cult. That's pretty much Rules # 1 through 14 in the *How To Run a Cult* handbook.

Something (possibly my brain) urged me to copy down the time, date, and address. There wasn't too much text so I managed to get it down word-for-word in shorthand. I wanted to see what this was. It had an enticing feel to it. Is this some sort of party? Is it just a bunch of college kids getting drunk and hooking up? Okay! Where does the line form? They'll probably let me in without a school ID. I still look young enough to pass for a student without getting the third degree over it.

There was also a flyer for somebody giving away puppies "no questions asked." I don't want to think about why that frightens me.

Once I got back home, I looked over my scribbled note and it occurred to me that this probably isn't a house party. For one thing, it's being held in a place called "The Dungeon." Haven't heard of it before, and I couldn't find any info online, either. I'm lucky they put the address down.

It hit me just then that this may not be a normal get-together. Think about it, dummy: "Cult." "Dungeon." How much clearer could this be? This is a bondage club, isn't it? "MBC"? Well, the last two words are either "Bondage Club" or "Bondage Cult." What about the M? "Massachusetts"? Wait, no, it's probably "Masochists'" or "Masochism." (Yikes, "masochists" is disturbingly close to the name of my state. That may explain why we all stay despite the winters.)

So there probably won't be any actual sex, but it will be an experience. Any sort of play or experimentation is welcome right now. Strip me down to underwear, handcuff me to something, spank me, anything! My curiosity has gotten the better of me. I must have seen this flyer at the exact right time and place, because I'm having a hard time believing that I'm considering this.

What's required of me? Do I have to bring someone? I gotta be honest, I'll probably walk into the place, see what's happening, and then walk right back out again. Hopefully, I'll have enough courage to go through with something, if I can get in at all. This has all the makings of being an embarrassing face-plant, like the time I drove to New York just to see the place and then didn't get out of the car because I couldn't find a place to park. But, they put up a flyer, didn't they? They must want people to show up and check it out.

I got a call from Mom, asking if I'd like to go to dinner with her this weekend, just to catch up. I didn't have anything planned. May as well. Plus, I think it might be about time for me to consider opening up to her about how I've decided to change the way I live. I'm sure she'll be supportive as long as I don't slip up and say anything about sex.

I certainly won't mention anything in regards to the bondage club. If I opened up about that, I'd be getting chained up for sure: she'd handcuff me to a pipe in her basement until I'm forty.

JUN 19 (FRI)

I brought my final inventory of books to be donated to Miriam's office today. She said she was glad I ran the idea for the new computer past her first, rather than just kowtowing to Winston's demands. If we were to get a new machine for the library, it would have to be a second-hand one donated by some state agency that didn't need it anymore, rather than a top-of-the-line model that just came on the market. Would have been a huge waste of funds, and a waste of a few good encyclopedia sets from the reference section as well.

"Of course," she said, "Winston wouldn't have cared since he's going back to his other school at the end of the year. Our problem, not his, right?"

I thanked her for sticking up for me on Tuesday.

"Hey, people like you and me, we have to watch out for each other."

Huh? People like me and her? That's a strange thing to say. What do we have in common? I'm almost thirty and she's about fifty, I think. I'm in the library. She's the principal. I'm white. She's black. I'm Jewish. Oh! So...

"Actually, I haven't gone to temple in years and I consider myself agnostic," I reluctantly explained to her. I didn't know just how religious she was, so I decided it might be best to hold back on my appreciation for the sushi with imitation crab sticks. Come to think of it, I'm not even certain if imitation crab is kosher or not. Yeah, it's crab, but it's imitation.

Miriam thought this was rather amusing. Seems a lot of people make that mistake due to her name. "Look," she said, "I know. I saw those books you had in your drawer. If you want to keep it a secret, don't worry. I've got your back."

What.

No. No way. No friggin' way. She's...

As I walked back to the library, I thought, there has to be some sort of explanation other than what I'm thinking. Maybe she thinks I'm a lesbian. That has to be it, right? Those books she's talking about are obviously the ones Zena gave me, so it has to be related to that. Miriam just thinks I'm reading about dating women and meeting women and having heterosexual intercourse with women. Because of that one about heterosexual intercourse. That one with "For Beginners" in the title.

Okay, she's not a lesbian after all. But what other possibilities could there be? Simply being single isn't a secret. That just leaves... unbelievable. Miriam is a virgin, and she knows I am, too. I have no idea what to think about this, because I'm still sure in my heart that there's a misunderstanding. This can't be. It just can't. She's twenty years older than me. This is unreal. But, admittedly, not unprecedented.

I spent the remainder of the day dumbstruck, until I got a text at about one o'clock. Never thought I'd hear from this person again: it was Ingrid, the woman who used to live on the floor above me and Willow.

The text read, "its ingrid can u babbysit 2nite? greg & me r going out 4 anniversery & babbysitter canceled plz txt back"

Hmm. Do I really want to do this? On one hand, I had planned to be at that speed-dating thing last night, so I didn't schedule anything for tonight. And I don't say "no" to easy money, even if it'll probably only be about thirty bucks. But, babysitting? I'm not sure that's something I would excel at, and this might signal the start of a trend of me watching people's kids. Don't want that.

But, money is money. The runt'll probably be in bed most of the time anyway. Okay. I texted back "From what time to what time do you need me?"

She replied, "huh?"

"When should I be there and for how many hours will you need me?"

126

"lol b here at 7 i don know how l8 well b out!"

"Okay. I'll be there a little bit before seven. See you then."

"y do u txt like a gameshow host?"

Huh? Game show host? Are game show hosts known for texting with capitalization, punctuation, and correct spelling? I didn't want to go any further down this road, as I knew any answer I got would be unsatisfactory.

I showed up at Ingrid's new apartment at 6:52. It's a half-hipstery place with lots of campy tchotchkes: fridge magnets depicting mascots for long-extinct products, framed reprints of faded cigarette ads from the 1950's, a John Turturro-themed shower curtain, a non-digital clock. I'd never actually met her husband Greg before. He's got this big, fluffy, almost Bozo-esque semi-circle of gray hair from ear to ear, and the rest of his scalp is bare. Looking at him head-on, it looks like he has koala ears. He also has a bulbous nose and a gray mustache, which only further the koala illusion.

They greeted me and called Darrin, their son of seven years, into the room. The speed of Darrin's footsteps seemed to suggest that he was perhaps a quadruped. Maybe he was a set of twins referred to collectively by a single name as some sort of new frontier in the "Let's give our kid a weird name" arms race. But, no: one child with two legs. And an iced coffee.

At 6:58, I called it: Audrey Perlmutter has now officially spent more time seeing children drinking coffee than she has spent being touched by males. Sorry, Tim, you did your best. When I looked through the fridge later, there was a distinct lack of any sugary or high-fructose-corn-syrupy beverages. Even the ice cream was that soy-based stuff. Nice try, but you're not going to raise the next Trader Joe if you give him a plastic cup of ice cold New England Hummingbird Food every so often.

The anniversary-celebrators (if there's a better word for that, I have yet to learn it) took off, and it was just me, Darrin, and two hours before bedtime. I didn't get to stay up past eight until I was eleven. Let me say that babysitters these days have it really freakin' easy. Darrin just played with his tablet computer for the next two hours. I think he was playing that game where you're supposed to throw cows into a giant metal funnel and they get sucked into a pipeline until there are enough of them stuck in the pipe to successfully clog a giant radiator and prevent the Eskimo's igloo from melting. Pretty sure the title is "Fevered Hallucination: The Game."

I did ask the kid if he wanted to play a card game. He said no. Well, I tried.

Spent my time waiting for nine o'clock going through their bookcase, looking for anything I might find entertaining. They had a coffee table book filled with photos of handmade paper notices stuck to walls and poles. "Lost Dog," et alia. The photos were organized by city, which I appreciated. One person in New York was selling a pair of nail clippers for 75 cents. He drew a picture of them and had little tear-off strips at the bottom with his phone number on them.

Nine finally rolled around. I ushered Darrin to his room, and he wanted a cup of water before bed. Ugh. Okay, fine. I could use one, too. I went to get a drinking vessel from the cupboard and what do I see? Seven plastic cups, each a different color: dark blue, green, purple, orange, light blue, red, and yellow. It would be so easy for me to disassemble the stack and rearrange them in proper rainbow order. I resisted, and instead retrieved the green cup for myself and the dark blue for Darrin.

I brought our cups of water back to his room where he was hiding under his desk, using a blanket stuffed in the drawers above his head as a curtain. Inside, he was pounding away on the tablet, and he informed me he was in his "super-secret fort". *Super*-secret? I'm a little impressed with myself that I was able to find something that secret by complete accident, but I guess I was tipped off by the bold, primary-color dinosaur print that adorned the main secret entrance.

Darrin suddenly wanted a bedtime story. I suddenly wanted a tubal ligation. I spent five minutes making up a yarn about a salt shaker. It was the only salt shaker in the restaurant that didn't have a pepper shaker at the same table. The other shakers looked down on it and all said that there must be something wrong with it.

Darrin asked if a pepper shaker ever showed up, and if they lived happily ever after.

Sure, why not. G'night.

That poor kid. Imagine the sorts of idealistic lessons from Fantasyworld he's being taught. How long is it going to take him to overcome all that well-meaning, but completely inaccurate, bull? I wanted to tell him what life is really like. He needs to learn that he's not special, he's just different from everybody else, in the exact same way everybody else is. He needs to know that looks are important and that money does buy happiness if you're smart with it and have enough of it. He needs to hear that nine times out of ten, while you won't be able to tell whether it's good or not, you can judge a hell of a lot about a book by its cover. And oh yeah, ducklings don't turn into swans when they grow up.

Yet, if I sat him down and explained all these things to him that he'll need to know as soon as possible if he wishes to make his way in the world, I'd be the villain. If you want to be the good guy, you have to keep telling them "believe in yourself" and "reach for the stars!" Kid, the closest star is a hundred million airless miles away. You'd be vaporized before even coming close enough to reach for it.

It's a little past eleven as I write this. May as well see what's on TV.

JUN 20 (SAT)

Ingrid and Greg didn't make their return until around two this morning. Thankfully, I was given a ride home. I was very sleepy and in no condition to be walking, especially at that hour.

After she parked the car to let me out, Ingrid fished through her purse looking for cash, eventually asking if I could take an I.O.U. on this one.

I had a proposal instead. Ingrid and Greg are the type who go to parties with their friends and co-workers every once in a while, so I asked if she could bring me along to the next one. "You know, I'm just looking to meet some new people, if you get what I mean. Just introduce me to some of your single friends and we'll call it even." She agreed, but with the caveat that it could be a while. They're all going out to stay at their cabin on Martha's Vineyard next month, so it won't be happening soon. I took what I could get. A party is a party.

It's funny. All this time, I've felt love and sex were like a party and I was the only one who wasn't invited. Well, if I have to crash this thing, I will. Sure I'll be late, but I still have time.

Isn't it just too perfect how the only party I'm not supposed to be fashionably late to is the only one where I don't show up early? I suppose I'll have to be unfashionably late. As long as I get in, I don't mind since I'm already used to being unfashionable. What's important is being there, being included, being alive. To paraphrase a pair of phrases, "Better late than dead."

I showed up for dinner with Mom about six minutes early. It was at a Chinese place in Attleboro, about halfway between Ridgeway and Railhead. Had some time for wandering around the parking lot and taking in the sights. It's amazing how little there is available to occupy yourself with when you need to kill some time. I looked at all the Massachusetts plates on the cars, comparing the last digit to the month of registration and making sure they all matched up. She pulled into the lot around ten past.

Once we had our table, I ordered my usual lo mein and boiled dumplings. I didn't want a drink, as a money saving measure. Why get watered-down soda for two dollars per glass when I can just get real water for free?

"Are you sure you don't want anything?" Mom asked.

"Yeah, I'm sure," I said in reply.

"Are you, though?"

"Yeah, I don't want anything to drink."

"Not even tea?"

"I'm fine. Okay?"

Right after we ordered, I got up to use the restroom. When I returned to our table, there was a cup of tea at my seat. "I got the waiter to bring it while you were gone. It's good for you, you should drink it," Mom explained.

I poured some of my ice water into the cup to cool it down. She asked why I was doing that. "It's because we don't have any milk or cream," I said. She was afraid other people in the restaurant would see me doing this and think I'm weird. Well, they'd be well-informed, at least.

She told me more stories from her job, about how one of her co-workers was facing D.U.I. charges for driving his car into someone's fence. I mentioned that Natasha was in an accident herself a couple of months ago, and admitted that I've been worried since then: "The whole incident made me realize that you never know when it could all end. Anything can happen, anytime, good or bad."

Our meals arrived. "How did you get here anyways?" she inquired.

I told her I have a subscription to a car rental service.

"Oh, is that the one whose logo is a Z on wheels?"

"Yeah. The one with the horizontal lines behind it, so as to indicate speed."

As we kept talking, I felt the urge to confess. I like confessing things, I must confess. It feels good. After I shared my life story with Rosita and the others, I felt relieved even though I hadn't done anything wrong. After I discussed Natasha's misfortune with Mom, I mentioned that I've been thinking about dating, maybe finding someone who can make me happy. I didn't tell her everything, just the sanitized version.

"Does this mean that you've changed your mind about having kids someday?" she said with a twinkle of hope in her eye.

I let her know (again) that if she wants grandkids, that's Rebecca's department. I hate children.

"How can you hate children? *You* were a child!" GASP! NO! REALLY? I was a child? Gee, looks like I was wrong! I guess I don't hate kids after all! Of course, that speaks to another problem: she sees me today and forever as a child. I'm still going through those rebellious teenage years. I'm nineteen-teen and I ran away from home to live with Willow, but I'm gonna learn my lesson and come back home any day now, just you wait.

Mom then pointed out that I'm constantly surrounded by kids as I work at an elementary school. Uh, where do you think ninety percent of my revulsion is rooted? I should know better than her that kids are malicious little heat-seeking gremlins who think the national pastime should be the "I'm screaming louder than you" game.

I did also make it known that I haven't been having a very easy time out there so far. I'm worried that maybe nobody will want to give me a chance, just like before. She assures me that it isn't my fault, it's just that having Asperger's makes it harder for me than most others. Ay Dios mio, *that* again.

When the meal was over, and I hugged her goodbye, she felt the ticklish area under my arms. It caught me off-guard and I made a noise that sounded like Paul Shaffer's pet myna bird.

"Just feeling your ribs," she admitted. "You're still not eating enough. Did you see Dr. Yiu?"

"Yes. She says I'm healthy and my blood work backs it up."

"Well, you still need to eat more, you're too skinny."

"Thanks, Mom. Love you, too."

I didn't believe my mother and my psychiatrist about how I supposedly have Asperger's syndrome. But, after the events of the last couple of months, now I'm starting to think that maybe they were right. Perhaps I'm not a misdiagnosis. Perhaps...

Does everyone think I'm disabled? When people meet me for the first time, do they think I'm autistic? Is it possible that I exhibit visual and aural and behavioral signs of being autistic, but I don't realize it because... well, because I *am* autistic? Is this the least little bit possible, and if so, would anyone ever tell me?

So many things would make sense. It would explain why nobody even gives me a chance to prove myself. It would explain why I've never been promoted at any of my jobs, despite working harder than everyone else. It would explain why, at the age of 29, I've never had a kiss or have even been on a date. It would explain why Lynn's and Angie's first reactions were to suggest I pay for a stud. Could an explanation so perfectly awful really be possible?

I'll never know, though, will I? I could ask everyone I know, and they'd never tell me the truth if it were the case, so I'd get the same answers either way. "No, of course you're not! Don't be ridiculous." There has to be a way of figuring this out. I have to find a person who I know would tell me the truth, even if it were something they think would upset me.

Either way, as far as I know right now, there are two possibilities. Scenario A is that people see me as a disabled person, and because of that, I'll almost certainly never have any sort of physical intimacy without there being a cash transaction. Scenario B is that I'm just undateable on my own merits. What an embarrassment of riches.

JUN 21 (SUN)

All day, nothing happened. Went for a walk. That's all.

Spent about an hour on the phone, though. Ange called from her car on her way back from DJing another wedding, this one in Watch Hill, a ritzy not-quite-Newport in the furthest corner of that torn piece of copier paper that is Rhode Island. She says she's been reading up on poker recently and wants to enter a tournament. She wants me to enter, too. From what she's read about them, she's come to the conclusion that the more inexperienced at poker a person is, the better they'll do in a tournament. Ideally, people won't be able to read me as well if I have no idea what's going on. I get what her reasoning is, but I'm not sure it'll hold up in practice.

She also suggested that I not go to Amsterdam. Instead, she wants us to go to Vegas. Angie wants to hit the casinos and loot the poker tables. I'm not a gambler, I don't like the odds. But, I wouldn't mind putting one coin in a slot machine and winning five coins, then walking away. Of course, if I left a casino with four more coins than I entered with, I may end up getting shot in the head by security. Pretty sure it's legal for them to do that in Nevada. My actions would be considered robbery and the casino would be acting in self-defense.

Also, there was the other legal thing Las Vegas is known for. Ange looked it up online, and there are a couple of male brothels outside of Vegas, but not necessarily in the city itself. She assures me that I don't have to worry about contributing to human trafficking, because it's legal. Hmmm.

For my money, Vegas carries a seedy aura about it, even though the closest I've ever been to it is Chicago. If I have to travel a thousand miles for sex, I'd rather it be Amsterdam. Might as well kill two birds and get "go to Europe" off my list at the same time. Plus, I just want to leave the country for a vacation, not the planet.

I gave Ange the rundown on my thoughts from yesterday about how others see me. I feel a bit relieved. Angela says I don't come across disabled to her. In fact, she says I seem completely normal, not even timid. I'm inclined to believe her because she says she doubts that I even have Asperger's. I don't know why that makes it more credible, but she sounds damn sure of it. She said my demeanor and composure at the after-hours party were as natural as can be. She was really not expecting that from me. Quite frankly, I wasn't either.

I'm starting to think this Amsterdam thing isn't going to happen, at least not this year. I can still go to Europe next summer. Maybe I won't even need Amsterdam. Maybe I can go to England or Italy or France. Maybe my boyfriend will come with me.

JUN 22 (MON)

Tonight was my blind date. More accurately, tonight was when it was scheduled. It didn't happen, though.

I took a taxi to the restaurant, a place called Skylight, and was there fifteen minutes early.

It was only 5:45. The tables were all empty. There were two Baby Boomer couples at the bar. One of the males was the type who spoke as if he wanted everyone in town to hear what he was saying, gesturing wildly and wagging his index tentacle like a jellyfish with a Napoleon complex. I figured I might as well sit at the bar, just so I could keep an eye on the TV while I waited. The local news was on. They had one story about a ninety-year-old woman who lives alone in a house with two cats and was mistakenly sent a water bill totaling nine-million dollars. Oh my God, how important! No wonder they needed to call out their investigative journalist for this one. Well, thank heavens they were able to sort everything out (and simply by making a single phone call, no less!) Now I can sleep tonight.

The bartender asked what my poison was. I ordered a Sprite, claiming I had to drive later. "I'm only here because I'm waiting for my blind date to show up. Don't worry, I'm sure he'll have a few."

In return, I received a glass of ice and clear, flavorless liquid. I'm sure there was Sprite in there somewhere, possibly even enough to be measured in ppm. I looked at my phone. Its clock read 5:50. Just gotta wait.

So I waited. And kept waiting. 6:05, no problem. We're all late from time to time. Five minutes isn't a big deal. The bartender seized my glass while my gaze was averted and took the opportunity to refill it, adding a second glass to my tab. Uh, thanks.

At 6:10, I was starting to get anxious. If he was going to be late, couldn't he have at least called? Or texted? Maybe Natasha didn't give him my number the way she gave me his. I should send a text to him, then. Wellllll, not *yet*. It's still only ten after. These things happen. Give him a little breathing room.

The bullhorn down on the other end of the bar was getting pretty animated now, saying something like, "And I told him, 'Excuse me, which one of us is the expert on roller coasters again? That's right, ME. Now SHUT the FUCK up, and get the HELL out of my way!' And everybody starting cheering." I have no evidence otherwise, nor do I know what he was talking about, but I have no doubt that whatever happened didn't happen like that.

I was cautious with my soda, taking only a tiny sip once every minute or so, lest I get charged for a third without my consent.

At 6:15, I was done sitting back and doing nothing. Time to send Willis a text. I punched the following message into my keypad: "Hey, are you still gonna make it to Skylight? -Audrey" My phone is an old model with traditional telephone-style buttons. It has an alternate function where you can spell out a word using the keys and it selects the most commonly-used word from possible combinations. That's how I accidentally told my sister that the sidewalks in Ridgeway were "pretty gay" back in January, when I meant to say they were "pretty icy." My name isn't in its database of English words, so I have to use the longhand method of typing out its letters with multiple keypunches (pressing 8 twice for U, 9 three times for Y, and so on.) The phone seems to think "cuesey" is a word, though.

Now I just had to wait for a reply. I kept checking my phone to keep an eye on the time.

6:19.

6:22.

6:25. Okay, okay, maybe he's driving here right now and he can't send me a message. Makes perfect sense.

6:30 rolled around and the national network anchor showed his mug on the TV to give us some happy fluff about pandas or something. I was getting mighty impatient waiting to hear back. I sent out another text, this time to Natasha.

At 6:41, I heard back from her. She told me got in touch with Willis and he isn't going to make it. He won't say why, but he didn't want to say it to me himself.

Oh, is that so. Wow, wotta shocker. My jaw hit the floor so hard I think I chipped a tooth. (Luckily I've already got a shoulder to match.)

The bartender came around again to grab my glass, but before he could pour me another, I asked if I could just have the bill instead. "My date's not coming after all," I explained.

He told me it was on the house. I guess, given the circumstances, he couldn't bear to charge me for two glasses of ice with watered-down Sprite in them. I left a tip anyway.

By now, a couple of tables had filled up, and the people who were already at the bar when I showed up still hadn't left yet. Decided I should head towards the bathroom first as a misdirection, then surreptitiously leave through the exit to the back deck. I just didn't want those other people to see me walking out by myself after sitting at the bar alone for nearly an hour. When I opened it, the back door squealed so loudly that for a split second I thought I had set off an emergency exit alarm.

I'm not feeling down about it. I'm not. He's never met me before, so I know I didn't do anything to drive him away. If he's so undependable that he never shows up for things and doesn't even bother to call, then I'm better off having never met him.

JUN 23 (TUE)

It was the last day of school. About friggin' time.

The library has a card catalog that nobody uses anymore. Once the computer came in and took over its duties, it got decommissioned and moved behind the counter. I keep snacks in there every so often: candy, granola bars, and the like. I file them under V for "victuals" (or "verboten", seeing as how I'm not supposed to have food in that room.) I guess snacks should go under S, but I mostly use it as a lost-and-found for all the crap the kids leave behind, so the S drawer is always filled up with things like staplers, spoons, a scarf, scissors. Plenty of space in the V drawer, though. Nobody around here ever loses anything beginning with V.

Once the kids were out the door, I emptied out the card catalog and gave Lynn, Rosi, Natasha, and Jeanette first crack at whatever misplaced items they wanted to keep.

The way I see it, once the students are gone for the summer they've surrendered it, and we were just gonna throw it all out anyhow.

"I tell ya, it is so good to have those kids out of the way so that I can go back to normal for a couple of months," Jeanette said to me as she fished around through the scraps and sundries, seeing if anything was worth salvaging before she walked away.

I didn't quite get it, so I asked her to elaborate. She did, saying, "You know, using gender-neutral pronouns in awkward ways. Pretending I'm engaged to a man without actually saying so. If just one of those kinnygart'ners finds out my fiancée is a woman, we'll have psychos down here marching around with handwritten signs in no time. Trust me, Audrey, they wouldn't rest until the school gives us both the boot."

Aha, so Jeanette's a lesbian but she's trying to keep it on the QT. She's doing a good job because I didn't have a clue.

Um. Something isn't right. Did she say…?

I asked what she meant when she said "both". Seems she was mistaken about my sexual preference as well. I had to clarify that I'm kind of into guys but they've just never been into me. That was uncomfortable to spit out. See ya in August, Jeanette. Enjoy the green glow-in-the-dark calculator and the cartoon cat bookmark.

Rosi was feeling a little irked. The kids in Mrs. Sanders' class spent the day making drawings of their favorite moments and events of the school year. One of them drew a picture of Rosi. "She drew me with bloody claws! Can you imagine? Does she think I'm mean?" she fumed. She calmed down a little when I suggested that those little red lines were probably supposed to be her fingernails.

Her attitude turned on a dime when Aristide Love stepped into the room. Mr. Love is the fifth grade teacher that Rosi's been crushing on for a while now. He's got a strong, full-bodied voice that makes John Lithgow sound like Lisa Simpson. If that's not enough, he doesn't let his marriage get in the way of his… what's the term? Well, he's a male, and he's still relatively young and good-looking, so it can't be "sluttiness" or "creepiness." "Healthy appetite," that's it. If he's ever broken his vows, I wouldn't know, but it wouldn't come as a surprise to anyone.

Love cracked some joke which caused Rosi to open a can of fake laughter, one made from individual "Ha!"s, clearly delineated as if each one was its own sovereign entity. What can I say, she's not an actress. Then, he suggested Rosi consider joining him on his annual trip to Seattle in July. Whoa, hold up.

"Uh, aren't you married?," I asked.

"Hey, I'm married but I'm not dead!" he said, half-laughing. Keep talking like that and you may end up wrong on both counts. He has this way of speaking to Rosi that straddles the line between jest and sincerity perfectly. He could just be joking, but I have to assume that's only if she doesn't take him up on any offers.

While Rosi and Love were keeping each other distracted, Natasha leaned over the counter and whispered, "Hey. I'm really sorry about your date last night. I'm pretty steamed at Willis for doing that."

Lynn was suddenly all questions. "You went on a date? Why didn't you say something? How'd it go?"

"It was a blind date," I told her. "So blind that we never even saw each other. I'm not counting that as my first date, by the way." So, my record remains unbroken. Number of dates I've been on: zero with a capital 0.

I asked if Natasha knew why Willis never bothered to wash up on shore. As far as she could tell, he was out with his friends and just decided he'd rather keep the status quo than meet me. Or call to cancel. I showed Natasha my phone, just to make sure I had the right number. She gave it a once over and said, "Yeah, you've got his number."

Boy, did I ever. I couldn't have been more right in assuming he was a thoughtless slacker. Looking on the bright side, at least I wasted my time by myself instead of with him.

Lynn told me not to let it get me down. "At times like this, when I get lonely, I always take comfort in remembering the good times."

Did she forget who she was talking to? "I don't even have any memories," I reminded her.

From ten feet away, Rosi got a stunned look. "You have amnesia? I knew it, I *knew* one of these days a book was going to fall off the shelf and konk you on the head."

"No, that's not it."

"It was that globe, then. Why do they even keep it up there on top of that cabinet where nobody can reach it?" (Actually, that's a good question, and one I've wondered about myself.)

So, I'm still sitting on square one. The good news is that school's out for the next two months. Not bad! I've got plenty of time now. Perfect opportunity for a new beginning. This is when things will truly begin coming together. And, when I come back in the fall, everyone is going to see a changed woman. They won't even recognize me. As of today, I declare that the Audrey of the past is officially no more. I still have a lot to look forward to.

This is only the beginning, I can tell. Things are really gonna get goin' now!

JUN 25 (THU)

Haven't seen Willow all day. This is the third time that's happened in the last few weeks. I'm not complaining, though. Anything that gives me more free reign over my own home is welcomed.

Went to the supermarket today, because we were completely out of food and c'mon, who the hell else is gonna go? The place was very crowded. Why are all these people shopping at 11 a.m. on a Thursday? Does anyone in this country have a nine-to-five job anymore? (Oops. Glass houses.)

The supermarket tends to cheer me up. Example: today I saw an arguing couple. They were having a loud disagreement in public over which of them was more inconsiderate. Sights like that are partially responsible for me spending half of my life believing there are worse fates than dying unloved. I am still not entirely convinced I was wrong.

Still, a few things put some sand in my joints. This store doesn't have a salad bar. They've got an olive bar, though. Is everyone really clamoring for olives more than salad? "Yeah, I'm gonna stop over at the supermarket for some lunch. Maybe fill up on olives at the olive bar."

There were cartons of lemonade over in the juice section. The label stated that it was "virgin lemonade". Why did they need to write that? That isn't even something I ask due to my personal teething troubles. I mean, who sees a carton of lemonade and immediately thinks, "Ooh! Alcohol! I can get drunk on that!" Not many people, I hope, otherwise there must be a lot of black-eyed kids out there, surrounded by the splintered remains of their lemonade stands. Maybe it just means nobody has had sex with the lemons. If that's the case, why won't their competitors make the same promise?

I had a redemption ticket for cans I recycled, so I went to a manned register instead of the self check-out. Got in line behind a guy who looked about twenty-five, maybe older. Hmmm… Seems halfway decent. Doesn't look like a complete trog, at least. Hair wasn't too short or too long. It was just right. Clothes weren't too sharp or too trashy. Just right. I'm not Goldilocks, but I guess I'd be okay with sleeping in his bed.

I thought back to that half-sentence I just barely sight-read in one of Zena's books. "Something something people you just meet standing in line at something, something!"

Well, they sound sure enough about it. But is it good advice? Ya know what, I'll do it, I thought. I will flirt with a stranger in a store. I wasn't even going to take it seriously. If for some reason it seemed like we might not get along, I would give him a fake number. Now to find an opening... Not a lot in his groceries to work with. This was the "12 items or less" line, after all. Let's see: 2-liter Coke, frozen burritos, eggs, coffee filters, Italian bread, a bag of sugar. Think, Audrey, think! Okay, I got it.

"You're not gonna drink all that soda yourself, are ya?"

He looked at me through the corner of his left eye. He said, "No." Then he turned away.

Wow. Flawless. "You're not gonna drink all that soda yourself, are ya?" I gotta remember that one. I may need it again, just in case I come across someone I'm *really* interested in.

Watched *Jeopardy!* I'm not overjoyed or shocked by it, it's just that the exclamation point is in the title. One of tonight's contestants has a comic book collection totaling more than 40,000 items. Another one takes his family to Disneyworld every year. These are not people who need to be on a game show winning money. I've applied to be on *Jeopardy!* three times. You have to take an online test on a certain day at a certain time. And then... I don't know what happens. They never emailed me after I took one, not even to tell me how many questions I answered correctly. My results must have been either dreadful or spectacular. I figure it would be smart to not put the absolute best players on. Don't want to give away *too* much money, right?

I never know how much I'd want to wager for the final question. If the category is something like "16th Century Philosophers," I think I should go with a low amount. Then, the clue often ends up being something like, "Giordano Bruno, found guilty of heresy, was burnt at the stake in 1600 in Rome, the capital of this modern-day boot-shaped country whose citizens are called 'Italians'."

Then the host says, "Good luck."

Then I yell, "I COULD'VE GOT THAT!"

I guess that's a lesson in taking risks. Easy to say when it's not my money, right?

JUN 26 (FRI)

Things did not go well at the "cult meeting". It was definitely not the sort of experience that I, or anyone else for that matter, could have expected.

I showed up only five minutes early. It's hard to kick the habit of being punctual, especially if you're really looking forward to something. I guess I knew in the back of my mind that this very well might not be what I was hoping for. My heart was still beating a little faster than normal anyhow. I used the extra five minutes to take some deep breaths and compose myself.

"The Dungeon" turned out to be named that simply because of its location: the basement of a building it shared with a bar on the ground floor and the ruins of a defunct travel agency on the second. The man behind the bar showed me to the door that led downstairs, marked "Staff only beyond this point". Pretty secretive. They must be trying to keep something very private. I liked where this was going so far. But then, why print those flyers? Were they just hoping to lure in new members in a coy "Wellllll, I guess you can come in since you're already here, but don't tell anyone" sort of way?

The hallway to the staircase seemed a skosh too thin to meet the modern building codes. There was bronze and silver metallic paint on the walls in thick stripes and four-pointed starbursts. If I had to guess from the decor, I'd say this place used to be a recording studio in the 50's and 60's, and a cocaine den in the 70's. Probably enough trace amounts of the stuff left behind the walls and under the carpets to qualify the building for a few million in foreign aid. The stairs led down to a small, dimly-lit vestibule occupied by a shadowy figure in a black hooded cloak. Wow. This was looking very, very good! Granted, it was a little frightening, and the person before me was a bit imposing even if it was solely due to her clothing.

"Your name?" she asked.

"Audrey." Damn. I was caught off-guard by the presence of this foreboding-looking person and my thoughts of whips and ball gags. I wanted to say "Jessica", but too late now. I guess I'm Audrey.

I was asked who sent me. Uh-oh, did I need an invite from a member? Well, I have an emergency card prepared to be played in exactly this sort of situation. "Sean," I said. (It's a well-known fact that in Massachusetts, there was a law on the books from 1980 to 2002 mandating that every fifth male baby born in the state must be named Sean.) It worked.

"So, this is your first time, huh?"

As in what? My first time here or my first time at any one of these places? Well, doesn't matter, either way the answer is "yes," so that's what I said.

She wanted me to hold still so she could give me the stamp, which I assumed was one on my hand. "We don't have an actual stamp, so we just use this washable marker," she explained in a way that sounded like she was trying her best to maintain a sinister aura of mystery, despite using the words "washable marker." She pulled out a thick scarlet Crayola and made a check mark not on my hand but dead-center on my forehead. I said it seemed like a little too much pageantry just for a stamp to get back in.

"It's not for that. It's a 'V' for 'virgin.'" My pupils must have constricted at record speed because she followed that up with, "Relax, it's just so the other members know to make sure you have an extra-good time."

Okay. That's... uh... "I'll be right back, I have to go to the bathroom." I darted back up the stairs and ducked into the ladies' room to inspect my new marking. Was this a misunderstanding? Could it be that she was asking if it was my first time having sex? Why else would she draw this big V on my forehead? Maybe it's not to be taken literally. Maybe it really does just mean I'm new to the cult. But still, "extra-good time"?

Then, a thought occurred. Oh my, is this actually an orgy? Could it be possible that I was lucky enough to stumble into an actual, legitimate sex party? Don't jump to conclusions now, Audrey. Cool down, you're shaking. Composure. Of course, easier said than done (especially when somebody just drew on your face in a way that makes you look like you've got angry eyebrows.)

After about ten minutes of attempted nerve realignment, I went back downstairs and found a group of people sitting at a table in the room just beyond the door guarded by the cloaked woman. There were five people at each of the table's long sides, men on one and women on the other. Is there some sort of system in place here? Do things get sorted out through a schedule so we all take turns? Maybe drawing numbers from a hat? I thought these things were supposed to be a free-for-all. Well, whatever. If this is how it's done, I'm not complaining.

Took a seat and was greeted by the "cult members." They got some small talk out of me, then I decided to start getting a feel for how things worked around here. "So," I said, "do I take my clothes off myself or does someone help me with that?"

That got some laughs, and one guy said "I've been asking that question myself since my first meeting!"

Huh? They thought that was off-color office humor? What's going on here? I definitely do not see any sort of chains or bondage gear around, and nobody's getting naked. I was trying to figure out what kind of thing I was in store for, when the woman in the black cloak emerged from the next room with a rotund bearded man in a red robe and a fez. Oh no. He sure looks like a cult leader. Why oh why did I give my real name?

The bearded man held up his arms and announced, "Welcome, worshippers! Hail the Marty Baby!"

"Hail the Marty Baby!" replied ten people who were now starting to scare me.

"Tonight, the Marty Baby Cult greets Audrey, our first new arrival in five months. Everyone make sure to remember that Audrey is a 'virgin' here at the cult, as you all were once. If she needs something explained to her, be sure to help her out." I was gonna need a *lot* of help, and that became clearer with every word the fezzed one uttered.

I spoke up. Of course, what I really wanted to ask was what the hell is going on, but I already made the mistake of saying I was invited, so I had to be more subtle. "Is it okay if I ask why we're divided by gender?"

"That is how the Marty Baby wills it, first-timer," said one of the men.

I couldn't handle it anymore. What is this "the Marty Baby"? Am I even on planet Earth anymore? Again, I had to be nuanced in ferreting out information, so I said, "I'm not exactly sure this is what I was told it would be. Would someone mind explaining what it is we do here?"

They seemed more than happy to fill me in, and not in the manner I was expecting a few minutes prior. Fez looked and sounded like explaining his group to outsiders was his reason for being. "Well, Audrey, I'm Marty, and this is my lovely wife," he said, gesturing towards the cloaked woman, who had dropped her hood by now. "We started this secret society so that people could appreciate and revel in the blessed imagery of the Marty Baby."

So, "MBC" wasn't "Masochism Bondage Cult," it was "Marty Baby Cult." Ohhhhh boy.

"We just look at pictures of your baby all night?" I asked hesitantly.

"No, Audrey. *I* was the Marty Baby! Everyone agrees that *I* was the cutest baby ever born, and so we all gather once a month to pay tribute to the Marty Baby."

What have I gotten myself into? His wife chimed in, "At our meetings, we come together and reveal to our members new photographs from the vast collection taken from his parents' family albums." The woman to my left handed me a photo. What the hell!? Marty wasn't even a particularly cute baby! He looked like W.C. Fields!

"We then take some time to admire previous photos, share any new songs or poems we wrote about the Marty Baby, and then Marty passes some of his profound wisdom onto us."

"And, of course," Marty added, "we always end each gathering with a friendly game of Marty Baby trivia."

As uncomfortable and spooked as I was, I asked if there were any refreshments.

"Apple juice!" several voices shouted.

Marty opened up a three-ring binder labeled "Heathen Conversion Log" and requested everyone's tallies for bystanders they attempted to reform in June. If memory serves, this was the point where I decided to bid them adieu, leaving them a gift in the form of a large puff of smoke and a smoldering, Audrey-sized hole in the door.

A minute or so later, I had caught my breath. I looked up at a starless night sky and yelled "This is all *your* fault!" to no one in particular. I might have been a bit lightheaded from my sprinting, but I think that comment may have been meant for the pleasure center of my brain (or torso.) On the bus home, I tried to erase my marking the best I could with some spit but all that did was smear it a bit.

Once I got back, I saw Wes had his car parked out front. Willow was bringing a big box of assorted clutter out to it. "Why are you getting rid of all that stuff?" I asked.

"Why do you have an upside-down A on your head?" she replied.

When I pop this cherry, nobody had better tell me I didn't earn it.

JUN 28 (SUN)

I met Angela last night for a spur-of-the-moment journey to a club called Firebird Landing. In case the blasé tone of the first sentence didn't give it away, I was unable to achieve anything of note.

Thought I'd try something new for an outfit, so I threw together a black necktie and a white men's shirt to wear untucked with my black skirt. I left the top button undone, so the knot of the necktie was down to just above nipple height, thus making up for my inability to make the thick end of the tie slightly longer than the thin end. I thought it would be a good look for me, something you might see a new wave singer like Fawn Clayton or Patti Smith sporting in photos from their respective heydays. Maybe I could pretend to smoke a cigarette once in a while just so I could take it out and make a show of flicking it away onto the sidewalk. I'm probably deluding myself. Anyone who took note of my outfit likely thought I was trying to look like a Japanese high schooler.

I took the regional rail into one of those almost-Boston towns and found my way to a sports bar where I met up with Ange. Everyone there was focused on one thing: hockey. The Bruins had made it to the Stanley Cup finals, meaning the ranks of their fans in June

143

had increased eightfold from what they were in April, sort of like what happens to Nantucket every year.

Forgot the name of the bar. Something half-heartedly Irish-sounding. Just once I'd like to see a bar in Massachusetts with a Polish or a Turkish name. Ange coaxed me into having some of what she was drinking. Ohhhhh alright, I figured, maybe this one will be the AACCKKHH. NO. Still hate alcohol. It still gives my uvula a very unpleasant burning sensation. Yes, seriously, "uvula." That was not meant to be wordplay.

Ange got the attention of the bartender and told her I just started drinking (I have?) and needed something to ease me into it, because the jumping-in-and-yelling- "Cannonbaaaaall!" method was not working. I showed the bartender my ID and she said she would mix something for me.

The game had been on for about fifteen minutes now. One of our guys took a shot and missed by a mile. The crowd groaned. Someone not exactly sure who he was mad at yelled out "Stupid fucking… hockey!"

The bartender came back and handed me my drink. There was more ice in my glass than there was on the television. I had a sip. Ehh. I didn't have anything against it. Wouldn't bother crossing the street for another, but I managed to down the whole thing eventually. Tasted like ice water with a soupçon of Juicy Juice and just enough alcohol to make its presence known without being annoying. Well, that was it: my first drink that I actually finished. I asked Ange what it was called. Even though she took a sip of it herself, she couldn't identify it. I hereby officially record it as The Nameless Drink. That is how I shall remember it.

Eventually, the two of us got into Ange's car and off we went. We didn't make it to the club until about 11:30, due to a detour. Ange had some, *ahem*, "business" she had to take care of, and I soon found myself sitting in a stranger's living room. Okay, only gonna take a second, I thought. She'll pay this guy for his, *ahem AHEM*, "marijuana" and we'll be on our way.

The hockey game was in its home stretch by now. Our host, I never caught his name, had decided to join us at the club, but he wanted to finish watching the game first. Sigh. He had the game on a DVR delay of about ninety seconds, I'd estimate, due to a minor distraction in the form of a call from his girlfriend. As a result, the cathartic cheers and angry shouts from the building next door gave away key moments of the game before we got our chance to see them for ourselves. The frustration this stoked in our host was amusing enough to just barely keep me awake.

144

The game was tied as the clock hit zero. Overtime. Dammit. The break in the action allowed our host to re-sync his DVR with the live broadcast, so I didn't have the time delay to keep me entertained anymore. Ange asked if I was sleepy. I said, "no," even though my eyelids begged to differ. Just end the game, already. Get me up and outta here, and I'll be more awake and energetic than a jackrabbit in a folksy simile.

Come on. Go Bruins. Go Other Team. I don't care whoever scores the next goal as long as it happens NOW. Finally, Other Team scored. Our host joined the rest of the city in the ceremonial Screaming Of The F-word That Registers On Seismographs.

The three of us were in Ange's car within minutes.

Firebird Landing was about the size of your average Wendy's, but it was so packed that maybe it just looked that way. I found my way into the crowd on the dancefloor. As far as I know, Ange just stood against the wall drinking and having a friendly chat with anyone close enough to make out what she saying. I noticed just then that I don't think I've ever seen her dance. Her, of all people. Who would have thought that between the two of us, it would be me dancing in the crowd of strangers and her stapled to the wall? Of course, I had my reasons now.

One thing I found rather unsettling was the number of people on the dance floor who were doing nothing except holding a beer. They just stood there, stone-faced, staring at the DJ. Why would you bring your drink into the middle of a crowd of people dancing, especially if you aren't even bothering to dance yourself? Accident waiting to happen. Hey, Magnet Shoes, if you feel the need to stand there like a support beam, just do it on the other side of the damn room. Or at home.

Then I caught sight of one guy who was neither holding a drink nor dancing. His pal was having the time of his life, but he stood there staring into nothingness, with a sort of longing look on his face. He seemed to be thinking, "What the hell am I doing here? Why did I let him talk me into this?" He certainly wasn't dancing with someone, that was clear. Okay, so I found someone who was alone. Bingo.

I spent the next half-hour trying to inch my way towards him. The crowd put up some formidable resistance, though. There was always at least one other human body between us. I was tempted to empty out the room by yelling "Everyone! Andy Richter and Flava Flav are outside and they're about to fight! And they're wearing tuxedos!" Yeah, that probably wouldn't have worked anyway.

I wouldn't be able to lure him over to me if he didn't know I was there. I could tell that if somebody started showing some interest in him, he would immediately take to it.

He needed somebody to brighten his day. He needed to feel wanted. He was like me.

That was, until his girlfriend came out of nowhere and told him she wanted to go home.

On the bright side, it was during the last couple of minutes of this that I noticed a blonde fellow who seemed to be gradually getting closer to my tiny section of the floor. This looked good. This was going to get interesting.

It was time for an experiment. I needed to find out if this was just my imagination telling me he was coming my way on purpose, or if those glances I was getting every few minutes were serious. I slowly worked my way through the crowd to what I'll call the "east" side of the room. (The DJ's stage would be de facto "north" in this scenario.) Blondie headed east. I made my way south. So did he. Then he went to the bathroom.

Okay. The big one. I went a little further into the center of the crowd, so that he might lose me. This was "playing hard to get," huh? Yeah, I can get used to this. Somebody is after me for once.

When he emerged from the bathroom, I immediately averted my gaze before he could catch me waiting for him. Sure enough, he immediately came right for me. It was like he was a child star from an 80's sitcom and I was a dancing box of Oxycontin. Incredible. Finally, he managed to get right next to me, acting the whole time like he wasn't even doing it on purpose, like I was just another person. My skirt brushed against his leg quite a few times as I waited for him to turn towards me and say something.

And I waited. And waited.

He's not gonna make the first move, I thought. I was getting impatient. I'm gonna have to do this, aren't I? Yeah, of course.

"Hey," I said at the first hint of a drop in the music's volume, "d'you wanna go outside?"

He said, "No thanks." What? WHAT? After all that, after he, and he, then, you gotta be, I, this can't, how does someone, this, he wasn't even, the HELL? I had to get some fresh air. I made my way to the exit.

I wanted to leave now. Thankfully, the club was about to close anyways. 1 a.m. already? That came fast. I guess I don't have to ask to be shuttled home prematurely, then. Ange was already outside making new friends. One was a chain-smoking woman who claimed to be thirty-four, but looked more like she was well into that decade of life when birthday cards tend to contain the word "nifty."

Thirty-four. Dear God. I hope I don't look like that in five years. I can't risk it. I'm trying to make the most of what I have left, but I'm not getting anywhere. Not even a kiss yet. It shouldn't be this hard.

Got a tap on the back. Turned around and why, hello! What did this young man want from me? You want me to take a picture of you and your girlfriend and seventeen of your closest friends, huh?

He handed me his Apple thingy. I politely told him, "I don't know how to work one of these things." It was true, but it was also Audrey-ese for, "Thanks for getting my hopes up and then asking me for a favor instead. I hate you. Get lost." He explained that all I had to do was aim the camera and press the little button on the screen. I guess I could have figured that out for myself if I wanted to. (I didn't want to.)

I snapped a pic, but like all photographs I've ever taken, it was not a good one. Everyone in the photo had a bright glow in their eyes, as if they were all watching TV in the dark while wearing glasses. I told the people to keep still so I can take another one. Click.

Same thing.

Good enough.

A realization hit me then: I haven't yet been to any actual parties. I don't mean places where you can't have conversations and get acquainted with people because YOU'RE TALKING LIKE THIS THE WHOLE TIME. WHAT? I'M SORRY I CAN'T HEAR YOU OVER THAT SAME BASSLINE THAT'S BEEN PLAYING FOR THE LAST THIRTEEN FUCKING SONGS. I mean parties on private property with people talking. I need to try meeting people. I need to try anything.

The guy who came with us wandered off with some other people, so Ange took me back to Ridgeway without any extra stops. I don't remember a thing about the ride home. I was still perplexed by how I could be so wrong about Blondie.

Today was kind of a wash, though. Did the laundry, went to the supermarket, cleaned. It kinda gets me down because I feel any day I don't get out there and try again is nothing more than lost time. Just finished the laundry before I began writing. Wish someone was here to help with that.

JUN 29 (MON)

Rosi rang me up to ask how my vacation was going so far. I told her about how I thought I was going to an underground BDSM club, but ended up at a post-modern art

147

project with a bunch of people who may or may not worship an erstwhile baby who looked like W.C. Fields. She asked if W.C. Fields is the place where all the portable toilets are kept when they're not being rented. She's a sharp one, she is.

"Would you even want that? I can't see you at some bondage club or a sex party. Those don't sound like very Audrey places," she said. (This isn't the first time she's made a comment like that. It seems that Y in my name makes for ease of use as an adjective.)

I also told Rosi about how I went to that club on Saturday. She thought maybe my approach is wrong and she suggested a new strategy: I should just pick out anyone I think I might like and offer to have sex with him. Gee! I can't see any way that could possibly backfire!

Clearly, I can't do that. It's uncouth. It's not the least bit romantic. I don't have the nerve. Besides, context is everything. Coming from me, it would just sound really unsexy. It just plain wouldn't work.

Well, that was my phone call. I'm pretty sure that something else of note happened, but I can't seem to recall... lemme see here... tryin' to put my finger on OH! Now I remember! Willow moved out!

All that time, she wasn't throwing things out, but packing them up. She and Wes have acquired their own apartment in the New Illsley district. I found out this afternoon when she was good enough to finally tell me. She figured she wouldn't bother letting me know until the last moment because that's just the kind of relationship we have. Awwww!

I was watching the news at noon when I found out. They were at that part near the end of the newscast where they go over entertainment news and recap the weather one more time, when Willow came home from work. She made a couple of round trips back and forth across the living room, carrying a cardboard box on each trip back outside. It was somewhere around Box #3 that I decided I should ask what was going on.

She looked at me, innocent as can be, and told me, "Oh, I'm moving into my new apartment with Wes in a couple days, and I'm just bringing the rest of my stuff to his place for now."

She brought her box outside and the sound of a cicada held the floor for the duration. Upon returning, she looked at my panicked face and said, "What? I didn't tell you?"

Did I ever feel stupid. I should have realized something was wrong, but I've been so pre-occupied making up for ten years of not thinking about sex that I didn't catch on to all the little clues. Her video games were all gone, for one. Fewer clothes filling up the laundry hamper. The fact that I've been regularly using the bathroom in my own home without being chided for it. Subtle things, really.

I reacted the way you'd expect me to: a calm, well-adjusted, mature panic attack. I went over to shut the door, as if that would enough to incapacitate her. Yeah, she'll never be able to open that door while holding that last box with both hands. Great plan. I even locked it for good measure. I tried to appeal to her better nature, crying out, "How am I going to live here if you're gone? I'd have to pay the entire rent by myself! Didn't you even think of that?"

"Not my problem," she said as she placed the box down on the ground and used her newly-freed hands to not only unlock the door, but open it as well. I had underestimated my adversary.

Her advice: if I need someone to come up with the other half of the cash, I should (Are you ready for this? Are you sure?) find someone else to move into the apartment to take her place!

I asked where she expected me to find someone on such short notice. She said I should get a boyfriend to help with that. Oh. Okay. Why didn't I think of that? It's so easy. Also, if all those people in third-world countries are hungry, why don't they just eat something?

I begged her to be realistic. I told her I don't have a boyfriend and I've never had one.

She picked her last box of stuff back up and said, "Suck it up and get over it."

She walked out. Didn't even come back to say good-bye. That's the last I saw of her today. The only things left in her room are her bed, an empty dresser, and trash. I started picking up her mess, collecting burger and taco wrappers by hand, despite not having any gloves. Or a rake.

So, what am I going to do without her? I can still make the rent for a while, but it'll have to come out of my savings. Can't keep that up forever. It might be time to finish that "Dear dying wealthy man with poor eyesight," letter I wrote as a joke a couple of years ago.

Well, I'm alone now. I don't have to keep everything that belongs to me in my room from now on. This place is mine. I've already taken spiteful comfort in moving one of my bookcases out to the living room. I dug out my CDs from the box under my bed and lined them up on a shelf built into the wall: alphabetical by artist, then each artist's releases chronologically. Absolutely perfect. With Willow's video game console and games gone, I had a spot for my Scrabble box. I never liked that tablecloth. Out ya go. Who put these candleholders here? They're not mine and it seems they're not hers. Nobody to complain when I throw them out, then! And this thing? I don't even know what it is, but it's useless and it's gathering dust. Yer outta here!

This is mine now. This place is under my jurisdiction. After all this time, I'm in charge. Though this will certainly provide some financial problems down the road if I don't find a new roommate, I have to say that I'm not disappointed. Willow was a friend when we worked together, but since we started living together she became a kind of a... well, to be polite, the Reverend Spooner might say she's one who "weren't at the stake."

"Suck it up and get over it." Can you believe that? I did get over it, years ago. That's how I ended up in the rut where I am now. All that wasted time, I was just sucking it up. And then, I got tired of my life sucking.

I needed a drink. I tried to create my own with what I had available in the house already. It's a glass containing a melted scoop of orange sherbet, a melted scoop of vanilla ice cream, Jones cream soda, and a tablespoon of Listerine. As for the name, I have no idea which names are taken already, so I had to come up with one I know nobody else has used yet. I'm calling it "June 29, 7:53 p.m."

I don't recommend it.

JUL 2 (THU)

It was speed-dating night, at long last. Rosi decided she'd be joining Lynn and me so that she could keep watch over us and judge my performance. Plus, there was the possibility that Lynn might have required our assistance getting home again. In Ridgeway fine, but coming from Boston that's too big a job for just me. As it turned out, Lynn didn't have a single drink, thank goodness. As for me, the only drink I'd be having was a cocktail mixed from equal parts risk, trust, and c'mon-this-had-better-work-already. Also, water.

While we waited at the station for our dawdling train to show its sorry caboose, Rosi had an idea: she'd hide under the table and feed me lines like Cyrano. As appealing as it sounded to not be the one with the big nose in that scenario, I had to pass.

"Then tell me," she said, "what if you are presented with a question regarding your sex life?"

If anyone was tactless enough to ask about sex in our five minutes of acquaintanceship, I would just have to tell them the truth: I am a virgin. And then, I would lie like a damn rug.

Here was my emergency all-purpose background story: I spent three years in a sexless relationship with a very religious man named Gabe. He refused to engage in any sexual intercourse outside of marriage, but he never seemed to be moving any closer to a commitment, either. Honestly, I hope it doesn't sound like I'm badmouthing my ex, but... I'm pretty sure he was gay and in denial. It's so obvious in hindsight. He needed me to be his "ticket to heaven", you could say. I did know about the "no sex" thing going into it, it was his faith and I had to respect it. It wasn't about that, it was about his lack of respect for me. He was also very possessive. Sometimes I'd look out the window at work and see his car driving through the parking lot. He wasn't coming in to see me, he was just making sure my car was there, and that I was where I was supposed to be instead of running off with someone else. I had to break it off, and I thought that would be it, but he kept trying to get me back for about a year after that. It was such a horrible ordeal, that I just stayed away from any relationship for a few years. Finally, my friends convinced me "You can't be scared off and put your life on hold just because of one psycho." So, that's why I came here, to make up for lost time.

"Oh," Rosi said, "so is honesty still the best policy, Miss Goody Two-Shoes?"

"Gee, I'm sorry! How many shoes was I supposed to be wearing?" Ok, that was a rather weak comeback on my part.

Lynn said she agreed with Rosi, that I have changed. "If I was told just a few weeks ago that one of the staff at Braun Elementary was making up elaborate stories in an effort to get laid, Audrey Perlmutter would have been last on my list of guesses."

They're right. I am changing. And I think I like it.

The train to Boston was fifteen minutes late, so we stood outside working up a sweat that none of us needed. It wasn't even that hot, but it was just barely humid enough that it creeps up on you and you don't even realize what's happening until your shoes start to overflow. The lateness didn't bother me too much beyond that, since we were set to arrive at our destination with fifty minutes to spare.

The Massachusetts Bay Transportation Authority could benefit from selling its inevitable tardiness as a positive. Maybe do an ad where somebody shows up late for a job interview and whips out a train ticket to show the interviewer. Then, cut to the applicant's first day on the job. The slogan: "MBTA. They'll understand."

We showed up about thirty minutes early, but that's just because of the limited numbers of evening inbound trains, and not due to my constant earliness for once. Our plan was to part ways inside: Rosi sets up camp at the bar while Lynn and I do whatever it is they make us do. That was before we discovered that the Irish pub was the sonic equivalent of the tropical bird cage at Southwick Wild Animal Farm. Music was blaring, a baseball game was on seventeen TVs, and the bar was shoulder-to-shoulder with young males who were all giving birth (at least that's what it sounded like.) The entire place was one room and to top it all off, two families were having dinner at the larger tables smack dab in the center of it all. So, this is where it has to be, huh? Great. Now I won't be able to make conversation here, either. Why not turn on a few vacuum cleaners, too?

Lynn and I each got a numbered sticker and a "scorecard", as they so sensitively called it. At this point do I even have to mention that the scorecard was made from that special type of glossy paper that refuses to be written on with anything less potent than a Sharpie? The guys would move from table to table in alphabetical order, and the ladies got to stay put. I was assigned to table B. Lynn was across the room and out of sight at table E. The "dates" were each five minutes long, and then the whistle blew. I wonder if anybody at the bar complained about that. "I beg your pardon, Ma'am, but your constant use of that whistle is distracting my friends and me as we try to make loud barfing noises at the television. Would you mind being a trifle more considerate?"

The first whistle blew and we were off. When we weren't busy shouting "What??" at each other, here were the things that my "dates" said that made it clear it wasn't going to work:

- "Hi, I'm Wally. So, are you saved or heathen?"
- "Hunh? Oh, sorry, I was just checkin' out that FINE-ass bitch over there."
- "If anyone like, sayyy… I dunno, the police happen to ask where I was tonight, you'll tell them I was here, right?"
- "When I heard that speed-dating was originally invented by the Jews, I had my doubts…"
- "[*Unintelligible, but my final estimate was 5.2 uses of "fuck" and variants per minute.*]"
- "I think *Hostel 2* was even funnier than the original. Not a lot of people do."
- "Hey, me again. It's exactly 8 p.m. now. You're still going to say I was here, aren't you? Okay. Just checking."

But, I accentuate the negative. It's easy to see why all of the above are unacceptable, but the other eight were surprisingly decent blokes, and I used my pen to carve an inkless circle around "YES" for each of them on my card. None of them were outstanding, but nothing was wrong with them, either.

Lynn was more selective, and only picked out six she thought she could see herself with. She helped me out by pointing out that one of my selections came off as "kind of a mama's boy." I returned the favor, letting her know that one of her six came off as "kind of a guy who may have hired a hitman to kill someone as we speak." Neither of us were swayed.

Rosi said she was able to keep an eye on me the entire time, and I didn't come off the least bit self-conscious to her. She said I looked like I was in my element. "I mean, you weren't great, but you were good! You took to it like a duck to wa–" she said. She then made that sucking-air-in-through-teeth noise which translates to "Oops." I guess I can't blame her for thinking I'd fall apart, but if I have a captive audience, then I'm fine. I didn't need to get anyone's attention, so I could just focus on the important stuff. Plus, it certainly helps knowing everybody was there for the same reason I was.

I like the idea of speed-dating, the participants were half-and-half (even if nobody really jumped out as anyone I was excited about,) but the atmosphere was an unmitigated disaster. All-in-all, not sure how I feel about this yet. I entered my picks on the site once I got home, and in less than forty-eight hours I'll be able to see if any of them said "YES" to me as well. Looking forward to it.

JUL 3 (FRI)

With Willow gone, I feel a little freer. Freedom comes with a price, and in this case, the price is the other half of the rent. Well, it's worth it for as long as I can hold out. It feels pretty good to use the bathroom with the door open. And, on top of that, it's summer. Normally, I'd have to squeeze the swollen wooden door into its frame by leaning my entire body against it. Not this year. Who says I don't count my blessings?

A thought crossed my mind the other day: if I'm having trouble introducing myself to new people, I need to create a scenario that will make discussion inevitable. Captive audience, just like speed dating. With that strategy in mind, today I sauntered my way down the sweltering streets, dodging the falling air conditioners and making my way to the same pharmacy where I bought you. I was going to buy some gum just so I could chat with a cashier as practice, if there happened to be a male on duty.

Two register counters were open. One was run by a pleasant enough lad cursed with poor haircut-related judgment, the other by a woman who smelled like she was trying to save enough Marlboro points to buy an electronic voice box. If I ended up being rung up by the guy, I'd try out some very low-key, under-the-radar flirting that I've been preparing. I stood in line and hoped the odds played out in my favor.

Three other customers were in front of me. As I slowly inched my way up to the front, I was going over lines in my head and so I didn't notice what was happening until I was next to be served. The male cashier was still ringing up the same elderly customer as he was when I got in line! I'd been waiting there for five minutes! What's the friggin' hold-up!?

"Sir," the cashier pleaded, "I can't change the price. I have no control over how much our products cost."

"All I want to know is why the brown eggs cost twenty cents more than the white ones! They're both eggs, aren't they? There's no difference! They're exactly the same! They should be the same price!" the customer wheezed in reply.

154

"Would you like me to put these back for you and get a dozen white eggs instead?"

"I don't want white eggs! They're not the same as the brown!"

Yeah, it was one of those folks. As expected, I ended up paying for my gum at Joanne Camel's register, and I schlepped my way out. The end.

NO! Not the end! I wasn't giving up on this. I had to try again. I marched myself down to the Newbury Comics a couple blocks away, and as luck would have it there was a guy my age at the counter. His nametag said "Leon." Alright then, Leon, you wait there.

Had to find something fast. Went to the jazz section, and grabbed a used Thelonious Monk CD that was a mere $3.99. I didn't really want it that much, but it was in my line of sight and only four bucks, so it won. I just needed an excuse to get to the register pronto.

Turns out, it was a perfect choice. When I brought it up to the counter, Leon commented that he was into Monk, but he hadn't heard this one yet.

I tried my best to sound "extra-friendly," you could say. "You know, I could burn a copy for you, if you're interested." Shit. I immediately realized I just offered to make an illegal copy of a CD for a person working in a music store. I win the moron prize today.

Leon said I didn't have to do that for him. My memory's a little hazy on what I said next, but I think I told him that I'd be happy to hear any suggestions he had for other discs I should consider buying. Except I tried to say it all sexy-like. I dunno, I can't tell if it was any good or not. He asked if I wanted to sign up for the email newsletter. I never thought this would come up, but I said I would.

He gave me a slip of paper to fill out. I wrote out my name and email, as clear as a bell. No cursive, no embellishments, nothing. Just plain, angular capitals and lowercase. I gave the paper back to Leon, and he squinted at it with a confused expression. He hesitantly asked, "Aud... rig? Audrig?"

Audrig!? Are you kidding?? That isn't even a name! Audrey. It's "Audrey". Why is that so fucking hard? I told him my name.

"Oh, like the plant," he said.

I give up. "Yeah, like the plant."

In the end, I didn't ask him out. I backed out, telling myself, maybe if I come by a few times, I can build a sort of rapport with him first. Of course, I didn't jump right in, that wouldn't have worked out. I'm laying the groundwork for future encounters. Give him some time to think about me. Let the memory of that moment get inside his... not head. It's already in his head. Veins? Sorry, I don't know where that metaphor was supposed to go when I started it. This wasn't a surrender, it was a tactical retreat. A retreat from a man who associates me with a carnivorous, singing plant from outer space.

I stayed inside once I got home. I have a video game version of Scrabble on my laptop that I'll play for practice, but since I got the actual board game out of the closet on Monday, I played that instead. I didn't have anyone to play with, so I played against myself. You thought I was gonna say the other thing, didn't you?

Normally the letters of the alphabet all work in congress to accomplish their goals. However, in a game of Scrabble the letters are no longer working as a team, but practically competing against each other; all of them, from the common, dependable A (worth one point) to the daring and coveted Z (a ten,) vying to be in the next word. The one- and two-point tiles find their ways onto the bonus squares only out of necessity and desperation. The rare and valuable letters are jealously guarded.

There's a lot of odd things about the game. For instance, a list of acceptable two-letter words came with the instructions, most of which do not get used by Anglophones in daily conversation. The only letter that can't be used in any of these words is V, so if you've got that tile near the end of the game, you're probably stuck with it since you can't find an available vowel for it anywhere on the board. There's also a list of words containing Q but no U. I shouldn't have to mention that most of these words are very foreign in origin.

So far, my best score in a game of Scrabble has been 446, against a computer opponent in the video game. Today, neither one of my scores came close. One of my trays even got stuck with a Q at the end, a devastating hit that penalizes a player ten points. But, what're ya gonna do if no U is available?

I'm tired of it all, really. I don't know, I just can't stand the thought of seeing all that from another angle, a third-person shot of me on the floor playing both sides of a game by myself just like when I was a kid. And yet, it's entirely accurate. That's exactly who I am.

When they say "accept yourself for who you are," I understand the sentiment. However, accepting myself is what I did for many years, and inside I was miserable. Acceptance is for that which can be accepted. My life as it was had been unacceptable. I'm not giving up. I'm not resigning myself to living my entire life this way. If I accept myself, I resign myself.

I got out a brush pen from Japan that I bought online a few years back. It was meant for Japanese calligraphy, the type that often gets displayed on motivational placards, but today it would be tasting a different tongue. I made a capital A, but didn't like how it came out. It looked more like one of my shoes than an A, actually. Tried again, slower this time. On my second try, I got it down almost perfectly. A few spots were kind of thin, but it didn't interrupt the flow for me to go back and fill them in a little. It was good enough to frame:

"Acceptance is Resignation"

I taped it onto the door to my room, so that I have to look at it every day when I get out of bed. And every morning, it will remind me that it's not over.

JUL 5 (SUN)

I didn't get a single match. Not one of the eight guys I picked liked me enough to want to go out with me.

I was frustrated enough to give up on this company immediately. I changed everything in that online profile they made me fill out. Then I deleted the profile. Then, to make absolutely sure, I cut up my credit card into thirty-six pieces and threw half of them in the trash and the other half in the garbage disposal. Tomorrow morning, I'm calling the credit card company and telling them I lost my card and need a new one with a new number.

I don't consider the speed-dates to be actual dates. Come on, five minutes with a person who didn't really ask to be with me in the first place? Rather, they're an opportunity for dates to be arranged later. Given that, my record so far for even going on dates stands at a perfect zero. How do I do it? It's a circle so perfect that it remains undisturbed even on a microscopic level. I picture little molecules with a perfectly smooth black line crossing them like they have slick new racing stripes. I am absolute chemical purity, unbreakable, impenetrable. If I could find a way to capture this essence of mine and incorporate it into the manufacturing of parachutes and bulletproof vests, I'd be a national hero.

Truth be told, I'm not down on myself right now. I'm feeling kind of good, considering the circumstances. It's a "Well, whaddidya expect, dummy?" feeling. It was something I could have easily seen coming, even though I did go in truly believing that I was going to come out ahead for once. So, I guess I'm not disappointed.

Okay, I am disappointed. While I don't feel like I've missed out on something or wasted an opportunity, it is a real blow to the spirit knowing that none of these men

157

wanted to see me again. Zero for eight.

I couldn't have scared them off with anything I said. I stuck to the most mundane, anodyne, milk-of-magnesia small talk topics imaginable: What town do you live in? How did you get here tonight? What do you do for work? How about that weather, huh? So, eliminating what I said, that just leaves everything else. I feel like I'm missing something crucial, something so important and basic that other people would never think to bring it up. It's like I've driven to work and pulled into the parking lot, only to remember that I somehow left my car keys at home. It's making me feel, well, stupid.

So, speed-dating was a wash. I may have to try again, but definitely with a different service, (preferably one that doesn't hold its events in a restaurant that sounds like a summer camp for morning zoo soundboards.) I'm sure I'm on the right track with this.

Got on my bike and went to visit that church again. Wrong day for that. There was some sort of outdoor service happening, and the presiding priest was mic'ed up so his words were broadcast throughout the entire churchyard. Couldn't put my finger on the language. I'd expect something like this to be in Spanish or Portuguese, but I picked out a lot of phonemes that weren't native to either of those tongues. I'd have to guess it was probably either Polish or an unfamiliar dialect of French. There were definitely a lot of silent Zs. I couldn't hear them, but I could sense their grave, foreboding presence in there somewhere.

It seemed kind of melancholy, but there were too many bright clothes and umbrellas for it to be related to someone's passing. I didn't come within forty feet of the nearest attendee as I walked behind all of their backs. One time-weathered fellow in the back saw me daring to enjoy the outdoors on a nice day and his scowling countenance slowly rotated to remain pointed at me as I walked along. "How dare you come within the general vicinity of whatever's going on here? Have you no respect?" is what he seemed to be trying to beam at me telepathically.

I stared right back at him and slowed my gait, as if to say, "If it's so important, why don't you pay attention to it instead of watching someone who isn't even bothering you?" He looked away. The nerve of him, judging me for minding my own business while he shows up for something solemn-sounding in a bright orange polo shirt and whiter-than-white shorts. When I blow this big blue popsicle stand, people had better not be mourning me while dressed like a Rubik's Cube.

I cut my visit short due to the service and took my walk in the cemetery instead.

158

Was able to ride my bike through the woods via that big swath of land cleared for the power lines. Hearing the electrical hum buzzing overhead tends to fill me with a vague enough sense of dread that it makes me feel alive. The pylons look down on you like a higher power (pun intended) knowing they have the ability to smite if they feel like it. "You dare to pass between our legs at will, you insolent plebeian? You just stay right there for a few years and we will give you such a tumor!"

The cemetery can be interesting every now and then, if you pay attention. For example, there are plenty of deceased men whose wives' names are engraved on their headstones without corresponding dates of death. Those women are still alive, and every time they visit their husbands' final resting places, they have that reminder of their own inevitable fates. At this cemetery, at least two of these women are named Audrey. Popular name for folks born in the 1930s. I saw a headstone from the Eighteenth Century of someone whose first name was Christmas. There's one that died out, probably for good. Imagine all the year-round caroling a kid named Christmas would hear in this day and age. (Oh Lord, imagine if Miriam had a relative with that name? Christmas Canada. He'd be working in indie films by the age of six.)

I don't want to be buried when I die. I want to be cremated. Bring my remains to the ocean and kiss my ash goodbye. I'm not comfortable with the idea of my cadaver taking up room in a cemetery. I don't even know if there'll be any room left by that time. Stiffs might need to be buried standing up, or maybe they'll have to introduce bunkcoffins. Plus, what would they put on my headstone?

- "She sure was around for a while, wasn't she?"
- "Her heart was too beautiful for her face to keep up."
- "If only her skin were as fiery as her sense of justice." (This one only works if I get locked in a walk-in freezer.)

I suppose that if I plan ahead far enough (and feel like spending money on something I'll never be able to enjoy,) I could pick my own design. Maybe my epitaph would be a secret code that kids could try to decipher, believing it will lead them to my buried treasure. When they finally break the code, it will only spell out something like, "Try getting the last word now."

Just came back from the 24-hour market. Had to pick up a few things for a little kaffeeklatsch I'm having in the morning. There was a mother in there with a child who looked to be about six or seven. The kid was drinking an iced coffee. It was 10:30 at night. I have no clue what's going on anymore. I feel like I'm living in the fall of Rome.

<u>JUL 6 (MON)</u>

Lynn and Rosi stopped by the apartment today. I thought it might be a good idea to just sit down with them and do a little bonding over some coffee. (I switched mine with Yoo-Hoo.) You know, just friends being close. And then, I would spring my nefarious trap on those unsuspecting chumps. I thought I'd convince one of them to take Willow's place and handle the other half of the rent for me. I'll charm them with java and these Italian cookies, I thought. Luckily, I'd pretty much straightened everything out following my roomie's departure, so the kitchen and living room were no longer attracting location scouts for upcoming natural disaster movies.

Once they arrived, Lynn was sporting a different haircut, one of those Cleopatra-type bobs that Fawn Clayton had for a while. She seemed quite pleased with her new look and was humming an aimless upbeat tune that sounded like "Take Five" in 7/4 time. While we were all gabbing over coffee, she was happy to inform me she got two matches from her speed-dates. Just two? While I didn't get a good look at most of the female participants, from what I did see, I'd have to say Lynn was the best-looking of the bunch. Yeah, I know, people have different tastes, but c'mon! Two?

They wanted to know how I did. I told them I got zero matches. Rosi was shocked by this, saying, "Inexplicable! I am inable to explic it!"

After a while, Lynn's eyes fell on the Scrabble box which I brought out the other day. She said we should play. I think she wanted to cheer me up after hearing about my results, or possibly just trying to change the subject. Rosi wasn't as keen to play, saying, "We all know Audrey's gonna win. Why bother?"

"You never know. You might be surprised," I said. Oh yeah, I was gonna take a dive. If I didn't throw this game, chances are Rosi would (for distance.)

On one turn, I had the tiles A, E, I, K, N, T, and a blank. I knew there had to be some way to use them all. Plus, there was an S on the board with a big, empty field in front of it. The Holy Grail. Aha! I could play all of my tiles and net an extra fifty points with "BEATNIKS", I thought. But, because I wanted to leave open the possibility of them playing with me again in the future, I made "KITES" instead.

Rosi cried out, "No fair! You stole my spot." You're welcome.

In the end, it was Rosi who came out on top. "YES! I DID IT! I actually beat Audrey! Do you believe in miracles! Do you be-LEEEEEVE in miracles!" At first, she celebrated like she'd just won a boxing match, but then she started throwing in things like "Four more years!" and "Burn, baby, burn!"

Lynn seemed less than pleased with the excessive celebration. Her eyes said to me, "You! You could have prevented this from happening." Don't worry, Lynn. The next one will be different. I'll show you true hell.

I must have put Rosi in a seriously good mood with that win, because she gave me her tablet. She told me her mom gave her a new one for her birthday and she wanted me to have this old one, since I don't even have a smartphone. Very kind gesture. I don't know what I'm going to do with it, as my laptop already does everything the tablet does, but with a keyboard. And, I don't need it to prop open the bathroom window, either, since I started using that wooden ruler from the junk drawer.

Before they left, both Rosi and Lynn said they'd have to "think about" moving in with me. I know it's a big decision, but so often I hear "maybe" when all I want is a "yes" or "no".

Wasn't feeling too down about the speed-dating results yesterday, but today it finally sunk in. A group of men who, like me, saw that gathering as their best hope, got to know me a little and none of them wanted to be with me. They're probably just as hard up for love as I am, and that still wasn't enough to get them to take a second look.

Often, I'll hear males claim to be at a disadvantage in the dating arena. Their argument is that we're the ones who make them fall in love with us, and that they have to pursue us, competing against each other for the prize.

I suppose I understand the reasoning, biased though it may be. However, there is a very big societal issue that is not addressed in this theory: men are expected to be aggressive, and women passive. If a woman approaches a man, something's off about that. She must be desperate, they'll whisper. It's just not the way things are done in our society. At least males have the option of advancing.

Women are expected to wait by the phone. We are told to attract males and entice them into approaching us. Oh, but you won't wait long because it's all so easy. Women can have sex whenever we want, they'll allege. It's the men who are after us.

So what if nobody's after you? Nobody ever addresses that, do they? In all the things I've ever read, heard, or watched regarding love and sex, I've not once caught a discussion on "What if nobody wants to be with you? Ever?" They just don't want to think about us. It would be better if the sight of us didn't keep de-rosing their colored glasses.

I confess, I can't specify who "they" are.

UPDATE. Text from Lynn: "u threw it didnt u?"

JULY 7 (TUE)

I'm having trouble figuring out this tablet. It takes me a while to adjust myself to new technology, but once I've been at it for a while I can usually make it second nature.

This one might be my Waterloo. It uses a touch-screen, which I've never been fond of. It's not a very responsive touch screen, either. On top of that, I thought I fixed the date and time display this morning but now it's claiming today is the eighth. Whoever manufactured this thing must have a backdoor deal going with the makers of Advil.

Got a text: Rosi and Lynn want me to go to the beach with them this Friday. I figure I might as well. I'm not a beach person, I get bored pretty easily there. But, I haven't been in years, and I want to get out of the house and spend time with friends, so I may as well. I need the sun.

There aren't any beaches around here, just ports and rocky shores, so it's a haul all the way out to Marshfield. It'll be fun having a nice long road trip with my pals. Maybe I can suggest we play a license plate game that I made up. And who knows, if they like it maybe they'll let me ride on the inside again.

On that topic, I went for another ride with Angela. Tomorrow she's taking off for California. We had another bar trip before her departure. She wants me to have a "real" drink at any cost. I've got the feeling she's determined to make a drinker out of me yet. I'm not sure why. She brought me to a Chinese restaurant with a bar in a small town about five miles east of the city limits. It looked to be the only thing on the block that was open and it was only nine o'clock.

Angela sat down at the bar. I took the stool next to her. The man on my other side got up and moved to the only other unoccupied stool. Angela ordered a drink (I forget the name) for herself and the same for me. I didn't ask for anything, but I figured her strategy was to drink both in the end.

I got my drink. It was a little smaller than an above-ground pool and filled with an amber-colored liquid with fumes that singed the hair off my nostrils. The glass came with a thin little wire of a straw that couldn't drop those last few micrograms it needed in order to join the coffee stirrer squad. I took a sip.

It was the worst yet. I managed to choke down that little sip somehow, following it up with a noise that can only be properly written out as a word balloon containing a picture of a seagull being strangled by a plastic six-pack holder. I tried again. It wasn't any better. I was slamming my hand on the counter involuntarily, trying to create enough noise and motion to distract my brain from the taste. I know alcohol is an acquired taste, but why the hell would I want to get used to the flavor of something that goes down tasting like a fruit salad does coming up? I kept going but I couldn't stand it and Ange volunteered to take the remaining nine-tenths off my hands.

"You have to start drinking," she still insists. Seems like a fool's errand, but she's certain that's the key to all this. I don't really want to drink, anyways. Even though I haven't been drunk yet, I still like being fully aware, having my senses fully-operational.

Ange asked about how my list of new things I want to try is coming along. I hadn't really thought about it in a while. She suggested I should add to it, and began throwing out suggestions for things that are never going to happen like "skydiving" and "getting a tattoo." She's kind of missing the point. I'm supposed to be trying things I WANT to do. I guess that's not as open-minded as it could be, is it? Of course, if I go skydiving and something doesn't pan out right, my mind will be so open that... well, I'll just leave it at that.

"Didn't you say something about ballroom dancing lessons before? How about that?" she asked. Oh yeah, that one completely got away from me.

She finished her first glass and went on, telling me she saw a flyer down at the yoga studio. There's a company has these little soirées once a month in Boston. Apparently, they have quickie lessons earlier in the day to teach you a few steps, then everyone shows up for a ball later that night. I had doubts. Her description made it sound pretty fly-by-night, like their ballroom would be a decaying former roller rink, complete with a DJ wearing sunglasses and a tuxedo T-shirt. Maybe the custodian would be good enough to keep the floor buffer on "low," so as not to drown out the music. Glamorous.

"It would still be a good way to meet people," she claimed. Well argued. She looked it up on her phone. The next one is the first of August. I had her text the site's address to me, just in case I change my mind.

I bid farewell to Angela once she dropped me off back home, wishing her luck on her journey. I waved goodbye and shouted "Tell Lexy I love her!" As she pulled away, I quickly followed up with, "But I love you, too, of course!" I hope she heard me. Leave it to me to mess up something as simple as saying goodbye.

163

UPDATE. I just figured out what's wrong with the tablet. Rosi had the time zone set as "China." Why? I don't think we'll ever know.

JUL 10 (FRI)

We all set out for the beach today, just as planned, with Rosi at the wheel of her brother's Near-Deathmobile and me in the passenger seat. I still don't trust that vehicle; it feels like it could die on us at any time. Rosi insists that all the noises are signs that it still has some "oomph" in it, but if we hit a pothole too fast, the only "oomph" will be the reading on the speedometer. Lynn and Zena shared the back with all of our beach gear, as the trunk was already full of emergency equipment, soda cans, and bags of clothes that will allegedly find their way to the St. Vincent de Paul bin one of these years.

The four of us had plenty of time to shoot the breeze. Rosi told me she's been reading this advice column and someone wrote in with a problem similar to my own. The columnist's answer was tantamount to giving up: pay for a sex worker. "Just go look up a male escort service online. It's not ideal, but it's something," Rosi said in an "It's not so bad!" sort of way.

I'd already made up my mind. "I'm NEVER going to an escort service. My cash could end up in the hands of human traffickers."

Zena pointed out that there are independent sex workers out there, but none of us had any idea how to find them. "They're good people. They do it of their own free will because they like it, and they hate trafficking just as much as anyone. You could argue that they even help fight human trafficking because they divert business away from it."

You're all kind of missing the point, I thought. Is a sex worker going to go to the laundromat with me to help fold my clothes? Or go for walks with me, holding my hand? Or help me with crossword puzzles? Or exchange little love notes written in secret code with me? That ain't how it works.

Zena continued, asking, "Didn't you say something about going to Amsterdam before? 'Plan Z,' you called it?"

"Well, I still haven't ruled that out entirely." I slumped back down in my seat, adding, "Besides, even if it's legal, I... I'm just not so sure about Amsterdam anymore, I guess."

"Okay, the trafficking thing is despicable. I agree," Rosi said. "But we all do things we don't want to do for money. That's why it's called 'work' and not 'play.' If we all got

164

to do what we want for our jobs, nothing important would ever get done. If it's legal and regulated, what's the big deal?"

"I'd probably just be helping him support his drug habit."

"Every time you shop at the supermarket, you're supporting the drug habits of upwards of thirty people." (No way I could make a counter-argument to that, so white flag there.)

I sighed. "Rosi, please. Don't devil's advocate me on this one. Besides, I don't know the rules but I bet they have to keep everything as super-hygienic as possible. A Dutch sex worker probably wouldn't even be allowed to kiss me." The last sentence squirmed its way out from my mouth in a guilty half-mumble, as if I didn't even mean to say it aloud.

That triggered some sort of cry of disbelief that sounded as if it were coming from twice as many people as there were in the car. Zena even let out a sizable "WHOA, where did THAT come from all of a sudden?"

Rosi wasn't done yet, oh no. "See! I told you! You want a boyfriend!" she announced with a schoolyard sing-songy edge.

I guess I can't rule out the possibility that I'm having a change of heart. Then again, even if by some miraculous series of accidents and natural mutations, I managed to find someone who was willing to give being my boyfriend a go, I'm sure it wouldn't take long before my eccentricities and blandness would drive him away. At this point, the sex is only about ten percent of what I want. Rosi's right but, more than that, I think I'm afraid of what would happen if I got what I want.

"I don't know what I want," I sighed just as we passed the sign welcoming us to our destination.

The town certainly had a New England seaside tourist trap quality: almost no houses more than one story tall, businesses refusing to repair their decayed signs out of stubborn nostalgia, elderly men in chairs on their front lawns smoking cigars and staring daggers into traffic intersections. Very much a "beach town" feel. As we got closer to the seawall, I eventually saw the first glimpse of that big, blue, hypothermia-inducing expanse of water. Probably the cleanest public toilet in town.

We somehow managed to find a parking space within a mere fifteen minutes, but it was a bit of a hike down to the beach from there. As expected, the place was crowded. You'd never know it was a weekday. My ears were flooded with the noise of hundreds of people talking, screaming, crying, yowling. My nose was clogged with the essences of salt water and sunscreen. My eyes were overcome by a nagging urge to find Waldo. The four of us were able to tiptoe our way through the throngs and claim a patch of land the size of a welcome mat right next to a rocky area at the very edge of the beach. Okay then, we had a spot. We could now begin our day of getting sand in everything we brought with us.

You'd think its proximity to the water would be a beach's main draw. However, less than one out of a hundred of the beachgoers were in the ocean at any given moment. Can't say I blame them given how frigid the water is. I don't get it. Is everyone here just to lie in the sun? They can do that at home, can't they?

As soon as we dropped anchor and got everything settled, I wanted to take some time to lie down and do my best to relax. Suddenly...

"Connor! You are SIX years old! Do NOT fucking argue with me!" Oh, did I forget to mention that we had staked our spot only about twenty feet from a mother who had a delightfully inexhaustible supply of things to shout at her misbehaving son? Her voice had a rich wheezing quality to it, as if Scotch tape were singing. We were truly in the presence of a diva.

Rosi was disappointed in my choice in swimwear, asking why I wasn't in that Chernobyl-pink two-piece she wanted so desperately to see me in. I just told her I forgot I had it. Well, half-true: I tried very hard to forget it and was nearly there, so let's just round off.

Lynn was curious about what we were referring to, so Rosi told her about our shopping trip. "I told her to pick out some underwear and she comes back with a pack of cheap granny panties. Really, Audrey, sometimes I'm not sure about you."

I requested that she not call them "granny panties" as it's a very negative-sounding name. When she asked if I had any better label to offer, I suggested "ankle warmers". She had to admit that was a pretty good spin on it. That's the power of picking the right words.

I brought that tablet for entertainment. I figured out how to download a book onto it, and was planning to get started on that, but the outdoors had other plans. The screen was completely unreadable in the light of day, even in the shade. Another plan burnt up in the sun.

For about an hour I attempted to nap instead. I was in that DMZ where you're about to fall asleep, when little Connor's mom finished her warm-up act and allowed her son to move on to the Satan-channeling portion of the show. This was as good a time as any to take a walk. Lynn jumped up to come along. Don't get me wrong, I love her, but she's not quite who I envision myself taking long walks along the beach with.

Our path hugged the shoreline as close as it could, right along that endless strip of wet sand that's perfect for writing in with something pointy. Lynn had this look on her face like she was trying not to laugh at a funeral for a distant relative with a comical name. ("I'm so sorry, I really *do* miss Uncle Nabisco!") I had to ask what was so amusing.

Lynn said she wasn't holding in laughter. She was just really happy. "It was what you said in the car, about how you wanted to be kissed." For a while, Lynn was worried that I was going to stray down a path of unchecked hedonism and casual sex for the sake of lashing out at society (off to a great start so far, aren't we?) but hearing me open my heart the slightest bit seems to have renewed her faith in the power of luv. She used the word "inspired" at one point.

Lynn wanted to know what sort of man I'm looking for, as far as looks go. Really, I have no clear-cut answer to this one. It's just so hard for me to envision myself with anyone, so I can't really tell what I want.

"As far as physical attributes, I don't really know what my type is. As long as he has good hygiene, is nice to me, and isn't an ill-mannered primate, then I think I'll have to take it. That isn't too much to ask, is it?"

"The sad thing is it shouldn't be," she remarked in sardonic, humming tone. "But what about the characters in those Japanese comics? Use them as an example." We turned around and headed back the way we came.

"That's different. Those are cartoons. They're not real. Even then, a lot of it really is about personality." I told her I'd think it over.

She pointed out a couple holding hands off to the right and asked, "How about him? Would you want him to be your boyfriend?"

"I don't even know anything about him." Granted, I do get jealous almost every time I see a display like that. If it gets to that point, I just think, "What difference does it make? If he wasn't with her, he'd be with someone else who isn't me." That doesn't help. I'm jealous of what they have, not who they're with.

Lynn still thinks I'm on the right track now. She says she's more convinced than ever that I've got something good in my future, thanks to my revived pursuit. "It's good that you're trying new things and being active about it instead of just waiting for the phone to ring. We all deserve to be loved, but you have to earn it."

"Oh? So, what did you do to earn your first love?"

She shrugged. "I dunno."

The others were having a lively discussion when we got back. Zena asked me what color she thought Rosi's bikini is. Rosi protested, "Zena says it's baby blue. It's not. It's cerulean, right?"

I suggested it may have been cerulean when she bought it, but the color has probably faded since then. Since they couldn't get a straight answer out of me, they had to go to Lynn for the tiebreaker. She said it "just looks blue." She also hasn't heard of cerulean before.

The family nearby was packing up and taking off despite Connor's objections. The mother grabbed his arm to drag him off. The child responded with a "NO!" full of such power and resonance that it would be better suited to Moses parting the Red Sea. Impressive, I'll admit. I guess his mom's not the only one with a set of pipes. The rest of our stay was quiet and uneventful after that.

Zena won the passenger seat on the way back. Lynn slept in back next to me. Rosi had a couple of close calls at the wheel this time (Friday evening traffic, of course.) There have been studies saying that Massachusetts has the worst drivers, but I think that's just Boston skewing the average for the whole state again. Though I will admit that if there were a campaign to change the official state nickname to "The Land That Turn Signals Forgot," I'd be in favor of it.

JUL 13 (MON)

Welcome to thirty.

Yes, it was my birthday. Not just any birthday, but one that ends with a zero. Exactly three decades have now passed since I "Here's Johnny!"-ed my way out of the womb, and what do I have to show for it all? A bunch of books for kids in an elementary school library and a two-minute massage.

I was hoping to ride this one out quietly, but Rosi shot me a "Happy birthday!" text. She says she remembers because I have the same birthday as her brother Tomas. If I recall correctly, Tomas is twenty-eight and his wife prepared to give birth to their first child this October. Perhaps Tomas could do me a favor and discover a cure for Alzheimer's in the next two years, just so I can be one-hundred percent sure my first thirty were a complete washout.

Rosi also sent a text pointing out that thirty in Roman numerals is "XXX." Clever.

Lynn, on the other hand, did not know it was a red letter day. We went for lunch and, for some reason, I thought it would be a brilliant idea to try another drink. I don't know what possessed me to try a piña colada, but maybe I just felt like it would lift my spirits a bit, damage a lobe or two. The waitress asked for my ID, looked it over, and wished me a happy birthday. Cover blown.

"Oh, it's your birthday? Why didn't you say anything?" asked Lynn.

I sighed a little. "You know how it is with birthdays. Besides, I'm thirty now. Thirty, and I still haven't... you know."

Lynn got that "Let's go git 'em!" look in her eyes, and said, "Hey, thirty is good! This is gonna be the year for you, I know it! Sure, it marks the end of a decade, but you can look back at that as the turning point!"

"I wouldn't get too comfortable with that nice, round multiple of ten. At the rate I'm going, I figure we're already staring down the barrel of thirty-one."

"Thirty-one's good, too!" She quieted to a whisper due to the public environment. "I hear that if you lose your virginity when your age is a prime number, then that guy will turn out to be your soulmate!"

That was a superstition I hadn't heard before. "Prime number? Really? Where did you hear that one?"

Lynn admitted she just made it up to make me feel better. "But wouldn't it be great if we could spread that around and it caught on? But it only works for girls. For guys, it has to be a sum of two square numbers."

I didn't like the piña colada, as expected.

Later, Lynn insisted on buying me a birthday gift. She said I should just pick anything out and she'd pay for it. I couldn't think of anything I wanted. At least, nothing she could give me. After lunch, we went over to Newbury Comics to browse the CDs, just because I figured she wasn't going to let this go.

Here's a sign I'm getting old: maybe when I was a kid I just didn't notice, but the world seems a lot racier nowadays. I was looking over the DVDs in the store. One looked like the most watered-down, kid-friendly pile o' nothin' ever made. The cover was a close-up of a dog wearing sunglasses in what I assume was Hawaii or California, due to the reflections of palm trees in the lenses. The title was "Cool Pooch". It was rated PG.

Why PG? What could be in that movie that would both deny it a G rating and be essential enough that it absolutely had to make the final cut? Does a Klansman burn a

169

cross on Cool Pooch's lawn? Is there a flashback to Cool Pooch's first LSD trip in the jungles of Southeast Asia? Does Cool Pooch walk through the cemetery at night to collect his thoughts regarding his illegitimate son, only to be beaten to a bloody pulp by a gang of grave robbers that he unwittingly comes across? Nah, it's probably something more like farting.

The store actually had a Style Council CD I'd been looking for, so Lynn bought that for me. I didn't want her spending her money on me, but I guess I did get her that Chia Pet for her birthday, so we're even. Lynn's birthday is February 14, Valentine's Day. She's such a sweetheart that it's only logical, *non*? Having worked in a school, I'm fairly certain that Valentine's Day was made up as a distraction to keep kids under control during those long winter doldrums. Dangle a carrot in front of them and you'll virtually eliminate the chance of a revolt. Then, adults felt the same way and co-opted it to make their lives a little less dreary, they way they did with Halloween and St. Patrick's Day. It's nice having something to look forward to.

Valentine's Day itself doesn't really bother me. It does grate on a lot of people's nerves, but from where I stand every day is Valentine's Day. Plus, I live in Massachusetts so the entire month of February is a dismal, grey stretch of pneumonia anyhow. That tends to overshadow everything else on the calendar.

Before we parted, Lynn wanted me to know that she went out with one of her matches from our speed-dating expedition. They had a great time together and they're going out again in a few days. I congratulated her, and I was genuinely happy to hear the good news, but I still had to try to smile. I don't smile a lot to begin with, and I suck at trying to force one. I must have looked like I was trying not to offend my host who so graciously invited me to dinner and claiming that I only needed to throw up so that I could make room for more.

Lynn, wherever you are right now, please know that I love you and am happy for you. I wasn't bitter. I am disappointed, but only in myself.

And so, that was how I spent the changing of the guard in "the tens place," as it's called. ("The Tens' Place" sounds like a club catering exclusively to stiflingly conceited people.) I think I've finally moved into that third stage of birthdays. When you're a kid, you love them because you get presents. When you're a teenager and a young adult, you don't care as much because you can buy things for yourself. Finally, you get to the age where you hate being reminded of how old you are. I still look really young for my age, everyone says so. I feel as young as I always have. Now, I think it's all about the sex thing. I feel like time is against me now.

Ange texted me from California. Says she's getting her first tattoo while she's over there and wants me to help choose what it should be. Here are her ideas:

1) "a hand-grenade with a black and hot pink yin-yang over it"

2) "a submarine in space, having an identity crisis"

3) "Orville Redenbacher's head and a ribbon bearing the words 'He Can Do Anything'"

As curious as I was to see how an identity crisis would be depicted in a tattoo, I voted for the grenade. I asked if Ange had any new ideas for "Hippo Campus." She said she had a better plan now: we should make a mascot for the Ridgeway Police Department who can teach kids about safety. Her current idea is "Chalky the Outline."

While I was writing this, Mom rang me up for the usual birthday salutations. She wants me to swing by this Sunday for a small family gathering in my honor. She says Rebecca will be there. This won't end well. When Mom and Rebecca are in the same room for enough time, there's bound to be a skirmish. The last time we all got together, Rebecca flipped out over Mom's constant questions regarding a TV show we were all watching. She doesn't ask about what's going on, or things relevant to the script. She just asks general questions about elements that are never explained to the audience. Questions like, "Why doesn't that girl wear contacts? She'd look so much nicer without those glasses."

Eventually this got to be too much for Rebecca to take and there was a frenzied quarrel. Rebecca went home mad, Mom went to bed mad, Dad walked the dog mad, and I thought to myself, "All this over a show called *Cutest Kittens On Earth*?" I guess it's a lot easier to be the mature one when you're not involved.

All along, I've been told by people (who aren't family) that I'm mature for my age. Maybe it's been my intelligence that's misled them all, the suckers. I've matured in all the boring ways, at least: temper, knowledge, rationality, responsibility. In the remaining aspects of maturity, I still lag far behind and now it's all a confusing mess. I'm only reputedly maturer. I'm only mixed-up Audrey Perlmutter.

JUL 15 (WED)

Forgot about this until I looked at the calendar yesterday: I have my gyno exam tomorrow. Despite not being "sexually active", as the medical texts like to call it, it's still

171

important to have a check-up every year. I'm actually not very good with doctor's appointments, and tend to put them off. I've only had nine gynecology exams so far.

Met Rosi for lunch today. She wanted to take me out shopping again, but I don't think spending money is going to help me, so I talked her down to just having a meal. She asked if I had plans for the week, so I told her I have a doctor's appointment tomorrow.

"What sort of appointment?"

"Gynecologist." Oohhh... why did I say that? Immediately, I came up with three possible barbs she could have stung me with, but she must have been feeling merciful today because she just let it go. Instead, I just ended up inadvertently zinging myself three times in my own head.

I admitted that I'm dreading it a little, as I'm still inexperienced. "I'm just worried that she'll know. She can tell, right?"

Rosi was doubtful, and asked "Are you seriously telling me you've never put anything in there?"

I did admit that wasn't quite the case, but never anything thicker than a finger.

"Wait, did you say 'A finger'? As in, one? And you're how many years older than me?"

"Three years and eleven months. But, I'm still kind of afraid that my trips up the one-way alley might not be... 'enough.' She is an expert, after all."

Rosi shook her head. "You worry about some weird things, Audrey." She wanted to know what I meant by "one-way alley."

"You know what a three-way is, right?" I said.

"Oh. Got it."

She did have an idea, though. She suggested I just acquaint myself with a, what's the commercial term again? "Marital aid." I immediately expressed my doubts that this was a good idea.

"Trust me, it'll be great. Your first time will be even better because it will get the ouchie part out of the way." Well, loathe as I am to ignore advice on intimacy and sexual health that involves the term "ouchie part," I still wasn't sure I was up for it. Problem number one with using a vibrator is that I have to buy one first. I felt like I could dredge up the courage to do that, but where would I get one?

Rosi said there's a sex shop right down the block and that I've probably walked past it hundreds of times. I remembered now. I actually went in once, because I needed a birthday gift for a young cousin and I thought it was a magic shop. The signs in the window were very confusing. Rosi thought that was hilarious, and she assumed her best Bullwinkle voice. "Hey, Rocky! Watch me pull a rabbit outta my pants!"

Once we were in the store, Rosi felt the urge to look at the porn DVDs, just so she could rattle off some of the more entertaining names. She asked me what my "porn name" would be. "I dunno. Uh, 'Jessica something' is okay I guess?"

"No, you don't get it. There's some formula for it. Something to do with the street you grew up on and your middle name or something. What's your middle name?"

I would not give it to her. My middle name stays buried alive. I refuse to even write it, whether in Hebrew, Latin, or shorthand letters. Rosi wouldn't give up and kept asking for it. Boy, was she ever asking for it.

Eventually, I got sidetracked going through some outfits they had on display. Rosi pointed out a maid costume and said she wanted to buy it for me. I didn't know what I could possibly say to that. It caught me so off-guard that I forgot to have an involuntary reaction. She asked if I have any fetishes, other than just the manga thing.

"Isn't there anything you might want him to wear? Or someone you'd like him to pretend to be?" she asked, her eyes wide with curiosity.

"I guess I could ask, but… what's the point of having someone you love do something for you if they're just going to be cringing and wanting it to end the whole time? I wouldn't be comfortable with that. And I wouldn't want him to think I'm weird," I told her.

Rosi said I was too cautious, and she went over to the vibrator section for some browsing. Well, can't argue with her on that. All my life I've been playing by the odds, following common sense. But, you have to take risks, too. That's what life is. Sense is what you make of it.

"Audrey! This would be perfect!" Rosi called out as she turned the corner, brandishing an object that looked to be missing its Husqvarna logo. Yikes. How to describe it… In a word: no. In two words: no way. "Come on! You know you want it!" she teased.

"Forget it! I'm not shoving something with the diameter of a soda can inside of me!" …is what a saner woman would have said only in her head instead of out loud.

"You know, they make these eight-ounce soda cans now. They're pretty popular, and they're a little thinner, too," she informed me. I don't know what that had to do with anything. Rosi was annoying me a little now. I was hoping to keep everything discreet, get in there and back out in no time. This was not how it was working out, though.

173

Instead, she pinballed all over the store finding interesting fluorescent objects to shove into my field of vision.

She eventually picked out a vibrator for herself and announced she was naming it "The Chancellor." By this time, I found one that looked normal enough, and Rosi began pestering me for what I was going to name mine. I must have insisted five times that I wasn't going to name it anything, but she kept badgering me. I hate that. Nobody takes me seriously. If someone asks me a question and I give them an answer they don't like, they just keep asking. I think I'm smart enough to make my own decisions.

Eventually, it got to me and I had to conjure up something to get her to shut up. I was irked enough to have a miniature outburst, shouting, "FINE! I'm naming it 'Sir Jitters the Caffeinated'! Happy?"

"In that case, would you like to keep shopping or bring Sir Jitters up here to pay for him?" That was the cashier, by the way, looking more amused than I think the employee handbook allowed her to in such a situation.

Rosi was behind me in line, ready to make her purchase. She asked the cashier if she knew the formula for a porn name. Her take on it was that you had to use the name of your first pet plus the street you grew up on. I've never had a pet, so I had to abstain (for a change…) Rosi's name is "T-Bone Poplar." She said it sounds like a guy's name, like one popular guy who gets to bone everyone. I said it sounded like an order to smash a car head-on into a tree.

After we left the store we were about go our separate ways, but I had to know something first. I asked her if we could do a trade-off. Since she knows I'm a virgin, I asked if she would mind telling me how old she was her first time. She wasn't embarrassed at all, telling me, "Sixteen. Honestly, the guy I was steady with at the time was starting to get on my nerves. I didn't even want to do it. But, all my friends were already gettin' it on, and you hear so much about how great and important sex is. I didn't enjoy it. It was all about him."

"You didn't orgasm?" (Can that be a verb? It has to be, right?)

"I don't even think he knew females had those." She had a look of derision and regret on her face like it had just happened yesterday. "I've always felt that I could have waited a little longer. Maybe I would have appreciated it more. Not until age twenty-nine, of course, but OH! Sorry, it's thirty now, isn't it?"

"Hey, I'm 'looking forward' waiting. You're making it sound like I'm 'holding back' waiting."

174

"Well, either way, you're not sexually active."

My heart skipped a beat. Those words. The doctor's going to ask me that tomorrow, isn't she? Damn. Vibrator or no vibrator, I'd have to tell her either way. Talk about an oversight, all this hassle and humiliation was for nothing.

I dunno. Now that I have it, I don't really want it. This sounds silly, and I should know better, but I feel a little ashamed. We all masturbate, every one of us. The proud are fooling nobody when they claim otherwise, as if having a partner should be the only acceptable method for enjoying an orgasm. They get approval for this façade due to mutual embarrassment on the part of their audience. Aside from sex, their nether-regions are supposedly completely inactive when they aren't busy pissing vintage wine and taking perfumed shits of gold.

Still, I feel like this purchase is taking it to another level. Like I'm becoming the caricature I know I'm not. Even if I'm alone, I just wouldn't feel comfortable...

You know what? Forget it. I can't do this. I won't even take it out of the box. I guess I'll just stick it on a shelf in the closet to be forgotten, lost to the ages. Yesterday's news. Banished to the ether. Gone.

UPDATE. Okay, fine, so I used it. What of it?

JUL 16 (THU)

The worst thing that happened at my exam today was on the way up the stairs. I normally like stairwells. They're a kind of vertical no-man's-land, not chained to any particular floor. Isolated and utilitarian, like *moi*. I was on my way up to the doctor's office on the fifth when I found my path obstructed by a couple descending hand-in-hand. We came within two stairs of each other, then they stopped and stared at me. I stared right back. For five seconds, I waited for them to let me pass. I guess they expected me to be the one to go back down to the second floor so that they wouldn't have to spend a single moment interrupting their human chain creating a closed-circuit connection between one railing and the other.

I finally said, "Are you going to let me go or not?" Their bond was severed for what must have been an excruciating 1.6 seconds for them. As I continued my ascent, echoed whispers climbed the walls.

"What the hell was her problem?"

Was that just one's rhetorical attempt to save face in the presence of the other?

They couldn't be so dense as to honestly not know what the problem was. But, you never know. It's possible that they just didn't know what to do as the situation presented a puzzle too difficult for them to calculate their way out of. If so, good luck in the revolving door. I won't be around to give you a hint when that brainteaser presents itself.

Once I arrived, I wrote out a check and forked it over to the receptionist. She had a few dozen of those rubber ducks like the one Rosi gave me lined up on a shelf behind her counter. People really do collect these. One had fangs and a Dracula cape. As non-threatening as it looked, something about a duck with teeth disturbs me.

I sifted through a bunch of magazines of no interest to me in the waiting room. I hate having to see all these glossy celebrity faces everywhere: waiting rooms, supermarket check-out lines, the pharmacy, the newsstands. It isn't enough having to put up with couples I come across in public every day; I also have to hear about these Hollywood ones, too. It's like driving behind a cement mixer. It isn't anybody's fault you're stuck there, but it's still a huge pain in the ass and it still makes you nauseous after a few minutes. I was about to start re-stacking the mags in chronological order, when the doctor showed up and said she'd see me now. I had to put that mission on hold.

Well, it's all in the name of getting the pill, so we're on our way towards that now. Dr. Ianovich did ask if I'm active, so I had to say no. I'm pretty sure I had my eyes closed at that moment. Reflex. Still, I made sure to ask for a birth control prescription anyways, because hey, ya never know. Anything can happen. It's important to be prepared.

I was tempted to ask her a bunch of questions, but I couldn't think of any. The sex advice I need is not to be sought here. I don't know where else to go, though.

When I came out, the receptionist was out to lunch. I dug around in my purse and pulled out Vaudeville, then left him there on the counter for her. Now he has someone who might appreciate him, and he can be with his own kind, no longer on the outside. One of the crowd. The odd duck no more.

I still had some unfinished business. I eyed the stack of magazines over on the table in the corner, with a gaze that produces the sound of a sword being unsheathed. I don't know why I do this, but I had to go over and begin sorting them chronologically. Again, reflex.

Now that I'd finished that, I noticed another table in the other corner. Maybe I was still on edge from just seeing Dr. Ianovich. I've noticed that when I'm nervous, this sort of behavior gets worse. I went over to the other side of the room, and began the same task, sorting the magazines with the newest on top and the oldest at the bottom. Then, I began walking from one table to the other, back and forth, to make it so that the weekly ones and the monthlies were on separate tables.

A voice said, "Excuse me."

I turned around to see a couple of women staring at me, probably patients. The dark-haired one of imposing stature asked what I was doing. The blonde looked frightened and confused.

I turned red and mumbled, "I was just sorting the magazines. It's my way of giving back to the community." I made a break for it, as if I expected one of them to yell, "Stop her! She's getting away!" at any moment.

JUL 19 (SUN)

A small tempest touched down in Railhead today in the form of a, ummmm, let's go with "spat." I showed up at my parents' place for our little family get-together and from there it just snowballed. It may have been the most unpleasant family dinner scene I've ever been present for, with second prize going to the time I told Rebecca that mushrooms were penguin meat. And, just like that incident, today I was the cause of all the fury.

I met my parents and Rebecca at the old house on First Street. I got a better look at recent additions to the home decor while waiting for dinner to be served. There was a new multi-photo frame in the living room filled with snapshots dug out of photo albums. Most of the pics were new to me. Mom pointed out a picture of me taken on the morning of my first day of third grade. I always hated going back to school after summer, and I looked completely defeated in that picture. I look like I'm trying not to cry. Cry as much as you can, kid, because when you're an adult you won't be able to. Even if you try.

"That's really the best picture of me that you could find?" I asked.

Mom explained to me, "It's just so hard looking for photos where you're smiling. There's even one where you're on a carnival ride, and…" She was laughing now. "Sorry, it's… It's just that you have the same hangdog expression you always have! I've never seen a kid so depressed to be on her favorite ride!"

Oh, I get it now. Funny.

For my birthday gifts, I just received gift cards. I'm fine with that, as there's nothing specific I really want for presents. Better that I can use these cards to pick out my own things than get something I can't begin to imagine using, like that "portable" twenty-pound wooden lap desk the size of a dresser drawer I got for my eleventh birthday. Well, I did use that a lot, to be honest. I just didn't keep it on my lap.

We ate dinner, and kicked around the usual small talk: Mom, Dad, and Rebecca all talking about what's going on at work and asking how my summer's going. They noticed that I was kind of down, so Mom asked what was wrong. That's always where things fall to bits: she always gives me the same useless platitudes and I explain how none of that helps. Eventually, she says she doesn't know why she bothers because I'm impossible to console and I say she shouldn't have asked in the first place if she knew this was going to happen. Rather than going into why I was feeling low, I should have asked if we could all cut to the chase and walk away angry right then and there. Save some time and energy.

"I've just been thinking about turning thirty. Everybody else my age is already taken, and I think it might be too late for me. I'm worried that maybe no one will ever love me," said the life of the party.

Rebecca, confused, said, "I thought you weren't interested in that."

"Well, I wasn't interested. For a long time. But, sometimes events in your life cause you to change your mind," I replied. I didn't look up from my plate. "I guess what I'm looking for is... just loving, laughing, letting someone into my life, leaving behind the loneliness. I just want to be with somebody I can love for once."

"Audrey, you have plenty of people who love you! We love you and we're with you right now," said Mom, apparently a twelve-hour drive away from the closest thing resembling the point.

That irritated me a little. It felt like I wasn't being taken seriously again. "I'm not talking about family love. I'm talking about the good kind of love."

Mom, suddenly with look of dread: "Wait, hold on. Are you looking for a male or female partner?"

"What? Yes, of course a male! Why wouldn't I be?"

"Well, you said you don't want children, and you've always been saying you're not attracted to men."

"Okay, that's true. But, I just thought that you would have known if..." I had to drop that thought. How could I expect anyone to else to know if I'm straight when I'm not even clear on the subject?

Instead, I said, "I just have no idea where I'm supposed to start. I feel like everyone has paired off already, and that every route I try leads to a dead end."

Mom tried to comfort me, bringing up her favorite topic. "It's okay, Audrey. You don't have it easy, but it's not your fault. It's just because of the whole Asperger's thing."

Couldn't stand it any longer. "I don't have Asperger's," I said, firmly.

What followed was a long, increasingly heated debate that drove Dad and Rebecca away after a little while. In Mom's defense, I was diagnosed by Dr. Kosciuszko fourteen years ago. In my defense, I was undiagnosed by Angela last month while we were discussing her strategy for winning a poker tournament. I had to have something better than that, so I told her that I've been going out to clubs with my friends for the purpose of finding unfamiliar men to have sex with. There! Does that sound like something a person with Asperger's syndrome would do? No, but it certainly sounds like something an idiot would say to her religious mother.

She took a sharp, cutting tone as she ran through a list of things that she disapproved of regarding all this. It only took fifteen minutes, so I guess she just wasn't in better form today. Eventually, it culminated with her asking how long I was planning to keep this up before I told her.

"I was kinda hoping to save it for your deathbed," I said. "That way, you'd die of shock and wouldn't have to suffer any longer. So, really, it was more for you than me."

Mom wanted to know how many guys I'd slept with so far. "That depends," I said. "Will a high number or a low number make this conversation end faster?"

That line angered her enough to get her to walk off, furious. "If that's the way you feel, then I'll do you a favor. I'm never meddling in your life again. Happy? No, of course not! You'll be never happy!"

I was alone at the table now, having alienated the rest of my family into leaving me. Job well done. Seems I'm not always the mature one after all, huh? Welp, not much else for me to do here, I thought. Guess I may as well take my leave.

Before I struck out for Ridgeway, I made a couple of stops. I wanted to give my business to a little Mom'n'Pop corner store I used to visit every so often. The same posters in the windows from more than ten years ago are still up, faded to the point where the only colors remaining are faint blue and black. I was pleased to see they were still in business, but the entrance bore a sign reading "SORRY CLOSED ON SUNDAY$" in stick-on letters. The last S was shorter than all the other letters as it was really a dollar sign that was circumcised on both ends. Just down the street, there was a new gas station. I went there instead, and bought a soda and a candy bar. Perhaps it's for the best. All the candy bars in the other store probably have nice, appetizing coats of dust on the wrappers. I bet the Sour Patch Kids in there have been hanging around long enough to be getting regular prostate exams by now.

I drove about a half-mile to the school down the road. Something possessed me to bring my snack here. I probably assumed this would be a good place to eat in privacy. Got out of the car and looked around. There wasn't anyone else here. Not another car. I guess a Sunday evening in July is probably the best chance you have for a result like that. Even if I couldn't enter the building, this was the first time I've ever had free reign over the school grounds. All it requires for me to be in charge is a complete absence of other human life in the vicinity.

This was my high school, the building I spent more time in as a teenager than any other, save for my own home. Now it wasn't even a high school anymore. A new one was built on the other side of town and this place was then demoted to a middle school just a year or two after I graduated. The building had a nice, clean visage facing the road, but out in back everything was a rusty, crumbling wasteland of brown dust and broken mesh fences. I walked around to survey the damage. The tennis court is cracked from one side to the other with brown weeds sprouting out of every crevice. The bleachers and scoreboard were removed from the football field, probably brought over to the new school. The concession stand was now just a canvas for an amateur graffiti artist who calls himself either "FLIZ" or "PUR", I couldn't quite tell which. The plants by the walls are all overgrown and strangling the rivets out of the nearby benches. It feels more or less like a ruin. It was like all those years I'd spent here never really happened. The past doesn't exist anymore.

On the way home I thought about that photo I saw and the little girl in it. Even at that young age, she was looking forward to one day being old enough to have her first boyfriend. Even though she wasn't attracted to boys, she always wanted a boyfriend. There's nothing she wants more than for someone to spend time with her and make her smile and tell her she's beautiful.

That little girl only cares about three things: playing, watching TV, and her books. She watches television and reads because she doesn't have someone to play with. She's been a good girl and obeyed the rules. She thinks she deserves something for that. The path from that girl to the woman I am now is as clear as can be.

Mom texted me while I was driving back. Her message read, "what if u get an std? u could get aids!!!"

Once I got home, I wrote back, "Then I'll get to meet Elton John. I'll ask him to play 'Levon' for you."

Her text arrived about two hours after she said she'd never meddle in my life again.

Congratulations to everyone who took the "over" bet.

Last week at the laundromat, I took a look at the bulletin board for once. Normally I don't bother as I figure it'll all be nothing but a bunch of business cards for plumbers and repairmen. This time there was a little quarter of an 8½ x 11 in there, decked out in Helvetica and declaring:

poetryreading   julythetwentyfirst   blackchinaroom   fortyfoursiegelstreet eightpostmeridiem

They know what p.m. stands for! I thought this might be a good crowd, a more intellectual group. That's more my type. I really think the clubs aren't gonna work for me. I recently got the sneaking suspicion that the conversation-erasing loud music in clubs may be used as a measure to cut down on the number of people being slapped for saying horribly sexist things. Those people aren't the sort I should be among.

But, at a poetry reading, you have to be able to hear people speaking. You have to hear the person on stage. Just imagine someone at a podium reading a poem she wrote about how making an origami crane is like growing up as an only child, all the while the room is being shook by a pounding, speaker-eroding bass and a robot voice repeating, "TYRANNOSAURUS REX. TYRANNOSAURUS REX." That wouldn't be poetry at all. It would be performance art.

I took a note of it, and tonight I went. Zena was the only one who joined me, as everyone else was busy. That's funny: too busy for a poetry reading? That's the sort of activity people will usually move things around for.

The Black China Room is a coffee house with a lot of abstract paintings and scattered remnants of a pan-Orient motif that suggest it was once a Chinese restaurant. There were lots of couches and other cushioned spots for sitting. The atmosphere was pretty relaxed, like being in a rather large studio apartment. Zena and I sat down on a couch by a window, just in case I needed to make a quick getaway.

My traveling companion began asking whether or not this was really about poetry. "Is this just another attempt to meet a man who'll finally make a woman of you?"

I didn't like that. "I'm *already* a woman, thank you, and I don't care much for that expression even it is only figurative. Please don't say it like that. And, as to your question, yes."

"Hey," she said, "what do you think of that guy all the way in the back?" She was referring to a male sitting by himself on the furthest couch from the stage, looking like he could use some companionship. I didn't get a real good look at him before, but I knew he was there. I told Zena to take out her compact and watch him using the mirror.

"Why? Wouldn't it be easier to get up and walk by him for a better look?"

"You'll see. Trust me. Just talk to me like normal while you're waiting."

We commented on the atmosphere in the room for a little while. After two minutes of that, a stunning young lass walked past us with a coffee in each hand. In Zena's mirror, we could see her sit down next to the guy in back and hand him one of the coffees. Zena wanted to know how I could tell his girlfriend was in line getting coffee.

"Because that's how it always works," I said. "Every time. I'm not even convinced all those speed-dates were single."

I noticed a few people gathered around a table close to the stage. They were all holding copies of a book. I thought I should check this out, so I got up and went over.

At the table was one guy selling copies of his new self-published book of poems. I figured I could repeat my "diplomacy through purchase" gambit that netted me a screen-print of a steamroller. This way, a person who I don't even know might want to help me out if I needed it. Maybe the book will be a good conversation starter. Who knows? I bought a copy of his book and the other one that was on sale. He was very glad to make the sale to a stranger, as everybody else seemed to be folks he was already quite familiar with. I brought my new possessions back to the couch.

The second book was written by someone named Ewen Tavitt and is a single paragraph that lasts all the way from the first page to the last. It's made up of short sentences, about two-thirds of which begin with "I." Here is an excerpt:

I think Manchester should burn. Leonard Cohen is the man for me. I gave blood twice. I'll never grow another Hitler mustache. I would be able to fly if I were a bird. Vandalia, Illinois is a place. I gave you everything and this is how you repay me. There is an octopus in Germany that can predict the outcomes of soccer matches. I don't know how to read. I'm a snowman. N-44. Bingo. I will drink the blood of that Australian singer, then I will be invincible. I can't stay long, trust me, be strong. I'm watching my weight. Hey hey, I'm the Monkees. I like to say the word "zoo." I have legendary tonsils.

It goes on like that for thirty-six pages. One sentence on page 24 is just the word "want" repeated eighty-one times, followed by the word "drugs." Somehow, I figured that out before I was done with page 1. I flipped through it, skimming the sentences wherever my eyes landed. Was this serious or not? It was funny. If it was serious, it would be funnier. I didn't want anyone seeing that I was grinning and giggling at this, just in case it was meant to be taken seriously. I had to hold the book up just high enough so that it covered my mouth.

I kept scanning the room for the next fifteen minutes, searching for a single guy in my age range who wasn't with someone already. Zilcho. It's amazing how I can enter any public arena and it suddenly turns into practice for a three-legged race. Finally, a woman got up on stage. She was the first reader.

Her poem was called "Machine." It sounded like it was a condemnation of recent technological innovations and how they are supposedly replacing human interaction and romance. I distinctly remember seeing this person using a smartphone just seconds after I walked into the room. Reader after reader went to the mic and recited their poetry. Every last poem that I heard had "love" as its focal point: how great it is to find love, how the world needs more love, how breaking up is so terrible, how love is what makes the world go 'round. The sad thing is that I'm sure all of these people hate mainstream pop music, which is essentially the same thing, but marketable. For the sake of creativity, will someone read a poem about cleaning out the garage or faking one's own death for insurance money? For artsy types, these people didn't seem to care much for imagination.

To keep myself busy during the intermission, I flipped through the Ewen Tavitt book for some funny quotes I could read to Zena. She was already on her second latte and I wanted to see if I could make her do a spit-take. I arbitrarily picked out a few sections to read.

"Okay, Zena, how about this: 'My turtle is more masculine than your turtle, therefore I win. I think the Great Depression was bad, but kinda good. Ringo Starr invented the Rolling Stones. I want my last name back. I cried at my own funeral. You know who sucks? Roman emperors. I can make boats out of boots. Ocean Spray: Crave the Wave.'"

Because I was reading all of this for the first time, I couldn't help but chuckle. Zena was having trouble keeping her snickering quiet as well. We must have gotten a little out of hand because when I was able to regain my bearings, it was clear that everyone in the room was staring at us. The man taking the coffee orders stepped out from the behind the counter and approached us. His nametag had the word "Ewen" on it, just above the word "owner". Uh, hi, Ewen.

He saw that I was reading from his poem, and asked what was so funny. I am not good with easing tense situations.

"Sir, if it's any consolation, I also like to say the word 'zoo.'" I tried so hard not to smile, but failed.

He asked me what the hell I knew about culture anyway. I kindly pointed out that the Kandinsky reprint by the restroom was hung upside-down, and I know because it's pictured in an encyclopedia I own. He told me he hung it upside-down on purpose and also that the encyclopedia is wrong. I kindly pointed out that these explanations cannot both be true. He kindly pointed out that I am annoying and should leave.

Zena and I amscrayed and had dinner at a cheapo café a short walk down the street. I was pretty disappointed, because I'd hoped I would get along with some of the people there, but I felt like they were all on the same wavelength and I was on a completely different spectrum. I'd even be willing to give it another chance, but I'm pretty sure that Black China Room isn't willing to open its borders to me anymore.

I guess I don't really belong in that sort of (ugh, don't make me use that word… Alright, fine,) "scene." Outside of my own circle of friends, I don't feel at all comfortable in any group. I'm just odd: all of the drawbacks of being average without any of the advantages of being normal.

I don't know where I fit in. Meeting new people is like keeping a secret: I never want this scene or herd.

UPDATE. I had to go throw up after I made a conscious decision to refer to a group of friends and acquaintances with similar interests as a "scene." My mistake.

UPDATE 2. I had to puke again after that last update.

JUL 23 (THU)

Why do we still have to shave our legs? You're telling me that after all these millennia of living indoors, the human body still hasn't caught on and evolved past this? I've seen the limit to how long and thick these hairs get on males. Is that really supposed to be enough to keep us warm in the winter? That's like wearing a section of fishing net as a parka.

Got a book I ordered online in the mail yesterday. Was reading it when, apropos of nothing, I shouted out, "COME ON! THIS IS GETTING RIDICULOUS!" I have no idea why.

I lied. Of course I know why.

Anyhow, it's Fawn Clayton's autobiography. Been out for a few years now, but I never picked it up because I kept waiting for it to show up on bookstore shelves. I love being able to pick something up in a store, bring it to the register, pay, and take it home. The feeling of bringing home a new purchase is great: anticipation coupled with a guarantee that things are going to go well. You know it's already yours. This must be the modern-day equivalent of bringing home a dead animal, since we don't hunt for food anymore. Also, your clothes don't get quite as bloody (as long as it isn't the day after Thanksgiving.)

The book is pretty great so far. I'm only up to when Fawn was almost as old I am now, when Wax Dolls parted ways and she started gathering a new group of musicians for her first solo effort. I've always been impressed by the wide variety of subject matter in her lyrics. She never really wrote about love all that much. She didn't paint a world where the greatest tragedy that could happen is a break-up that lasted only as long as a four-minute song. Her favorite topic seemed to be being driven to the brink of insanity by an everyday deluge of minor annoyances. Now who can't identify with that?

I've been giving it some thought, and I decided to go for the ballroom dancing lesson Angela told me about. I signed up online today. However, I don't have anything nice to wear for it. After shelling out for the dance, the lesson, the rental car, and the hotel, I wasn't in any mood to rush out and buy a fancy dress, so I rang up Lynn instead, asking if she had anything I could borrow. She said she has a few things I could try on, so I paid her a visit.

I still had an irritating little speck in the back of my mind from Sunday that I couldn't get rid of. There was something I had to know. While I was trying on this blue number she felt looked good on me (we agreed to disagree but it was the best we could do with what she had,) I asked, "Remember back when we visited Natasha in the hospital and then we had that talk? Did you really think I was a lesbian or were you just joking?"

"That was months ago and you're still thinking about it? Audrey, I'm sorry. I didn't know it had upset you that much."

I told her I wasn't upset by that, but by what happened when I visited my family. Also, what Jeanette said on the last day of school. Lynn seemed to understand my concern now. She claimed she was never really sure, but she always suspected I might not be straight, just because I never seemed to show any interest in men. Plus, I did tell her as much in my own words. Well, point for her.

She continued, "You still never answered my question from before: what sort of guy do you like? I don't mean personality or whether or not he likes you back. I mean looks. There has to be an answer."

I honestly didn't know what answer I could give. I can't get turned on by looks alone. I just told her that it's something I have to judge on a case-by-case basis. "I sort of always thought that I'd know he was the right guy when I saw him. But, I guess that's kind of a childish fairy tale notion, isn't it?"

"AWWWW! That's so sweet!" Ah, Lynn. When you have me on the spot, I can always count on you to be distracted by something lovey-dovey.

It is pretty strange when you get right down to it. How many other people have this problem? How common is it for someone to be presented with pictures of all sorts of sexy males and females and feel completely indifferent to all of them? Am I straight? Am I asexual? Some other, rarer, stranger thing in-between?

All those years went by and I believed that I didn't need affection just because of that. I told myself that love wasn't for me and that I could go without. "Love isn't a necessity," were the words I lived by. I was a fool. It's humbling just to admit that much. I guess I can't have my words and eat them, too.

JUL 25 (SAT)

DAMMIT, WHAT AM I DOING? I threw down the Sudoku book Mom gave me three Hanukkahs ago. I came across it and couldn't help starting one of the puzzles, only to break free of its event horizon when it occurred to me that I was doing a Sudoku alone at home on a Saturday in July.

Well, genius, what the hell else are you gonna do? Rosi's on a camping trip with her family, Angela's in the California desert, and I know Lynn's going to be watching the game with her new guy. I probably shouldn't bother Zena for a while after dragging her to that fiasco on Tuesday. I even tried texting Natasha but she never got back to me. Do I really need them, though? I don't need to be accompanied to, oh I dunno, the restaurant down the street, do I?

You're a grown woman, I told myself. You're changing your clothes, you're going to that restaurant, you're sitting at that bar, and you're talking to at least one guy. If I don't keep pushing myself out into public, then I won't get anywhere.

186

So that's precisely what I did. An hour or so later, I found myself marching into Il Costo. I caught a glimpse of the bar: it was a frigging sardine can in there! I slid myself over into the bathroom to think things over. Do I really want to go out there? Hey, the bigger the crowd, the more anonymity, right? Fewer people will notice when things go wrong.

Calm, deep breaths. Now get back out there and talk to a few guys, Audrey.

It was still jam-packed. So many people. I walked over to the bar, looking for a spot to sit down but there wasn't one available. It was a horseshoe bar, meaning that it's the type that makes a U-turn. And so am I. I went back in the direction I came from and right out the door. Oh well, there isn't anywhere to sit, I thought. That was all I needed to throw in the towel.

I stood outside by the door for a few seconds. Then I walked. I walked over to the side of the parking lot and took a sharp left once I got to the edge. I had to go back. If I'm not going to try, then I don't deserve sympathy. I told myself I'm going to go right back in, and I'm not leaving until I talk to at least one guy. After one complete orbit of the lot, I walked back to the entrance. I was determined not to run away from this.

Nice to see the old place again. Just the way I left it.

The bar was full enough that I had to stand by and wait for a stool. Very uncomfortable, leaning against the wall by myself, looking anxious. Luckily I have enough experience in that already. I'm an expert anxious-looker. A married-looking couple departed, and I finally got a spot next to a woman in a dark blue top with a face caked in a gram or two of swimming pool-colored eye shadow, enough to take a core sample. That meant I had an empty seat on my left side. Someone's gotta take it sooner or later, right?

Sure enough, I was right. In under a minute, a slightly-younger-than-myself gent had parked his bearded self right next to me. Well, as much as I dislike facial hair, I'm not in any spot to pass up an opportunity. And I wouldn't have, if one had been there. For the entire length of his stay, he was alternately watching the game on the big screen and texting on his phone. I did steal just enough of a glance to make out the words "awww! luv u so much" on the screen. That's life. This is life, these are life, those are life.

There was a menu at my spot. I decided to order a bowl of lobster bisque and a glass of water. It's not a good idea to buy something every time I want to go out, so I have to keep it cheap-like.

The whole time I ate, I kept my eyes in "scanning" mode, searching the other side of the bar for anybody who could be an open target. There seemed to be only two close to my age, talking with each other the whole time. One was obscured from my view by a support beam. I was determined to make eyes at the other one, but he managed to look in every direction except mine for the duration of my meal. It was just about when I reached the bottom of the bowl that the two of them made tracks.

The woman to my right must have been keeping track of the situation. Without prompting, she patted me on the shoulder and said, "Hey, you'll get 'im next time. Good things happen." She got up and walked out. Thanks, I think.

If only she had stuck around thirty seconds more, then she would have seen how prophetic her words were: the bartender handed me a glass of red wine. He said it was sent by the man in the striped polo shirt on the other end of the bar. Seriously?

Well, any port in a storm. I didn't want the wine, but I drank it anyways. (Yeah! The whole thing! Seriously! I hated it!) It wasn't the wine that mattered, it was how I got it. Someone sent me a drink. To think, I almost didn't even sit down. I almost left after doing nothing but use the bathroom. Courage pays off. I could not see my potential suitor anywhere at the bar, however.

When the bartender came by again, I asked for my bill. I gave him about a thirty percent tip, just so I wouldn't have to get coins involved. I then asked where the guy in the striped polo shirt was. Turns out he was on my side of the bar, way over by the wall. Ah, now I could spot him. He was obscured by a rather large man on his right.

Audrey, this may be it. He's definitely interested. To think, this only happened because I was able to work up the courage to come back.

I made my way over and scoped him out for a little while. Young guy. Didn't seem at all like someone who'd be interested in me, or vice versa. But, you take what you can get. And who knows, maybe he'd turn out to be sweet after all. ("Sweet" the way a person is sweet, not the way that everything that a college kid sees is "sweet.")

I caught a glimpse of some letters tattooed on his right arm. As I got closer, I could see they were Roman numerals. Ah, now there's a conversation-starter. After a quick decipher, it came out to be a date, most likely his birthday. Lovely. Now I had an ice-breaker and a pretty good line I could use.

I asked him if that was a date on his arm. He said "Yeah, my birthday."

I asked him if he'd like to have a date on his other arm.

"Huh?" he replied.

He didn't get it, so I had to take his left arm. I was hoping I wouldn't have to spell that one out.

"Hey, I'm not really interested, alright?" What? How did I screw this one up?

"But, you sent me that drink…"

"NO! I didn't buy you anything! Are you crazy? HEY! BAR GUY! Didn't I tell you to give that wine to the chick in the blue shirt?"

The bartender thought for a second, finally saying "Oh, you mean the other one? She left before I got the wine, so I thought you meant this one." (I'm "this one," it would seem.)

Striped Polo Guy pointed at my shirt. "Does this look like *blue* to you?"

"I'm sorry, sir, it does. I'm protanopic."

Polo Guy was livid now. "Hey, I didn't ask what God you pray to, just LEARN YOUR DAMN COLORS!" So this is the guy I thought wanted me, but it turns out he doesn't. Oh no. What a shame.

The bartender tried to explain that he's blue-purple colorblind, and, with the departure of the woman next to me, my lilac shirt left me the only "chick in blue" he could see. So I drank that wine for nothing. I was prepared to walk out right then and there, but then I stopped.

I made another U-turn and went back to Polo Guy, still cussing out the bartender. I looked across the counter and asked if his ID had been checked. The bartender told me that Polo Guy is in here all the time and they checked it before. I insisted he check it again. Then I pointed to the tattoo, saying "He told me this is his birthday. He's only nineteen and his ID is fake. If you don't believe me, use your phone to look up the numbers on the internet." Then I left.

So, I guess I fulfilled my minimal obligations: I went back, I sat at the bar, and I talked to a guy. Sure, I didn't initiate it, it didn't end well, and he didn't even want me near him. Bludgeoned by the colostomy bag of reality yet again.

JUL 27 (MON)

Back in April, not long after this all began, Zena said something about knowing a concept to be true but never realizing it simply because the thought never occurs to you. All other paths are unlikely, so the only remaining possibility is almost certainly the correct one, even if the facts aren't there in front of you.

I'm nearly done reading Fawn's book. I learned a lot about her and her songs and career path, but one thing stood out to me as a revelation.

Publicly, she had never been in a relationship during her career, and considered herself celibate. She lost her virginity at fifteen, and grew to dislike sex because of how her boyfriends treated her. In the book, though, she admits that during the recording of her fourth solo effort, she was in an intimate relationship with the singer for her opening act. She doesn't explain why she never admitted it. Maybe it was an image thing.

I always had this feeling that if she could make it then I could, too. I guess in my heart I knew it was too good to be true. But, because I couldn't confirm it, I wasn't aware of it. Would've been nice if somebody passed along the word about "You don't need love to be happy" meaning "…but if an opportunity comes along *for me*, I still get to take it." That might have come in helpful ten years ago.

Also, she wrote more than her fair share of songs about arson. Never caught on to that before, either.

I called Mom today. I thought I'd apologize for what happened last weekend. Getting caught up in the moment can cause you to say some rude things every so often. She apologized for overreacting, but she still doesn't want me having sex with anyone that I'm not familiar with. I just told her what she wanted to hear.

Mom never wants to talk about sex, and I'm willing to oblige her. She did ask again how many guys I've slept with. I relented and told her it was zero, that males still won't even give me a second look. She gave me usual bromides, it's just not my time yet, and so on.

There was one thing I couldn't let go, though. I pleaded with her, "If you were me, if you had just turned thirty and had never even been on a date, wouldn't you want to do something about it? Wouldn't you feel like you were missing out all that time? Can't you see things from my angle?"

"Trust me, I'm fifty-five. I may not have been in your situation, but I'm old enough to have an acute understanding of what you're feeling."

There ya go: the old "I'm older, so I automatically know better" dodge. (If only I could find a 56-year-old to take my side.) We're approaching this from two clearly different angles. However, if there's one thing I've learned from geometry, it's that it doesn't matter how acute you are, it doesn't make you right.

JUL 28 (TUE)

Raining out.

190

Plunked myself down on the couch for a nap around one-ish. It's the same couch that Willow and Wes would get busy on once in a blue moon, a moon that I might catch an unwanted glance of if I walked in at the time. I still plan on having it incinerated, but until that day comes I figure a quick snooze is okay when I get the urge.

I was wondering if it would be safe enough to take my pants off, when a knock on the door brought a swift end to that notion. It was Willow. She was crying. Oh my, let me guess: the kid dropped the caterpillar, I thought. She didn't ask to come in, she just did.

I asked what happened between her and Ronald McWallbanger. The event that set it all in motion was Willow being laid off from her job two days ago, so she doesn't have a steady source of income anymore. Then Wes provoked a fight over it. Today, he brought a girl from his job to their apartment and announced that she would be moving in, since she could afford to and Willow could not. Turns out they'd been seeing each other for quite a while now. Willow was no good to him without her money, so he decided to use this opportunity to drop her.

Damn. I couldn't help hugging her after that. She needed me, and she came to me of all people for comfort.

"What are you hugging me for? Do I look like I need a fucking hug? I need a place to live, freak!" Ah, what a touching half-second that was.

I'll cop to it, I've played the martyr every so often as I've related my experiences of the past few months. I've tried to be fair, but sometimes you just have to vent and let your true feelings out. Even if nobody else sees it, it helps to put your honest thoughts in writing. Makes it easier to cope, and it beats a lot of other methods that some people use for letting off steam. I'm not so blind as to think that the world really is out to get me, though, even if it feels that way at times.

However, I still maintain that I have far more reason to be upset than Willow does. 'Tis better to have loved and lost, and all that. And yet, the tears and distress brought on by a break-up elicit gallons of sympathy, whereas my thirty loveless years are seen as a sitcom punch line. Between the two of us, it's the one who had it all and lost it who no one would dare laugh at or slap with a crass, mean-spirited "Suck it up and get over it."

Oh dear, that's me on the cross again. "Hey! Idiots! Are you gonna help me out here or not? I can't nail in *both* my hands by myself!"

To me, this reads as a reinforcement of the notion that people who aren't sexually active are somehow inferior and therefore less deserving of sympathy. Or, maybe people just don't want to hear sob stories that they can't identify with. I guess that would explain my feelings as well.

I asked if she wanted anything to drink. She said she didn't, as she was certain I didn't have any alcohol. I fetched two glasses of water, just in case. I get very quiet when faced with these tough spots. I feel nothing I say will help, so it's best to just listen, and let the other person know you're there to hear them out.

"Aren't you going to say anything?" she spat.

"I don't think I should say anything. I tend to unwittingly say insensitive things in sensitive moments. It's practically a hidden talent." I took a sip of water. "I'd rather hear what you have to say."

"Well, how about a little encouragement, then? You know, tell me that it's going to get better."

"You don't need me to tell you that. You've already heard all those lines before." There were a few seconds of sniffling, before I added, "Why don't you just tell me how you feel. Whatever it is, just say it."

Willow said she felt used. She felt like she wasted her time on somebody who didn't love her. She wanted that time back.

She surveyed the landscape. "I see you lined up your CDs. Alphabetically, of course. How long did it take you to get those up after I left?" Then she noticed that I still had that bike I rescued stashed in what used to be her room. "How do you even ride that thing? You know that's a kid's bike, right?"

"Yeah, I was tipped off by the fluorescent multi-colored camo pattern. Luckily, the previous owner was a big kid and I'm a little adult." (Well, I'd like to think I'm more than just a little.)

The tears had stopped now. Willow looked down at her shoes, still tracking a little water across the floor I might add, and said, "I always knew you were smart, but you really hit the nail on the head when you decided to stay single."

"Well, I didn't choose a life of celibacy so much as I resigned myself to it. But now I'm fighting back."

"Not worth it, Audrey. They're all scum. I'm thinking of giving it all up and doing what you did: a life of solitudy." Yeah, that. Precisely.

I tend to say the wrong thing a lot. Perhaps it's because I have a hard time identifying with other people and relating to their problems. This was an exception. I told her that she can't make the same choice I did. My self-imposed exile was a massive, unforgivable mistake that cost me years that I'll never get back. I had to convince her not to give in just because she was miserable now.

"Audrey, I didn't mean that literally."

Oh. Okay.

She sat back down, nose pointed at a downward angle, eyes pointed at me. "You know, anytime you want to say I can stay here again is fine with me," she intoned.

Willow's parents live all the way over in Flottsham, next to Railhead. Neither of us has a car and I don't know if there's anyone else here in Ridgeway she could stay with. I could be her only hope right now. She was at my mercy.

All my life, I've felt like I've had no control. I've always felt small, pushed around, unable to stand up for myself. So what am I going to do about it? I could have said that she could stay here again, or I could have put some steel in my spine and told her to hit the bricks. And why the hell not? She's still behind on her half of the rent payments, and even now she's talking down to me. In my own home, no less.

I could have stood up for myself and taken a big step towards becoming a stronger, more well-adjusted adult. But, this wasn't the time for that. This wasn't about fetching the remote. Somebody genuinely needed my help, so I agreed to let her stay here.

I let her know she could stay for a couple of weeks, but not forever. If she still can't find a new job, she'd have to leave. If she has to live with her parents again, then that's how it would be. If she's able to pay her half of the rent again, she'll be welcome to come back, even if I have a new roommate.

She thanked me and seemed like she genuinely meant it. She said I'm a saint. "You're St. Audrey," she said. So I've heard.

UPDATE. Willow asked if I'd seen the gas cap from Wes' first car. I said I didn't know, even though I'm now ninety-nine percent sure that was the unidentifiable object I disposed of only hours after she moved out. She said it was no big deal to her, but Wes was always looking for it. Sentimental value. Oopsie!

JUL 29 (WED)

Something extraordinary happened today. Couldn't believe it. Somebody sent me a drink. No, not like what happened at Il Costo the other night, this time it was for me. Even better, it wasn't a real drink, so I didn't have to slam my hand against the counter to draw my attention away from the taste. It was a "drink" on the online dating site that Rosi enrolled me in when I had to sign up for the first speed dating event. It's basically a wordless message, an alert that someone who saw my profile is interested in me. I've actually been sending out messages to guys on that site from time to time, but I haven't gotten a thing back from any of them. This time, someone else made the first move. Now we're getting somewhere. Never thought I'd say this but, sure, I'll have a drink! Who's buyin'?

The guy in question goes under the username "ca°ean'ce°bee'." Haven't seen one with degree signs and apostrophes in it before. Well, I have a pretty good idea what his real name is: Jericho. His profile states that he's Jewish, and if you turn the letters into their corresponding numbers (A is 1, B is 2, etc.) and take a quick peek at the atlas, then it gives the coordinates for the city of Jericho, just north of the Dead Sea. I suppose he could have grown up there, but I suspect he's a clever guy named Jericho. I just wonder if he's clever enough to decipher "yerduA0713." There's a headscratcher. (Hint: It's spelled backwards! Don't tell your friends, though. Let them figure it out for themselves!)

The protocol for this seems to be that I send a "drink" in return to let him know it's mutual. That is what I did. I can't be too choosy, after all. Neither can he, it seems. His profile lists "Doesn't matter" for everything under what he's looking for in a mate. Doesn't exactly make ya feel special. I guess he could be like me, just hoping to get acquainted with some people and gauge them based on face-to-face conversation and interaction. Come to think of it, I did leave all those spaces blank on my page, too, except that for age I chose "24 to 40". Though, in the write-in section I was tempted to write, "No dumbasses, please." I decided that wasn't necessary, as "dumbass" isn't anyone's idea of an endorsement (I hope.)

Angela is back from her trip to California. She told me all about it on another long car ride. This one ended up bringing us to a carnival in Rehoboth. It was the normal sort of carnival: flashing lights and music devouring the air, creating a tiny meteorological enclave where night doesn't come. Games you can't possibly win without divine intervention. Booth workers deep-frying and sugarcoating any artificial food that the FDA lets escape from a heart-attack factory. And, of course, everyone holding hands.

I loved carnival games when I was a kid, but like most other things, the gloss wore off once I was old enough to figure out what was really going on. Ange ponied up for one immediately. It was a dart-throwing game, and she could not overcome the odds. However, Ange paid for seven darts, which automatically comes with a "medium-sized" prize whether you win or not. She got a stuffed fish and gave it to me. What to name it? When Ange was young, she had a goldfish and named it Paddington Bear, after her favorite book. So, I shall name my fish The Doubleday Roget's Thesaurus in Dictionary Form. I'll call him "The" for short. ("The" as in "The," not "Thesaurus.")

They had my favorite ride there: the Scrambler. But, I've been on that thing dozens of times before. I wanted something new. That's how I'm supposed to be living from now on. Ange had a suggestion for a ride we could try. It was the one known as Zipper. It's essentially a five-story-tall construction crane festooned with cages for the riders that flip upside-down at zeniths high enough to ensure death were you to jump from them. This had the potential to be the most horrifying thing I'd ever done. I'd seen this ride at nearly every carnival I've ever been to and had never even entertained the possibility that I could ride it. Well, now I was going to.

There was a sign at the entrance: "No single riders allowed on this ride." Friggin' hell. You can't even go on certain amusement park rides unless you have somebody with you.

We were – strapped is the wrong word – barred in behind a big metal beam which would serve as our seat belt. The door closed. We were now in a cage-like capsule without very much in the way of a view. This near-death experience didn't seem all that bad so far.

Approximately three seconds before the ride started moving, Ange said, "You know these things aren't regulated, right?" Oh, come on. Nice try. Does she really think that I'm going to fall for that?

Here's the abridged version of what happened next: I screamed. I shouted "NO!" a lot. I kept my eyes closed for the entire second half. It was pretty much a time-lapse re-enactment of the time my family brought me to see my cousin compete in the "Mr. Railhead" contest.

When we were released from our cage, Ange told me that her remark backfired and she ended up scaring herself instead. I admire her powers of concentration. It took my vertigo-addled gray matter a few minutes to even remember what she was talking about. I must have a gyroscopic stomach because I didn't feel the least bit sick coming off of that ride. My heart, on the other hand, was vibrating like a chihuahua whose warranty expired two days prior.

Ange wanted to play another game, which I was now onboard for since it was her treat. She picked the one where you fire one-hundred BBs at a 4 x 6" card with a red star in the center. The idea is to "knock out" the star with your scattershot machine gun fashioned to look like something out of a poorly-researched Western.

Her method seemed to be to fire one BB at a time and make a ring around the star.

Mine was to surrender to the unfair nature of carnival games and just go nuts trying to pulverize the target for fun. I noted that there were no prizes to be seen at this booth. Perhaps shooting them just proves to be too much temptation for the kiddies to handle. Or, it could be that belligerent adults will pay for a second round, then turn it into a game of "If I can't have one of those giraffes, nobody can!"

Ange carefully tried to squeeze out one projectile at a time, taking as much time as she liked. Perhaps her covert strategy was to get on the booth operator's nerves to the point where he'd finally give her a prize just to get her to go away. Having already unloaded my weapon, I received my consolation prize in the form of my target. I think I'll hang it up when I get home. I don't have one of these yet.

I don't remember how we got into it, but on the way back to Ridgeway, Ange told me that she was comfortable with me asking her anything at all. No matter how personal, it would be okay. She's known me forever and she wants open and honest dialogue whenever possible, complete transparency.

I told her I felt that way, too, and that she's welcome to ask me anything, anytime, and I'd give her the honest truth. In fact, I told Angela right then and there to ask me the one thing she always wanted to know about me. I wouldn't be offended in the least. I'd be honored.

"Well," she said, "I had that question answered for me already. For the longest time, I wondered if you were straight or not. Until we met up and did that yoga thing and you asked me for help getting laid, I didn't know."

Okay. So, altogether that makes Angela, Lynn, Jeanette, and... who else? Oh yeah, my mother! All of them thought I was a lesbian. Nobody seems to have any trouble with making that assumption.

It can't be that unusual, can it? To be in my position, I mean. Everyone seems to figure that there's another reason at work here. It could be that some people just refuse to believe that not everybody finds love at least once in their lives. It shakes their belief in a fair and just world too much. Maybe I should just give up again and see if the lesbian mafia will take me. I could be their token heterosexual member. My handle would be "Straight A", because I'm straight, my name begins with A, and I got good grades in school.

Hell, what was I thinking? "Straight A" is a *much* better code name than "Virginia Plain."

UPDATE. I've heard it can confuse a pet to change its name, but I'm thinking the fish should go by "Thé" (pronounced 'tay') instead. I don't think he'll voice any objections.

JUL 30 (THU)

Did the shopping again. Thursday is a good day for it, especially in the mornings. No crowds getting in the way. I suppose that in a supermarket, you don't really need an entire crowd to keep you from getting around, just one person who insists on walking a shopping cart straight down the dead center of the aisle with the precision and determination of an obsessive-compulsive tortoise (and the speed, as well.) People with shopping carts should be allowed to enter stock car races. They could go as slow as they want and still always win because no one would ever get by them.

On the other hand, there is a drawback to shopping at the off-peak hours: there was nobody to talk to again. Thought I'd give another go at trying to flirt with a perfect stranger. Not a good crowd at all. Everyone fell into one of three categories: too old, too young, or too female. Well, I suppose there was that pair of young primates in tank tops and baseball caps. One was using the motorized shopping cart even though it was clear that he had no trouble walking, and used the word "epic" about twelve times in the span of two minutes. The other seemed to have an irrational fear of laundry detergent and a ninety decibel laugh that brought to mind the image of Paul Prudhomme choking on his own tongue in a reverb chamber. And to think, those were my best options. The picture's lookin' a little bleaker every day.

Maybe it's better that way. I have no idea what to say. I'd probably just come out with something like, "Is that grapefruit juice? I had that once!" or "How about these tabloids, huh? 'Father Of World's Oldest Man To Re-Marry Despite Son's Objections.' Crazy stuff, huh?"

On my way to the register I happened to come across Miriam, of all people. I went over to say hello and have an impromptu chat, just so we could each catch up on how uneventful summer has been for the other one. It's always good to unexpectedly run across someone I get along with. Miriam, in particular, was a breath of fresh air given our unspoken common bond. I was feeling a little glum before, but it was comforting to know that one of my peers was on the same page as me, except her page was about twenty volumes further in.

While I was immersed in conversation, a man holding a couple of frozen dinners stepped in and said that the frozen foods section was out of steak tips, so he got roast beef instead. He put his right arm around Miriam, who introduced him as Parker.

I shook his hand. "Oh, uh, nice to meet you, Parker. So, how long have you two known each other?"

"We'll be married fourteen years next month," she replied. Okaaaayyy... Even though this made all the sense in the world, I was more confused than ever.

Had to find out, so I asked. "Say, Miriam, remember back when you said we 'have to watch out for each other'? I've been pondering on that one for a while, and I can't really figure out what you meant by it."

"You know, the manga," was her response. As strange as it sounds, it seems that Miriam is actually a fan of Japanese cartoons from way back. She even met Parker at an anime convention. Those books she said she saw in my drawer weren't the ones Zena gave me, but those two volumes of *Yoichi-san no Hanafuda* that I had stashed away.

"What secret did you think I was talking about?" she asked.

"I honestly had no idea," I said dishonestly. We bid our farewells and I went to the check-out line.

Come to think of it, Miriam has about twenty years on me. She was almost definitely having sex before I was even born. The idea that... well... It was unlikely, but not impossible. I guess I should have been rational enough not to believe something just because I wanted to feel better. I guess I also should have realized that just because she's usually "Principal Canada" doesn't mean she isn't also a "Mrs. Canada."

Later in the day, I had an appointment with my psychiatrist. It was good to confess again. I wanted to tell her all the things that have been going on in my head and in my life, but my appointments are really just check-ups, only fifteen minutes long, once every two or three months. They're mostly for determining whether or not I need any changes in my medication.

But, despite all the hubbub, there was one thing I wanted to discuss above all. For once, it wasn't sex. I asked if it was possible that I didn't have Asperger's syndrome. Maybe I was misdiagnosed since everyone was certain that I had to have some sort of disorder just because I'm not, for lack of better terminology, "normal." I know Dr. Kosciuszko has a much better handle on all this than I do. I don't really have any ground to stand on when I question her, since I don't know anything about psychology compared to her. Still, ever since I talked to Angela about it on that phone call, I feel like there could be a mistake.

On another topic, I told her that I think my medication isn't actually helping me, that it's only suppressing my emotions. Sure, without it I was inconsolable but if it "levels out" my mood, then is it possible that it's preventing me from being happy as well? She wanted to know if I felt it was causing me any problems.

"Well, I've been taking it for about ten years," I said. "I may have felt my eyes get a bit watery in some extreme cases, but I haven't out-and-out cried for about the same period of time. That can't be healthy, can it? I think that if something's causing me to deny my emotions, that it'll all come flooding back eventually." In addition to that, I never really feel happy, at least never for more than an hour or two. Perhaps the same pills that limit my sadness could be limiting my joy as well.

I suggested that it might be worth the risk to stop taking my medication, and that the happy times might outweigh the misery. If I can't risk having a few bad times, then I might never have any good times, either.

The doctor thought this was a pretty brash decision and that it could have some very dangerous immediate effects. I guess I can't argue with that. So, in light of this, I asked if there was anything she could prescribe that would actually make me happy. She told me she'd come back to me on that.

In the wake of that "drink" I sent, I decided that I should write to the male who could possibly be named Jericho. According to the site, if someone sends a drink and you send one back, then that is a green light for sending a message to the other person's account. So who says it has to be him who writes first?

I sent a note to him, just letting him know that I was interested in getting to know a little more about him. Done all I can do there, just gotta wait. I know I've said this before, over and over, but it's not over.

AUG 02 (SUN)

Saturday: The day of the dance. I decided to drive into Boston, rather than take the train. I figured it would be easier this way, because I packed a suitcase and had Lynn's dress on a hanger, wrapped in plastic. I didn't want to have to go toting all that around on the train and the subway.

The hotel I stayed in was rather nice. It had all the amenities that I didn't need. Better to have it and not need it, and so forth. The TV had an interesting selection, including a few channels that were just background noise. One was an endless loop of palm trees blowing in the breeze at night, accompanied by the sound of waves breaking on the shore. Look, it was Saturday afternoon, okay? What other choice did I have? It was either golf, cooking shows, or palm trees.

The lesson was not hard at all. I didn't come with a partner, so they paired me up with someone named Ethan. He was really nice to me. We had some friendly chit-chat, I don't recall the bulk of it but we got along pretty well. I somehow let slip that I like manga, and he mentioned he did as well. Not the same genres that I like, of course, but it seemed like a good start. I felt we were starting off on the right foot. (Well, one of us was, anyway. It was ballroom dancing and somebody had to lead.)

It took a while for things to get going, though. The instructor was having a bit of trouble with her wireless headset. She couldn't wander outside of a circle with a radius of about five feet, lest she suddenly become inaudible. The tech guy on duty never really got the issue settled, so she had to conduct a dance class from one end of the gymnasium only. I was at the other. It was like trying to learn the Twist from a lawn sprinkler across the street.

The foxtrot was the easiest for me. I caught on immediately. In my mind I pictured two right angles with overlapping arcs, forming a square with a football-shape inside. This was a cinch, or so it would have been were it not for my long stride constantly going one half-step further than it should have. Even though my timing was right, I was still messing it up because I have trouble taking normal-sized steps. Feet got tangled and a lot of tripping occurred, with nobody falling down. (Be thankful for the little things.)

200

I adjusted to it soon enough, though. I just needed to be more aware of the length of my steps. The lesson was two hours total and we were given the basic run-through of three different dances. Once it was over, I asked Ethan if he'd trip the wire fantastic with me that night at the ball. He said he was looking forward to it.

I didn't know anyone at the dance. I hadn't even thought of that until I arrived. Anxiety started forming in my stomach, but I had to keep going forward. I would forge ahead and not let my fears get the better of me.

I waited around for twenty minutes, my eyes trained on the door. I waited for Ethan, the one person who I'd know, to show up. When he did, he had a couple of guys with him. Ah, that's why he didn't have a partner. He came with his pals.

I took some time to give him some breathing room, maybe let him have some other dances first. I had a lot to drink, as the only beverage available was ice water. Yeah, they really did do this thing on the cheap. I probably drank about six cups, which isn't out of the ordinary for me. I usually drink a lot of water at home. Plus, it was really hot in there.

When I finally came over to his table, he seemed surprised to see me, as if he didn't really think I'd have the guts to show up. I asked if he was ready for a foxtrot, but he told me he was going to wait for a while and that I should come back later. Fair enough. Now that my schedule was clear for a little while, I had some time to stake out the territory. There were some chairs lined up against a wall, a few populated by the butts of some guys who looked all dressed up but with nowhere to tango. Alright, I thought, time to pick a wallflower or two.

Went up to the first guy and asked if he'd like to dance. He said he was just waiting for his partner to come out of the bathroom. Oh. Understandable enough. She might be the jealous type.

I spent the next few minutes trying to work the room, seeking out strangers and asking if they'd dance with me. I was pretty good, really getting beyond my shyness. I didn't have any problem with it because I figured there was no commitment involved. It would only last a few minutes and then they'd never have to see me again. One of them would have to take me up on my offer sooner or later, right?

The second guy I talked to said he wasn't there to dance. He was just taking pictures. He wasn't doing professional photography or anything, just a few snapshots with his phone. Ummm, okay…

The third guy said he wasn't in the mood for dancing. Why was he here?

The fourth said, "I'm not interested, thanks."

The fifth simply said, "Sorry."

The sixth told me he was just on his way out.

Around this time I thought I could use a visit to the bathroom.

I didn't really need to go to the bathroom. I just stood there in the stall and thought to myself, tried to give myself a pep talk. C'mon, Audrey, you can do this. So a bunch of guys who didn't seem to have anyone to dance with all turned you down. That doesn't mean you're going to have that same luck for the rest of the night. Besides, you still have Ethan. He said he'd dance with you later, didn't he?

I wanted to kill some time until "later" came around. I took some deep breaths. I kept telling myself "You can do this. Stop worrying. You worry too much. This will work out." It was more a mantra than a convincing argument, but it kept me busy inside that stall.

Ethan wasn't at the table with his two friends from earlier. I found him on the dancefloor. I sat back at a chair against the wall and watched him for a couple of dances. I got my phone from my purse: it had been fifty minutes since I spoke to him last. Close enough. He's already on the floor, so I may as well make my move.

I strode up to him with purpose. My head was held as high as I could muster. Once the song was had ended, I gave him a tap on the shoulder and asked if I could cut in.

Throughout this diary, I've been paraphrasing the quotes as best as I can remember them. I'm pretty good at recalling conversations as they happened, even if it's not word-for-word. But, I doubt I'll ever forget the exact words I heard next: "You know, just because we took the lesson together doesn't mean we have to dance together."

I was surprised by this, to say the least. "Well, then," I said, defeated, "thank you for a lovely time." I went to the back of the room to vanish into the background for a few moments so nobody would see me leave right away.

I walked back to the subway station.

I went down the stairs.

I waited for the next train for twelve minutes.

The subway didn't go all the way back to my stop at this time of night. (It was only about nine. What the hell is wrong with this city?) I got as far as I could before moping my way back to street level and catching a cab. The ride was only five dollars, so I tipped two bucks, an extra twenty percent for wasting the driver's time with such a short ride.

Back in my hotel room, I took a bath. Might as well appreciate the uninterrupted flow of hot water while I have the chance. When that was over, I put on clean underwear and turned on the TV like it was just another night. It didn't work.

I lied face-down on the bed. I cried. Not just tearing up a little, I actually cried. Despite my medication's best efforts, for the first time in ten years I cried.

This isn't even about sex anymore. This isn't about men or romance or love, either. This is about me.

Is it possible that I'm even more undesirable than I thought? Am I really so repulsive that nobody will even share a dance with me? The more I try, the more ground I feel I'm losing. How can it be this hard? What the hell is wrong with me? I'm garbage. I must be.

In an emotional sense, it was the worst night of my life.

Today: I didn't bring my white noise machine with me, so I slept with the palm tree loop on. Packed up everything immediately once I woke up. Just threw it all in the car and set off for home. All day, I've just been going around like a ghost, like the air is just passing through my body. I'm not even here.

It's that feeling again. It's been a decade but I remember it perfectly now: the feeling that everyone and everything is out to get me. I didn't feel this way when I was suppressing it all. It was unhealthy, but at least I wasn't aware how unhappy I was.

On my way home, I saw a liquor store that was open. It was that magical window of time on Sundays when it's not immoral to sell alcohol in Massachusetts. I pulled into the lot, marched in, and bought a single bottle of beer. I forget the name. It began with H. I figured today was probably an ideal time to become a drinker in an official capacity.

Once I was home, I was only able to get through half of it. I didn't get sick or tipsy, I just hated the way it tasted. No way am I gonna get used to this. It was like somebody stuffed an old wallet into a blender and set it to "liquefy." It had no effect on me. I didn't feel better. It's not worth it.

AUG 03 (MON)

I'm starting to think this isn't going to happen. Looking back, it's been three months and I'm exactly where I was when I started. Not even a single date. I remain completely pure, immaculate. Vinyl enthusiasts want *Zenyatta Mondatta* remastered and re-released on my fingerprints.

Pretty boring day. I brought that tablet Rosi gave to me to the park. Those things must be made for the indoors because outside the screen was still very hard to read, even though it was partly cloudy. I tried to take a photo of myself, but I all could make out on the display was a shiny white triangle which was my nose.

Once I got home, I attempted a few more snapshots in the more photography-friendly indoors. Stomach-turning. From now on, I refuse to be photographed without the supervision of a make-up artist, a hair stylist, and an undertaker. That one kinda sorta okay-ish pic that Rosi snapped for the speed-dating site was still in the tablet's photo gallery. Hey, wasn't I planning on trying that again?

I searched the internet and found a new company that organized these events, and they didn't require that I create a profile or upload a picture or any of that crap. All they needed was some standard info and my credit card number. It took me only about five minutes total, and I'm now registered for another speed-dating event next week. It requires me to go to Boston again, though.

On its website, the company touts itself as "A way for young professionals to meet and hopefully find the right one! Acclaimed and award-winning, we've been operating in the Boston area for two decades! We're your solution for finding dates without having to sort through the riff-raff!" (For "professionals" they sure use a lot of exclamation points.)

Well, I'm not a professional but I'm not riff-raff, either. I notice ninety percent of these companies use words in their names like "Elite," "Exclusive," "Professional," "Successful." Knock it off and just own up to it: "Rich." It's the little things like that, repeated again and again, that bring me down. Death by a thousand papercuts. It helps reinforce the notion that I just don't fit in anywhere and that my options for finding love are not quite what you'd call numerous. Well, should anybody ask if I'm a professional, I'll lie. I'll make up a good one, airtight and plausible. Something like, "Yes."

I didn't feel right, though. Something was off. Is this really a viable solution? For the next hour, I had this nagging sensation in my heart, like I had just wasted money on something I didn't want. I picked up the tablet again. I had to do some research.

Found my way to a tourism website. I typed in A-M-S-…

Learned some interesting things. Amsterdam's city flag is a luscious red background with a black censor bar bearing three crosses resembling the letters "XXX". Really. That is the flag of Amsterdam. (Oh, how cute, notebook! You think I'm joking!) I know that it wasn't created with that intention, but maybe it's time to at least consider a redesign, huh?

"XXX." Thirty. Once again, it's all about the letters.

I kept searching site after site until I finally found what I wanted: there are male sex workers as well. The site I found claimed they work in clubs for the most part and are estimated to make up about ten percent of the market.

I went to look up prices on flights to Amsterdam. I'm thinking it may be time for me to look over this as an option. Aer Lingus has a pretty good price, but if I have to do a layover in Ireland, they might confiscate my birth control. They treat the stuff like anthrax over there.

It's too expensive, though. I don't know when I'd have the time. It's such a hassle getting a flight and a hotel and packing and lining everything up and...

Yeah, I guess I'm talking myself out of it already, aren't I? I think I had better sleep on this one.

AUG 04 (TUE)

What a frigging roller coaster.

It started with coffee with Lynn and Rosi today at that very same Starbucks where I had that cappuccino all the way back in April. Today I got a bottle of lemonade.

Lynn was sunnier and more vivacious than usual, which is really saying something for her. She looked relaxed and was laughing in a particularly boisterous manner. She had a smile big enough to attract elephant poachers on the prowl for ivory. Everything was going well in her world, it would appear.

While sipping her coffee, Rosi suddenly got a startled look. She swallowed and said, "I just thought of something! What if Mr. Love and Coach Bucket were gay and got married and hyphenated their names? Do you know what it would say on their mailbox?"

"I suppose their mailbox would probably say 'The Love-Buckets,' if that is what you were getting at," I replied. "Why do you ask?"

"I was wondering if I should hyphenate my name when I get married," she explained. "'The Love-Sandovals' and 'The Sandoval-Loves' both sound kind of off. 'We're having dinner with our friends, the Sandoval-Loves!' The Sandoval loves what? That has the potential to turn into an Elvis and Costello routine."

Lynn tried to explain that the comedy duo is Abbott and Costello, but Rosi insisted she had heard the name before. She didn't believe me when I told her Elvis Costello is a singer. Lynn wanted to prove it to her by looking it up online, so I handed her my tablet.

She was still giggling a little when she took it from me. She turned it on and a disgusted look washed across her face. "Aer Lingus," she said in a biting voice usually associated with the phrase "You make me sick." It would seem that I didn't close the browser from yesterday.

She shoved the tablet into Rosi's line of sight and told her to "Look at this," then followed up by reading the screen out loud: "Departing Boston, changing planes in Dublin, final destination Amsterdam." Her eyes were pointed directly at me, as if I was the one who needed to be told what was going on.

I asked her if she'd mind keeping it down. Then I reminded her that the Amsterdam idea was hers originally.

She had a furious look in her eyes as she responded, "Yeah, well, I'm sorry I ever brought it up. I was an idiot for even mentioning it. It's a horrible idea and I'm sorry I said anything." (She had elected to not keep it down, by the way.)

Rosi had been left speechless. Her expression said she really did not want to be present for this. That made two of us. I reflexively shielded my face with my hand, as if that would be sufficient camouflage.

Lynn put her elbows on the table and leaned in toward me. Judging from the look I got, I'm quite certain now that she secretly has heat-vision. She did bring the volume down a notch or two and, as if she were interrogating me now, said, "After everything I heard you say in the car on our way to the beach, you're seriously thinking about giving up? Did those words that I was moved by really mean nothing? Were you just trying to look noble?" I swear I could see the makings of a tear in her eye.

I told her that it's a hopeless situation. Everyone in my age range is already spoken for, and the few who aren't wouldn't want anything to do with me. On top of that, if history is any indication, no guy will ever make the first move, and I'm too shy to do it myself. It's a lost cause. I have to come to terms with it.

Lynn stood up and walked over to the trash to throw out her cup. She then ordered us into Rosi's brother's car. She told Rosi to take us to the bookstore in the Mars Avenue strip mall. I sat in the back.

Freed from the constraints placed on our conversation by the coffee shop setting, Lynn didn't hold back. She barked from the passenger seat, "I'm NOT letting you give up. You're NOT wimping out on this," and plenty of other supposedly motivational things delivered with the anger of a woman scorned. I must have really disappointed her.

I asked why she was bringing me to a bookstore, and expressed my desire not to take on anymore useless advice books. She said she wasn't buying me anything. Instead, I was buying something for her. I didn't get it. As we disembarked from the car, I could tell from Rosi's face that she was just as in the dark as I was. This was not something they had planned in advance. Lynn was genuinely livid.

Lynn brought us to the magazine rack, and handed me a women's fluff-piece mag and a fiver. "Buy this for me," she ordered, "and don't leave this building until you ask out that guy working the reg." I turned to see this guy in question. He was actually a little cute.

I asked how Lynn knew him. She said, "I noticed one of the guys who works here the other day, and thought he might be a good match for you. And, uhhhhh... Okay, now that I give him a second look, I see that this isn't the guy in question. Never mind, just as good. Go."

Aside from my chosen target, one other register was open. It was tended by a sixty-something woman. Each register was busy and I was next in line, so I had a fifty-fifty shot at winding up at the correct counter. I hate those odds.

Don't know either of the cashier's names, but for brevity's sake, I'll call them Granny and Mark. I don't think I should have to clarify which is which. So, which cashier was next to take a customer? You got it. I gave Granny the magazine and the money, cursed under my breath, thanked her, and walked away. The *k'TUNK k'TUNK* of my shoes echoed in my head as if I were being led down a hallway to the electric chair.

They say you have nothing to lose in these sorts of situations. Well, at that moment, I was feeling even worse than I did yesterday and I didn't even get to try. I was ready, I really was. I was going to do it, but luck had other plans. I left the store and stood by the car until Lynn showed up. Rosi was nowhere to be seen.

Lynn snatched the mag out of my hands and fed it into the car through the open slit atop the passenger side window. "Are you TRYING to make me mad now? Is this funny to you? Do you think I wanted to spend five bucks on tips for making my October an 'autumn-tastic' one?"

I tried to defend myself, pointing out that I didn't have any say as to which register would be open next. Lynn grabbed me by the shoulders and told me I'm smarter than that. She said I'm the smartest person she knows, and she knew I could rig it so that I'd end up at Mark's counter. I'd just have to think of a way.

She then spun me around so I pointed in the direction of the store again. "You told me you've always wanted to be a writer, right? Now, we're going back in there and you're buying a copy of that *Completely Braindead Guide to Getting Published*. And you're paying with your own money as punishment for screwing up the first time! Now go back in that building and try again!"

Alright, I thought. I have a captive audience, it's all set up for me in advance. I cannot afford to miss this chance again. I marched back in for Round Two.

I found the *Completely Braindead Guide to Getting Published*, and gave it a quick skim:

"Completely Braindead Lesson One: If you're not talking or eating, keep your mouth closed! You can't get published if you get caught in the rain and drown!"

Naw, I'm kidding, but wouldn't it have been great if it actually said that? Lynn and Rosi were still pretending to carry on a chat over by the magazines. They could have tried a little harder. As I passed by, I swear I heard Rosi saying "blah blah conversation blah talking to you blah blah." I couldn't see the piercing gaze Lynn had trained on me, but I felt it.

Again, there were customers at both registers and no line. This time I would employ strategy. I waited behind a nearby rack of bookmarks as the woman at Mark's register finished up her order. She picked up her book and took one step towards the exit. That's my cue. I came out from around the bookmarks, audibly brushing past them. The rack could have fallen down, but it didn't. Yes! It was clumsy, but not a big mistake. It's like it didn't even happen.

I tried to smile as naturally as I could, and placed my book down on the counter. I didn't even have to do anything. Mark took one look at the book and everything went into motion. "Ooh, I should get one of these!" he said.

I asked if he was a writer. He said he was "trying to get some writing done" but didn't quite know what to write about. I estimate that I was able to keep the conversation going for about three minutes. I was getting somewhere! Of course, it helped that I mentioned I was writing as well (okay, I bent the truth a little) and that I just finished a short story (that wasn't true either) which was a follow-up to a murder mystery parody I had published in *GAMES* magazine (LIAR!)

Okay, enough dilly-dallying. Big moment. I took my change from him and said, "You know, I could help you come up with some ideas, if you'd like. Are you doing anything later?"

He had a hesitant look on his face as he said, "Uh, juuussst workiiiiiiinnng..." Ah, so that's how it's gonna be.

I tried to keep the cool I had maintained so far, and not let any sign of disappointment surface. "Alright. Well, I'll be on my way and maybe I'll see you around. Thanks for everything." I made my way to the door, picturing myself leaving the private eye's office in a black and white film.

k'TUNK k'TUNK.

I waited by the door of the car until the girls showed. Lynn came rushing out and gave me a hug that would have been embarrassing even in private. I was smiling. I was proud. This wasn't like the pharmacy or Newbury Comics or the line at the supermarket, this time I actually asked somebody out. Even though I had asked people out before, and had always been turned down, this time I was filled with a renewed sense of hope. I was closer than I've ever been before.

I didn't get a date, but I didn't care. I was over the moon. "That couldn't have gone any better!" said she who is I.

Rosi looked even more flummoxed than before. "Yes. Yes, it could have. He could have actually agreed to meet you later."

"Well, he didn't say 'no,' specifically," I explained. "Maybe he was trying to keep his options open for some other time." Wow, was that *me* trying to put a positive spin on something? Who are you and what have you done with Audrey?

Lynn was back to her bubbly self again, effervescent as ever. On the ride back, she couldn't stop saying how proud she was of me and how well I handled myself. I felt like I did her a huge favor. So it was a mutual exchange.

I wanted to do it again. I wanted to rush out to the next place that caught my eye and have another try right then and there. But I decided once was enough for today. I don't want to buy another thing I don't need just yet.

The moral of the story: Lynn can be really friggin' scary when she wants to be.

AUG 05 (WED)

Willow asked why I have a shredded slip of paper taped to my wall. I told her that it's a souvenir of the time I fired a BB gun at a piece of paper with a star on it. I haven't made her laugh in a year or so, but that was enough, it seems.

She's been a lot nicer to me than before. It's like back when I worked at the store with her and we got along just fine. I've been so pleased with it that I was motivated to go out and buy a pack of cigarettes for her, just to let her know that I forgive her. Also, I wanted to take another shot at asking out the cashier, the one Rosi describes as "the Asian one with the haircut that makes him look like Hitler's evil twin." (Um, "Hitler's *evil* twin"? So then Hitler would be the... Never mind. I'm guessing she may not have thought that one through all the way.)

I couldn't tell which area of the Far East he descended from but I'm pretty good with patterns, especially where language is concerned. If I could see his nametag, I'd likely be able to tell if he's Chinese or Korean or Japanese or Thai, I thought. I'll say, "That's an unusual name! Is it from Xxxxx?...." Then I could use that as the springboard for conversation, ask him if he was born here or there, has he ever been there, just let the conversation take its own shape.

He was in. He was at the register. There was no line. Great, so I'll just march right up and see what his name is...

"Chris." Ooooof course.

Seeing all those hundreds of varieties of smokes behind him gave me an idea. I told him I wanted a pack of cigarettes. I didn't ask for Willow's brand, though. Instead I asked for a pack of Compass Point Lights. I had a plan in mind: if I could keep some cigs on me when I go out, perhaps I could get to know some new people if they come up to me outside of a club and ask me if I've any to spare. These are Natasha's brand, so if that doesn't work at least I can unload them on her.

I had to devise some other scheme, so I asked him if he smoked. He said he doesn't.

I let out a demi-giggle and said, "You know, I don't either. I'm just buying these cigarettes for someone else."

STUPID. STUPID. STUPID. STUPID. STUPID. STUPID.

"Your friend is over eighteen, I hope," he said while giving me a knowing smile. Oh! I'm not being kicked out? This might work out after all! He's smiling, isn't he? And there I was, worried that I had made another faux pas like the CD-burning remark.

His smile was enough of a glint of hope that I just asked right then and there if he was interested in doing anything later, when his shift was over.

"Oh, geez, I'm afraid I already have a girlfriend, so..."

I wasn't as focused as yesterday, so I immediately stepped back a little. "Ah! Say no more!" I said, suddenly back to my self-conscious self. I fumbled to stuff my change into my pocket, dropping coins and forgetting how to fold a dollar bill in half. It was so clumsy it looked intentional. It could have appeared in black and white on an infomercial with a red X superimposed on it.

"Well, I'll still see you around," Chris said.

"Maybe!" I called back as I darted out.

That's a shame. I really thought he liked me. You think you're getting somewhere, then you pop the question, and it's right back to the starting line. Story of my life: ask and ye shall recede.

So, I guess I can't go back to that embarrassment, I mean, establishment anytime soon. I needed to boost my mood after that, so I stopped over at Newbury Comics later in the day and Leon was there. Alright, a first chance at a second impression. I went to find another cheap used CD, so I could make a little small talk. I went over to the used bin and dug in looking for something I might like, perhaps The Style Council or The Smiths if anything was available. I flipped through the S section: Split Enz, Shriekback, Stiff Little Fingers, Saints, Squeeze, Snakefinger,... They were all out of order. Why couldn't they just be alphabetized like everything else?

I couldn't help it. I figured I'd just put the S's in order, then get back to my mission. It was only about fifty CDs. It didn't take long but,... you know, that N section would take even less time. I thought it over, but then Leon came down the aisle and asked if I was finding everything alright. He even used my name. He remembered me from before! Good sign. I told him I was fine, not looking for anything in particular. He thanked me for sorting out the S bin for him.

I bought a used compilation CD. Still couldn't ask him out yet. I need to handle this one just right. I have to wait until I think he's familiar enough with me and spring the trap at the right moment.

So, I got turned down two days in a row. I've been here before, but I have to keep going. As the heroin addicts say, "I'd rather lose the fight than quit."

AUG 09 (SUN)

Oh my. I'm sorry. I went three days straight without an entry, didn't I? Forgive me, notebook. I'm just not as into it as I was when this all began. The novelty is starting to lose its luster and, on top of that, not much has happened. Some days, I just have nothing to say. I have, however, gone to a few more stores to flirt with the employees. Found myself in a pet store yesterday and bought a can of fish food for my excuse. All for naught, though. Every last one of them told me that they're already seeing someone. I guess that was readily apparent, as I would have written had anything good came of it.

On the bright side, I have a can of fish food now. Given his current food intake, I think Thé is set for life.

On Friday I got a text from Zena that seemed promising. She asked if I wanted to join her at a pool party today. Well, I say it "seemed" promising, but it wasn't the type of pool party I was expecting. Once we arrived, it turned out that the only attendees were all members of Zena's family. Older ones. It was a family party at her grandparents' house. Would have been nice to have known that ahead of time, especially given my choice of attire.

I finally wore that retina-searing pink bikini Rosi egged me into buying. She came along, too. Lynn couldn't make it as she and Dustin (the guy she met speed-dating) went to New York to see the Mets play, even though I was sure their season ended in June.

Zena's relatives were all ensconced on the patio chatting over drinks and gossiping about this and that. Zena wanted us to be sure we didn't offend her grandfather. "I'm gonna have to ask that you keep a civil tongue," she said. "If there's one thing my grandpa won't have, it's swearing."

She asked about my luck with asking out guys working at stores this week. When I gave her the news, she wanted to know why I was giving up on them so easily. "Just because he's seeing somebody else doesn't mean you can't still get him, you know?"

Well, I suppose she's right, but only technically. It's really just a way of giving me the brush-off when they say that. If they don't like me, I can't make them like me. Plus, I don't want to "steal" anyone's boyfriend. I can't ruin someone else's relationship. That's not the right thing to do.

I tried to keep my hair as dry as possible as threw myself into the water feet first. Zena settled herself in a deckchair with a book. Talk about role reversal, huh? Rosi rummaged through a basket of pool toys, looking like she was searching for something in particular. I asked what was up and she told me she was planning to shoot me with a squirt gun the moment she found one. Instead, she ended up settling for a floating basketball hoop and a spongy foam ball. I should note that the way she chose to play the game involved the ball bouncing off of my head more often than the backboard. I was considered a three-point shot.

Zena said her grandfather doesn't allow squirt guns at the pool. He hates guns that much. "Tattoos, guns, and swearing: he won't put up with any of them."

"Really old-fashioned type, huh?" Rosi said as she attempted to try on a pair of children's goggles she found.

"Oh yeah, he's up there in age. He even fought in World War II. He was in the navy." Really? The navy? But she just said that he hates... Oy, never mind.

I stated that I liked that. It's nice to know there's still a few gentlemen out there in the world. I guess that's the sort of guy I'd like to date. Not necessarily somebody old-fashioned, or a deluded soul who wears a top hat and carries a jeweled walking stick, referring to others as "my good fellow." Just a man who's considerate and chivalrous. He can be a little naughty without being out-and-out crass.

The rubber strap on Rosi's goggles broke. "'Crass'?" she asked.

"You know what I mean, every sentence is effin' this and effin' that and so on."

"Aud, I've heard you say f— uh, the F-word plenty of times." She caught herself, just in case any stray ears were picking us up.

"Please tell me you can see the difference between using the word for emphasis and using it as a replacement for commas."

I was resting my head on my hands at the edge of the pool when Rosi dove in and, well, so much for keeping my hair dry. I expressed my disapproval through the fine art of shrieking. She said I was too uptight. "You need to relax. Take it easy. That's how I live, I don't let the little things bother me."

I suggested that maybe she wasn't the best person to advise me on taking life a little more in stride. For one example, I reminded her of the time she brought the flag from Mrs. Sanders' room to the dry cleaners (following a chowder-related incident,) then forgot to pick it up. The class had to recite the Pledge of Allegiance to one that she drew on the blackboard.

Zena burst out laughing. "I remember that! It was the size of a postcard and had twelve stars and ten stripes! You didn't even use colored chalk!"

After a while, I pulled myself out to towel off and get a little sun. I think Rosi's score was 24 at that point. Couldn't help but notice that Zena had barely moved from her seat since we arrived. I asked if she was going in the pool or not. She said she wasn't. Okay, so she just wanted come here to lie in the sun?

"You can't tell anyone this, but since you told me your secret, I guess I can trust you." Wow, I'm getting a ton of mileage out of this whole secret thing. Maybe if I sent out some emails to a few CEOs, I could get some insider trading info.

Rosi was swimming laps, so she wasn't able to hear Zena whisper, "I can't swim." Ah, of course. She didn't go in the water at the beach either, did she? I took the reclining deckchair next to her and reclined the hell out of it. (Oh sorry, I should have written "heck.") Then I inquired into the possibility of teaching Zena some of the basics of swimming.

"I'm interested, but I can't do it. I don't have it in me." She put her book down and asked me how I'd like to die. I asked if I should take that as a threat. She was serious, though: if I could choose my own method of dying, what would it be?

Thought it over for a couple of seconds and came out with, "I guess my ideal way of checking out would be by getting a fatal heart attack in the middle of my five-thousandth time having sex. Failing that, I'd go for Dr. Kevorkian's method." Zena admitted that was a pretty good choice, but she wants a quick, painless death to take her out while she's asleep, and she doesn't want to know when it's coming. I asked why she brought it up.

Zena gave another look around to make sure we still had our element of privacy. "Don't laugh. I've always wanted to go skinny dipping. I even had a great opportunity once, with a guy I really liked, no less. And I blew it because I can't swim." She told me how she wanted to just jump in the water like Rosi and I did, but she's scared of everything that could go wrong.

I told Zena she shouldn't worry about drowning. If she just learns to swim one step at a time, she'll be fine and the water won't scare her anymore. Plus, you don't need someone else's consent and mutual physical attraction to take swimming lessons.

Bonk.

"I'm outta the pool, Rosi! That doesn't count!"

"Yes it does. It's after halftime."

My next-chair neighbor remarked that I've been talking a lot about sex recently, postulating that I may have developed an obsession. I told her it's fine, I have obsessions that come and go all the time. They infiltrate my every thought and action. I don't just obsess, I revel. I assured Zena that things would work themselves out before too long. Hopefully not the way they did last time, though.

"You know, Audrey, we're the same age. I see people like Pedro and Jeanette getting engaged and I start thinking to myself that maybe I slipped up. I'm turning thirty-one in only a couple of months. Maybe I'm too late. All that time I spent in college, I think I was just sleeping with all sorts of guys as a power thing. I didn't date anyone until I was eighteen, then I wanted to have as many boys as possible. I didn't really outgrow that. If you look at it like that, you and I are actually quite similar."

I said we aren't similar at all. We're polar opposites... but, I guess the North Pole and the South Pole do have more in common with each other than they do with any other place on Earth.

Zena giggled a little, shaking her head as if she couldn't believe I would make that analogy. "Polar opposites, then. That's us."

Final score: 33.

AUG 11 (TUE)

Entertainment media has a funny way of coloring our world. It can create and wet-nurse legends and stereotypes until they become big enough to accept a place in our collective consciousness. Media can even dictate our morals to a certain degree. For instance, you hear all the time in movies and TV that money isn't everything, family is what's truly important. I used to believe that, but then one day I realized who was telling me that. (Hint: It ain't middle-class folks writing all those sitcoms in their free time between shifts.) One of these days, someone's going to pitch a show about a family that may not get along but they all just love each other sofuckingmuch even if they pretend they don't and they're gonna do just fine, and the title will be *Put Down Your Pitchforks, Peasants!*

Similarly, when you're so desperate to be loved that people can tell you're completely devoid of hope, everyone who's already found love is quick to point out, "Hey, love isn't everything! Just look on bright side! It's not so bad!" To your ears, it sounds like "Trust me, *not* being in the quicksand isn't as glamorous as it seems," while you're scrambling to grab hold of a vine. Then, when they think your back is turned again, they go back to their songs and movies centered around how love is the most importantest thing in the whole wide world. They tell their significant others that they can't live without them. They say love is all you need. Who do you think you're fooling?

Tried asking out a guy who works at a sushi place in the mall food court today. He said he's flattered but taken. That's six guys I've asked out in the last week. Six guys at six different stores, all with girlfriends ("all" being the guys, not the stores.) Unbelievable. No, what am I saying? Completely believable. While I sense that I'm getting the hang of it, I also feel like there's a map of Ridgeway with six red pushpins in it down at the police station. A detective in a smart pantsuit leaves a lip-print on her styrofoam cup, stares at the map, and asks, "Where are you going to be next, you psycho?"

I did see Leon at Newbury Comics again. I didn't ask him out, though. I'm still playing it strategically with him, letting him get used to me. Seems to be going well, he's friendly enough. I get this inexplicable good feeling from him, like it's going to work just as long as I don't screw it up by asking if he'd like me to burn a CD for him again. No, knowing me, I'd probably say something like, "You know your name spelled backwards is 'Noel,' right?" Now there's a pick-up line.

As for online dating, I doubt I'm going hear back from possible-Jericho. It's been far too long. He would have written back by now if he was still interested. Maybe another opportunity knocked for him. If so, good for him. As for me? I'm still not taking any steps forward. No progress at all. You try to spread your legs and you just end up taking a giant step sideways.

Went for a ride with Angela tonight. All in all, it was a nice ride. The sky was clear and the moon full. Out in the suburbs, away from the light pollution, everything had that bluish moonlight tint to it.

She packed her pipe and offered it to me, and this time I actually hit it. It was horrid. It tasted like garbage and nature got together and had a barbecue in my mouth.

Ange told me she had mouthwash somewhere in the car if I wanted it. Yes, please! In the pitch-black night, she somehow fished it out of the backseat while keeping one hand on the wheel. She gave me the bottle on one condition: I couldn't spit out the window because she has trouble getting it to close again. I'd have to wait until we hit a red light, then open the door to spit. Okay, great. I took a swig immediately, swirled it around, gargled... swirled some more... gargled a little more... We're kinda into the burning stage now, Ange. When's the next light, Ange!?

Then I remembered we were on Route 44 and the next traffic light could be ten or fifteen minutes away. After I emitted a string of panicky squeaks and made some Kermit-like hand-flails, my driver got the picture and pulled over to the side of the road just so I could end up spitting into a stranger's driveway.

Between laughs, Ange told me, "If you can handle that, you can definitely handle a peppermint schnapps!" Who frickin' said I could handle that?

There's an online radio show she thinks I should write in to for advice. I don't know if that's a good idea. I don't have the patience for more time-tested pat-on-the-head attaboyisms amounting to "Aw, you'll do jus' fine! You just keep on keepin' on, okay?"

I feel like I have a problem that requires serious advice, but there's none to be given. The only choices are to keep trying or give up. Giving up means never getting what you want. If you decide to keep going, there's no guarantee you'll ever get it, no "yes" or "no," there's only "maybe." And whichever path you choose, the problem just keeps tearing you up inside. There is no answer to be had. Just "maybe."

I thought back to what Ange said last time about how I should feel comfortable asking her anything at all. I figured the time had come for me to play that card. I do not know what possessed me, but I asked her how many guys she's had sex with. She gave a few more details than I had hoped for. I was only uncomfortable because it reminded me of how much I've been missing. One of those things where you instantly stop and ask yourself, "Why did I do that?"

I don't believe I'm trying to have sex because I want to impress anyone. I'm not doing this to try to make it a competition. I'm just trying to make myself a little happier is all.

UPDATE. I didn't notice before, but Ingrid texted me while I was out with Angela. I didn't think she'd come through for me, but she's going to a party this weekend. A bunch of her friends and acquaintances from college are getting together, so it looks like I'm in. Finally. It's about time I made it to the party.

AUG 13 (THU)

Chewing gum and earbuds don't mix. If you have enough trouble properly screwing those little bulbs into your ears on a normal day, try keeping them where they're supposed to be with your jaw clenching every three seconds.

I learned this the hard way while listening to my mp3 player on the train into Boston today. I only had the earbuds because they came free with the player and I didn't want a pair of headphones falling out of my purse at an inopportune moment. I had to be extra careful tonight, as it was my second exercise in speed-dating. I couldn't afford to have anything out of place.

On the subway leading from the train to my destination, I ended up in a seat facing a couple who were holding hands and being all kissy-kissy. They spoke and acted as if their lives depended on making sure everybody in that subway car knew how much they loved each other. It was an antagonistic, almost spiteful affection they exhibited, like they were playing characters at a costume party in an attempt to win the "People You Just Want To Pound On With a Cold Bostitch" prize. I had to really go out of my way to keep my eyes fixed elsewhere, like on a sign informing riders that they can "learn English as a second language in your spare time!" (What's wrong with that picture?)

I showed up early as always. Once it got going, it was the usual chit-chat: where from, how far, what music, the same ol' time-tested, focus-grouped small talk. I just think I should play this close to the chest so that I won't scare anyone off. Better to let them think I'm normal than know I'm boring.

When you do this with a lot of people back-to-back, the patterns start emerging in pretty sharp contrast. For instance, if you ask what type of music somebody likes, nine out of ten people will give you an answer containing the word "everything". Really? You like almost *all* types of music? Even Baroque? Enka? British music hall acts? How many Gregorian chants are on your mp3 player?

The first time I speed-dated, nobody really stood out. This time there were a few characters worth remembering. One had a nametag that looked like it read "Tony-O", but the O had a slash through it. He corrected me, explaining that he is "Tony Minus Zero".

"I'm called that because I am the whole package, I am missing nothing," he said, emphasizing each syllable as if it were the most important syllable in the entire sentence. I couldn't dignify that in writing so on my scorecard I just listed his name as "???". He wore a tight T-shirt and his hair was in a crew-cut, which is kind of a relief since usually this whole crazy name bullshit is the sort of icing on the cake you expect from someone dressed like a breakdancing Gypsy in a Mel Brooks movie. Thankfully, he was the worst of the lot.

There was one person who I did feel I bonded with. His name was Godfrey, which immediately struck a chord with me as that name almost rhymes with mine. Audrey and Godfrey. See? Close enough for a pop song. Closer, even. He also works at a school: a private school in Norwood. I asked him about music, and he didn't give me that "everything" line. He said he likes jazz, and even knows who Vince Guaraldi is. He says he wants to be a writer. He doesn't drink. He's too good to be true.

The way we talked felt like I was having a conversation with Lynn or Angela. It was as if we were old friends catching up after not seeing each other in a while. It only lasted five minutes, but the best five consecutive minutes I had all night. When we had to part ways, he even said "See you later!" Oh, is that so? Well, in that case…

One other person who left an impression on me was Errol. He had bad skin, not kinda splotchy under the flashbulb like mine, but broken out all around the upper-left quadrant of his face, above and next to his eye and ear. But, more importantly, he could barely stand to look me in the eye. He was much quieter than everyone else, and I could just barely hear him.

I'm making an assumption, but this guy could well be in the same spot as me. Of course, next to Errol, I'm just another average person who gets nervous in certain situations. My shyness is a nuisance that I'm trying to shake. His was crippling. If only my mother and psychiatrist could see this. This is closer to what Asperger's really looks like. He certainly didn't come off as a guy who had a lot of girlfriends, if any at all. I put him down as a "yes." This is someone who I want to give a chance to. I couldn't stand the thought of him coming away from this empty-handed, the same way that I did a few weeks ago. Granted, I would have penciled him in as a "yes" anyhow, as there wasn't anything really wrong with him. I held him up to the same standards as everybody else: he didn't seem to hate me, he wasn't obnoxious, and he didn't say anything that led me to believe he'd one day end up chasing me with a blender-chainsaw hybrid device of his own design.

Still, I knew that if he didn't like me, he wouldn't even know I wanted to get to know him better. That's how the speed-dating game is played, right? Well, yes, but this company did things a little differently. I was only able to narrow my picks down to five. A mutual "yes" wasn't enough anymore. Now I'd have to make it into some guys' top five lists *and* have them in mine as well. On top of that, there were twenty people to pick from for each gender. This way, the more choices there are, the fewer matches there'd end up being. What a poorly-designed system. It's almost as if they want things to go badly so that people will have to keep coming back again and again and holy shit I just figured it out. Bastards.

In the end, I went with Godfrey, Errol, and three other guys who I feel I got along with well enough (one is from Ridgeway, even.) Still, I'm not very hopeful. In order to get a match, I'd have to make into at least one of their top five lists. I don't like my chances, even on a purely statistical level.

On the train ride home, I thought a lot about Godfrey and how well we got along. I have a good feeling about him. Ya know what? I honestly felt like he was into me and wanted to see me again. He had to have put my name down, I just know it. This time, things are going to go well! I'll overcome the odds and the cynicism and see him again and win his heart. Cynics. Ha! What have they ever been right about, aside from almost everything in recorded history?

The train pulled into Upper Ridgeway station a little before 12:30 a.m. Five people got out. I was the only one who walked down the platform without holding someone's hand.

AUG 14 (FRI)

Willow left for her parents' house today. We were able to put everything she had in her dad's truck and her mom's minivan, (except her bed which is still at my place.) Her folks were fine with taking her in and thanked me for helping her out. They tell me they really hated Wes, though. Repeatedly.

Maybe two weeks was an unfairly short stretch of time for expecting her to find a new job, given today's hiring practices. I remember when I applied to the supermarket all those years ago, it was in March and they didn't even start scheduling interviews until June. I wasn't hired until July. (Yes, it was a normal supermarket, not a front for a government-owned uranium storehouse.) Still, I had to show Willow that she wouldn't be able to push me around anymore. Any longer than two weeks and she would have started taking root again. Can't let her get too comfy. I'm not any closer to solving the rent problem, though.

I got a last-minute invitation to dinner today. Rosita wanted me to meet her family. Didn't have any other plans, so why not? She picked me up in her usual mode of transport, which was still rattling up a storm. I asked if she was the least bit concerned about all the noise.

"Stop worrying, it'll be fine," she assured me. "Driving is like making love. If you're not making a lot of noise, you're not doing it right."

Oh my God, EVERYTHING is like making love! Mopping a floor is like making love: it's tough to get in the corners but you have to keep at it. I don't know what I just wrote but it sounds feasible, doesn't it?

Rosi turned on the radio. One station does a "retro" night on Fridays, playing songs that were popular when I was still just a sprout. I was in luck, they were playing "Nursery Rhyme" by Fawn Clayton. I turned the volume up a little, saying this was my favorite artist.

My chauffeur unleashed one of her stand-alone "Ha"s. "Fawn Clayton? What is this? Thirty years ago?"

"No. It's never thirty years ago. That's not possible." Plus, this particular song was only twenty years old.

Once Rosi brought me to her house, she introduced me to the two cats who have made their home with her family for eleven years: a peach-colored one named Mr. Meowsers and a piebald named Screaming Banshee Skull of Blackest Midnight. It seems

220

Rosi and Tomas each got to name one of them. "Yeah, I was kinda doing the goth thing for a little while back then," she explained.

A heavy-set woman who I'd guess was around forty-five or fifty came down the steps. Rosi introduced me, and the woman glared at me as if she couldn't believe I had the nerve to show up for the dinner I was invited to. "Oh. So this is the famous Audrey who I've been hearing so much about. The young [*Spanish word I didn't recognize*] who's trying to lead my Rosita astray, dragging her to the nightclubs and the sex shops."

"Mama, please, you said you wouldn't do this."

The woman went on, saying that I was welcome to have dinner in her home for the night, but she didn't approve of my libertine ways. She made her way into the kitchen to get back to preparing our meal. Nice to meet you, too.

Rosi took me into the living room to explain what was happening: her mom found the vibrator that she bought. Upon being confronted, Rosi's first instinct was to claim I bought it as a gift for her. Mrs. Sandoval is still under the delusion that her daughter is as pure as every brand of bath soap claims to be, and that I'm to blame for anything naughty that she gets caught doing. I kinda figured all that out from the context (just short of the vibrator.) I guess tonight's plan was to pretend that Rosi was me and that I was Salome of the Seven Veils on a three-day Kahlua bender.

I met Tomas once he came back from wherever he was. I thanked him for always letting Rosi use his car, thus helping me get to where I needed to go once in a while. He didn't know what I meant by that. Seems like Rosi couldn't bring herself to admit that the celery green Explodesmobile Alero was really hers. She finally admitted she bought it back in May for $700.

A pregnant woman with short blonde hair slowly carried herself downstairs, step by step. She was introduced to me as Tomas's wife Karen. She had a depressed air about her, as if she couldn't believe that she of all people had been cursed to tote around that little freeloader. She definitely had a bad feeling in her gut. I tried to make conversation with her while Rosi helped her mom by setting the table.

"Have you two picked out a name yet?" I asked Karen.

"Captain Do-Nothing of the Goodship Freeride over there wants 'Enrique.' I'm leaning towards 'Dad Sucks' myself."

It was right around then that I decided I should just avoid discussing the baby. Rosi's mom shouted out to her from the kitchen, warning her to be careful with the glasses. The response was "You don't need to tell me that, Mama. I have everything under control."

SMASH. Wine glass down.

Aside from listless Karen, we all spent dinner on the edges of our seats awaiting Mrs. Sandoval's next salvo against me. She said that she hoped some of Rosi's ways would rub off on me (so to speak.) "Rosi's such a morally upright girl. Did you know she left her first boyfriend because he tried to pressure her into sex?"

I smiled, replying, "As a matter of fact, she did tell me that. That was when you asked me if I enjoyed my first time, wasn't it, Rosi? She's so cute and naive, always full of questions!"

Tomas laughed, adding, "Oh yeah, naive she most certainly is! A couple years ago, she drew Snoopy on one of Karen's dental dams because she thought they were Shrinky-Dinks!"

Rosi glared at him, saying "You swore you wouldn't tell anyone!" Then she requested that her mother stop discussing morals. "If that's all you talk about, Audrey's going to start thinking that you don't want her here."

"You should take up a hobby like Rosi has. She spends her spare time roller skating now. She told me she's going to join a skating league."

That caught Karen's attention. She asked if by "skating league" Mrs. Sandoval meant "roller derby," and if Rosi had a name picked out yet.

Rosi rolled her eyes and muttered, "Catherine Wheels."

Mrs. Sandoval wagged a pair of salad tongs at me, telling me that if I found something worthwhile to do then I might not feel the urge to sleep around like [*another word I don't know.*] Rosi shouted something to her in Spanish. Her mom answered in kind. It went back and forth like this for a short while.

I tried to adjust the barometric pressure by joking, "Wow, sure hope you're not talkin' about me!"

Blonde-haired Karen, looking more Nordic than a sauna full of ABBA, came out of nowhere and said, "Mrs. Sandoval can't believe someone who looks like you is doing a different guy every night, and Rosi just told her it's because you walk right up to strangers in truck stops and say you'll do anal."

Everyone else at the table stared at her in horror. Rosi in particular was astonished and sputtered, "Karen, you know Spanish?"

After dinner, Rosi suggested we play Scrabble. Her mom really likes the game, so it was an opportunity to get myself into her good graces. As there's a maximum of four players, Tomas and Karen played as a team. This time, I wasn't holding back. From the very first turn, nobody else even stood a chance of catching up to me. I was able to use all seven of my tiles once (to form "PRONATOR", which of course drew a challenge from guess who.) For my last word I was able to make "TAU." Rosi's mom challenged me on that one as well, and I explained that tau is a letter of the Greek alphabet. She asked if I learned that word walking the streets.

Rosi snapped. "Mama, enough! Audrey's not who you think she is. She's a... very cautious... individual." Yikes. My heart stopped for a second. Cuttin' it kinda close with the V-words, there. She continued, "She didn't buy that vibrator for me. In fact, it was my idea to go to that shop in the first place."

Mrs. Sandoval didn't flinch, but her eyes gave away her shock. "I knew that," she responded. So many people in this world can "knew" anything after you've already confessed.

Rosi even threw in that I visit their family's church once in a while. Tomas was perplexed and asked, "Wait a sec, aren't you Jewish?"

"Well, yeah, but I appreciate the beauty of the churchyard. I find it relaxing. Plus, given how my family gets along, our brand of Judaism is more along the lines of Punch-and-Judyism."

Nobody got the joke. I was born too friggin' late.

Everything went smoothly after that. Rosi's mom trusted me now that she knew I liked to stop by her place of worship once in a while, even if it isn't to worship. Before I left, she gave me a hug and said, "You seem like an okay girl. I may have judged you too harshly before, and I'm sorry. But mark my word, if you end up corrupting my little Rosita, you will rue the day. You hear me? Rue! The day!" Already on it. I'm well-versed in day-rue.

On the ride back, I had to ask Rosi why her father wasn't around. Just like the other night with Angela, I instantly regretted it.

She didn't mind, though. Her dad's quite alive and on a business trip right now. "I didn't tell you? He went to Japan. I thought you'd like that." She uncorked a big grin and said, "Maybe I can have him bring you back something!" I told her not to bother, I don't want to impose like that.

I rolled up my window to cancel out the rattling noises from the outside of the car. We were passing by a chain of Jersey barriers and the echo was starting to get to me. I mentioned that I appreciated how she stood up to her mother, and thanked her for not getting into any specifics regarding my love life.

"Stop worrying about it so much. I think you'll be better off if you just accept yourself for who you are and get over it."

"Getting over it is what I did ten years ago, and it was the worst decision I ever made. It didn't help a damn thing, it only made it all worse because I lost an entire decade waiting. If I accept this, then that will be giving up all over again. Acceptance is resignation."

"Oh! That's an oxymoron!" Rosi shouted with delight.

"No, it's not. When you resign yourself to something, you accept it as being inevitable. They're synonyms."

"But when you start a new job, you accept the position. When you quit, you resign. Aha! Got you there, didn't I?" Huh. It is kind of contradictory if you look at it that way. She won this round.

I do accept myself. That which is true I accept to be true. I can't deny the facts. But, just because I accept the facts doesn't mean I'm going to accept the reality. I can't just let the facts fall where they may, I have to take control of what they're going to mean.

Tomorrow night is the party. I think things are about to change. It's not over.

AUG 16 (SUN)

Okay. I think I'm ready to write about last night.

I was all ready to go, dolled up and set to mingle at the party. Then I got the phone call. It was Ingrid. She told me that she and Greg had elected to stay home, as Darrin had "a tummy bug." Wow. Thanks, Darrin. Next time I watch you, I'm telling you the bedtime story about the little boy who spontaneously combusted from not falling asleep fast enough.

Alright, ya know what? Who needs 'em? I told Ingrid that I was going anyway and had her give me the address. I had been looking forward to this, and if I can still go then I have to go.

Things were already well in gear when I arrived. Not early for once. I spent about ten minutes roaming about the one-story house, trying to look like I had a purpose in doing so. I was just trying to get a lay of the land (among other things) and see what type of crowd I was dealing with. I was still kind of nervous, so I hid in the bathroom to collect my thoughts, a familiar strategy by now. I don't think I've ever been in a room

224

I've wanted to clean more. I didn't want to touch anything, and I'm now considering sending the soles of my shoes to the Center for Disease Control. My entire reason for being in that room was to relax for a few seconds but I was so afraid of accidentally coming into contact with any object, that it was all I could think about. I opened the door back up by getting some toilet paper and using that as a buffer between my hand and the door handle.

After exiting the mildew-storage room, I saw a small group of people, male and female, gossiping away in the center of the living room. There were enough of them that I might be able to slip in undetected, and their location was perfect. But, how should I ingratiate myself with all these people when I don't have anyone to introduce me? Still haven't learned how to fly in the ointment. Maybe I'll just pretend to be texting someone until I overhear something that I can add my two cents to. Felt like it might work at the time. One problem with that strategy: as it turns out, the only thing that people I don't know talk about in my presence is other people I don't know. I'm not infiltrating my way into any of those conversations. All I can do is stand nearby and eavesdrop, hoping there'll be a hook that I can use to pull myself in.

I stood by, listening intently for any angle I could exploit. It really felt like I didn't belong there, (which I guess was true,) waiting it out for something I could recognize. I cringed hearing one fellow say, "Aw, yeah. He's a wicked good aahtist." Yes, he said "wicked." It's a stereotype, but plenty of people around here really do talk like that. This must be how Australians see "G'day!" or how Mexicans feel about "¡¡¡GOOOOOOOOOL!!!"

Sooner or later, I was noticed. A couple walked in from the other room, came up to me and asked who I was. I told I was there as a friend of Ingrid. "She said she was going to meet me here, but I'm still waiting for her to show up." I'm actually a little proud of that. Not a bad excuse for why I was alone.

The guy said to his lady, "Honey, do you know any Ingrid?" She did not.

"Oh, you must know Greg, then," I said, feeling a renewed unease. They claimed not to have heard of him, either. Oh dear. "Didn't you go to school with at least one of them?"

"Maybe," the woman said, seemingly unsure of what to make of all of this. "We went to BU. Where did they go?"

Luck was on my side at that moment. A sudden burst of hearty laughter arose from the clique I was keeping an ear on. With this unexpected distraction, I took the opportunity to ask what was so funny. I missed the joke, but it was an ongoing story, so I listened in as one bald and portly fellow related a tall tale of how he (and I'm not kidding, he actually said this) knocked a "karate-looking" guy's teeth out with his first and only punch and was awarded a black belt on the spot despite having no training in martial arts.

Now, I think I've met far more than my fair share of nuts with fantastic stories to tell. Of all the exaggerators I've come across, the scariest of these was the incident where a college classmate saw fit to inform me of a man stalking his girlfriend and leaving threatening voices on her answering machine, but with *his* voice. Because you see, he uh, had this computer program or something, that uh, changed his own voice into, like you know, other peoples' voices! Even less credible was a co-worker once related the yarn of how he was paralyzed from the waist down and spent a short stretch of his life in a wheelchair. However, one day he was home alone and fell out of the chair. He then "taught [himself] to walk again" as he really needed to go to the bathroom. So, I guess what I'm saying is that I'm used to this sort of thing. Too used to it. I figured I'd just try to blend in with the crowd and give the delusional sense of machismo a pass for now.

The conversation somehow turned to a poll in a weekly news magazine asking people over the internet what they considered to be the ten most important events in world history. One of the most popular answers was a recent celebrity wedding. Somebody rightly scoffed, and went off about "kids these days," not that she was necessarily wrong even if it does lack generational perspective. So, rather than the wedding, what would this woman consider to be one of the ten most important events in the history of the world?

"What about when the space shuttle blew up?"

Yes, what *about* when the space shuttle blew up? That stands right there beside the Exodus from Egypt, the discovery of the New World, the Crucifixion, the invention of paper, and the harnessing of electricity, doesn't it? Who are these people? What college did Ingrid graduate from anyway? Was it Frank & Jimmy's Discount Diploma Bonanza University? Maybe I sound like I'm being too harsh but, remember, I'm writing this with the benefit of hindsight.

While my mind was trying to find a way of making sense of that one, I lost track of the conversation and someone was telling a joke now. It was an anti-Semitic one, featuring a Jewish genie trapped in a piggy bank. Okay, *now* I had something to be legitimately upset about. Couldn't say anything, though. Had to go along with the crowd, heh heh. Oh, yeah, good one.

I figured it was time for me to make a move, so I interjected with, "Okay, I just heard this joke the other day. Trust me, this is a good one." They got quiet, but it was a suspicious kind of quiet. The looks on their mugs seemed to be more curious about who I was than what I had to say.

I went against Rosi's advice and told the fish joke. Nobody got it. Instead, it was a lot of blank stares. I remember getting a warmer response way back when I told that joke about the breakdancer who got mauled by a pit bull. (Punch line: "Hey, man! Gimme some skin!") I'm lucky that one didn't get me kicked out of Hebrew school.

I tried to rescue myself with one I came up with on the taxi ride over: "A fortune-teller walks into a clothing store and the woman working there says, 'Lemme guess: you're a medium.'"

Nothin'. I do admit that one still needs some fine tuning.

"Who did you say you were again?" someone asked.

"I'm a friend of Ingrid. And Greg."

"Who are they?"

"Didn't any of you go to school with them?"

The Space Shuttle woman asked where this "Ingrid and Greg" were. I told her that they couldn't make it.

"So, what are you doing here, then?"

They all stared. Fourteen eyes all on me, waiting to hear what I would say next. I was the most interesting person in the room. My wish had come true in the most ass-backwards Twilight Zone way possible. It took me a little while to gather what I wanted to say. I had nothing prepared for such a situation, so I just said the first things that came into my mind.

I told them I wanted to meet new people. I wanted to meet someone who liked me. They didn't seem very satisfied and kept staring silently. I told them I don't know what I want.

I pulled my still-unopened pack of Compass Point Lights out from my purse and made my way for the door as calmly as possible, spanking the box to pack down the tobacco the way that exceptionally annoying people do for ten minutes straight. A perfect excuse to go outside. I guess my smokes had a dual purpose. I heard a voice from the group expressing his disappointment that "no good-looking women ever want to crash the parties I go to," and a few people laughed.

That hurt. I don't know why, but it killed me inside. If anything, it was the laughter that hurt more than the comment. I stepped across the threshold, thinking, go on, laugh. Laugh at someone for wanting the luxury of being normal. Laugh at me for wanting to be loved. What a horrible crime that is!

Even now, I still haven't figured out what the hell was going on. I looked at the house number once I was outside. Yeah, it was right. I walked a few houses down to the street corner. There was a street sign that confirmed this was the right address. How did none of these people know Ingrid or Greg? I was just a party-crasher.

I retraced my path back to the house and stood there on the front lawn, living out the metaphor. Unfamiliar figures milled about in the illuminated windows while I stood there in the night, the outsider. I was alone, not invited to the party, and literally on the outside looking in. It was so perfectly emblematic that it had to be another dream. I wasn't going to wake up, though. Still, I couldn't walk away without doing something supremely immature.

I threw the door back open and yelled, "HEY! Who owns this place!?"

One guy on the far side of the room raised a hand.

"Your bathroom's a fucking rat's nest, you filthy shit!" I slammed the door and walked down the street, leaving my bad dream behind me. I'm counting that as my first experience with lucid dreaming.

I walked back home. It was only about a thirty-minute walk. I didn't have the shoes for it, though. Once I made it back inside, I immediately took them off, making sure they were far enough away from anything that the infection the soles might have suffered in the bathroom wouldn't spread.

I fell face-first onto the couch, and spent the night there. I didn't want to go into my room. I didn't want to have to exert the effort of standing up, walking twenty feet, and opening a door, only so I could fall down again. I didn't want to see my lonely, empty bed. I didn't want to be in the same room as my mirror. And I didn't want to admit it before, but I really am ugly.

I stayed on that couch for ten hours, only seven of which I slept through. I only got up when I had to use the bathroom. I wasn't yet ready to lie on a couch soaked in my own urine. At least that's enough for me to know I still have one smithereen of pride left.

I didn't leave the apartment today. This little area is mine, it's where I'm safe. This is where I really belong. A place for everything and everything in its place. I don't like things to be out of place.

AUG 17 (MON)

There's a thunderstorm right now. We haven't had many so far this year. It's only

228

the second one by my count. I shut off all the lights for a while and pretended it was a blackout. The microwave clock display stayed on because it's too much trouble getting to the plug. I brought out that tiny book light that I never use, just so I could see my own writing. I'm by the window now, waiting for lightning strikes.

I always thought it was kind of strange how people fear lightning. The odds of getting struck are so statistically small, that we use it as a yardstick for how unlikely other things might be. Example: "Doctors say you're 56 times more likely to get struck by lightning than develop SCA (spontaneous Canadian accent.)" The concept of lightning is pretty scary, though: a sharp zigzag that falls out of the sky and immolates anything it grazes at a speed too fast for anyone to dodge. It's a rather apocalyptic thing when you think of it that way, like a creature out of some unintentionally funny sci-fi novel.

So, even though the likelihood of getting struck by lightning is almost nil, that probably contributes to the fear. Similarly, any day on this Earth could be your last. Something nobody expected happens, and you're gone. In that way, lightning is a perfect phobia: it's proof positive that all you need is for a single thing beyond any one person's control to go wrong and then it's all over. The plane crashes, the building catches fire, la revolución breaks out. So many things you never got to do, all because you were the one that was chosen at random to lose out.

A few hours ago, I found out I didn't get a single match from Thursday. Not even one. Again.

I needed something to pick me up. I went to that same café that I ate at with Lynn after our hospital visit. Kept having short conversations with the waiter, then asked him out when the check came. He said, "maybe some other time." Yeah, I know what that means.

It wasn't really a "no" per se, but it sure as hell wasn't "yes". Just "maybe". The cruelest word in the English language.

There's nothing I hate more than false hope. If you want to say "no", just say it. Just tell someone, "I don't want to go out with you, so I won't. That's the only reason I need." Just text someone and say "I don't want to talk to you anymore. Please don't write back." I don't need to hear "maybe". I knew it was "maybe" beforehand, otherwise I wouldn't have asked. Have a goddamm heart and just put me out of my misery.

This working-up-the-courage-to-flirt-with-strangers thing doesn't have the same uplifting quality that it did a couple of weeks ago at the bookstore. I thought I'd at least be hitting some sort of runner's high with that by now, but no such luck. The shock of the new has turned into the familiarity of years past.

Ingrid called to find out how I liked the party, so I asked why nobody there had heard of her. Turns out that when she said "a bunch of friends from college" were having a get-together, she meant "one friend from college (the guy I called a "filthy shit", as it would happen) and *his* friends who she has never met." That figures.

Par for the course, nothing of interest was on TV. Before the storm broke, I was tempted into watching a documentary. I was hoping it was going to be a crime doc, but it turned out to be about sex addiction. Beautiful people with beautiful problems. There's no escaping it. It really is everywhere.

I shut the TV off. Before I shut the lights off, I went fishing through the papers on the table and I came across the list: my original list of things I wanted to do for the first time. That was what this was all about, wasn't it? I'd forgotten all about it.

Look at this pathetic thing. What did I cross out? Coffee. Alcohol. Dance lessons. Gee, that was all so wonderful, wasn't it? And up at the top is still the one I really wanted from the beginning, and I haven't even gotten close to it.

What the hell is wrong with you, Audrey? This wasn't about finding love but somehow you made it that. You took something as simple as losing your virginity and turned it into some futile, melodramatic quest for love. The only thing I've lost is the thread. Do I really want to go on trying in vain like one-hit wonder acts that keep making albums nobody buys because they can't stomach the thought of going back to having jobs? How long am I expected to wait for lightning to strike? I can't let the perfect be the enemy of the good. Doing something is always better than doing nothing.

Time to get back to basics: don't worry about dating and holding hands and kissing and such. Get the first one under your belt and worry about all that later. Just have sex. Just do what Angela suggested and go to Nevada, the Devil's Quadrilateral. Or, I shouldn't even have to say it by now, Amsterdam. So what if it upsets Lynn? She's not the one who has to live with this. She'll never have to feel this way. She'll never be in my position. I'll do what I know is the wrong thing first, then pretend I'm sorry and ask for forgiveness later, just like when senators pay for sex.

Well, I'm all out of time for that now, since school starts up again next week. I guess I'll just have to see about going to Amsterdam in the winter during the Christmas break, or maybe the February one. I don't know what the Netherlands is like in winter, but I'm sure it beats riding it out in a giant, Massachusetts-shaped block of ice for four months straight. Then again, the Thanksgiving weekend is good, too. The sooner the better. I can just add a couple of personal days to it and I'll have enough time.

That's that, then. Time to start planning. I guess deep in my heart I always knew it would come to this.

AUG 20 (THU)

I had a mission today. Following those speed-dating results, I had to reach out for anything I could. So, yesterday and the day before I went to Newbury Comics to finally ask Leon out. He wasn't there Tuesday. He wasn't there Wednesday. Today he was there. This was gonna be the big one. My long game was about to pay off.

Picked up a three-dollar, used CD single and brought it to the register in record time. He still recognized me from the other times. We had a little chat about that and this, just asking about what the other has been up to. It was going quite well.

I didn't ask him out, though. I was about to spit out a "Do you..." but was interrupted. From the back room a woman called out, "Hey! Don't get *too* friendly with the customers! You aren't a free agent, ya know!" Leon laughed and assured her that he was still hers.

I should have seen it coming. Every time. Every.

Single.

Fucking.

Time.

What was the point of even continuing the conversation? I coughed up my cash and went home. Just another tally mark in the "loss" column.

An idea hit me. I looked up the contact information for the speed dating agency (the second one) so that I could give them a call. I asked the woman who answered if there was anything they had for people who didn't get any matches at all. I was hoping for perhaps a partial refund or possibly even a discount on future events. She explained their policy regarding this.

"What we do is, we offer our discounts to the daters who get the most matches. That way we keep the popular ones in and offer the best options to the other daters," she said.

"But if they get lots of matches, then they're less likely to be back, because things worked out for them."

"Uh, you could see it that way."

I asked if there was a reason she couldn't have just answered my question with "no."

I also made some suggestions for similar discounts they could offer, like fifty percent off event attendance at Boston venues for people onboard the International Space Station. Maybe free drinks for twenty-year-olds, as long as they can provide valid ID proving they're twenty-one or over. She hung up on me, and she was right to. I was being an incorrigible asshole to someone who didn't deserve it. I didn't feel better about myself, like I had power or confidence. I felt bad about going out of my way to make someone else's day a little worse. I don't know how people who act that way on a daily basis can live with themselves.

The phone rang a few hours ago. It was Lynn. She wanted to know if I could be ready to go out in fifteen minutes or so. I had gotten reasonably tarted up in preparation for Newbury, so I was already in good condition for a night out and said, "Sure, I'm ready. Where are we going?"

Lynn wanted to have one last get-together with the girls before school started up again next week. She already knew what she wanted to do. There's a weekly Trivia Night at this bar and grill on Watford Street. She figured that if I could be on her team, we could actually win. Our team ended up being a trio, as everyone but Natasha was unavailable.

On the ride over, Natasha asked if I'd done anything interesting recently. I mentioned that I ate at a house full of people who think I'm a truck stop hussy. Then, I crashed a party when the people taking me couldn't make it. Lynn asked if the party was any fun. I simply said that it was a graveyard smash.

At the bar, I was in charge of signing us up to compete in the trivia game. We'd have to write our team's name on a new slip of paper every time we answered another question, so we wanted to keep it short. I convinced them to go with "LAND", which stands for "Lynn, Audrey, and Natasha, dammit!"

While waiting for the game to start, I watched the huge TV. Three talking heads at a sports desk were going over some football stuff, and it must have been live because the captioning left much to be desired:

"AND FOR ME TO BE OPEN ABOUT INTERROGIE FY THOME SIGH MY WORK ETHIC FWHUNL. LIKE THE WAY BLCHNTS ON IS TASHGTL."

I don't know how live closed captioning is done but it must be hard, so I shouldn't jump down the captioner's throat about it. Maybe pro football just has a lot of new recruits from vowel-hating Eastern European countries this year.

I tried making eyes at someone on the other side of the bar, hoping he'd notice me. He did, and he didn't hesitate to look away from me with a dismissive eye-rolling motion. If he rolled his eyes any harder, they would have flipped over and turned into dollar signs.

Once the game was underway, it became clear that Natasha knew her history and Lynn could tackle the sports questions. There wasn't really much in the way of ones I could answer at first, and it didn't help that there were a lot of questions about movies and celebrities. Plus, I just wasn't on my game. I was still feeling low. It was one of those moods where I don't want to do anything, especially move a muscle.

In the third round, my time to shine had finally arrived with this question: "If you're in a ship on the Black Sea, and you travel through the Bosporus past Istanbul, which sea do you enter next?"

I wrote down "Sea of Marmara," and handed it in before any other teams. I couldn't wait for this one, I was sure I'd be the only one who'd get it, unless there were cheaters among the crowd. With those smartphones, it's basically an honor system.

I looked at the captioning on the TV again. "OHAVER LTDRRM," it read.

When the quizmaster read the answer, it was the "Mediterranean Sea." He went on to the next question, a sports one. Lynn handled it while I went over the facts with Natasha regarding the tiny Sea of Marmara, contained entirely within Turkey's borders. She said I should say something about it, but I disagreed. When the contest began, our host told us that we couldn't register any complaints over the answers.

"Don't be such a wallflower," Natasha said. She got up and took her concern to the quizmaster's table. After a few seconds, she turned to me and shouted, "Audrey! Tell him what you told me."

I got up and went over to the table, and explained why the quizmaster's answer to the Istanbul question was wrong, and how there's a small sea between the Black Sea and the Mediterranean. He said it didn't matter because he doesn't write the questions and everybody got it wrong anyways.

"That's why we're here," Natasha tried to tell him. "If your answer was right, we'd have gotten the point." He said we should sit down and this wasn't up for discussion. Lynn had joined us to hand in her answer to the current question.

Our host looked directly at Natasha and let out a stern, "Look, lady. The answers are final. Now sit down!" They locked in a stare.

I suggested to the quizmaster that he learn to be more polite to a lady. He replied by saying he would start as soon as he saw one. That did it.

My pals held me back as I called him anything I could remember from my emergency list of creative obscenities. I used every known swear and bodily fluid in a compound word at least once, preceded by adjectives like "festering," "cloven-hoofed," and "slope-browed". Then I said a few mean things as well. I never thought the day would come when Lynn would be carrying me out of a bar.

Once we were back in the car, Natasha asked if it was alright if we could make a stop at the store down the street before heading home. She wanted to pick up a pack of cigarettes. I would have offered her mine, but I left them at home.

When she got out of the car, I had some time alone with Lynn, who was sitting up front. She asked if everything was alright. I said I was fine.

"Seems like you're not 'fine' at all. Are you sure about that?"

I snapped at her, "I know how I'm doing, okay? Why does everybody second-guess me at every turn?" Shouldn't have said that. I said I was sorry immediately, and that I was just sick of getting absolutely nowhere. I hate having every single avenue be a dead end.

I should have stopped talking right then and there. Instead, I felt the need to shoot my mouth off, and I gave away my plans.

"I guess what it really comes down to is having someone there to help you get through life. Having that loving human touch letting you know that even the bad times are still worth it. Knowing someone misses having you around even though it's only been a few hours. I feel like an entire life without that isn't worth living. I'm thirty now. It's only going to get harder for me the longer I go on. Nobody's going to give a chance to someone my age that nobody else wanted." I got a bit misty-eyed. I choked up a little.

I apologized. I told Lynn I couldn't keep it up. I wasn't quitting, but I didn't have the strength to keep running on an empty tank after all these years. If I can't have the real thing, and I can't pay someone to love me, then I have to take what I can get and pay for sex. That's the best I can do.

"Audrey, shut up. You're gonna make me cry."

"Please, Lynn, I need you to understand. I have to go to Amsterdam. I'll go in November, just… fuck, just give me a break."

That was the last thing that was said until Natasha came back. She saw us both in very different moods than before she left, and asked, "What did I miss?"

I said it was nothing, just me whining about being lonely again. I tried to put a little life into my words, as if it were just another ho-hum chat between friends.

After Lynn got dropped off, Natasha asked if I wanted to move to the passenger seat. I said I was fine where I already was. She knew something was wrong.

She asked if I wanted to talk about it. I said I didn't. She asked if I wanted to be alone. I said I don't.

AUG 21 (FRI)

I left a message for Angela a few days ago about the possibility of going to the Netherlands with me. She called me back today and said that she's planning on spending Thanksgiving with her family instead. I suppose I should've known better. It was kind of stupid to think people would be joining me on my jaunt to the Zuider Zee rather than celebrating the carving of the turkey and the cranberry gelatin mold with their folks. I wonder how I'm gonna break it to mom and dad that I won't around for this year's feast.

Ange has another wedding to DJ this weekend, this one on Block Island. That brought us to the topic of her possible engagement. She's pretty sure Lew is planning something elaborate for the proposal, but she can't figure it out. It may involve getting a bunch of strangers to pull off a Broadway-esque dance number in a public setting.

She's thrilled that I'm going to Amsterdam, though. She says wishes she could be me. I have no idea how that works.

After I hung up, she texted me regarding another tattoo idea: a rabbi in a karate pose. Okay. I think I can whip something up.

After last night, I needed something to clear my head. I took the bike up to the park by the reservoir again today. It was pretty cool for August, the sky was overcast and foreboding. There weren't any families having a beach day by the shore, just a few folks reading, walking, sitting on benches together and staring out at the water.

There's a playground in the park as well, one with a swing set. Nobody was around in that corner, so I figured I'd go over and sit down on one of the swings. Figured it wouldn't hurt to just let the swing do its thing a little bit. I eased back and forth, ever so gently. Things got out of hand rather swiftly and in a couple of minutes, I was swinging as high as I could, just like I did back when I was a kid. It felt good, but due to the unusually cool wind, the joy was brief.

I dragged my feet a little to slow down. Friction... and... dismount! Stuck the landing. Not bad, I wasn't out of practice at all.

I heard clapping. A young woman came out from the nature trail in the woods behind me, applauding. "Nice job, but aren't you a little old for these, kid?"

Not this again. "Don't call me 'kid,' okay?" I called back to her.

She made her way over to me, asking, "What's the matter with you? You don't want to go back to school, right?"

I didn't give her my age, but I did declare that I was quite certain that I'm older than her. When she asked for a numerical figure, I relented and told her I'm thirty. She was impressed and complimented me on looking so young.

"So what are you doing on the swing set? Having a second childhood?"

"No, just getting around to finishing up the first one." I sat down on some nearby playground equipment, one of those things that isn't quite a jungle gym, and said, "It isn't so great, you know. Nobody respects you, everyone treats you like a lightweight. There's no point in looking young if you don't look good, if you've got a big nose and big ears and splotchy skin tone."

"Oh, I get it. Love problems." She leaned against the thick metal pole to my left and, like it was nothing, said in a warm voice, "Wanna tell me about it?"

What? Do I want to talk about it? What's wrong with this woman? She knows nothing about me. I'd never seen her before in my life. Chances are I'll never see her again.

Actually, I thought, that's kind of perfect. Why not? I basically just gave her the abbreviated version, telling her how my looks and shyness make it so I can't get a date in a calendar factory.

"Well, we all have our flaws. Sometimes you can't fight them, like with looks. Sometimes you can, like shyness," she advised.

My brain had a violent reaction to that, silently screaming, "Shyness isn't a flaw! It's a character trait, you dolt!"

She continued, "A friend of mine from high school had a similar problem: she just couldn't start a conversation with anyone. She was always afraid that people were going to be mean to her."

Well, it's a mean world we live in. I asked how she handled it.

"I don't know," she said. "We kind of lost touch after graduation. I went to Quinella and she went off to a college in Amherst. Not UMass, the other one. What's the name of the other college in Amherst?"

"Amherst College?"

"Yeah, that's the one. Maybe I should think about looking her up again, just for ol' times sake."

She told me she had to go. She shook my hand and wished me luck, adding, "By the way, I never got your name."

"It's Jessica," I said.

"No kidding! Mine, too!" With that, she left.

I sat there for a while, under a cool gray sky and observed my surroundings. There was a stone marker at the edge of the playground. I'm not sure if it had been there before and I just hadn't noticed it until today, but it seemed brand new, so I went over to read it. The engraving on its smooth surface began "IN LOVING MEMORY OF." It instantly reminded me of the gravestones for those two Audreys, alone and waiting to die. It even used the same typeface. You can tell from the right leg on the R, always a dead giveaway.

It was smooth and polished enough for me to see a reflection of my silhouette in. There she was: the woman that everyone still treats like a child. I'm an adult, just give me a chance to prove it. That child in that photo from third grade should be nothing more than a loving memory by now. So what the hell was I doing on this playground?

Lynn texted me later today: "thought about W u said last nite. if going to Amst. is W u think is best for u then I cant object." (The capital W is her texting abbreviation for "what". Like "watt". Get it?)

Before I could think of an appropriate reply, she sent another one: "u deserve to have some fun. u didnt let me down."

AUG 23 (SUN)

Willow never bothered to send a change of address to the folks who send her the TV Guide, so it still shows up in our mail. Usually if I'm bored and waiting for something I'll try my hand at the crossword. They're much harder than you'd think, but only due to the constantly recurring clues referencing TV shows nobody has ever heard of. I still have no idea what the name of the nun was on *Just The Ten Of Us* and I can't be bothered to look it up. (That was a real show? I thought TV Guide just made it up to fill in empty spaces on Saturday afternoons.)

I was doing the puzzle today and felt drawn to the horoscope on the facing page. I never read the horoscope. I don't know why, but today I did. Something just compelled me to look over to the side and see what fate the zodiac had determined for me.

CANCER: Don't go poking around in others' affairs, otherwise you could become an unwitting partner-in-crime! Also, is it time for some new wheels? Maybe you should do some research on how much your current car should go for and start looking at those new models for next year.

What the hell am I supposed to do with that mess!? I don't have a car! It's bunk. I don't even know my own future, so how can the stars know anything? What does it matter which sign the sun is in today? Heavenly bodies and astrology and fate: all lies. There's no such thing as fate. Fate is something that can't exist by its own definition, because it's always off in the future, never in the present or past. It's just a word. All you can do is look for patterns and make an educated guess. And that's what really scares me.

What am I gonna do. What the hell am I gonna do. Nothing fucking works. I don't know any men who are available and all my attempts at meeting new ones all fall flat.

I didn't get a single match from speed dating. Ditto online dating. The clubs are too loud. The bars are too scary. I feel like I just don't fit in anywhere. Everyone I ask out is already seeing someone. I still haven't even been on one date. I couldn't even get anyone to agree to spend three or four minutes with me for a dance. I really missed the boat on this one, didn't I? I hid myself away, nestled within the safe vice-grip of knowing that love would work itself out the way it seemed to with everybody else, and now the world has already been paired up.

This isn't an extraordinary request. I'm not trying to win the lottery or become a famous singer or marry a millionaire. I just want what everyone else has. Doesn't everyone need to be loved?

I haven't done anything to deserve this. I haven't done anything to invite this. And yet, I know in my heart that it's all my fault.

But, it's just the same old self-pitying shtick as always, isn't it? Why am I even writing this? No one will ever see it. No one but me can even decode it. So why do I do it? Why bother?

I've lived so much of my life feeling completely resigned. I don't know if I even want to have sex anymore. I'm not even sure I want a boyfriend. I just think all I've wanted all along was to feel accepted, not resigned.

Shit. It really is an oxymoron.

AUG 24 (MON)

On the Monday before the new school year begins, all the faculty has to get together for an in-school meeting known as "Professional Development Day." There's nothing necessary about it, at least not for me. Just the usual "welcome back" sorts of activity: go over the same things as every year, meet the new staff, get our stories straight.

The biggest news this year is that Rosi is the new first-grade teacher, replacing the newly-retired Mrs. Finch. She's quite excited about her new position, but she seems to be ignoring the drawbacks. I told her she's not going to be able to just roam about the school at will anymore, and that she'll have to monitor recess professionally instead of joining the students and teaching them the "Who can hit the other person the softest?" trick. When I first saw her, she had just finished yakking it up with Mr. Love.

"Yeah, I know what you're thinking: he's married. But, I'm pretty sure his wife is headed out the door any day now," she informed me in a confident manner. "He's too good for her, anyway. He told me she's actually mad at him because of his medical condition. Something called 'wandering eye syndrome.'"

I decided to let her figure that one out for herself and instead asked, "Do you think he's really interested in you, or is it possible that he just tries to chat up anyone who he thinks might be available in order to improve his chances?"

"You mean like you're doing?"

"That's completely different. I'm desperate. My point is that even if you two get together, what makes you think it's gonna last?"

She breathed a heavy sigh through her nose and admitted that she really didn't know if Mr. and Mrs. Love were having marital strife. He was probably just joking about it for flirty purposes. "I'll be honest with you. I don't really like him as much as I make it sound. I've been thinking it over. Maybe I only like men who are already taken because when they reject me, at least I'll know it's nothing to do with me. A long time ago, somebody I loved said something that hurt me pretty badly and..." She didn't finish the sentence.

Rosi hypothesized that maybe she wants to be rejected because she's afraid of what would happen if she ended up falling in love with the wrong person. As usual, I didn't know what to say, so I used that old line about how we always want what we can't have. "Tell me about it," was her answer to that. Well, I guess we all have our own problems, don't we? I decided this might not be the best time to tell her about my travel plans.

Speaking of which, I finally got to see Lynn face-to-face again for the first time since Trivia Night. She was her usual bright and sunny self again. She greeted me like nothing was wrong and we just made small talk at first, pretending there wasn't anything of note that had happened recently.

It was going to come up sooner or later, so she brought it up. She whispered, "I still think you're stronger than this."

I apologized. I was sorry that I disappointed her but, strong or not, I'm not invincible.

She hugged me, saying, "I guess I just wanted to believe that true love isn't dead. I was kind of pinning my hopes on you. I think that's why I didn't want you to give up."

I told Lynn I'm not giving up, but I just can't keep waiting anymore. She needs to think of it in a purely statistical sense and separate from everything else. It's an outlier, an anomaly. "You know, just because a scant few people have to be alone all their lives that doesn't mean that love is dead," I added. "All it means is that life isn't fair. It's always been that way, so just don't worry about it.

"Besides, maybe this is what I need to get me started. I need some help. Once I get back, I'll be ready to get right back out there. The icicle glistens brightest when it's melting."

She smiled and asked who said that line. I told her I made it up.

She said it wasn't very good.

I got to see Jeff one last time. Now that he's finished with his training as a T.A., he's going to be working at Mooreland Middle School as a sixth grade Social Studies teacher. But, in Mooreland, the school year doesn't start until the first Wednesday of September, so he was able to drop by and see the gang again and bid his farewells. He asked me how I liked Europe. I told him that the closest I got to Europe was an Irish pub called Paddy O'Furniture's.

Jeff began to mimic Winston's mannerisms and speech. "Oh! So you did go to Europe! Yes, I'm certain that I've seen Paddy O'Furniture's on a map of Europe before. Ireland is a jewel, but my favorite country is still Amsterdam." I did that stupid laugh again.

"As it happens, I actually might be going to Amsterdam in November, over the holidays. Just for a few days, though." Telling him that felt like a confession, even though he had no clue what was going on.

Anyhow, Jeff said he just wanted to stop by and give his hellos and goodbyes to everybody before he had to leave. Plus, he wanted to give Jeanette the key to Tench's vending machine so she could restock it from now on. So, he had the key this whole time, eh? Hmmm, I sensed a pattern...

I asked Jeff if Vice Principal Tench was secretly gay. He said he had no idea. "Why? Did he ever do or say anything to let on that he was?" he asked.

"Well," I said, "it's just that you're giving the key to Jeanette, and she's a lesbian. And Tench gave the key to you, and you're gay. So I figured maybe it was just a... you know, tradition you were keeping alive."

"Audrey, I'm not gay."

I recoiled a little and said, "Yes, you are!" What!? Why would I try to correct him on that?

Jeff wanted to know why I thought that, so I told him how I heard it from Chuck. He said he wasn't surprised, then told me that Chuck also said his brother went on a secret NASA mission to the moon to re-plant the American flag after it got knocked over by solar winds. Chuck also claimed that Miriam has a nipple ring and that Natasha gave a reading at Junior Seau's funeral. He just made up stories about other people to get everyone's attention.

I couldn't help but see the parallel to my own life, and told him how Lynn, Jeanette, my best friend from childhood, and my mom all thought that I might be a lesbian just because I'm not seeing anyone. "So, I guess we have that in common, then." Here I was upset that everyone was wrong about my sexuality, and I turned out to be just as guilty. I guess I learned my lesson.

He told me, "Don't feel bad. It's not an isolated case, ya know. I actually met my first girlfriend because my Dad thought I was gay. He had me go out with his co-worker's daughter. I think he may be planning something like that again because I haven't been seeing anybody for a while." Yeesh. Maybe I should have just let Mom keep thinking I wasn't straight. She could have done some of the legwork for me.

It was good to see Winston is gone and that a new permanent vice principal is in place. They called him Mr. Sutton. I didn't talk to him, but from what I observed he seems like one of those types who'd prefer that the students like him than obey him. He's a gray-haired male who'd rather act his BMI than his age, and comes off a tad rougher than his suave predecessor. It's clear that the older women are already warming up to him, acting all swoony and "Winston who?" At least he's in their age bracket.

Is he any easier to stomach than Winston, though? Well, he spent most of his time flirting with almost every woman in the room. He even said to Mrs. Harmon-Lewis, "Your name is Alberta? No kidding! I love girls named after states!" Where do they keep coming from and how do they keep ending up here?

I showed Angela that karate rabbi I drew. Turns out her text message was one character over the limit. It was supposed to be a rabbit.

AUG 26 (WED)

First day of school today. Back to the library counter and living day to day six feet under the hanging mercury lamps. My path crossed George's on my way in this morning. He asked me what the matter was. "What makes you think that something's wrong?" I said.

"Well, ya look even worse than usual."

George is really getting up there in years. On the day he passes, I'm sure I'll miss him at first. I'm a terrible shot.

I had to label and shelve the new books that came in. There was a new alphabet book, so I thumbed through it just to see what was on the X page, and guess what? It was a xylophone! Swear to God! While I was keeping busy with this task, Jeanette brought in her morning kindergarten class so that she could show them the library.

"Class, this is Miss Perlmutter. Everyone say hello to her!"

A chorus of junior bipeds chanted, "HELLO, MISS [*speaking in tongues*]." A couple of them did say "missus."

"Hi, kids. How are you today?"

"GOOD."

Just once I wish they'd say, "OH, YOU KNOW HOW IT IS. SAME OL', SAME OL'. CAN'T COMPLAIN, I GUESS." It would have to be in perfect unison, though. Otherwise, it wouldn't work. I doubt they could pull it off.

Once Jeanette finished her state-mandated spiel about how reading is an adventure, she led the kiddies back out. Before I could have even two seconds to myself, in walks Mr. Sutton. He couldn't wait to introduce himself to me, giving me one of those extra-tight handshakes that no right-thinking adult with a properly-wired human brain would do on purpose. Okay, you're a male and you think you're hot shit, we get it.

Gave him the standard introduction. He gave a big grin and said, "Oh, please, 'Mr.

242

Sutton' was my dad. Everyone can just call me 'Oliver.'" Oh God, how I hate that line. This was not going to be pleasant. (The thing is, I didn't even call him "Mr. Sutton." I just said, "I'm Audrey. Nice to meet you.")

I kept going about my business, bringing over some of the new books to their designated spots on the shelves. He followed me over and asked me all about what I do here and the like. He kept tossing out inane questions like "Now, tell me, have you read all of these books yourself?" and "D'you ever take naps on the shelves when there aren't any kids around?"

Come back, Winston. All is forgiven.

All this could be glossed over were it not clear that he's the type who doesn't stop to think before opening his mouth. Rather, he instantly lets fly the first line that comes into his mind without regard as to whether or not it's any good, constantly throwing out whatever's on hand in the hope that something will get a response and never letting up. I felt I could stand to be more affable, so I gave a pity chuckle every now and then. Coming from me, that's a rave.

Then, he made a more obvious play. He asked me my age and followed up with, "When I was that young, they still hadn't discovered the G-spot yet!" Pal, when you were my age, they still hadn't discovered North America yet.

This was a first. A new man walks into my life and instantly takes a liking to me, throwing clichés and other goofy lines at me. He was definitely not even close to my age, though. Clearly in his sixties, but acted much younger. He was wearing a paisley tie and a suit that was kinda bright beige, if that's possible.

Before he left, he said, "Mr. Perlmutter's very fortunate, I can tell you that."

"Please. 'Mr. Perlmutter' was my father. Call me 'Ma'am.'" He thought that was a pretty good one. I tried to be friendly when we were talking, but I'm actually quite serious about that.

So, a guy takes an interest in me and he starts flirting, but he's twice my age. I guess I technically got what I asked for again, didn't I? It's like when the woman who sang that "And I never want to hear that song again" song lost her hearing in that fertilizer explosion. Maybe I should take a look at my priorities here. When I'm seventy Sutton will only be one-hundred.

I did take note of his hands. Wedding ring. Maybe I'm being shallow, but sometimes a dead end can be a relief.

Rosita dragged herself into the library before lunch break. "Aggh! I'm starving! I didn't have time to make lunch this morning and I have no money on me. Audrey, please tell me you're hiding a candy bar in your, uh, V-area today."

"Excuse me!?"

"You know, in the card catalog. I know you keep food filed under V," she said. Oh. I didn't have a thing. Year's just begun, after all.

Rosi and I made our way down towards the lounge and she practically snapped at me, saying that if I do have candy hidden somewhere, she should have it rather than me. "You eat all that chocolate and never gain a pound! Do you realize how jealous I am?"

Somebody's jealous of me? Over something as inconsequential as chocolate? Remarkable. The face is always greener on the other side. I offered to trade: my metabolism for her complexion.

I told her about Sutton once we were in the lounge. I felt a little bad about not liking him when it was so obvious that he was trying to impress me. She said it was actually good that I felt that way.

"I was afraid you were going to instantly fall head over heels for the first guy who so much as looked at you. This is healthy. You're not automatically taking the first answer to your problems just because it's there." That's actually a pretty good argument. I still feel a little bad about it, though. It feels like I'm being an ingrate. Who knows, maybe if I got to know him, we might even get along pretty well after all.

On one hand, he's running unopposed. On the other hand, there's a ring. I guess I'll just do what I always do when somebody on the ballot is unopposed: vote for a write-in.

I gave Rosi some money and she charted a new course for the cafeteria. She went out and Natasha came in.

"How's the first day back, Agent Plain?"

"Pretty boring, The Sentinel. Just the way I remember it. First days are always like this, I suppose."

She procured an orange soda from the secret vending machine and sat down across from me. I didn't have anything to say and neither did she, at least for a while.

Two restrained women without much to say sat there for a few minutes, alone. She ate half a sandwich she brought with her while I just stared at a blank page in my sketch pad, occasionally making an uncertain mark, only to erase it seconds later. I could only imagine what was going through her head.

Without provocation, Natasha spoke up and said, "I'm sorry things aren't working out for you."

"Thanks."

244

She finished her sandwich, and told me, "I'm not trying to make you feel bad when I say this, but I was talking with Zena the other day. She agrees with me. She thinks that going around having anonymous sex with lots of different guys is probably something you shouldn't take up as a hobby."

Zena said that? ZENA? "Why on earth would she say such a thing?" I asked, trying to remain as subdued as possible.

"She just says it's wrong. You could end up getting hurt. It's not for you. She says what you need is a stable relationship."

My blood was boiling. For Natasha to feel that way, fine. She's religious, she's monogamous. She practices what she preaches. I expect that from her and I can respect her point of view, even sympathize with it. But for Zena to say such a thing?

Zena. Zena, who has been with scores of men while I haven't had a single one. Zena, who has been out there having fun all this time, doing things I could only dream of. I never got to explore or experiment. I've had to go through my entire life doing everything by myself. Compared to her I have nothing, not even memories, and she wants to take even more away from me?

I said nothing else, stood up, and walked out. I heard Natasha say, "I'm only looking out for your best interest," as I left.

I walked past Zena's office on the way back to the library. The door has a laminated poster on it to which someone applied a sticker that reads, "NURSES CARE!" with one of the R's as an "Rx" symbol. She told me she liked sleeping with guys as "a power thing." Is that all this is to her: power? Does the thought of someone like me having sex somehow take away from what she's accomplished? Would it diminish her or make her feel less special?

Did she even enjoy any of it? Could someone like her possibly appreciate the idea of being desired?

I'm fueled by pure spite now. If it were anyone else then I could handle it, but if Zena doesn't want me getting laid, then all bets are off. I began doing research on flight-and-hotel packages for Amsterdam the moment I got home. As soon as I get the chance, I'm getting those personal days scheduled in November. Forget the money problems. Forget the moral dilemmas. This comes first.

The wait is over. I'm going to do this.

AUG 28 (FRI)

I did it.

I just wanted to get that in writing.

I didn't have time for a full entry yesterday, as it was late and I had to get to sleep. So! Ummmm, here's how it all happened…

When I came in to work yesterday morning, there was an envelope taped to the library door. I didn't like the look of this, and instantly assumed it was going to contain a note beginning with those seven dreaded words, "Can you do me a favor and…" Thankfully, I was wrong, but there was no way I could have guessed which seven words were inside. It read:

ASLEEP TEEM EVENS HOTTING EARN URBAN ASTUTE

Made no sense at all. On top of that, it was signed "VOLE ?"

Vole, huh? Okay, so I guess that rules out the lemmings. In retrospect, I could have figured it out right then and there but I was not in the mood.

All morning I went about my business in the usual manner for the most part. I looked at the note a few more times. All these words mean something, but what is "HOTTING"? Is it even a word? Couldn't stand it. Had to look it up. Whaddya know, "hot" can be a verb.

³hot \'hät\ *verb, transitive* [mostly Southern US, British] : to heat (usu. used with "up") | **hot·ted; hot·ting**

Well, I learned something new. So, did a Southerner or a Brit leave this note for me? When I first read the note, I thought maybe Rosi was playing a prank on me, even though it wasn't in her handwriting. But why would someone just having a laugh go out of their way to use such an uncommon word when "HEATING" would have done just fine?

I showed the note to Lynn at lunch, but she couldn't make out what it meant, either. "It has to be a code or a puzzle. I'm sure somebody wants you to solve it for them," she surmised. "It could be that you're supposed to figure out which word comes next in the pattern. That might be why there's a question mark at the end." I asked her if she recognized the handwriting. She could not.

I flattened out the folded page on the table. Okay, each of these words had to have been chosen for a reason. I tried looking at each word individually. I tried looking at pairs to find what they had in common. But, no matter what I tried, my eyes kept being drawn back to that one word. "HOTTING." Why would anyone use that word for anything?

247

I analyzed it, letter by letter. The H is necessary, otherwise they would have picked something like "rotting". The O is required as well, because they could have gone with "hitting" instead. Could have been "hosting", so T isn't replaceable. And it had to end with "ING", because they didn't just use "hot" or "hotel" or something else. Every letter is absolutely necessary.

Then, I realized it. "ING". It's not about the word at all. It's about the letters.

I knew what the message was, and I knew who wrote it as well.

I asked Lynn if she had any plans that night. I'd need her to keep an eye on me, just in case my hunch about who sent the note was wrong. "Why? What's going on?" she asked. I handed her the paper again so that I could explain that I had been asked out on a date.

But, was it really going to happen? Everything else I've done that came close to this had been scuttled at the last moment, so what would be different now? Before he met up with me, he'd probably end up diving into an empty swimming pool or getting caught in a Chinese finger trap or gluing a model airplane to his face.

And there was something about that handwriting. I know I've seen it before. Something told me a woman wrote it.

Oh God. What if a woman did write it? What if this is all just a prank after all? The floodgates in my mind were open, and out came the deluge of "What if?" drenching my synapses. I quickly ran out of legitimate concerns and, for the rest of the school day, began worrying about scenarios that only the most ardent of paranoiacs (i.e., yours truly) would imagine. The prize-winner: "What if he uses his smartphone to secretly record me and then sells it as stock footage for local news stories about facial moles?"

Around one o'clock, I came to terms with the fact that this probably wasn't a joke. I was just making excuses for myself to back out of it. After all this wishing and waiting, I couldn't run away. I was actually going to go on a date. This wasn't some speck of optimism on the horizon, it was real and it was only a few hours away.

Lynn assured me that everything would go just fine. She was convinced that I would have a good time. I was still uneasy about it all. I said that my stomach was in knots and my legs were starting to shake a little. Lynn walked over to me, stood at arms' length, and put her hands on my shoulders. She had a look in her eyes, austere yet hopeful. I knew this was important. She glared directly at me and delivered her inspirational words.

"Audrey, if you do not go on this date, I will homicide you to death. I will bring you to Hawaii and throw you in a volcano and it will be legal because you are a virgin. Do you understand me?" I told her I understood and that her fingernails hurt.

Lynn stationed herself just around a corner on the west side of the school. Her view of the statue out front was unobstructed from there. I told her to wait for my signal that everything was okay. (The signal was me raising my arm above my head and waving it as if I were trying to get someone's attention. I came up with the idea for that subtle maneuver myself.)

Looked at the clock on my phone. 6:53. Early, of course. I waited it out looking at that note again. "VOLE ?" Really? Okay, if you say so.

I looked up from the note and was suddenly struck with terror. A familiar-looking man was coming down the street. No, it can't be. Not that guy. But, he... he's married, isn't he?

Luckily, he passed right by me. Oh, thank heavens. I was afraid my date would be Sutton, but that wasn't even him, just a jogger with similar hair. Since I only met him this week, my memory still doesn't have a lock on his face yet. The thought of having my first date be with that cretin made my heart race, and not in the fun way. I was too preoccupied with breathing a sigh of relief to notice someone had walked right up behind me.

"Hi! How's it going?" a voice said.

As I was already a nervous wreck, it was just surprising enough to startle me into screaming a little. "Don't sneak up on a woman like that!" I told him between deep breaths.

It was who I thought it would be: Jeff. There he was, dressed sharp in black and white like he had just stepped out of a manga. I admit I was underdressed compared to him, but given the venue, I didn't quite know what to expect. After all, in his note, he asked if I would please meet him near the statue in front of Braun at seven o'clock. That was it. (Finding an anagram for "tonight" must have taken him a while. Good job.)

I asked what he had planned. "Where are we headed? You don't need me to do the Jumble for you, I hope. Because if that's what this is all about, forget it."

He thought he should let me choose where we should go. Hmm, so the choice is mine, is it? What am I in the mood for? What do I want?

Why sushi, of course. Informal yet classy. Adventurous yet familiar. Upscale yet affordable. Off to Lucky Cat. As we walked down the block, I turned around and waved to Lynn. Jeff asked what I was doing. I said I thought I saw a cardinal.

Over dinner, Jeff explained that he and his roommate in Mooreland can't move into their new place until September 1st, the same day as his faculty orientation meeting. He came back to Ridgeway for the weekend to get the rest of his stuff. As it turns out, Mooreland is only a two-hour drive from here, if the interstate isn't congested. You could take the commuter rail instead if you change trains in Boston, but both methods come out roughly equal in length.

For once, I didn't just inhale everything on my plate and finish in under ten minutes. We talked, mostly about things at Braun. I told him how everyone is doing, and we traded some stories. I thought he was going to die laughing when I told him the one about Rosi drawing the flag on the blackboard. He was surprised he hadn't heard about it before.

I felt like we "connected" as they say. It was like, well, I don't really have anything to compare it to. He seemed to genuinely want to get to know me. Everything about me. He even said, "Please don't think less of me for it, but I don't even know how to spell your last name. How does that go?" Geez. Nobody's ever asked before unless they were filling out paperwork.

I spelled it out for him, making it a point to let him know there's no silent A. He then pressed me for my middle name, but I wouldn't budge. My middle name is not getting out anytime soon.

Actually, I did open up just a tad. "Let's just say my initials spell a word and leave it at that," I said, hoping the mystery would be enough to satisfy him.

Before the check came, the waitress asked if we wanted dessert. That was the signal I was waiting for. I was supposed to give a smooth, alluring "I was thinking we could have dessert at my place." Instead, it came out as a jagged "Let's hav-, uh, have that in *my* house!" The judges gave it a 3.6. Poor execution, but it made it in the water. Jeff paid up and we set off.

I was mindful to shorten my stride so that Jeff could keep pace with me. Our path took us over that footbridge that crosses Quirk St. You get a great panorama of the office skyscrapers over in New Illsley, accented by the red radio tower lights glowing like a neon umlaut on a sign for a European nightclub. It's underlined by the headlights and taillights on I-595: red lights heading in one direction, white lights in the other. Drivers heading in opposite directions on the same stretch of road, and neither side even knows that the other is there. Well, sure, they know it, but they aren't aware of it.

"What a beautiful view out there," were Jeff's exact words. That could have been a good time for me to accept that as a compliment or for him to say something like, "I wasn't talking about the city." But, the presence of "out there" put to bed any notion of those things coming to pass. Just as well, that sort of thing is too corny for me anyways. Too much like a bad movie.

As we descended the stairs, he used the opportunity to take my hand. I had no idea what to say. I just took it for what it was, like it happened all the time, but I wanted to say something. I think I wanted to say, "Thank you."

When we came back to the apartment, I asked Jeff not to sit on the couch. I'm still planning on giving it a Viking funeral.

"Oh, so should we go into the kitchen?" he inquired, sounding a bit perplexed. I pushed open the door to my room and suggested he sit on the edge of my bed. I have no idea how I did that. I felt like it was an acceptable thing to say to him. He walked into my room and I followed with my body leaning forward, as if my head and heart were dragging me in while my legs were distracted by something else.

We sat on the bed side-by-side, both of us looking straight ahead. It was kind of tense. I couldn't think of anything else to say. Jeff saw the mutilated 4 x 6" target from the carnival up on the wall and wanted to know what it was. I told him it was a poster. I pointed at Thé over on my bookcase and claimed he was my new pet.

Well, I'm outta things to talk about.

"So," he said, trying to put an end to the silence again, "I heard from one of your friends that you just started dating again after a few years of not seeing anyone. What made you change your mind?"

I didn't really want to tell Jeff the whole story of Natasha's car getting hit and setting off my quest to find love out of fear of death. Not exactly upbeat stuff and I wanted to keep things light. I just told him that I thought about it for a while, and then a chain of events, and then domino, domino, domino, and here we are.

Yeah. After all that, here we are. I turned to look at him. I think I was going to offer him a glass of water but when our eyes met, I lost my place.

I looked directly into his eyes. He has a face that I'll always be able to recognize. I noticed tiny distinguishing marks all over it: a lone freckle here, a little thin brown spot (mole? scar? birthmark?) there, a tiny bump on one bottom eyelid. It was still an unremarkable everyday face, unglamorous and average and normal. It was perfect.

I didn't want to wait for him to make the first move. The way I saw it, there were no more formalities or uncertainties to inhibit me from taking the next step. We had already gone to dinner, he had already held my hand, and now he was sitting on my bed. I didn't have a problem initiating anything.

On an impulse, I put one hand behind his head and pulled it over for a kiss. My mouth was open, his was not. I think my tongue went into a nostril a little. There ya go: my first kiss. It only lasted three or four seconds. As always, I apologized reflexively. "I was just trying to be spontaneous," I said, covering my eyes with my hands.

Jeff responded saying that he was sorry, too. "It was too late for me to react once I realized what was happening. I'm a little out of practice with this. I'm not sure what to do next, really."

I suggested that he should treat me like he treated his other girlfriends. He came clean and admitted that both of his girlfriends were from his high school years. He dated them for only a few months each, but was still pretty young, so he didn't try to get very far with either of them. After that, he just wasn't able to find a new girl due to his lack of money, so he decided to put everything on hold until he could "finance a relationship," as he put it.

"Didn't you ever worry that you might never earn enough for that?" I asked. "Don't you think you should have gone out there anyways and taken the risk?"

"If a guy isn't financially stable, women won't even consider dating him. That's all love is worth now. You just wouldn't understand how bad it gets out there."

I grabbed his shoulder with my right hand, leaned into him, and said, "You wouldn't understand how much I understand." It looks kind of dumb writing it out, but it was a lot more effective when I said it. That's probably because I punctuated it by climbing on top of him and eventually wrapping my tongue around his. I was going to make him understand.

We kissed for a while. I really have no idea if I was doing it right, but I didn't get any complaints. When we decided we'd had enough of that, Jeff mentioned he didn't remember to bring any condoms. I told him not to worry because I had it covered, getting that box that I bought back in the spring.

"Plus," I added, "I'm taking the pill on top of that, so no need for concern." I started unbuttoning his shirt.

"Yeah, but you have to be safe. Wouldn't want you worrying about catching something from me," he replied.

"Wait, didn't you just tell me you're a virgin?"

He seemed a little shocked that I said that and pleaded, "Hey, could you keep it down? I'm twenty-seven. Don't use that word."

I had Jeff's shirt off now and started working on his belt and pants. As per his request, I quieted down just a little, telling him, "Don't worry. I'm thirty and I'm a virgin, too."

"I don't believe either one of those things," he said to me. "You're saying that to make me feel better, aren't you?"

I had him down to his underwear at this point. "What makes you think I'm lying?" I laughed.

"There's no way somebody as beautiful as you isn't getting asked out at every turn. You'd have to have will power beyond belief."

I don't get compliments that often, so I have trouble knowing what to say in response. Instead I wanted to keep things moving forward, so I told Jeff he should take my clothes off. He was very cautious, making sure to ask before he put his hands in any new places.

It wasn't long before I told him he didn't have to keep asking anymore. Sometimes, words are worth more when they're left unsaid.

So I won't bother saying what happened next.

This morning, I woke up with Jeff's arms wrapped around my waist. I would have stayed there for hours if it had taken him that long to wake up, but I really had to pee. I thought I could wriggle out vertically, but that was poorly thought-out. I actually did pretty well for a while, but my ankle brushed against his face and I had to explain myself.

When I came back out from the bathroom, Jeff was still in bed and staring at something on his smartphone. Just seeing him there made me think, wow, this really happened. Someone else is in my bed. He spent the night with me. It was so cute the way he was giggling at the video he had playing.

He saw me watching him from the doorway, and informed me, "Oh, I was just watching this Japanese kids' show from the Seventies. Some guy dressed as an octopus wails on his friends with a length of pipe and then tries to steal their stuff."

Neither of us had anything planned, so we spent the day together. As wonderful as today was, nothing really notable happened. We went to lunch, we went to the park by the reservoir, stopped to pick up a few things at the supermarket (the Halloween stuff is already out in full force,) we went to dinner. It was almost normal. There was a small surprise, though. Before we did anything else, Jeff insisted we go back to his mother's house so that he could change his clothes and get his car. He looked very uncomfortable going out in public wearing the wrinkled shirt and pants that spent the night on my floor.

He exhibited a fixation on getting the crease just right while he was ironing his pants. That explains a lot, then. All this time I just thought he went out of his way to dress well, when he just has mild obsessive-compulsive tendencies. I suppose I can relate to that, but at least he didn't insist on ironing things in alphabetical order.

That's right, we also stopped by the school at one point. We had a short walk through the same playground we kept watch over together that one day. The blacktop area had a new design painted on it: a map of, not the fifty, but the contiguous forty-eight states in bright pastels with white borders and coastlines. Massachusetts and Cape Cod were rendered in loving, crooked detail while poor Rhode Island was just a lavender rectangle. Jeff noted that the two peninsulas of Michigan were mistakenly given different colors and that a non-existent lake had formed in Illinois. Pretty sure that was just bird crap, though.

I was in such a good mood that I jumped onto the playground equipment and walked across the balance beam. I invited Jeff to come up and swing across the hanging rings. He decided he'd rather watch. I went across the rings and made it to the other side on my first try without touching the ground once. Take *that*, people twenty years younger than me! Jeff laughed at how pleased I was with my success. With a big grin, he told me I was acting like a teenager and that he didn't know I had this side to me. I didn't know I could do that, either. I've always been too busy acting like an adult. And a child.

I'm writing this in bed right now. It's about eleven o'clock.

Jeff looked over a while ago and asked what language I'm writing in. I don't think I'll teach him my shorthand code. I've gotta keep some secrets, after all. But who knows, maybe if he's around enough he'll be able to figure it out for himself.

AUG 31 (MON)

I maintained radio silence all morning. I figured I should just break the news casually, like it wasn't news at all. Not make a big fuss over it.

Lynn and Jeanette were already chewing the fat in the lounge when I arrived for lunch. I walked right past them and sat in the corner at that little ledge along the window. A few other teachers were in the room, so I wanted to keep this clandestine.

Just as I suspected would happen, Lynn came right over to ask how my date went. I said I'd let her know once Rosita showed up. Well, that was kind of a giveaway, wasn't it? Made for an uncomfortably quiet half-minute, though.

"You're really not gonna tell me until Rosi gets here?"

"Nope."

Rosi burst in, seemingly in the middle of an unpleasant day of first grade hi-jinks. I learned later that one of her more tech-savvy tykes had replaced every last piece of clipart on one machine in the computer lab with a photo of Don Knotts wearing an astronaut helmet. Knowing Rosi, she may have been steamed that she hadn't thought of it first.

The four of us were all clustered in one corner. Jeanette was there with us, so I had to choose my words carefully and hope the others would do the same. I informed my colleagues that I had a date with Jeff on Friday night.

Rosi seemed a little surprised by this. "So he just asked you out? Out of nowhere? Just like that?"

"What can I say? Sometimes things change in an instant," I said. "Anything can happen, anytime, good or bad." I went on, telling them about dinner and how we just had a great time. We really have something going, you could say.

Lynn leaned in, demanding to know how it ended.

I tried to tamp down a smile as I said, "Yeah, about that. We decided we're going to see each other again, but... It was only the first date, after all. I didn't want the word getting out that I'm easy."

I'm pretty certain Lynn's trembling hands were positioning themselves for "strangle mode," so I quickly told her I was kidding. Ah, there was that look of relief again. It almost rivaled the one from the restaurant booth.

"Don't ever do that to me again. You know what I'm capable of, so that's for your own safety," she warned me with a bright smile. Poor Jeanette must have been wondering what her deal was.

It had to have been a bit of a spectacle with all these faculty members crowded into one corner of the room. The three or four others in the lounge probably thought the young ones were all cooing and drooling over some new tech toy I acquired. No surprise then that when Miriam opened the door her attention was drawn to us. She came straight toward our little gaggle and called out, "Okay, okay, what's the big deal over there?"

Uh-oh. Had to think of something fast. I was able to get out, "I,... I was..."

Rosi leaped two feet in the air and triumphantly shouted, "AUDREY LOST HER VIRGINITY!"

Then, nothing happened. Nobody moved. Pretty sure a tumbleweed rolled by.

Miriam did her best to stifle her chuckling. "Oh my. Uhhh, congratulations, I guess!"

"Thank you," I said.

"You do know that I'm still here and that putting your hands over your face doesn't change that, right?"

"Yes. I am aware of that."

I decided this would be a good time for me to get back to work. I picked myself up and forged a path to the door while trying my best to avoid eye contact with the teachers at the other tables. I heard their snickering and faint whispers, and I could have turned around to get the final word before leaving the room. Really burn them by saying something like "Oh yeah? Well... you're all dumb!" But that's a childish thing to do, to passive-aggressively get in a last dig before running off. It's not what a mature person does.

And just what the hell do they have to laugh about anyway? I don't have any reason to feel bad. For the first time in a long time, I don't feel bad at all.

Rosi texted me about ten minutes later, saying, "I screwed up and broke my promise. I'm really sorry."

I wrote back, "No need to apologize. You promised not to say that I AM a virgin. You said I'm NOT one, so you kept your word. Thanks for all your help."

Natasha brought her class to the library today to check out books for the first time this year. She was busy showing them all around, and didn't have much time to talk with me. Before she called for her little runtbuckets to line up for the march back to the classroom, she did have one thing to say to me.

"Audrey," I heard from a distance. I turned to see Natasha glaring at me. For a few seconds, she looked like she didn't know what she was supposed to say.

She gave me a thumbs-up. "Good job," she decreed. I had no idea how to react to that, so I just mirrored the gesture to let her know everything was fine. It was an exchange as strange as it was terse. Uncomfortable, yet comforting.

Once the day was done, I popped by Lynn's classroom to see her again but she was nowhere to be found. As it would happen, she was waiting for me outside and accosted me from around a corner of the building just after I exited. She brought me over to a secluded spot behind the school for privacy reasons.

She had a nervous canter to her voice, very unlike her. "It was me, alright? I set it all up. I saw you and Jeff talking last week and you seemed to get along, so I asked if he'd want to go out with you."

"So you heard him tell me that he's not gay, huh?"

She said she didn't. She just noticed a few visual cues that showed he was interested in me. "I knew he wasn't gay, so I talked with him about going out with you. I could tell he was really into you. Just the way he looked at you. After you were done talking to him that day, he was still looking over at you from time to time to see what you were up to."

Lynn had Jeanette write the note, because she knew I'd recognize the handwriting of all my closer co-workers. It was Rosi's idea to use the jumbled letters. (Oh, so Rosi *did* know about this after all, huh? Her acting abilities are improving.) She said she couldn't come up with an anagram for 'tonight.'

"You did," I reassured her. "I looked it up. 'Hotting' counts as a real word."

She perked up upon hearing that. "Oh! Fantastic! I knew you'd figure it out, but I was ready to give you a few hints if it looked like you were stuck."

All weekend, I had a feeling something was up with that note. Stuff like that doesn't happen in real life. It isn't realistic. I asked why such an elaborate plan was needed. She looked down at her shoes for a second or two, then looked back up and sheepishly told me, "If Rosi and I set up the date for you, then... I guess I was afraid you'd feel like you weren't doing it yourself. I wanted you to be asked out. I wanted you to be confident. But you were going to find out what happened sooner or later so I figured I may as well come clean now. It feels good to confess."

"How come you didn't just tell Jeff to ask me out himself?"

"He was going to, but there was a miscommunication. When I approached him with the idea, I sort of told him that I'd handle everything and that I was going to make you think it was a blind date, and it just got all messy from there. I guess it worked out in the end, though."

I gave her a hug and thanked her over and over.

Then, she added, "And, while we're on the subject, Iiiiiii kinda told Jeff that there was no way you wouldn't put out. You know, just to make sure that he would ask." Turns out he didn't need to.

I wasn't in too much of a rush to get home, as I knew Jeff was probably packing up the rest of his things at his mother's house before leaving. He wasn't here when I showed up, but after a half-hour he finally came around. His car was empty, though.

Turns out, he was shopping. During the weekend we spent together, we talked about all sorts of things and along the way I mentioned how much I dislike my knees, even the way they look under tights or stockings. So, he bought me a gift: a pair of really long socks that go up to the thighs. They're gray with a sort of three-diamond argyle vignette on the front of each one. I tried them on and, can't even believe it myself, I like how they look on me.

I felt kind of dumb for not thinking of that sooner. I might never have thought of it. I guess I'm gonna have to buy a shorter skirt one of these days. Perfect for autumn.

I asked Jeff why he didn't have anything loaded into his car yet. He told me that he didn't really come back for the rest of his things, that was all taken care of already. He only came back so that he could go out with me. That's it.

Jeff left around 7:30. We hugged, we kissed, we said how much we'll miss each other. Thankfully, it won't be long. We decided that he'll come back on Friday afternoons so that we can spend the weekends together. Despite that, it wasn't easy letting him go.

As he drove off, I kept hoping he might turn around and come back. I knew that wasn't going to happen. It was unrealistic and unreasonable. What's the point of hoping for something like that? Instead, I stood there on the sidewalk as he took off down Reilly Street, his car slowly shrinking as it made its way towards the horizon, turning into a tiny period at the end of a promise.

I kept standing there, my eyes playing tricks on me. I kept telling myself that I could still see the dot. It must have been ten minutes before I went back inside. I sat down in front of the couch, my chin on my knees. My eyes were watering up for another almost-cry. A good one this time. Even though he wasn't with me, I wasn't sad at all. I mean, he'll be back in only a few days. I'll just go on with my life, waiting for him, and knowing I have someone waiting for me.

It's not autumn for another three weeks, but the first of September is always the unofficial start. As surely as spring brings rebirth, the heat of summer must follow, and then the colors of autumn arrive. If you look at the grand scheme of things, I'm not that late at all. Sure, my summer may have ended, but I'm still in my spring.

I think this is a good place to end it. It's September, summer is over, school has started again. Most importantly, there's only a few pages left in you, notebook. I want to thank you for putting up with me all this time. I guess I didn't really make it easy on you.

Plus, I guess things have worked out for me after all. I mean, I didn't win the heart of some trophy pretty boy with plenty of experience or a well-muscled adult services section cover model who proposed to me at Disneyland. I didn't get an impossibly effective make-over that turned me into the most desirable and sexually-active woman in the city. Santa Claus didn't show up at the last minute and score the winning touchdown. What did happen was that I got a normal-looking guy who I can share a slightly abnormal relationship with. It's not a conclusion fit for a romance novel, but it's more than enough for me.

Life isn't a romance novel or a Broadway musical or a manga. Sure, there wasn't a Hollywood ending, but there's really no ending at all, is there? Just because you're out of pages doesn't mean everything's settled. I still have plenty of other problems, like what I'm going to do about the rent. I'm pretty sure Jeff can't pay half of the rent at two apartments. But, a new school year has started, I guess I'm seeing someone now, and I still have a lot more things I want to try for the first time. Maybe Jeff can be there when I try iced coffee for the first time. Or maybe I'll just have an actual milkshake. Vanilla, maybe. That goes with every flavor, I hear.

So, I still have a lot to look forward to. I have something to look forward to every week, in fact. Of course I'll miss him during the week, but absence makes the heart grow fonder, they say. Say, I just realized Monday is Labor Day. I guess we're having a three-day weekend, aren't we?

On my way to the teachers' lounge for lunch today, I saw that the kids in first grade already have drawings taped up in the halls depicting places where they had seen things that looked like letters of the alphabet. One depicted the letter N in a closed gate sporting a cautionary diagonal plank like a guard holding a staff, meaning to protect but also inadvertently isolating. One girl divined the shape of an L from the figure of someone sitting down against a wall and enjoying a beautiful sunny day without a care in the world. Another was able to make out capital R's marching in lockstep as she watched other backpacked students trudging into the school that morning, all trying to keep up with their peers. One boy drew a fire escape suggesting a grand Z as it ascended a building, assuming its untouchable place in the sky above.

I walked on to the lounge in an A-line skirt that stops right at the knees, as usual.

This evening, I went out for dinner with the ladies from school. The regulars were all there: Lynn, Zena, Rosi, Natasha. Jeanette and her fiancée were there as well. The little gathering was their idea and dinner was on them. How can I say no to that? They wanted to let us know that they've scheduled a date for their wedding, and we're all invited. Furthermore, Jeanette's not keeping it a secret anymore. If any of the kids or their parents ask, she's not denying it: she's engaged to marry a woman. Her sex life isn't hurting anybody, so why acquiesce to the small-minded boors who want her to feel bad about it just because it makes them uncomfortable? She's not ashamed of it, and she's going to stop acting like she is. Brava!

Zena was expressing her irritation over constantly receiving junk mail for "Lena Swanson." Lynn felt that was worthy of a "told ya so," lecturing her, "That's what you get for always writing that showy, loopy Z of yours! Maybe it's time you came to terms with your true self, and join me and the other L-girls!" Our school nurse was then called "Lena" for the rest of the night.

I was getting a lot of questions about Jeff, particularly from Rosi and Zena. I admit that I didn't have answers to a lot of them. Rosi didn't mince words, coming out and asking, "So, what's the sex like? How is he in bed?"

"Incomparable. I say that because I have nothing to compare him against. I mean, I enjoy it. I'm not complaining, but we're just getting started, so…"

"What's he say about you?" she interrupted.

"Oh, I can't, really…" Well, I'd like to think that I'm incomparable as well. There's the power of choosing your synonyms again. I'd rather be "incomparable" than "matchless."

Zena had an interesting question: "Are you still planning on going to the Netherlands? Or is that not on the agenda anymore now that you have a boyfriend?"

I had to explain that I'm not really sure if Jeff is my boyfriend. "Oh yeah," she responded, "he's just a guy who you have a lot in common with and you like spending time with each other and you have sex. That's not what a boyfriend is." Natasha actually laughed at that. Really!

260

Honestly, I haven't necessarily ruled out visiting Amsterdam someday. I still have to see Europe, don't I? I just can't go right away. I'd have to find a time when it would be good for Jeff to go, too. If we're still together, that is.

I don't know what will come about. What Jeff wants and what I want may be two very different things, but I'm still pretty sure I can't have a years-long relationship with him. However, things do change. Sometimes they change because we force them to, and sometimes they change on their own without us even noticing. Still, some things stay the same.

It's said that "the only constant in life is change." I don't believe that. People will say that when there's a problem that can't be resolved through reasonable and viable means, so they have to try to wait it out. I know that we have to accept the fact that some things will just always be. That's why I'll always be Audrey with the small eyes and the big nose and the annoying voice. I don't have to appreciate these things just because they're part of who I am, but I can overcome them. I know I'll never be beautiful, and I'll never be sexy, but that doesn't mean that I can never feel that way. The scarcity makes those few times all the more special.

My name is Audrey Perlmutter, and I can't wait to feel beautiful again.

www.ingramcontent.com/pod-product-compliance
Lightning Source LLC
Chambersburg PA
CBHW072210170626
46813CB00003B/869